HELLENIC STUDIES SERIES 95

POETRY AND THE POLIS IN
EURIPIDEAN TRAGEDY

Recent Titles in the Hellenic Studies Series

http://chs.harvard.edu/chs/publications

POETRY AND THE POLIS IN EURIPIDEAN TRAGEDY

Jonah Radding

Center for Hellenic Studies
Trustees for Harvard University
Washington, D.C.
Distributed by Harvard University Press
Cambridge, Massachusetts, and London, England
2022

ISBN: 978-0-674-27853-0
Library of Congress Control Number: 2022946145

For my parents

Contents

Contents

Acknowledgements

I MUST THANK FIRST OF all Sarah Nooter, who spent many hours reading and discussing Euripidean drama with me, advised me throughout the process of writing the dissertation from which this book derives, and continued to support me as I made revisions. Her counsel has been unfailingly astute, and delivered with the utmost kindness and grace, making for not only a better final product of this, but indeed a more enjoyable experience for me.

I have benefitted from the generosity and wisdom of many colleagues and mentors. Jonathan Hall's guidance concerning many questions of Athenian history and identity have been vital. I will forever appreciate the exacting attention and insightful comments given by Shadi Bartsch-Zimmer and Mark Payne. Marianne Hopman, Anne-Sophie Noel, and Angeliki Tzanetou provided ample encouragement and necessary insight on the best way to frame some of the questions I have pursued in this book. Adele Teresa Cozzoli first taught me how to work with fragments, a skill that turned out to be crucial. Thank you as well to Casey Dué Hackney and Jill Robbins for shepherding this book through the editorial process, and to the anonymous readers whose feedback has helped smooth over some of the many wrinkles present in the original manuscript. William Blake Tyrrell first instilled in me a love of Latin and ancient Greek, and then spent many summers reading with me, helping me get my languages up to speed; without him, this project would never have begun.

Nor could I have completed this project without the ample love, support, and inspiration that friends and family have always provided. My parents, Charles Radding and Maureen Flanagan, first taught how me to ask questions, and then how to begin to answer them with rigorous thought and attention. My father has read and re-read every word of this book many times, bringing his expertise to bear on questions of style and structure, and convincing me to get rid of what needed to be cut. Beyond taking on such drudgery as proofreading bibliographies, my mother has always helped buoy my spirits over the years, suggesting that everything would come out good in the end; it seems she was (as per usual) right. My sister, Sarah, has been a model for how to be a human, always combining generosity of spirit with an admirable ability to get stuff done. Both of my children spent countless infant hours sleeping on top of me and essentially giving me no choice but to revise first my dissertation (Gaia) and later this manuscript (Elio). The love I share with my better half, Ashley Telman, preceded and endured this entire project, and without it I feel I could hardly stand, let alone have written a book. She will forever be the most beautiful star in my sky.

Introduction

MOST CRITICS AGREE THAT EURIPIDEAN tragedy addresses a wealth of political questions, and that it successfully incorporates and engages with a variety of ancient Greek poetic traditions. Nevertheless, these topics and questions have generally been treated separately.[1] In this book, I focus on the intersections of politics and poetry in Euripidean tragedy in order to address a number of questions that can only be answered when they are examined together: to what extent is poetic exploration a political exercise for Euripides (and vice-versa)? How can the poetic sub- and inter-texts of Euripides' plays alter the audiences' perceptions of the political issues that lie within? And finally, what do these intersections of poetry and politics tell us about Euripides' understanding of the poetic tradition he inherited, and of its place in the Athenian *polis*? Ultimately, I contend that the political issues addressed in Euripides' tragedies are inextricably related to his employment of choral lyric genres such as paean and epinician, and to his engagement with canonical poetic texts such as the *Iliad* and Aeschylus' *Agamemnon*. As I argue throughout this book, we consistently see Euripides recast these traditional poetic genres and texts in order to dramatize and illuminate political questions that are central to his tragedies.

To begin, it is important to understand that the politicization of choral lyric was a powerful dramatic tool because these songs were often used as vehicles for transmitting specific political values and ideas. In fact, Euripides' public would have regularly experienced and even performed choral lyric[2] in highly politicized settings. Paeans were songs that typically exalted and promoted

---

[1] As Donald Mastronarde said in 2000, "[i]f some in a previous generation made the error of seeing only the 'literary' side of Greek tragedy, this does not justify falling into the opposite extreme of recognizing only a 'non-literary' side." (Mastronarde 1999–2000:23–39). With some exceptions, for example Wohl 2015, this divide between political and literary studies of Euripidean tragedy remains the rule, especially for monographs. For example, Torrance 2013 specifically examines Euripides' engagement with other poetic traditions, but generally eschews any discussion of politics, while none of the chapters in Carter 2011 addresses any of the tragedian's use of other poetic genres and traditions.

[2] For a discussion about the widespread participation in choral performances in classical Athens, and the extent to which these were woven into Athenian culture, see esp. Bacon 1994–95; Swift 2010:36–39; Weiss 2019:181.

specific ethnic or civic identities and bonds,[3] and our evidence suggests that Athens made great use of them both within and outside the *polis*. Epinician odes regularly worked to mediate tensions between Olympic victors and their communities, and the two 'epinician' plays examined in this book (*Heracles* and *Alexandros*) were produced at a time when Alcibiades' celebration of his athletic triumphs—including an epinician ode attributed to Euripides—was a hot-button issue in Athens.[4] When Euripides uses paeanic or epinician song in the fabric of his plays, he also evokes political questions or ideals that were implicit in them.[5]

Put differently, because poetic genres such as paean and epinician were political in nature, they contained an inherent potential to shape an Athenian audience's understanding of political questions. This potential is actualized when Euripides invokes these poetic traditions in dramatic contexts that recall the specific political and civic spheres in which these genres were regularly employed. A contemporary example of a lyric genre (hip-hop) employed within a dramatic work can help clarify the point. Not all hip-hop is necessarily political in nature, but the genre is frequently associated with expressions and/or constructions of Black or subaltern identities in the United States.[6] The language and rhythms of hip-hop might be used in musical theater without necessarily bringing any social or political issues to the foreground. But when the musical *Hamilton* uses hip-hop as its poetic backbone in the process of reinventing a familiar story about American identity and values, we see a fusion of politics and poetry that becomes a vehicle for social self-reflection.[7] Similarly,

---

[3] I discuss this in some detail in Chapter 1, but for the fullest articulation of these ideas, see Rutherford 2001:85.

[4] See especially Kurke 1991. Even though epinician performances were no longer en vogue by the end of the fifth century, the two 'epinician' plays examined in this book—Heracles and Alexandros—were produced at a time when Alcibiades' celebration of his athletic triumphs, which included an epinician song attributed to Euripides, was a hot-button issue in Athens. I address this issue at some length in both Chapters 2 and 5.

[5] Or, to put it in Jaussian terms, embedding different lyric genres within a tragedy sets up a "horizon of expectations" that includes specific types of political discourse, which may then be "maintained intact or altered, reoriented, or even fulfilled ironically" (Jauss 1982:23).

[6] The topic is vast and the question is, of course, tremendously complex, but as a starting point see e.g. C. Smith 1997; Ibrahim 1999; Clay 2004:1351–1356; Gause 2003; Hill 2009:103–106; Harrison 2012; Rubin 2016; Gill 2019; Guillory 2019.

[7] See, for example, Herrera 2016. Kajikawa 2018:482 argues that "Miranda's use of hip hop as a lingua franca for the entire production is fundamental to Hamilton's political thrust, sounding out the distance between the United States' ideals of liberty and justice for all and its ongoing realities." Cf. also the comments by Oskar Eustis, the artistic director at the Public Theater, quoted in Mead 2015: "What Lin is doing is taking the vernacular of the streets and elevating it to verse. That is what hip-hop is ... Lin is telling the story of the founding of his country in such a way as to make everyone present feel they have a stake in their country ... By telling the story of the founding of the country through the eyes of a bastard, immigrant orphan, told entirely by people of color, he is saying, 'This is our country. We get to lay claim to it.'"

Euripides' *Ion* operates as an exploration of Athenian and Ionian identity, and within this tragic exploration we see lengthy and innovative paeanic songs. Since lyric paeans were instrumental in forging varying notions of Athenian and Ionian identity in the fifth century BCE, the paeanic twists and tones of the play become closely associated with these questions of identity, and thus affect the audience's interpretation of those questions. In other words, the poetic and political dimensions of *Ion* inform each other, and should in turn inform our understanding of the drama as a whole.

The invocation of both the *Iliad* and *Agamemnon* in *Iphigenia at Aulis* is a different, if related, phenomenon. In particular, they are not choral lyric genres, but single texts with which Athenians engaged almost exclusively as spectators. Still, Euripides' employment of the *Iliad* and *Agamemnon* had similar political potential. Both were canonical texts with which his Athenian audiences were intimately familiar.[8] And although most of the *Iliad* is not situated in the world of the *polis*, much of the action takes place within "political fields,"[9] and the poem was often understood to provide lessons on political and military leadership.[10] Greek tragedy itself, of course, often and overtly explored political questions, and in a manner that was especially relevant to the Athenian *polis*;[11] almost everyone agrees that Aeschylus' *Oresteia* is a prime exemplar of that tendency. Thus, when he alludes to specific aspects of the *Iliad* and *Agamemnon*, Euripides draws on these texts to sharpen his critiques of Athenian democracy.

The technique is one that modern writers and artists continue to exploit to great effect. Looking again to hip-hop, an especially poignant example is offered by Public Enemy's "Fight the Power," a song that permeates Spike Lee's *Do the Right Thing*, a cinematic exploration of race relations in New York City in the late 1980s.[12] Throughout the film, a character named Radio Raheem regularly appears, always playing "Fight the Power" on a boombox. At the end of

---

[8] In the case of the *Iliad*, this is certain. Beyond the regular competitive performances by rhapsodes at the Panathenaic festival, Niceratus' comment in Xenophon's *Symposium* that he "heard [rhapsodes] nearly every day" (*Symposium* 3.6: ἀκροώμενόν γε αὐτῶν ὀλίγου ἂν' ἑκάστην ἡμέραν) strongly suggests that performances of Homeric epic were readily available for those who were interested. The case of *Agamemnon* is somewhat more complex (and one I address at greater length below, in Chapter 5), but suffice it to say that the constant and often subtle allusions to the *Oresteia* in both tragedy and comedy suggest that audiences at the City Dionysia were reasonably "competent" in their knowledge of Aeschylus (Revermann 2006b).

[9] I borrow the term from Hammer 2002:26.

[10] I address this question at length below in Chapter 5, but the conviction expressed by Plato's *Ion* that he has "learned [how to be a general] from Homer's works," (*Ion* 541b: ἐκ τῶν Ὁμήρου μαθών) and the fact that similar ideas come up repeatedly in Athenian literature of the fifth and fourth centuries, suggests that this viewpoint was at least relatively common.

[11] For a thorough overview of this question, see esp. Carter 2007:64–89.

[12] *Do the Right Thing*, directed by Spike Lee (1989, Universal City, CA: Universal Pictures).

the movie, when Sal, a white pizzeria owner, smashes the boombox (referring offensively to "Fight the Power" as "jungle music"), a riot ensues in which Radio Raheem is killed by the police and the simmering racial tensions of the neighborhood are laid absolutely bare. The song's use in the film has been read in different ways,[13] but it unquestionably influences the way that any audience understands the political message of the film, even when those interpretations differ dramatically.[14] More recently, Mat Johnson's novel *Pym*[15] presents itself as a sequel of sorts to Edgar Allen Poe's *The Narrative of Arthur Gordon Pym of Nantucket*. By "invert[ing]" the deeply racist tropes of Poe's novel,[16] Johnson manages to create a satire of constructions and "pathologies" of race and identity in the contemporary United States. Just as Johnson and Lee draw on individual texts in order to tease out powerful political points, so too does Euripides by presenting *Iphigenia at Aulis* as a prequel to the *Iliad* and *Agamemnon*.

Examining this range of plays allows us to develop a holistic sense of the political dimensions of Euripides' re-elaboration of the poetic tradition, since we can see that he uses two very different types of intertextual engagement for similar effects. Indeed, whether he was working with choral lyric genres or canonical texts, we can see that Euripides consistently employed a range of poetic forms in conjunction with specific (and intrinsically related) political questions, just as contemporary authors and artists have continued to do. Moreover, these plays were all performed before spectators who possessed a great deal of experience with choral lyric and with Homeric and Aeschylean poetry. As such, the audience must have been able to perceive, at least on some level, the entanglements of poetry and politics in Euripidean tragedy.

This is especially true because in all the dramas I examine in this book, we see that Euripidean tragedy uses various poetic traditions—Homeric epic, Aeschylean tragedy, epinician and paeanic lyric—as literary devices that help the audience reflect on civic and political issues of great relevance in Athenian society. These intertextual processes are not, of course, identical. In the case of Homer and Aeschylus, the tragedies prompt reflection by recasting the plots,

---

[13] For example, as an encouragement to fight against abusive power structures in the United States (Mitchell 1990:898); or more generally as a vehicle for critiquing the oppression of African-American people and voices (Gibson 2017:190–193).

[14] See for example Stanley Crouch's 1989 review of the film for the *Village Voice* (Crouch 1989), in which the critic refers to Public Enemy as "Afro-fascist race-baiters" immediately before launching into a broader meditation on the fascistic elements of Lee's film. And compare to a more recent review from The New Yorker (Larson 2014) in which Sarah Larson quotes President Barack Obama's comment that "*Do the Right Thing* still holds a mirror up to our society" and later argues that the film's music "perfectly reflects the film's power."

[15] M. Johnson 2011.

[16] To paraphrase Weaver 2012:134.

characters, and conflicts of canonical texts. With paeanic and epinician song, conversely, we see Euripides rework choral lyric genres that are intimately related to the principles and values explored by the tragedies into which they are woven. But in each case, the poetic traditions embedded within the tragedies function as a framework through which the audience can consider, and even reconsider, contemporary issues and ideologies.

Moreover, much like Miranda, Lee, and Johnson, Euripides uses his poetic materials to address political questions that were especially pressing for his Athenian audience. *Ion*, a play that reached the stage in a period when Athens was desperate to (re)establish solidarity with its Ionian allies, presents a myth of Ion's origins in which Athenian and Ionian ethnic identity are completely fused. *Heracles* and the fragments from *Alexandros*, both contemporary with the controversy surrounding Alcibiades' Olympic victory and celebration, employ epinician language as they grapple (as epinician odes themselves did) with the mix of envy and admiration that a hero or victor can provoke among his peers. And at a time when debates about the efficacy of Athenian democracy had reached a peak, *Iphigenia at Aulis* uses Homeric and Aeschylean backdrops to throw into relief some of the issues with contemporary democratic politics and leadership.

These intersections of poetry and politics have several ramifications. Most obviously, we see that the poetic engagement that is evident in Euripidean tragedy is not merely a product of the poet's interest in the literary tradition, but that it is often closely related to the social and political questions explored within these plays: in Euripides, even poetic allusion contains political dimensions. This in turn suggests that Euripides' employment of earlier poetic traditions, even when they are buried beneath the surface, actually plays a fundamental role in the conceptual framework of each play, and that the political dimensions of Euripides' tragedies cannot be fully understood when examined separately from their poetic sub- and inter-texts. At the same time, however, the politicization of poetic interplay works to open up questions about the way these poetic traditions were used or understood in Athenian society, Euripides' own relationship with them, and whether they were adequate or effective vehicles for political thought.

Each chapter of this book focuses on the extensive use of a single poetic tradition in at least one of Euripides' tragedies, and argues that the poetic sub- or inter-text is intimately related to, and should influence our interpretations of, the political issues explored in those plays. In chapter one, I demonstrate that Euripides uses paeans in his *Ion* in a logical setting but in a problematic manner: paeans are an ideal poetic vehicle for creating the various civic and ethnic bonds that the play purports to forge, but the paeanic songs we actually see in *Ion* only serve to undermine these bonds. In the following chapter, I discuss the role of epinician poetry in *Heracles* and the fragmentary *Alexandros*, particularly in relation to the dramatic problem of integrating the two epony-mous heroes into the *poleis* of the tragedies. As I argue, these plays use epinician language and ideologies as a framework through which to view the problem of integration, with differing conclusions. In my third chapter, I argue that the echoes of the *Iliad* in *Iphigenia at Aulis* serve to bring into focus a radically new vision of authority within the Achaean army, and in so doing, the play high-lights problematic aspects of the dynamics of power in democratic Athens. In chapter four, I return to *Iphigenia at Aulis* to examine Euripides' inversion of the Agamemnon/Clytemnestra relationship in Aeschylus' *Agamemnon*. Here, I argue that while Aeschylus presents deceptive speech as a peculiarly 'female' mode of communication, *Iphigenia at Aulis* reveals it to be a common instrument of male political speech, and thus dramatizes an issue of growing concern about deceit in the Athenian political sphere.

In my concluding chapter, I reverse the direction of the lens, so to speak. Here, rather than looking at how Euripides' poetic backdrops help frame the political issues in his tragedies, I examine the manner in which the political dimensions of the plays open up space to debate the use of poetry in the *polis*, and reveal Euripides' complex relationship with the traditions he reimagined. I argue that in all four cases, the civic and political outcomes of the plays chal-lenge the mainstream, Athenian reception and conception of the specific poetic forms. In other words, just like *Hamilton* and *Do the Right Thing* open up questions about the place of hip-hop in American culture,[17] so too does Euripidean tragedy ask his audiences to reconsider the place of paeanic, epinician, Homeric, and Aeschylean poetry in Athenian society. Looked at in this light, Euripides appears as a post-modern poet, at least as Umberto Eco defined the term: one who recog-nized not only the literary traditions that preceded him, but also his audience's recognition of those traditions.[18] Just as importantly, we see that the relation-ship between poetry and politics in Euripidean tragedy appears truly reciprocal, for both aspects illuminate and are illuminated by the other, each becoming a more powerful force in the process.

Studying the political commentary implicit in the poetic sub- and inter-texts of Euripides' plays does not mean attributing to him a well-developed set of political ideas, nor does it mean that his tragedies consistently reflected

---

[17] Kajikawa 2018:474 suggests that "through its many intertextual references to hip hop, *Hamilton* suggests that the Founders and famous rappers are cut from the same enterprising cloth." On *Do the Right Thing*, see e.g. Gibson 2017:191: "the disagreement between Sal and Radio Raheem is as much about solidifying hip-hop as a respectable musical genre as it is about the intensified racial tensions sprawling in Brooklyn."

[18] Eco 1984:39. Translation from Italian by author.

the same set of ideas. His perspective is likely to have changed over the course of his long career, and depending on what he was reacting to when writing a specific play. Moreover, in most cases, Euripides appears just as interested in asking questions as providing answers. The important thing, however, is that Euripides' invocation of poetic modes and narratives invited his audiences to reflect on current issues with a certain intellectual distance, to recognize incongruities in Athenian society and politics, and indeed to think about the ways that poetry and politics were intermingled in the Athenian *polis*.

1

The Paean and Euripides' *Ion*
A Song for Athens and Ionia?

THE CRISES AND QUESTIONS OF identity in Euripides' *Ion* have long proven an irresistible topic for critics, and for good reason. The tragedy fuses two conflicting and ideologically loaded notions of Athenian identity: the myth of autochthony, according to which Athenians were descendants of the original and earth-born inhabitants of Attica;[1] and the idea that the Ionian Greeks shared an ethnic identity with the Athenians by virtue of their common descent from or association with Ion.[2] Each notion provided its own distinct advantages. Autochthony granted the Athenians a certain chronological superiority over the rest of the Greeks and bolstered a sense of democratic equality among their own civic body,[3] while the idea of a shared ancestry had long been used by Athenians

---

[1] Depending on the tradition, the Athenians' mythical ancestor was known as either Erichthonios or Erechtheus. In short, Erichthonios/Erechtheus was said to have been born from the earth in Attica after Hephaestus' aborted rape of Athena resulted in the god's semen spilling on and impregnating the earth. According to the myth, Cecrops was the king of Attica at the time, and it was to him (or his daughters) that Athena entrusted the infant Erichthonios. For a reasonably coherent version of the myth, cf. Apollodorus *Bibliotheca* 3.14. On the meaning and importance of this concept in fifth-century Athens, see esp. Montanari 1981; Rosivach 1987; Loraux 2000; Connor 1994:34–44; J. Hall 1997:53–56.

[2] Within these traditions, Ion is generally presented as the son of Xouthos. While Xouthos was decidedly not Athenian, Ion was either provided autochthonous descent through his mother, Creousa (daughter of Erechtheus; this genealogy is already presented by Pseudo-Hesiod fragment 10a, 20–24), or connected to Athens by virtue of having served as a military leader (cf. Herodotus 8.44.2). Regardless of the details of the Athenians' and Ionians' shared origins, Solon's claim that Athens was the "oldest land of Ionia" (fragment 4a, 2: πρεσβυτάτην γαῖαν ['I]αονίης) makes it clear that the idea of a shared ethnicity existed long before Euripides' time. For more on the subject, see Robertson 1988; Connor 1993; J. Hall 1997:42–44 and 51–53.

[3] Cf. Isocrates 12.24; Plato *Menexenus* 237e–238a; Rosivach 1987; Connor 1994; Loraux 2000:33–38. It is also worth noting that the Athenian conception of autochthony did not arise until much after their theorization of a common Ionian ancestry: while Solon already speaks of Athens' conception of Ionia in the early sixth century BCE (see above, note 2), we hear nothing of Athenian autochthony until after the advent of democracy in the early fifth century (see esp. Rosivach 1987).

and Ionians alike to justify Athenian involvement in Ionia and the Cyclades.[4] At the risk of oversimplifying, one might state that the myth of autochthony was relied on more heavily in the democratic sphere of internal politics, while Ionianism was exploited within the external sphere of Athens' dealings with its allies and subjects.[5] These two myths were for the most part mutually exclusive; when one was emphasized, the other was by necessity marginalized.[6] In *Ion*, however, Euripides resolves this dichotomy by "purifying" the bloodline, removing the non-Athenian Xouthos from Ion's lineage, positing Apollo as his natural father, and maintaining the Athenian Creousa as his mother. In short, Euripides' play poses Ion as both an autochthonous Athenian and the eponymous founder of the Ionian race.

The timing of the play's production adds urgency of these questions. The play was likely performed shortly before, during, or immediately after the revolt of many of Athens' Ionian allies,[7] so the mythological promotion of these allies' descent from Athens would surely have been of interest to many members of the audience. But *Ion* also coincides with the rare and brief periods in which the requirements of Pericles' citizenship law of 451/450 BCE were eased,[8] suggesting

---

[4]   Cf. Herodotus 5.97.2; Thucydides 1.95.1; 3.86.3. See also Barron 1962; Barron 1964:46–48; Connor 1993; Bremmer, 1997:12; Alty 1982:1–14.

[5]   On the "elite" and "imperialist" associations of Ionianism, cf. Connor 1993:200–204; Dougherty 1996:252–254. On the "democratic" associations of autochthony, cf. Connor 1993:204–206; Connor 1994; Dougherty 1996:254–257; and especially Rosivach 1987:302–306.

[6]   See esp. J. Hall 1997:53–55; and Connor 1994.

[7]   The precise year of production cannot be established, but the tragedy can in all likelihood be placed within a limited range. Metrical considerations (i.e. the percentage of "resolved" trimeters; see esp. the table in Caedel 1941:70) suggest that *Ion* (25.8 percent) was performed after *Trojan Women* (21.2 percent) and before *Helen* (27.5), or between 416/415 and 412/411 BCE. The metrical criterion is, of course, approximate, and earlier scholars attempted to ante-date *Ion* based primarily on historical considerations (cf. e.g. Owen 1939:xxxvi–xli). In more recent years, however, scholars have generally placed *Ion* in the later years of that range, i.e. between 413 and 411 BCE. Scholars who lean toward 413 BCE include: Diggle 1981:306; K. Lee 1997:40. For a compelling argument in favor of 412 BCE, cf. Zacharia 2003:1–7. For 411 BCE, see Walsh 1978:313–315. Martin 2010 proposes a date of 411 BCE or later. And 410 BCE has been proposed by Klimek-Winter 1996, and is followed by Bremmer 1997:12.

[8]   The law was "eliminated" during the Oligarchic coup of 411 BCE (see Lape 2010:21n76), but shortly before that (ca. 413 BCE), Diogenes Laertes 2.26, tells us that Athenians changed the law so as to allow Athenians to "marry one woman and to have children from another" (γαμεῖν μὲν ἀστὴν μίαν, παιδοποιεῖσθαι δὲ καὶ ἐξ ἑτέρας). Note the emphasis in the Greek on the wife being a citizen; whether or not the "other woman" was required to be a citizen is open to interpretation, though the construction of the sentence (*astên ≈ heteras*) implies that the second woman was supposed to be an Athenian as well. Lape 2010:263–265 argues that this was the original intent of the law, but that because of various difficulties (e.g. the unwillingness of Athenian citizens to "sacrifice their daughters to a life of concubinage" [264]), the application of the law was probably fluid. Ogden 1996:72–75 provides a good overview of the "bigamy law," but is noncommittal in his assessment of potential collateral effects.

that concern about the purity of Athenian bloodlines may also have been at a peak. Given these contexts, it is obvious that Euripides is broaching delicate and highly relevant subjects. It is thus crucial to remember that questions about Athens' autochthonous and Ionian identities are in the foreground from the very beginning of the tragedy, would have remained in the minds of the audience throughout, and are ultimately posited as the framework through which to read the play's exploration of Ion's identity.

Whether the play's Apolline genealogy was a Euripidean innovation or an adaptation of a less well-known myth is still the subject of debate. Plato's uncritical citation of the very same bloodline a mere twenty-five years after *Ion* was produced,[9] and the likely existence of the cult of Apollo *Patroôs* as early as the sixth century,[10] suggest that the story pre-dated Euripides in some form.[11] Regardless, Euripides appears to be the first to fully articulate this mythological tradition, and the fact that he does so in terms that are overtly political has suggested to most scholars that *Ion* deliberately presents a merger of two distinct myths with the potential to resolve, or perhaps challenge, highly charged issues of identity.

Scholars have examined this tragic fusion of identities from a number of different angles. Many have focused on the tragedy's implications for Athenian and Ionian identity, variously arguing that *Ion* functions as a critique of Athenian politics of identity[12] or a patriotic celebration of Athenian autochthony and its

---

[9] Plato, *Euthydemus* 302d, names Apollo as Ion's father and cites this as the reason that Athenians and Ionians celebrate Apollo *Patroôs*. As Shapiro 2009:271, points out: "[t]his does not sound like a recently invented genealogy."

[10] For more on the cult of Apollo *Patroôs* in Athens, the foundation of which is typically dated to the 6th century BCE, see Thompson 1937:77–84, who identifies a structure in the Athenian *agora* from the 6th century BCE as a temple to Apollo *Patroôs*; de Schutter 1987, who generally follows Thompson's identification of the temple; Hedrick 1988, who notes that there are "grave problems with the standard interpretation" of the archaic temple to Apollo *Patroôs* and that "even [its] existence" is not "beyond doubt" (p. 191), but who nevertheless does not dispute the Peisistratid foundation of the cult. *Contra*, see Lawall 2009, who puts forth a strong argument that the temple of Apollo Patroos in the *agora* should be dated to the end of the fourth century BCE, and even doubts the existence of the cult in archaic or classical Athens.

[11] Shapiro 2009 argues that several heretofore unidentified figures found on mid-fifth-century Attic vases are in fact Ion in the presence of Apollo, an identification which, if correct, would essentially prove that Euripides is working with an established Attic tradition.

[12] Loraux 1993, for example, argues that the tragedy exposes the uncertainty of Athenian origin myths, and contends that by making a woman (Creousa) solely responsible for "carrying the weight of autochthony" (236), Euripides fundamentally undermines his own genealogical creation. Others insist that the play's emphasis on ignorance, violence, complex notions of bastardy, or the final and presumably prolonged deception of Xouthos, who continues to mistakenly believe that Ion is his natural son, all function to question not only Athenian civic myths but indeed the process of Athenian mythmaking. See Saxonhouse 1986:271–272; Farrington 1991;

successful merger with Ionian identity.[13] Still others, perhaps heeding Kevin Lee's warning about the difficulty of "finding in the play any simple critique of its implications,"[14] have looked not for the play's ultimate message but rather at what it can tell us about perceptions of identity in contemporary Athens. Susan Lape, for example, has used *Ion* as a lens through which to examine notions of citizenship in classical Athens,[15] while Zeitlin and Mueller have considered the manner in which these identities are expressed and recognized by the characters in the play.[16]

One related problem that has gone unaddressed is the manner in which paeanic song is used to express identity in the tragedy. Doubtless the difficulty of approaching the topic, due not least to the nebulous nature of the genre, has dampened enthusiasm for analysis of this sort. But there are numerous reasons to believe that such rocky terrain could bear rich fruits: first, because *Ion*'s two paeanic monodies are both used to affirm false versions of Ion's identity—and hence Ionian identity—a curious dynamic considering the play's obsession with the topic; second, because these two paeanic songs also contain sharp and overt rebukes of Apolline music; and third, because it seems that paean-songs were regularly used in fifth-century Greece to define or propagate civic or communal identities, particularly within the context of Athenian/Ionian relations. In other words, while fifth-century paeans were a common poetic vehicle for the advancement of politically expedient notions of shared Ionian identity, *Ion* uses paeanic song to present blatantly false versions of Ion's descent-lines. This divergence of form and function, repeated twice, is no mere coincidence. As I argue, the fictional nature of *Ion*'s two paeanic songs suggests that even as the play presents the audience with a convenient merger of Athenian/Ionian identity, *Ion* also challenges the audience to consider the legitimacy of such mythical constructions, and thus undermines the very merger of identities that it purports to dramatize.

Hoffer 1996. Patterson 1990:66–68 argues that by making Ion a "bastard" child of Apollo and Creousa, Euripides "exposes the ironies of Athenian social conventions and pretensions" (67).

[13] This more positive interpretation was popular among earlier scholars. Cf. Owen 1939:xxxiii who asserts that the play was intended to "gratify the pride of the Athenians and to make closer the bonds that linked the Ionian cities with Athens." More recently, a number of scholars have added nuance to this interpretation, perhaps none more cogently than Dougherty 1996:250 who contends that Euripides successfully proposes "a new world in which Athenians emerge as both autochthonous and Ionian, simultaneously democratic and imperial." Along these lines, see also Zacharia 2003:44–102; and Swift 2008:94–100.

[14] K. Lee 1997:36.

[15] Lape 2010:95–136.

[16] E.g. Zeitlin 1996:285–338; Mueller 2010.

1. From Hermes to Athena: The Importance of Being Ion

Ion opens with Hermes standing before the temple of Apollo, and by the end of his prologue the audience is already prepared to see the play explore complex questions of collective identity. Hermes begins by mentioning "[the] famous city of the Greeks / named after golden-speared Pallas"[17] and its autochthonous ancestors (*Ion* 10–11). In the following lines, we learn of Apollo's rape of the Athenian Creousa and her secret parturition and abandonment of his child (*Ion* 10–27), a tale that prompts Hermes to spell out Athens' heretofore unbroken line of autochthonous descent. Creousa is the daughter of Erechtheus (*Ion* 10–11) and a descendant of "earthborn Erichthonios" (*Ion* 20–21: γηγενοῦς / Ἐριχθονίου). Her child, as it turns out, will continue this line, for Hermes had rescued and delivered the infant to Delphi shortly after his birth (*Ion* 29–40). Ion's true identity, however, remains a well-guarded secret.

The tricky question of the boy's identity dominates the remainder of the prologue. Hermes specifies that the Pythian priestess had raised him even though "she did not know Apollo was his father, nor who his mother was, and the child does not know his parents."[18] Now a young man, he remains at Delphi and serves as "the god's gold-keeper and loyal steward of all things" (*Ion* 54–55: χρυσοφύλακα τοῦ θεοῦ / ταμίαν τε πάντων πιστόν). The fact that Creousa is on her way to Delphi with her husband Xouthos presents an additional complication. Both wish to consult the oracle about Creousa's inability to conceive, a question that will force Apollo to engage in a certain amount of subterfuge:

> δώσει γὰρ εἰσελθόντι μαντεῖον τόδε
> 70 Ξούθῳ τὸν αὑτοῦ παῖδα καὶ πεφυκέναι
> κείνου σφε φήσει, μητρὸς ὡς ἐλθὼν δόμους
> γνωσθῇ Κρεούσῃ
>
> *Ion* 69–72

> For when Xouthos comes to his oracle, [Apollo] shall give
> 70 the child to him as his own, and shall say he was born of him,
> so that when [Ion] comes to the home of his mother
> he shall be recognized by Creousa

---

17 *Ion* 8–9: ἔστιν γὰρ οὐκ ἄσημος Ἑλλήνων πόλις, / τῆς χρυσολόγχου Παλλάδος κεκλημένη. All translations by author unless otherwise specified.

18 *Ion* 50–51: οὐκ οἶδε Φοῖβον οὐδὲ μητέρ' ἧς ἔφυ, / ὁ παῖς τε τοὺς τεκόντας οὐκ ἐπίσταται.

The plots—both Apollo's and the tragedy's—seem intentionally convoluted, and are the first indication that the unveiling of the boy's true identity will be the central conceit of the tragedy, and no simple matter. Indeed, according to Hermes, Ion will have to pass from one fictional identity (orphaned slave of Apollo) to another (son of Xouthos), before eventually finding his true identity as the son of Creousa, descendant of Erechtheus.

Moreover, we learn that the boy will come to be the progenitor of the Ionian Greeks, a fact that will have major consequences for the Greek world:

> Ἴωνα δ' αὐτόν, κτίστορ' Ἀσιάδος χθονός,
> 75 ὄνομα κεκλῆσθαι θήσεται καθ' Ἑλλάδα.
>
> *Ion* 74–75

> [Apollo] shall see to it that he be called Ion,
> 75 founder of the Asian land, throughout Greece.

Here Ion's name is spoken for the first time[19] and his association with the Ionian Greeks is immediately and explicitly stated.

The full implications of Ion's combined Athenian and Ionian lineage are vast, and would no doubt have been well-understood by Euripides' audience. But they are not explicitly stated until Athena, filling in for Apollo, finally arrives at the end of the play to confirm that Ion is indeed the child of Apollo and Creousa (*Ion* 1560), and thus ensure the long-anticipated happy ending:[20]

> λαβοῦσα τόνδε παῖδα Κεκροπίαν χθόνα
> χώρει, Κρέουσα, κἀς θρόνους τυραννικοὺς
> ἵδρυσον. ἐκ γὰρ τῶν Ἐρεχθέως γεγὼς
> δίκαιος ἄρχειν τῆς ἐμῆς ὅδε χθονός
>
> *Ion* 1571–1574

> Take this child and go to the land of Cecrops,
> Creousa, and set him on its royal throne.
> For he is born of Erechtheus' stock,
> and it is right for him to rule over my land.

---

[19] A few lines later Hermes will reiterate that he himself is "the first of the gods to name him Ion" (*Ion* 81: Ἴων' ἐγώ ‹νιν› πρῶτος ὀνομάζω θεῶν).

[20] For an excellent analysis of the "psychagogic" effects that the many and complex vicissitudes of the play would have had on the audience's desire to see Ion and Creousa finally find themselves, see Wohl 2015:19–38. Wohl argues that these effects would actually cause the audience to yearn so greatly for the reunion of Creousa and Ion that problematic questions of ideology might be obscured, and celebration encouraged. While this may have been the case for some spectators, I argue here that the issues of identity are problematized to such an extent, not least by the paeanic songs in the tragedy, that they would be difficult to ignore for much of the audience.

By declaring that Ion's divine parentage equates to autochthonous descent, Athena essentially confirms Creousa's earlier exclamation that with Ion, "Erechtheus has risen again!" (*Ion* 1465: ἀνηβᾷ δ' Ἐρεχθεύς). In short, the Athenians may now include Ion in their lineage without contaminating the purity of the line.

Just as crucially, Athena verifies the existence of Ion's descendants and emphasizes their importance for Athens:

οἱ τῶνδε δ' αὖ
παῖδες γενόμενοι σὺν χρόνῳ πεπρωμένῳ
Κυκλάδας ἐποικήσουσι νησαίας πόλεις
χέρσους τε παράλους, ὃ σθένος τἠμῇ χθονὶ
1585   δίδωσιν· ἀντίπορθμα δ' ἠπείροιν δυοῖν
πεδία κατοικήσουσιν, Ἀσιάδος τε γῆς
Εὐρωπίας τε· τοῦδε δ' ὀνόματος χάριν
Ἴωνες ὀνομασθέντες ἕξουσιν κλέος.
Ξούθῳ δὲ καὶ σοὶ γίγνεται κοινὸν γένος,
1590   Δῶρος μέν, ἔνθεν Δωρὶς ὑμνηθήσεται
πόλις κατ' αἶαν Πελοπίαν· ὁ δεύτερος
Ἀχαιός, ὃς γῆς παραλίας Ῥίου πέλας
τύραννος ἔσται, κἀπισημανθήσεται
κείνου κεκλῆσθαι λαὸς ὄνομ' ἐπώνυμον.

Ion 1581–1594

And later still
at the allotted time [Ion's grandchildren]
shall settle the Cycladic island cities
and the sea-side lands, which give strength
1585   to my land. They shall colonize the plains
of the two opposing continents, Asia
and Europe; and, named Ionians in his honor,
they shall obtain great glory.
You [Creousa] and Xouthos shall also share
1590   a family: first Doros, after which the Dorian city
shall be celebrated throughout the land of Pelops;
and second Achaios, who shall be the ruler
of the coastland near Rhion, where the people
shall be distinguished by his eponymous name.

Several details stand out in this description: the Ionians' descent from Ion and Athens' concomitant status as "mother-city" of the Ionian allies is reaffirmed;

Athenians and Ionians alike are given primacy—both chronologically and genealogically—over the Dorians and Achaeans; and perhaps most intriguingly, the Ionian colonies that make up the Delian league are said to "give strength" to Athens. Whether this last point is a reference to Ionian military assistance or, as Hoffer suggests, to the tributes upon which Athens so heavily relied,[21] it is explicit that the mythical origins promoted by Ion are closely related to the propagation of real Athenian alliances in the Cyclades and Ionia. Implicit is the idea that the Ionian Greeks themselves win "great glory" on account of both their privileged descent from autochthonous Athenians, and their present status as allies of the city. In essence, just as the tragedy is coming to an end, Euripides doubles down on the identity-politics of the play, framing them not only as essential to the tragic plot, but also as the foundation of the ties that had long bound Athenian and Ionians in a military alliance. Perhaps most importantly, Athens' hegemonic role in the Delian League is subtly justified by the play's (re)construction of Athenians' and Ionians' shared ancestry.[22]

2. Ion's Paeanic Monody:
False Identity and Internal Criticism

Just after Hermes primes the audience to expect this specific, identity-driven, and highly topical dramatic itinerary, Ion arrives onstage and begins to perform the (false) identity given to him by Apollo. Appearing before the audience for the first time, with a bow and Apollo's *stemmata* in hand (cf. *Ion* 108, 522), Ion takes after his heretofore unknown father.[23] The scene is playful, and as Anne-Sophie Noel has recently argued, can be seen as Ion "acting like Apollo," and thus taking a step towards actualizing his true identity.[24] At the same time, however, both his song and his actions underscore the fictionality of his current dramatic identity, and the discrepancy between his real and perceived identities is immediately thrown into sharp relief.

Indeed, the Apolline object to which our attention is most drawn is the laurel broom with which he sets about cleaning the temple. As he sweeps, Ion introduces himself and the setting with a series of recitative anapaests.[25] The first lines are appropriately rich in Apolline imagery: Ion sings of the temple's

---

[21] Hoffer 1996:313–314.
[22] See e.g. Bremmer 1997:12 who notes that an analogous (and deeply political) emphasis on Ionian descent from Athens seems to have taken place in Samos around 439 BCE, shortly after the Samian revolt.
[23] Wasserman 1940:601; Wolff 1965:172; Zeitlin 1996:292.
[24] Noel (forthcoming).
[25] K. Lee 1997:168. On recitative anapaests, cf. E. Hall 1999:105–108.

sacred tripod (91), Delphi's prophetic workings (92–94, 98–102), the Kastalia's "purifying waters" (96: καθαραῖς δὲ δρόσοις), and of the laurel branches (103: πτόρθοισι δάφνης) with which he is making the temple's entry "pure" (105: καθαράς). All this is reminiscent of the Delphic Septerion, a festival at which an ἀμφιθαλής κοῦρος (a young man with two living parents) re-enacted Apollo's post-Pytho purification by burning down a small hut in front of the temple at Delphi, traveling to Thessaly to purify himself in the river Peneius, and then collecting branches of laurel before leading a procession to Delphi, branches of laurel still in hand.[26] Ion's first appearance thus reminds us both of his father Apollo, whom he physically resembles, while with his words and actions he mimics the Septerion's ἀμφιθαλής κοῦρος.

All this is most incongruous with Ion's own assessment of his actions and origins:

> ἡμεῖς δέ, πόνους οὓς ἐκ παιδὸς
> μοχθοῦμεν ἀεί, πτόρθοισι δάφνης
> στέφεσίν θ' ἱεροῖς ἐσόδους Φοίβου
> 105   καθαρὰς θήσομεν

Ion 102–105

> As for me, I toil constantly at the tasks
> I have carried out since childhood, with laurel
> branches and sacred bands[27] I shall make
> 105   the entrance to Phoebus' temple pure

Much like the ἀμφιθαλής κοῦρος, Ion is involved in an act of purification that he describes as a sacred duty.[28] This service to Apollo, however, is not a one-time engagement, but a life-long endeavor. Moreover, Ion's explanation for his eternal servitude reveals a stark contrast between himself and the Septerion's traditional re-enactor:

> ὡς γὰρ ἀμήτωρ ἀπάτωρ τε γεγὼς
> τοὺς θρέψαντας
> Φοίβου ναοὺς θεραπεύω.

Ion 109–111

---

[26] On these rituals, cf. Plutarch *De defectu oraculorum* 417e–418d; Rutherford 2001:201–205; and Burkert 1983:127–130. Rutherford 2001:112 also draws the parallel between this scene in *Ion* and the Delphic Septerion.

[27] Following K. Lee 1997:171.

[28] Plutarch refers to the ritual as a λατρεία (*De defectu oraculorum* 417e8); Ion uses the verb λατρεύω three times later in the monody (*Ion* 124, 129, 152) to describe his relationship to Apollo.

> For since I was born motherless and fatherless
> I serve the temple
> of Apollo that raised me.

Ion claims to be without either parent, thus theoretically disqualifying himself from the role of ἀμφιθαλής κοῦρος. Of course, the dramatic irony here is thick. The audience knows that Ion was by no means born "motherless and father-less." In fact, the father he so closely resembles has been a constant (if evanescent) presence in his life, while his mother is soon to arrive at Delphi. As a result, there is a subtle but multi-tiered emphasis on the striking incongruity that exists between Ion's real and supposed identities.

At this point, Ion shifts from singing in anapaests to performing a lyric monody, one which overtly identifies itself as a paean at the end of the first strophe:

125 ὦ Παιὰν ὦ Παιάν,
   εὐαίων εὐαίων
   εἴης, ὦ Λατοῦς παῖ

Ion 125–127

125 O Paean, o Paean,
   blessed, blessed
   may you be, o child of Leto.

As Rutherford has noted this is "the only true παιάν-refrain in extant tragedy,"[29] the clearest formal marker of the genre. The appearance of a paean would not be surprising for an Athenian audience. To begin, the paean was the song that was most closely connected to Apolline cult[30]— Pindar, for example, refers to "seasonal paean songs of the children of golden-distaffed Leto."[31] Delphi itself "must have resounded on many occasions of the year to the choral paeans performed by both local choirs and foreign *theoriai*."[32] In short, the Delphic

---

[29] Rutherford 2001:111.

[30] This is evident simply from the sheer number of paeans dedicated to Apollo as compared to other deities, especially if one considers that songs for Asclepius would fall under the umbrella of Apolline cult. See also Photius, who tells us that Proclus had identified the paean as a type of song that "in antiquity was assigned to Apollo and Artemis" (*Bibliotheca* 320a22–23: τὸ δὲ παλαιὸν ἰδίως ἀπενέμετο τῷ Ἀπόλλωνι καὶ τῇ Ἀρτέμιδι).

[31] Pindar fragment 128c: "ἔντι μὲν χρυσαλακάτου τεκέων Λατοῦς ἀοιδαὶ / ὥ[ρ]ιαι παιάνιδες." In my translation I closely follow Furley and Bremer 2001 vol. 1:83.

[32] Furley and Bremer 2001 vol. 1:83. Calame 2009 argues this on the basis of Philodamus' *Paean for Dionysus*, but even more compelling evidence is provided by Bacchylides 16.18–22 (also cited by Furley and Bremer 2001 vol. 1:83, and vol. 2:22): δ' ἵκῃ παιηόνων / ἄνθεα πεδοιχνεῖν, / Πύθι'

setting and the propagation of Apolline imagery in the first part of the song strongly suggest the performance of a paean. Moreover, as we shall see below, paeans were regularly used as a means to express communal identities, precisely the stakes that Hermes had just outlined in the prologue. As such, the genre corresponds neatly to both the dramatic plot and setting, and the Athenian audience would be deeply primed to understand Ion's monody as a paean.[33]

At the same time, Ion's song contains a number of elements that fit uneasily with the genre. Above all, fifth-century paeans were typically performed by choruses of young men,[34] and there is no parallel for Ion's solo paean.[35] Moreover, the evidence suggests that classical paeans took place in communal contexts and "had the integrative function of articulating a sense of community among the members, and of expressing this sense before the polis as a whole."[36] Indeed, whether they were sung to prepare an army for battle,[37] in celebration of a victory won,[38] by *theôriai* at Apolline festivals,[39] or for apotropaic purposes,[40] classical paeans were always performed by groups of men who represented and advanced the interests of their communities. Conversely, by singing alone, proclaiming his orphanage, and even celebrating his status as a temple slave, Ion emphasizes his lack of ties to any *oikos* or *polis*, thus divorcing his song from the social contexts with which paeans were generally associated. Even on the basic level of form and function, Ion's song presents a number of idiosyncrasies.

Ἄπολλον, / τόσα χοροὶ Δελφῶν / σὸν κελάδησαν παρ' ἀγακλέα ναόν ("and you come in search / of flowers of paeans / Pythian Apollo, / which the Delphic choruses / sing beside your glorious temple").

[33] *Contra*, see K. Lee 1997:172, who calls this a "Delphic Hymn"; and Furley and Bremer 2001 vol. 1:322–323 (and esp. fn 14), who argue that "the cultic refrain of Ion's song is intended by Euripides to show Ion's deep familiarity with the type of songs which rang out constantly at the oracle." In my view, it is far less likely that the audience would come to this conclusion than that they would simply interpret this song as a "solo" paean, given the presence (and eventual repetition) of the paean refrain surrounded by a number of other paeanic elements.

[34] See Rutherford 2001:85 and 58–68 on the performance of paeans in general; Furley and Bremer 2001 vol. 1:90–91.

[35] Even other "tragic" paeans are sung by or with the chorus. Cf. e.g. Sophocles *Oedipus Tyrannus* 151–215; Sophocles *Philoctetes* 827–838; Euripides *Heracles* 687–700, etc.

[36] Rutherford 2001:62. See also Rutherford 1995:115–116; Furley and Bremer 2001 vol. 1:88–91 (following Rutherford 1995); and Ford 2006:284–285.

[37] As we see in Aeschylus *Persians* 392–394, and in Pindar's second *Paean*.

[38] E.g. Pindar *Paean* 2, which has the double function of celebrating a past victory and preparing for a future battle.

[39] Rutherford 2004:67 defines *theôriai* as "sacred delegations ... sent out by their city-states to perform religious functions abroad," but see also Rutherford 2013:4–6 for a broader discussion of the importance and origins of the practice. Examples of theoric paeans include in all probability Pindar *Paean* 5, *Paean* 6 (at least the first two strophes), and *Paean* 7b and Bacchylides 17 (if it is indeed a paean, on which more below).

[40] E.g. Pindar *Paean* 9; the paean in the parodos at Sophocles *Oedipus Tyrannus* 151–215.

The second strophe continues in the same vein and culminates in the same refrain, thus hammering down on the song's paeanic credentials. But the puzzling aspects of the first strophe are also magnified:

κάλόν γε τὸν πόνον, ὦ
Φοῖβε, σοὶ πρὸ δόμων λατρεύ-
130 ω, τιμῶν μαντεῖον ἕδραν·
κλεινὸς δ' ὁ πόνος μοι
θεοῖσιν δούλαν χέρ' ἔχειν,
οὐ θνατοῖς, ἀλλ' ἀθανάτοις·
εὐφάμους δὲ πόνους
135 μοχθεῖν οὐκ ἀποκάμνω.
Φοῖβός μοι γενέτωρ πατήρ·
τὸν βόσκοντα γὰρ εὐλογῶ,
τὸν δ' ὠφέλιμον ἐμοὶ πατέρος ὄνομα λέγω
140 Φοῖβον τοῦ κατὰ ναόν.

ὦ Παιὰν ὦ Παιάν,
εὐαίων εὐαίων
εἴης, ὦ Λατοῦς παῖ.

Ion 128–143

A beautiful toil, o Phoebus,
I render before your home,
130 honoring this oracular seat.
It is a glorious toil for me
to hold my hand in service to the gods,
not to mortals but to immortals;
nor do I tire of laboring at
135 auspicious toils.
Phoebus is to me as an ancestral father;
for I praise the one who feeds me,
and I call him by the name of father, beneficent,
140 Phoebus of this temple.

O Paean, o paean,
blessed, blessed
may you be, o child of Leto.

The focus of this strophe is obviously on Ion's toil (*ponos*) at the temple. Such a topic is, in a sense, standard for paeans,[41] but typically, the *ponos* to which a hymnal or paeanic chorus refers is the very act in which it is engaged—the song and dance.[42] Here, on the other hand, Ion is singing of his janitorial duties. This unusual use of a paeanic motif underscores the unconventional nature of his paean. The incongruity is further highlighted by the fact that Ion calls his toils "auspicious" (134: *euphāmous ponous*). The paean itself was considered a form of *euphêmia*,[43] so by using this adjective to refer to his mundane task, Ion again seems to be using a paeanic formula in a most unusual manner. Here we see Euripides overtly manipulating the generic conventions of the paean, and in so doing he draws the attention of the audience to the innovative nature of the song itself.

In this vein, Ion's words about Apollo are crucial. Ion says he looks at Apollo *as* a father:[44] a father in "name," but not, it would appear from his formulation, in reality. He recalls his earlier claim to be "motherless and fatherless" (109), and affirms this fictional identity by referring to Apollo as "τὸν βόσκοντα," a term that befits a shepherd rather than a parent.[45] The irony here is again obvious,[46] for of course Apollo actually *is* his father.[47] This underscores a crucial aspect of Ion's song: throughout the paean, but especially in the second strophe, Ion is intent on defining himself, and the definition he gives himself is erroneous. Rather than stressing that he belongs to a community of Athenians or Ionians, or indeed any community, Ion instead defines himself as a temple slave who does not know who his actual parents are. His paean thus "symbolizes his

---

[41]   Rutherford 1995:130 notes that this is "a theme that can be paralleled in nondramatic paeans," pointing to Simonides fragment 35b.6 (=*PMG* 519), and Pindar *Paean* 7b.21–22.

[42]   As Rutherford 2001:249 indeed notes regarding Pindar's seventh *Paean*. But cf. also Pindar fragment 70c.16 (a dithyramb): πόνοι χορῶν.

[43]   Rutherford 1990:173 makes a similar point ("there seems to be an association between the word εὔφημος and its cognates and the paean-refrain"), and the examples he cites point to how close this association was: rather than speaking of "singing a paean," a number of ancient authors simply say (*ep*)*eufêmeô paiana* or even simply (*ep*)*eufêmeô* (Aeschylus *Persians* 389; Aristophanes *Knights* 1316–1318; Euripides *Iphigenia in Tauris* 1403–1404; *Iphigenia at Aulis* 1467–1468; Macedonius *Paean* 3).

[44]   The line could of course also be interpreted as "Apollo is my father," but given the emphasis on Ion's ignorance of his origins, it seems unlikely that the audience would think that was Ion's intention, and very likely that the double-entendre would instead add to the sense that Ion is using his paean in a most unconventional manner.

[45]   Euripides uses this term several times in *Phoenissae* as well (*Phoenissae* 396, 400, 405), but here too it is used to emphasize an individual's (i.e. Polyneices') exile and lack of community. To my knowledge, *Ion* is the only case in which Euripides uses βόσκω to refer to an actual parent; he generally uses the more appropriate τρέφω.

[46]   K. Lee 1997:173, also notes it.

[47]   Though at the end of the play Apollo will refuse that name, for all intents and purposes.

isolation from community,"[48] and it celebrates the fictional identity that Apollo has imposed upon him. The song is marked by a constant tension between his real and fictional identities, and it insinuates this potential artificiality into paeanic myth. It provides the first strong, if as yet implicit, challenge to the paean's ability to properly define or propagate origins.

At this point, Ion's monody changes tone and becomes an "astrophic song"[49] that is unmarked by the paean refrain (144–183). In this section of the ode, we see Ion chasing birds from the premises, bow in hand (154–179), lest they sully the temple he has been cleaning. Among those that Ion abuses is a swan, Apollo's bird, whose "beautifully-resounding songs" he threatens to "bloody" (168–169: αἱμάξεις... / τὰς καλλιφθόγγους ᾠδάς) with his arrows.[50] While there is undoubtedly an element of humor in this scene,[51] there is also a sense that Ion has exceeded the bounds of propriety: to kill one of Apollo's swans "would surely constitute a form of sacrilege."[52] Even more disturbing, though oft over-looked, is his preface to the threat:

> οὐδέν σ' ἁ φόρμιγξ ἁ Φοίβου
> 165   σύμμολπος τόξων ῥύσαιτ' ἄν.

Ion 164–165

> Phoebus' lyre, your accompaniment,
> 165   will not protect you from my bow.

On the surface, Ion's dismissal of the lyre's ability to preserve the swan may seem reasonable enough; the average musical instrument offers little protection against arrows. Moreover, there is a playful side to the statement, for Euripides appears to draw on the well-known *"palintropos harmonia"* of the bow and the lyre, the idea that the two (Apolline) instruments were in many ways complementary.[53] On another level, however, Ion's claim that his own weapon is more powerful than Apollo's lyre is troubling, and seems particularly out of place in a paean. If taken literally, it seems that he is downplaying the power of Apollo's musical abilities in the midst of an Apolline song. Though the claim is made to seem insignificant by both its triviality and its playful allusivity, it

---

[48] Rutherford 1995:131.

[49] K. Lee 1997:171.

[50] With αἱμάξεις I follow the manuscript reading, though Diggle 1981 accepts Nauck's emendation of αἰάξεις. For recent defenses of αἱμάξεις, see Kraus 1989:36–37; Mirto 2009:229; and Harris 2012:514–515.

[51] As is emphasized by Knox 1979:259; and Zacharia 1995:49–50.

[52] Furley and Bremer 2001 vol. 1:323

[53] Noel (forthcoming).

epitomizes the tension with which Ion's paean is laden, and returns the focus to the very act in which Ion is engaged: the performance of an (especially peculiar) Apolline paean. By closing his paean with a subtle but direct denigration of Apolline music, Ion draws further attention to his song, and indeed the paean itself, and suggests that the play will not only focus on the question of Ion's identity, but also on the poetry through which this identity is transmitted.

3. Paeans and Identity in Classical Greece

3.1 Ionian Paeans in the Fifth Century

While the formal oddities of Ion's paean stand out on their own, they become most evident (to us) through direct contrast with authentic (i.e. non-tragic) fifth-century paeans. Here it rapidly becomes apparent how boldly Ion's paean defies the standards for a genre that was consistently deployed to promote and celebrate communal, and in particular Ionian, identities. An excellent starting point is provided by Pindar's fifth *Paean*:

35	[Εὔ-]
	βοιαν ἕλον καὶ ἔνασσαν·
	ἰήϊε Δάλι' Ἄπολλον·
	καὶ σποράδας φερεμήλους
	ἔκτισαν νάσους ἐρικυδέα τ'
40	Δᾶλον, ἐπεί σφιν Ἀπόλλων
	δῶκεν ὁ χρυσοκόμας
	Ἀστερίας δέμας οἰκεῖν·
	ἰήϊε Δάλι' Ἄπολλον·

Pindar *Paean* 5.35–43

35	[The Athenians]
	took and inhabited Euboia.
	Iêie Delian Apollo!
	And they settled the scattered
	flock-bearing islands and held
40	much-famed Delos, since
	golden-haired Apollo gave them
	the body of Asteria to settle.
	Iêie Delian Apollo!

This paean, of which only ten other lines remain (five of which are the paean refrain seen in lines 37 and 43), was almost certainly intended for a theoric pilgrimage sent from Athens to Delos.[54] The surviving strophe emphasizes Athens' early settlement of Euboia, Delos, and the "flock-bearing" Cycladic islands,[55] all of which were Athenian allies and members of the Delian League. In what appears to be an "assertion of Athenian claims to leadership in the region,"[56] Pindar emphasizes the allies' descent from Athenians. Just as importantly, the Athenian colonization of Euboia and the Cyclades is said to be explicitly endorsed by Apollo, the god to whom the song is dedicated. As such, the paean suggests that Athens' hegemony of the Delian League is justified by its status as mother-city and its appointment by Apollo's divine will. It is a powerful promotion of shared Ionian identity, and a stark contrast to the "isolation" that Ion projects in his paean.

While the scarcity of Athenian paeans, and of paeans more generally, does not facilitate the task of confirming that Athens regularly used these songs to reinforce solidarity among their allies via claims of kinship, we may use other evidence to buttress that argument. Pindar's second *Paean* is another ode that provides an interesting comparison to Ion's paean. While this ode, composed for the city of Abdera (also a member of the Delian League), focuses primarily on "performing [Abdera's] civic identity,"[57] and perhaps even creating it, the paean also shows the city forging ties with a broader community. After opening with an invocation of the city's mythical founder Abderus, the poet states his intention to "pursue this paean for the Ionian people" (Paean *Paean* 2.3–4: Ἰάονι τόνδε λαῷ / παι]ᾶνα [δι]ώξω ...). This may be the only instance that the word "Ionian" is found in all of Pindar in reference to a group of people,[58] so we may assume that the poet's choice is not casual and that he intends to emphasize Abdera's ties to a community outside the *polis*.

A large lacuna from lines 6–23 follows and unfortunately obscures much of what the poet may have done in this regard. But the contents of the first epode

---

[54] The context alone (settlement of Euboia and the Cycladic islands) points overwhelmingly to the Athenians, an assumption that is supported by the various surviving scholia (e.g. Σ 35: ἀπὸ Ἀθηναίων). Scholars generally agree on this point, and on the fact that it was destined to be performed in Delos. Cf. Rutherford 2001:296–297; Kowalzig 2007:84; D'Alessio 2009:146.

[55] On the identification of these islands as the Cyclades, cf. Rutherford 2001:295.

[56] Rutherford 2004:85.

[57] D'Alessio 2009:157.

[58] With the probable exception of another paeanic fragment, in which we read only "'Ιονι [-" (cf. Rutherford 2001:346), though of course this only increases the possibility that Pindar considered the idea of Ionian identity to be particularly appropriate for paeans. It is fair to say that Pindar's mentions of the "Ionian" sea in *Pythian* 3.68, *Nemean* 4.53, and *Nemean* 7.65, are distinct from the second *Paean*'s references to an Ionian people.

(directly after the lacuna) confirms the colonial and communal character of the song:

> νεόπολίς εἰμι· ματρὸς
> δὲ ματέρ' ἐμᾶς ἔτεκον ἔμπαν
> 30 πολεμίῳ πυρὶ πλαγεῖ-
> σαν. εἰ δέ τις ἀρκέων φίλοις
> ἐχθροῖσι τραχὺς ὑπαντιάζει,
> μόχθος ἡσυχίαν φέρει
> καιρῷ καταβαίνων.

Paean Paean 2.28–34

> I am a new city; but all the same
> I gave birth to my mother's mother
> 30 when she was struck by hostile fire.
> If anyone helps his friends and
> stands up fiercely to his enemies,
> the toil, arriving in due time,
> will bring peace.

Pindar boldly insists that the chorus is connected to both a local community—the city of Abdera—and a broader, colonial one. The former connection is obvious: the chorus actually embodies and speaks in the voice of Abdera. The remarkable phrase "I gave birth to my mother's mother" has caused much consternation among scholars,[59] but what Pindar refers to here is actually Abdera's re-foundation of its own mother-city Teos after the latter had been burned to the ground.[60] In this context, the gnomic lines that follow about "helping one's friends" gain new meaning: they specifically encourage the idea of mutual assistance between mother-cities and their colonies. *Paean 2* thus provides another important contrast to Ion's song.[61] Abdera's relationship with its "mother" may be peculiar, but unlike Ion it certainly does not consider itself to be "motherless," nor is there any doubt that the chorus, and by extension the city, is composed of members and representatives of a broader community.

---

[59] Grenfell and Hunt 1908:83 incorrectly saw this as a reference to Athens. In this identification they were later followed by Bowra 1964:41, and others.

[60] Radt 1958:33–39, was the first to make the point that the "mother's mother" is certainly Teos. This stance is by now the consensus; cf. Dougherty 1994:210; Rutherford 2001:268–269.

[61] In fact, Pindar may broach much more far-reaching issues of political unity between Teos and Abdera later in the paean. The text is highly fragmentary, but there appears to be an attempt to smooth over difficulties faced by the citizens of Abdera in receiving a "second wave of colonists" from Teos. On this, see esp. D'Alessio 1992:73–80 (quoted here from p. 75).

A similarly colonial, and indeed Ionian, dynamic emerges in Bacchylides 17. There has been a great deal of debate regarding the genre of this ode, with scholarly opinion divided between dithyramb,[62] paean,[63] and some mixture of the two.[64] The strongest arguments in favor of its identification as a dithyramb remain its classification as such by the Alexandrian scholars, its presentation of the narrative "*ex abrupto*,"[65] and its (possible) performance in a circular dance (*kuklios choros*).[66] None of these arguments is unassailable. Even its identification by the Alexandrians does not constitute definitive proof of its genre, for we know from a marginal comment on P.Oxy. 23.2368 that Callimachus and Aristarchus disagreed over the classification of another Bacchylidean fragment (23b), with the former arguing (successfully) in favor of dithyramb, and the latter in favor of paean.[67] Meanwhile, a number of the ode's elements are decidedly paeanic, such as the poem's dedication to Delian Apollo,[68] its emphasis on Theseus' transition into adulthood,[69] and its structural similarities to the section of the *Homeric Hymn to Apollo* which describes the invention of the paean.[70] The most paeanic moment of all, however, comes at the end of the poem, when Theseus' youthful companions celebrate his success by "singing the paean" (Bacchylides 17.129: παιάνιξαν). This small but significant moment has by no means sufficed to banish all disagreement on the question of genre, but it is certainly enough to demonstrate the ode's paeanic side: no one present at the poem's performance on Delos could listen to it without at least thinking of paeans.

Beyond the question of genre, the poem itself is a fascinating example of Athenian mythmaking in an Apolline context. It was performed by Ceans at

---

[62] Ieranò 1989; Calame 2009:esp. 177–179.

[63] Merkelbach 1973:45–55; Maehler 1997:167–170; Schröder 2000; Pavlou 2012.

[64] This is essentially the argument put forth by Tsagalis 2009. But I would also place in this category scholars who mention the controversy but eschew assigning a generic definition to the ode, such as Kowalzig 2007:88–94; Fearn 2011:210–217; and Fearn 2013 (despite its dithyrambic title, Fearn hedges on the question of genre, generally referring to the song—and its brethren—as a "circular choros"). An entirely different possibility is presented by Schmidt 1990, who argues that the ode is in fact a *hyporchêma*.

[65] Comparetti 1898:27. More recently, Calame 2009 has relied mainly on this point in identifying the ode as a dithyramb.

[66] Fearn 2011:210 notes that it was "probably performed by a circular chorus," though he does not claim this as proof of genre. On the dithyramb's association with circular choruses, cf. Pindar fragment 70b.1–5 (= *Dithyramb 2*); D'Angour 1997; and Fearn 2007:165–174.

[67] Maehler 1997:167; and Fearn 2007:205–212. For fuller arguments against the ode's identification as a dithyramb, cf. Schmidt 1990:26–29; Schröder 1999:130–137.

[68] Maehler 1997:168–169.

[69] Burnett 1985:28–37.

[70] I.e. *Homeric Hymn to Apollo* 397–501, in which Apollo takes to the sea in the form of a dolphin, leaps aboard a Cretan ship, and demands that the Cretan sailors follow him to Delphi and sing the first paean-song. On Bacchylides' many allusions to the *Hymn*, see Pavlou 2012:518–526.

Delos,[71] most likely in the 470s BCE,[72] but the myth in question is clearly Athenian in origin. Theseus is aboard a Cretan ship as one of the fourteen Athenian youths who are to be sacrificed to the Minotaur. When Minos begins acting aggressively towards one of the young women, Theseus intervenes (17.8–50), at which point Minos demands that Theseus prove his descent from Poseidon by retrieving a ring he casts into the sea (17.50–81). The Athenian hero does not hesitate, and as soon as he takes the plunge he is accompanied by dolphins[73] to the bottom of the sea to the home of Amphitrite (81–101). After witnessing a dance of the Nereids and receiving gifts from Amphitrite (101–118), Theseus returns safely to the ship (the ring is never mentioned again) where he is celebrated with the aforementioned paean. He thus symbolically anticipates his defeat of Minos and the Minotaur and his liberation of Athens from its grisly debt to Crete. Just as importantly, he proves his divine heritage. And unlike in Ion's paean, there are no longer any doubts about his paternity.

It is easy to see how this validation of Theseus' divine heritage would appeal to Athens, but it is less apparent why the Ceans should be celebrating Theseus' defeat of Minos, particularly since it is Minos whom the Ceans typically regarded as a mythical founder.[74] Kowalzig and Fearn have both demonstrated the serious ideological ramifications of Bacchylides' theoric ode, in particular Theseus' substitution of Minos as the Ceans' "culture-hero."[75] Even more crucially, Bacchylides fuses Athenian and Cean identities. This he does most cleverly at the end of the poem by transitioning directly from his description of the Athenian paean song (17.129) into a call for Delian Apollo to rejoice at and smile upon the Cean chorus (17.130–131). Such a "merg[er] of choral identities ... suggests an imposition of an Athenian, albeit mythical, identity onto the Ceans by means of their theoric performance."[76] Put slightly differently, the Cean chorus mimics the song performed by Theseus' companions and thus transforms itself into a chorus that self-identifies as Ionian, with Theseus serving as their "mythical *khorêgos*."[77]

Even beyond that, their narration of the myth in an Apolline theoric context implies that the actual Cean chorus celebrates Theseus' success in the same

---

[71] Ieranò 1989:158; Maehler 1997:168–169; Kowalzig 2007:88; Fearn 2013:135.

[72] On the date, cf. Käppel 1992:181–183; van Oeveren 1999; Fearn 2007:243. In all likelihood, the composition of Bacchylides 17 occurred after Ceos had joined the Delian League as a founding member in 478 BCE: cf. Reger 2004:748.

[73] It is perhaps not a coincidence that dolphins also appear on a number of Cean coins from the Archaic era: cf. again Reger 2004:748.

[74] Fearn 2013:141. Minos' founding role is celebrated at length in Pindar *Paean* 4 and Bacchylides 1.

[75] Fearn 2013:141.

[76] Fearn 2013:142; a similar point is made by Kowalzig 2007:89.

[77] Fearn 2007:255.

manner, and indeed for the same reasons, as the mythical Athenian chorus on board the ship. This final point is confirmed by the opening lines of the poem, in which Bacchylides most ostentatiously alters the identity of Theseus' wards:

Κυανόπρῳρα μὲν ναῦς μενέκτυπον
Θησέα δὶς ἑπτά τ' ἀγλαοὺς ἄγουσα
κούρους Ἰαόνων
Κρητικὸν τάμνε πέλαγος·

Bacchylides 17.1–4

The dark-prowed ship bringing Theseus,
steadfast-in-battle, and the twice-seven
splendid Ionian youths
cut through the Cretan sea.

Other sources are generally quite firm in noting that the "twice-seven" youths saved by Theseus were Attic or Athenian.[78] In ode 17, however, it is a tribute of *Ionian* youths that are sent to the Minotaur. The chorus, made up of Ionians from Ceos, is thus implicated in the very act of salvation about which they are singing, and so too are the other Ionians who were present at the theoric performance, which is to say a healthy portion of the Delian League. Meanwhile, the Ionians themselves "are subject to the finest ideological trick," for in celebrating their liberation from Minos, they implicitly sanctify the tribute imposed on them by Athens.[79] As in *Paean 5*, we see here a paeanic song performing an act of myth- ological mediation between Athens and its colonial allies by promoting their shared Ionian identity.

Paeans were by no means the only way to achieve this type of mediation, as is evidenced by the straight-forward appeals for military aid on the basis of Ionian kinship made by both Athens and its allies throughout the fifth century BCE.[80] But while these diplomatic appeals generally occurred strictly in times of need, the use of paeans as a mediatory mechanism seems to have been regular during the fifth century. Athens may have been sending such theoric choruses to Delos since Solon's time,[81] and by the classical period this certainly occurred at least

---

[78] It is explicit in Isocrates 10.27; Diodorus Siculus 4.61.3; and Plutarch *Theseus* 15. And it is implicit in Euripides *Heracles* 1327 and Plato *Phaedo* 58a11.

[79] Kowalzig 2007:91. Kowalzig applies the logic only to the Cean chorus, but given the opening lines of the poem, and the Delian context in which it was performed, it seems reasonable to extend this implicit debt to all the Ionians.

[80] Cf. Herodotus 5.97.2; Thucydides 1.95.1, and 3.86.3; Barron 1962; Alty 1982; Bremmer 1997.

[81] Rutherford 2001:297; Kowalzig 2007:84. Our source for this is Polemon Periegetes fragment 78 Preller (= Athenaeus 6.234e–f), who tells us it was stipulated in Solon's *kyrbeis* (tablets) that a theoric delegation of *Dēliastai* was to be sent to Delos each year.

once a year.[82] Moreover, by the time *Ion* was produced, Athens' commitments to Delos had been further increased by their decision to repurify the island, and to establish the penteteric festival to Apollo on Delos in 426/425 BCE.[83] It is significant that Thucydides tells us that "the cities brought choruses" to this festival (3.104.3). Hornblower calls this increase in theoric activity on Delos "evidence of an Athenian desire to reaffirm the 'Ionianism' of the Delian league."[84] And while we do not have any concrete evidence regarding the songs performed at this festival, paeans were certainly the most obvious generic choice for a festival to Apollo on Delos. Indeed, it is easy to imagine that songs similar to Pindar's fifth *Paean* would have been the ideal choral vehicle for effecting Athens' desire "to bring Ionian cult within her control."[85]

Furthermore, two sources tell us of the great impact such *theoric* delegations had: Xenophon's Socrates boasts that no city can match the splendor of Athens' choruses, such as "the one sent to Delos," while Plutarch, even several centuries after the fact, specifically recalls the splendid *theôria* that Nicias led to Delos.[86] In other words, theoric delegations to Delos left a lasting impression on all parties involved. As such, it is probable that much of Euripides' audience would have understood the important role paeans played in promoting intra-Ionian relationships, and would have associated this genre with the mythological setting and goals of *Ion*. In this light, it is somewhat ironic that the only paean we have seen that does not stress the idea of a shared Ionian identity is the one sung by Ion himself, the singer who most embodies the special relationship between Athenians and Ionians that the play is advancing.

---

[82] Plato tells us that during Theseus' voyage to Crete with the fourteen Athenian youths who were to be sacrificed to the Minotaur, "the Athenians had made a vow to Apollo, as they say, that if they were saved, they would lead a *theôria* to Delos every year, which they still now send to the god each year." (*Phaedo* 58b: τῷ οὖν Ἀπόλλωνι ηὔξαντο ὡς λέγεται τότε, εἰ σωθεῖεν, ἑκάστου ἔτους θεωρίαν ἀπάξειν εἰς Δῆλον· ἣν δὴ ἀεὶ καὶ νῦν ἔτι ἐξ ἐκείνου κατ' ἐνιαυτὸν τῷ θεῷ πέμπουσιν.) On other potential occasions on which Athenian choruses would be sent to Delos, cf. Rutherford 2001:297–298. For a more detailed account of Athenian *theôriai*, particularly the annual trip in celebration of Theseus' celebration, cf. P. Wilson 2000:44–46; Rutherford 2004; and Rutherford 2013:304–308.

[83] Thucydides 3.104. This was the second time that Athens had "purified" Delos, the first instance having been affected by Peisistratus in what Andrewes 1982:403 calls "a notable assertion of Athens' primacy among the Ionians cities."

[84] Hornblower 1991:521. But see also Hornblower 1992. And along the same lines, Constantakopoulou 2007:71–73.

[85] Hornblower 1992:195. P. Wilson 2000:46 also notes that paeans would seem to be the "most appropriate" genre for these festivals, though his reasoning is based on cultic grounds rather than political ones.

[86] Xenophon *Memorabilia* 3.3.12; Plutarch *Nicias* 3.4–6. On both passages, cf. P. Wilson 2000:45. On Xenophon, cf. Rutherford 2004.

3.2 "Local" Paeans in Fifth-century Athens

While Athens' exploitation of paeans to further its interests among its Ionian allies is adequately attested by our sources, the genre's connection to questions of local, Athenian identity is a more difficult case to prove. Given the paean's role in community-building and the general importance of Apolline cult in civic matters throughout Greece, and especially among the Ionian Greeks,[87] one might expect to find evidence of Athenian paeans that asserted their autochthonous identity. Alas, this is not the case. The chief problem here is that besides the scanty fragments of Pindar's *Paean* 5, there are only two other fifth-century Athenian paeans from which any words survive.[88] One of these is an extremely fragmentary paean to Asclepius written by Sophocles,[89] of which fewer than twenty words can be salvaged. It is intriguing to note that despite these scant remains, the word "Κεκροπιδῶν" (descendants of Cecrops) does appear—an obvious reference to Athens' earliest origins. But since the paean was dedicated to Asclepius it is difficult to connect this to civic cults or the promotion of Athenian identity.[90] The other fragment (Pindar fragment 152hAc = *Paean* 7c [c]) somehow pales in comparison to the remains of Sophocles' paean: only four, possibly five, words can be established with any degree of certainty. Among these, the presence of "δᾶμον Ἀθα[να ...]" hints that civic identity may have been stressed in this ode, but any argument based on such paltry evidence is inevitably doomed to uncertainty.

Equally frustrating is the lack of any source that mentions performances of paeans for Apollo in Athens. The Thargelia festival would seem to be the ideal setting for such songs:[91] not only was the festival dedicated to Apollo, but it included choral competitions,[92] and was one of the occasions on which young Athenian males could be enrolled in the phratries, with a concomitant oath to

---

[87] On Apollo as a civic god extraordinaire in Ionia (but in particular Apollo Delphinios in Miletos, for which we have the most evidence) see Graf 1979; Graf 2009:106–116; Gorman 2001:168–186; most exhaustively, Herda 2006; and more briefly, Herda 2011.

[88] This does not include paeans found in tragedies, though none of those are performed by "Athenian" choruses.

[89] Sophocles fragment 1b Page, preserved in an inscription in the Athenian *agora* from the second century CE. On the inscription, see Oliver 1936.

[90] Considering the scholion to Pindar's fifth *Paean* which mentions a son of Erechtheus (Σ 45: Πάνδωρον Ἐρέχ[θεως]Αἶκλον), one might see a pattern of mentioning autochthony in fifth-century Athenian paeans. The small sample-size and lack of context, however, renders it impossible to form any solid conclusions in this regard.

[91] On the festival, see Parke 1977:146–149; P. Wilson 2000:32–34; and P. Wilson 2007.

[92] There were two choral competitions, one for men and one for boys. Tribes were grouped in pairs in order to form the choruses, making for a total of ten choruses, five in each competition. Cf. Lysias 21.1; Antiphon, 6.11; Aristotle *Athenian Constitution* 56.3; P. Wilson 2000:33; and P. Wilson 2007:156–157.

Apollo *Patrôos* guaranteeing the purity of the child's Athenian origins.[93] This marriage of Apolline cult, choral performance, and citizen-initiation, would seem the perfect occasion for paeans. Nevertheless, until recently scholars have generally insisted that the competition featured dithyrambs.[94] It must be said that the basis for this claim is extremely tenuous, for it consists merely of a very late reference to a competition among *kuklioi choroi* at the Thargelia.[95] In fact, there is very little evidence of any sort regarding the festival, but we cannot simply take *kuklioi choroi* to mean "dithyrambs."[96] On the contrary, as Wilson has argued, this term refers primarily to the shape the chorus takes during its performance, and its use specifically "avoid[s] any more explicit generic, or cultic, markers."[97] Athenians would have used this term to refer to dithyrambs for Dionysus, but also for Apolline songs such as Bacchylides 17 and Pindar's fifth *Paean*.[98] As such, it is extremely unlikely that the competition at the Thargelia consisted solely of dithyrambs, and by extension extremely likely that it included the performance of paeans.[99]

All that still tells us remarkably little about whether or not Athenian paeans were used to express notions of their own identity, and how. Our only recourse, then, is to examine paeans that were performed in other Greek *poleis*. The evidence is not ample, but it is suggestive: Pindar's second and sixth *Paean*, for example, both center around expressions of self-definition,[100] but *Paean 4*

---

[93] Such is the case in the fourth century BCE, at any rate: cf. Isaios 7.15–16; Andrewes 1961:5–6; Cromey 2006:59–62; Graf 2009:108.

[94] Hamilton 1990:222; Ieranò 1997:248; Osborne 2004:222.

[95] *Suda* and Photius *Lexicon*, s.v. Πύθιον: οἱ τῷ κυκλίῳ χορῷ νικήσαντες τὰ Θαργήλια ("those who won in the [competition of the] circular chorus at the Thargelia").

[96] P. Wilson 2000:314n22, points out some problems with this line of reasoning, a discussion he continues in P. Wilson 2007:164–169, where he notes that "the word διθύραμβός is *never* used of" the songs at the Thargelia (167, italics in original). More recent explorations of the question have underscored how problematic it is to universally understand "dithyramb" for "*kuklios choros*": cf. Fearn 2007:165–174; D'Alessio 2013; and Ceccarelli 2013.

[97] P. Wilson 2007:168.

[98] P. Wilson 2007:177–178.

[99] As many scholars have suggested, e.g. Rutherford 2001:33n37, who states that the Thargelian chorus mentioned in Antiphon 6.11 "may have been a παιάν"; Ceccarelli 2013:160n35, follows Rutherford and states that "both in Delos and at the Athenian Thargelia the songs performed will have included dithyrambs, but also paians." Another possibility for the performance of paeans at the Thargelia resides in the "presumably choral" dances of the *Orchestai* (P. Wilson 2000:33). Somewhat incredibly, even less evidence exists for these performances than for those of the aforementioned competition, though we can at least presume that Euripides, who as Theophrastus tells us (fragment 119) was once a cupbearer for the *Orchestai*, knew more about them than we do.

[100] On *Paean 2* see esp. Dougherty 1994 and Radding 2021:273–278. The case of *Paean 6* is considerably more complicated, since even the most basic questions about the poem—including whether or not it was a single poem or two separate songs that have been merged—are still uncertain.

provides perhaps the simplest example of how the performance of paeans served to reinforce local civic and cultural identities. Like Bacchylides 17, *Paean 4* was composed for the Ceans, but unlike Bacchylides' poem it was most likely performed on Ceos,[101] and it presents a mythical structure which emphasizes the Cretan roots shared by all Ceans. Perhaps most importantly for our context, the ode sets upon these shared mythical roots the grounds for remaining dedicated to the civic community.

Pindar's approach to the topic is clever. He begins by noting the island's poverty and its lack of horses and oxen (4.27). He then gives an example of a foreign hero (Melampous) who had contented himself with the relative poverty of his homeland (4.28-30).[102] Finally, Pindar makes his point and illustrates it with an origin myth:

> τὸ δὲ οἴκοθεν ἄστυ κα̣[ὶ – ⏑ –
> καὶ συγγένει' ἀνδρὶ φ[⏑ – ⏑ –
> στέρξαι· ματ[αί]ων δὲ̣[⏑ – – –
> 35   ἑκὰς ἐόντων· λόγο[ν ἄν]α̣κ̣τ̣ος Εὐξαν[τίου
> ἐπαίνεσα̣ [Κρητ]ῶν μαιομένων ὃς ἀνα[ίνετο
> αὐταρχεῖν, πολίων δ' ἑκατὸν πεδέχει[ν
> μέρος ἕβδομον
> Πασιφ[ά]ας ‹σὺν› υἱοῖ̣σι·

Pindar *Paean* 4.32-39

The third triad of the poem, in any case, is clearly meant to be performed by an Aeginetan chorus and focuses on Aeginetan identity and origins. On the civic aspects of *Paean 6*, see again Radding 2021:279–290; along with Rutherford 2001:325–328; and Kurke 2005:105–119.

[101] On this, see especially Rutherford 2000; Rutherford 2001:292–293. *Contra* see Käppel 1992:146–151, who argues that the ode was destined for performance on Delos on the basis of a reference to Artemis in the opening lines of the poem, the fact that the paean's extensive praise of Ceos seems more appropriate for a Panhellenic context, and because a mention of the Graces must refer to reciprocity between Delos and Ceos. None of these arguments is unassailable (cf. Rutherford 2000:610), and it is particularly hard to see why the praise of Ceos would be more fitting for Delos than for a local context. What is more, Käppel's arguments are far outweighed, in my estimation, by the mention of a specific locality on Ceos (Karthaia, 4.13–14), and especially by the fact that much of the poem is dedicated to the idea of not leaving Ceos (see below).

[102] These lines, in particular 4.28–29 (ἀλλ' ὅ γε Μέλαμπος οὐκ ἤθελεν / λιπὼν πατρίδα μο[να]ρχε[ῖν] Ἄργει), have been subject to various interpretations centering around the question of whether Pindar is saying Melampous left his home (Pylos) or not. The tradition with which we are most familiar states quite plainly that Melampous did in fact leave Pylos (cf. Herodotus 9.34), and indeed Käppel 1992:132–140, tries to reconcile Pindar's lines with this tradition. But D'Alessio 1994:64, points out that Käppel's reconstruction "simply makes no satisfactory sense," since it posits the following logical construct: 1) my homeland is poor; 2) Melampous left his homeland to accept a share of rule in Argos; and 3) it is best not to leave one's homeland.

> For a man [it is always best][103] to love
> his home city, [hearth,][104]
> and kin; but to foolish men [belongs
> 35   a love] of things afar.[105] I praise the
> word of King Euxantios, who when the Cretans
> sought him refused to rule and to have
> a seventh share of the hundred cities
> with the sons of Pasiphae ...

Pindar's point is that it is better to remain at home, as Euxantios had, rather than seek fame and fortune abroad. Euxantios was the son of King Minos and Dexithea (the last surviving Telchinean), and is essentially the mythical progenitor of the Ceans.[106] The fact that Euxantios refused a share of the Cretan kingdom—the greatest Aegean power in that mythical time—is a poignant reminder for the Ceans that not only are they all descended from a common lot, but that it is one that has traditionally kept its sights focused on home. Pindar simultaneously emphasizes ethnic homogeneity and the tradition and benefits of loyalty to one's community.

    In closing the poem, Pindar goes even further. In the final twenty lines, we learn that Euxantios had once spurned an offer to rule a portion of the Cretan kingdom, and the Cean chorus actually adopts his voice to stress his reluctance to "utterly abandon the / mandates of my native gods to make / a run at wealth and hold elsewhere / a great inheritance."[107] This choral act is similar to that which we saw in Bacchylides 17, in which the Cean chorus embodies and thus identifies with Theseus' "Ionian" companions. In the case of *Paean* 4, however, the effect is altogether different: rather than placing themselves within a broader, Ionian, context, Pindar's chorus represents a figure with which all Ceans—and indeed only Ceans—could truly identify. Beyond being a simple appeal for loyalty to one's homeland, which D'Alessio correctly identifies as an endorsement of political stability,[108] Pindar's poem forcefully promotes the

---

[103] D'Alessio 1991:99 has suggested that the last four syllables of line 33 may be integrated with the words "φέριστ' ἀεί," a proposal that works both logically and grammatically.

[104] Following the proposal of ἑστία as the missing word in line 32, made by Wilamowitz 1922:472. The sense in any case must be something of the sort.

[105] Following the translation suggested by Rutherford 2001:283.

[106] Cf. Rutherford 2001:288–289 for a discussion of the myth and its variations, the most notable example of which is found in Bacchylides 1.112–128.

[107] Pindar *Paean* 4.46–49: ἔπειτα πλούτου πειρῶν μακάρων τ' ἐπιχώριον / τεθμὸν π[ά]μπαν ἐρῆμον ἀπωσάμενος / μέγαν ἄλλοθι / κλᾶρον ἔχω;

[108] D'Alessio 2009:164.

cohesion of the Cean people through an emphasis on kinship that is embodied by participation in a choral community.[109]

Like the "Ionian" paeans discussed earlier, *Paean* 4 presents powerful assertions of a community's shared identity, and it too stands in contrast to the strange paean with which Ion introduces himself to the audience. In Pindar's paean, the divine paternity of the city's founding hero is fully articulated and certain, and these origins are explicitly used to reinforce communal solidarity. Ion, on the other hand, emphasizes the uncertainty of his origins and his isolation from community, asserting instead an identity that the audience knows to be an Apolline fiction. The number of contrasts between Ion's monody and traditional paeans suggests that Ion's song deliberately eschews the genre's typical promotion of origin myths and civic unity. And the fact that Ion closes his puzzling song with a singular critique of Apolline music certainly draws the audience's attention to the idea of Apolline song itself, an implicit provocation which paves the way for Creousa's more explicit critique of Apolline music later in the play.

4. Ion and the Accumulation of False Identities

4.1 Oracular Deceptions

With Creousa's arrival at the end of the *parodos*, the play's exploration of Athenian and Ionian identity only widens. Ion instantly recognizes Creousa's "nobility" (237: γενναιότης), but does not realize her relation to him; mother and son are united in ignorance. She relates to him her background and the full story of her autochthonous lineage (260–282), an excursus that brings into focus (once again) the centrality of Athenian identity in the play. Soon thereafter, Ion inquires after Creousa's present circumstances, an exchange that recalls fifth-century Athenian citizenship laws:

> ΙΩΝ: πόσις δὲ τίς σ' ἔγημ' Ἀθηναίων, γύναι;
> 290   ΚΡ: οὐκ ἀστός ἀλλ' ἐπακτὸς ἐξ ἄλλης χθονός.
> ΙΩΝ: τίς; εὐγενῆ νιν δεῖ πεφυκέναι τινά.
> ΚΡ: Ξοῦθος, πεφυκὼς Αἰόλου Διός τ' ἄπο.
> ΙΩΝ: καὶ πῶς ξένος σ' ὢν ἔσχεν οὖσαν ἐγγενῆ;

Ion 289–293

---

[109] For much more on the manner in which *Paean* 4 promotes civic solidarity on Ceos, see Radding 2021:267–273.

> ION: What Athenian husband married you, woman?
> 290   CREOUSA: He is not a citizen, but a foreigner from another land.
> ION: Who? He must have been born a noble man.
> CREOUSA: Xouthos, born of Aiolos the son of Zeus.
> ION: And how did a foreign man acquire you, a native woman?

Ion's initial assumption that Creousa married an Athenian seems innocent enough, but his response upon learning that Creousa has married a foreigner suggests that Euripides has framed the question quite intentionally. Although Xouthos is a grandson of Zeus and thus a perfectly appropriate match for Creousa "[f]rom a mythic or aristocratic perspective,"[110] Ion is surprised that a "xenos" had been allowed to marry the "native" queen. He appears to be operating on the notion that civic endogamy is the norm among the elite classes in Athens,[111] a condition that in all likelihood arose only after Pericles' citizenship law of 451/450 BCE.[112] In short, Ion is oddly familiar with Athens' fifth-century citizenship laws,[113] and he places the tragedy's questions about identity within this decidedly contemporary context.

The remainder of the episode focuses on Ion's own history (308–329), and on Creousa's decision to ask Apollo about the fate of her child (330–369). Unbeknownst to the two characters, these subjects are closely related, and the discussion naturally serves to set up the eventual *anagnôrisis*.[114] Just as importantly, both topics bring into focus another theme that had been introduced by Ion's paean and that quickly becomes one of the tragedy's focal points: fictional identities. In Ion's case, the fictional identity is already known to the audience, for he simply relates the same story of orphaned servitude that he had told in his paean. Somewhat more surprising is the fiction that Creousa creates. In the process of explaining her oracular request, she gives the details of Apollo's rape and the subsequent birth and abandonment of her child, but she does so under

---

[110] Lape 2010:29. See also Loraux 1993:201–202.

[111] Lape 2010:29.

[112] One effect of Pericles' law, regardless of whether it was the primary motivation for the regulation, was surely to curb marriages between Athenians and non-Athenians. On the matter, cf. Boegehold 1994:62–63; Connor 1994:36–38; Lape 2010:23–24. Humphreys 1974:93–94 suggests that eliminating such marriages was actually the main goal of Pericles' law, though Patterson 2006:282, correctly points out that we know too little about the frequency of such marriages to suppose that this was a serious motivating factor.

[113] Lape 2010:29 and 107–108.

[114] Wohl 2015:29 argues that, since "Euripides often uses stichomythia to lead up to a recognition scene," the dialogue between Ion and Creousa actually "build[s] our anticipation …[by] teas[ing] our expectations."

the guise that this had occurred to a friend of hers (338). Both Ion and Creousa present themselves inaccurately, Ion by revealing the bogus status he had been supplied by Apollo, Creousa by concealing her suffering at the god's hands. The first episode thus picks up on the paeanic propagation of Ion's fictional identity, creating an uncomfortable blend of fictional identities and Athenian origins, confirming that this problem is a current that will flow through the tragedy.

The following episodes only see the complexities of identities and origins deepen. Xouthos leaves the oracle and enthusiastically greets Ion as his child (517). Ion is taken aback at this strange behavior, and he remains nonplussed even when Xouthos relates the prophecy that the first person he met on leaving the temple—Ion, of course—would be his natural son (530–537). Rather than celebrating with his newfound father, he asks after his mother (540). Disappointed to learn that Xouthos knows nothing of his maternal origins, Ion wonders if he wasn't, perhaps, "born from the earth as a mother" (542: γῆς ἄρ' ἐκπέφυκα μητρός;). Xouthos rejects this proposition out of hand, pointing out that "the ground does not bear children" (542: οὐ πέδον τίκτει τέκνα). The irony here is again obvious, for we already know that Ion's maternal ancestors were in fact born from the earth, but the important point is that just as Ion acquires a new fictional identity, Xouthos actually suggests that the entire basis of Athenian identity is also an impossible fiction.

This blend of Athenian and other fictional origins is drawn out in the rest of the exchange, and in terms that are again relevant to late fifth-century Athens. Xouthos offers to bring Ion with him to Athens, an offer at which Ion first balks because of issues of identity:

> εἶναί φασι τὰς αὐτόχθονας
> κλεινὰς Ἀθήνας οὐκ ἐπείσακτον γένος,
> ἵν' ἐσπεσοῦμαι δύο νόσω κεκτημένος,
> πατρός τ' ἐπακτοῦ καὐτὸς ὢν νοθαγενής.

Ion 589–592

> They say that famous Athens
> is autochthonous, born of no foreign stock,
> so that I shall succumb to a double sickness
> as the bastard son of a foreign father.

Ion here contrasts his new, but still fictional, identity to the purity of Athenian autochthony. Xouthos manages to convince Ion to leave Delphi by proposing to introduce him to Creousa and Athens as a *xenos* (654) and "sightseer" (656: θεατὴν), but here we simply see the replacement of one fictional identity with another, both of which are constructed in opposition to Athenian identity. Thus far in the tragedy, these two thematic strands—Athenian autochthony and fictional (Ionian) identity—have been consistently placed side by side, if not fully woven together.

The contemporary nature of the play's identity-politics is expressed even more poignantly as the father-son discussion draws to a close. Although Xouthos finally convinces Ion to join him in Athens, he cannot allay all of Ion's concerns:

> εἰ δ' ἐπεύξασθαι χρεών,
> ἐκ τῶν Ἀθηνῶν μ' ἡ τεκοῦσ' εἴη γυνή,
> ὥς μοι γένηται μητρόθεν παρρησία.
> καθαρὰν γὰρ ἤν τις ἐς πόλιν πέσῃ ξένος,
> κἂν τοῖς λόγοισιν ἀστὸς ᾖ, τό γε στόμα
> δοῦλον πέπαται κοὐκ ἔχει παρρησίαν.

Ion 670–675

> If I may pray for one thing,
> let my birth-mother be Athenian
> so I may inherit from her freedom of speech.
> For when a foreigner comes to a pure city,
> even if he is a citizen in theory, he acquires
> a slave's mouth and has no freedom of speech.

Ion's use of the term *parrhêsia* ("freedom of speech") confirms again that the civic context in which the tragedy takes place is that of fifth-century Athens.[115] Ion's recognition of "maternal inheritance" suggests that he is defining himself as a metic,[116] as does is his reference to Athens as a "pure city" in which foreigners have no political place. The *polis* Ion imagines is Athens in the late fifth century, and it is within this context that the play's (re)construction of Athenian and Ionian identities must be seen.

4.2 Creousa's Anti-paean and Ion's Tragic (Identity) Crisis

In the next episode, we see the problems with Ion's fictional origins build up to a tragic crisis that is both expressed within and prompted by paeanic song. Despite Xouthos' injunction that the chorus keep silent about his newfound son (666–667), the Athenian women reveal the plot as soon as Creousa returns (752–807). The tragedy swiftly takes on a sinister tone. Creousa's *Paidagôgos* is

---

[115] Somewhat surprisingly, the term practically does not exist in extant literature before Euripides.
[116] On Ion as a metic see Kasimis 2018:26–48 (and 34–38 on this scene in particular).

convinced that Creousa will be "cast out of the house of Erechtheus" (810–811: δωμάτων τ' Ἐρεχθέως / ἐκβαλλόμεσθα)—that her childlessness and Ion's arrival will result in her alienation. The situation is not yet unsalvageable, but it appears to jeopardize the easy solution Hermes had envisioned in the prologue, and casts doubt on Apollo's prophetic powers and his ability to control the narrative. Things do not seem to be working out quite as planned, and for a myth that relies on Apolline descent to establish a common link between Athenian autochthony and Ionia, it is perhaps troubling that the god in question seems less than reliable.

The *Paidagôgos* then provokes even more uncertainty by suggesting that Xouthos began engineering this plan years ago, after coming to Creousa's home as a *xenos* (813–814) and learning of her inability to bear children:

        λαβὼν δὲ δοῦλα λέκτρα νυμφεύσας λάθρᾳ
820   τὸν παῖδ' ἔφυσεν, ἐξενωμένον δέ τῳ
        Δελφῶν δίδωσιν ἐκτρέφειν. ὁ δ' ἐν θεοῦ
        δόμοισιν ἄφετος, ὡς λάθοι, παιδεύεται

        ....

825   κᾆθ' ὁ θεὸς οὐκ ἐψεύσαθ', ὅδε δ' ἐψεύσατο
        πάλαι τρέφων τὸν παῖδα κἄπλεκεν πλοκὰς
        τοιάσδ'· ἁλοὺς μὲν ἀνέφερ' ἐς τὸν δαίμονα,
        †ἐλθὼν δὲ καὶ τὸν χρόνον ἀμύνεσθαι θέλων†
        τυραννίδ' αὐτῷ περιβαλεῖν ἔμελλε γῆς.

                              Ion 819–822; 825–829

        He took a slave to bed in secret and begat
820   the child, and gave him to some Delphian
        to raise. And he was brought up, devoted,
        in the house of the god, to avoid detection.

        ....

825   The god did not lie, Xouthos
        did long ago by raising the child; and he
        wove such a web, that if he were caught,
        he could ascribe it to the god ...[???][117]
        ... he planned to install him as tyrant of [our] land.

A false mother is thus added to the false father Apollo had already granted Ion, and the implications of Xouthos' (theorized) act of identity-formation are

---

[117] K. Lee 1997:254 deems this line "incurable."

massive. In the eyes of the Athenians onstage, Ion, the son of a foreigner and a slave, is the key cog in a years-in-the-making conspiracy to usurp the throne of the Erechtheids and establish tyranny. His identity is ever-shifting and tenuous, and the fictions surrounding it have themselves become an overtly politicized tragic crisis.

Just as troubling is Apollo's role in the affair. The question of Ion's identity has become confused, rather than clarified, by Apollo's prophecy, and Athenian interpretations of his oracle only muddle the situation further. Although he mistakenly acquits Apollo of lying, the *Paidagôgos* suggests that the Delphic oracle can be exploited in order to create false identities and to advance political aspirations. The idea that Apollo's will can be so brazenly manipulated for political purposes is certainly distressing in a play that explicitly deploys an innovative Apolline myth to advance Athenian aspirations, particularly since the tragic audience was accustomed to seeing these same mythical pretenses exploited in very real political contexts. Even though we know the *Paidagôgos* is incorrect and that Xouthos has reported the oracle as he received it, this in turn reminds us that Apollo himself has lied. Apollo's will, which Hermes has explicitly stated would be crucial to the successful fusion of Athenian and Ionian identities (cf. *Ion* 67–68), is steeped in deception and subject to human misinterpretation. Euripides thus emphasizes Apollo's unreliability in the matter of establishing origins and identities, and he casts doubt on the very mechanisms upon which his creation of a new Athenian/Ionian identity resides.

Creousa then reconnects these troubling dynamics to paeanic song. She can no longer contain the secret of Ion's birth, which she has kept so long, and to disclose it she resorts to a monody that is undoubtedly "a complement to Ion's."[118] Numerous scholars have classified her song as an "anti-hymn,"[119] but I believe it is more accurate to call it an anti-paean. To begin, Creousa's monody abounds with elements that recall Ion's paean:[120] like Ion before her, she introduces her song with a series of recitative anapaests before turning to lyric anapaests;[121] when Creousa names Apollo, her invocation is the very same one Ion had used in his paean-refrain earlier in the play (127, 143, 885: ὦ Λατοῦς παῖ); Ion introduces his ode by addressing the sun which puts the stars to flight (81–85), and Creousa calls on the "starry seat of Zeus" as her witness (870: τὸ Διὸς πολύαστρον ἕδος); while Ion's song sees him rediscover his *aidôs* with regard to the temple birds

---

[118] Barlow 1971:48.

[119] Larue 1963; K. Lee 1997:257; Furley 1999/2000:188–190; Furley and Bremer 2001 vol. 1:327.

[120] See Fernández Delgado 2012.

[121] To be more precise, Creousa begins with three lines of lyric anapaests (859–861) before turning to recitative anapaests (862–880) and then again to lyric anapaests (881–892). Cf. K. Lee 1997:257, and Furley and Bremer 2001 vol. 2:317.

(179: κτείνειν ὑμᾶς αἰδοῦμαι), Creousa uses her song in order to let go of her aidôs and reveal her secret (861: αἰδοῦς δ' ἀπολειφθῶ); and Creousa even recalls Ion's false claim to be "motherless and fatherless" (109) when she mistakenly asserts that she is "bereft of home, bereft of children" (865: στέρομαι δ' οἴκων, στέρομαι παίδων). This mirroring has two principal effects: first, in recalling a song that was overtly paeanic, it shows that Creousa's song is intimately related to the genre; second, by drawing on some of the more disturbing elements of Ion's monody, Creousa builds off of his paean to create a far more problematic image of Apolline music.

The hostile yet intimate relationship between Creousa's monody and the traditional paean-song is further exemplified by her subversion of a number of paeanic themes and topoi: most obviously, while her song is dedicated to Apollo, it serves not to praise or propitiate the god, but rather to "reproach" him (885: μομφάν); the structure of the monody mirrors the typical structure of cult paeans, except that the closing prayer is replaced by a curse against Apollo;[122] and references to Apolline music, singing, and even the paean itself appear throughout the ode, but in an overtly critical context. This is clear from the very first lyric anapaests of her song:

> ὦ τᾶς ἑπταφθόγγου μέλπων
> κιθάρας ἐνοπάν, ἅτ' ἀγραύλοις
> κεράεσσιν ἐν ἀψύχοις ἀχεῖ
> μουσᾶν ὕμνους εὐαχήτους,
> 885 σοὶ μομφάν, ὦ Λατοῦς παῖ,
> πρὸς τάνδ' αὐγὰν αὐδάσω.

> *Ion* 881–886

> O you who stroke the sound
> of the seven-stringed *kithara*, which
> peals out from lifeless rustic horns
> the loud-sounding hymns of the Muses,
> 885 a reproach for you, o son of Leto,
> I call out before this light.

The importance of Creousa's invocation must not be understated: in beginning her condemnation of Apollo, Creousa turns directly to, and indeed only to, his musical aspect. Her reference to the *kithara* and the emphasis on sound (ἀχεῖ,

---

[122] Rutherford 2001:74–75, notes that "cult παιᾶνες" typically consist of an opening section in which the god "is directly appealed to," a narrative section which describes an "aretology of Apollo," and "a closing prayer." On Creousa's "curse," cf. LaRue 1963:136.

εὐαχήτους) make Apolline music the central motif of Creousa's proem, and it is a theme that remains prominent throughout the ode.

Creousa follows this "musical" invocation with a striking description of her rape by Apollo and the subsequent birth and (presumed) death of their son. Her former pain and terror are palpable: she screams out for her mother as the god assaults her (893); in giving birth to her son she is "wretched" (897: δύστανος); and she leaves the child in the very spot Apollo "took [her], wretched and miserable in a miserable union" (900–901: μ' ἐν λέχεσι μελέαν μελέοις / ἐζεύξω τὰν δύστανον). It is on this awful note that she then returns to the subject of Apolline music:

> οἴμοι μοι· καὶ νῦν ἔρρει
> πτανοῖς ἁρπασθεὶς θοίνα
> παῖς μοι καὶ σοί.
> τλᾶμον, σὺ δὲ ‹καὶ› κιθάρᾳ κλάζεις
> παιᾶνας μέλπων.

Ion 902–906

> Woe is me! Even now my child
> and yours is gone,
> a feast seized by birds.
> And you, wretch, just pluck your kithara
> and sing paeans!

The return to Apolline music closes the ring that Creousa had opened at line 881. In both lines she describes the god singing (μέλπων), a coincidence that confirms that, in this section at least, Creousa is deeply concerned with Apollo's music, and that the songs themselves—his paeans—draw her ire. The stanza functions as a meta-poetic but overt condemnation of Apolline music.

Creousa's image of Apollo singing a paean has other effects as well. Given that he both opens and closes this strophe singing, it appears that she imagines Apollo singing his paeans throughout her own performance; the two songs are, in a sense, coextensive. More importantly, Creousa's condemnation of Apollo's paeans recalls Ion mocking the god's music in his own monody. Creousa's critique is more poignant. While Ion's lack of reverence for the god's music was odd, he was at least playful in dismissing the power of the god's lyre. Creousa, on the other hand, overtly condemns Apollo's song as an accomplice to her own unjustified suffering. Here, it is important to note that both of the tragedy's Apolline songs challenge the very notion of the paean, first with regards to its efficacy, and second with regards to its reliability. Given the associations between the paean and the questions of identity that have been emphasized throughout the tragedy, the paeanic deprecation of paeans subtly undermines the play's supposed fusion of Athenian and Ionian identity.

Immediately after condemning Apollo's song, Creousa moves on to focus on his mantic attributes:

> ὠή, τὸν Λατοῦς αὐδῶ,
> ὅστ' ὀμφὰν κληροῖς
> †πρὸς χρυσέους θάκους†
> 910 καὶ γαίας μεσσήρεις ἕδρας.
> εἰς φῶς αὐδὰν καρύξω·
> Ἰὼ ‹ἰὼ› κακὸς εὐνάτωρ,
> ὃς τῷ μὲν ἐμῷ νυμφεύτᾳ
> χάριν οὐ προλαβὼν
> 915 παῖδ' εἰς οἴκους οἰκίζεις·
> ὁ δ' ἐμὸς γενέτας καὶ σός †ἀμαθής†
> οἰωνοῖς ἔρρει συλαθείς,
> σπάργανα ματέρος ἐξαλλάξας.

Ion 907–918

> *ôê*, I call the son of Leto,
> who dispenses his divine voice
> at golden thrones
> 910 and the midmost seats of the earth,
> I shout this song out to the light:
> *iô iô*, wicked bedmate,
> who took no favor
> from my husband
> 915 yet settled a child for him in my home;
> and my child and yours, †ignorant one,†
> is gone, carried off by birds,
> casting off his mother's swaddling-bands

Despite the transitional nature of these lines, there are numerous reasons to associate Creousa's rebuke of Apollo the prophet with her condemnation of Apolline music and his paean. To begin, prophecy is a recurring motif in fifth-century paeans. It is a regular subject in Pindar's paeans,[123] so it fits naturally in the context of Creousa's paeanic song and is germane to her description of

---

[123] Rutherford 2001:174–175.

Apollo singing a paean. Moreover, the structure and many of the features of these lines are by now familiar: both this and the earlier stanza begin with an invocation of Apollo as son of Leto; in each case, the invocation is followed by a narration of Apollo's crimes, though this time Creousa recounts his present offenses rather than his former ones; and Creousa continues to juxtapose her own suffering (916–918) to Apollo's actions (912–915), even using the same word (ἔρρει) and image (an avian assault) to describe her son's death. The structural and thematic similarities between the two stanzas mean we do not simply cease to hear Apollo's paean when Creousa turns to denigrate his prophecy; his song still lurks in the background.

More specifically, the association between Apollo's paean and his prophecies is clearly established in an Aeschylean fragment to which Euripides seems to be alluding:[124]

[ΘΕ]:
τὰς ἐ<μ>ὰς εὐπαιδίας
νόσων τ' ἀπείρους καὶ μακραίωνας βίου,
ξύμπαντά τ' εἰπὼν θεοφιλεῖς ἐμὰς τύχας
παιῶν' ἐπηυφήμησεν εὐθυμῶν ἐμέ.
5 κἀγὼ τὸ Φοίβου θεῖον ἀψευδὲς στόμα
ἤλπιζον εἶναι, μαντικῇ βρύον τέχνῃ·
ὁ δ' αὐτὸς ὑμνῶν, αὐτὸς ἐν θοίνῃ παρών,
αὐτὸς τάδ' εἰπών, αὐτός ἐστιν ὁ κτανὼν
τὸν παῖδα τὸν ἐμόν.

Aeschylus fragment 350

[THETIS]:
[Apollo allotted][125] to me the blessing of children
both free from disease and long of life,
and having told of all my god-loved fortunes,
he sang a paean and greatly cheered me.
5 And I expected Phoebus' divine mouth to be
unlying, abounding in its mantic craft;
but the one who sang those hymns, who was
present at my feast, who said those things,
is the same one who killed my child.

---

[124] = Plato *Republic* 383b. Rutherford 1993:91n41 was the first to recognize the allusion.
[125] From "ἐνδατεῖσθαι," Plato's introduction to the lines of Aeschylean verse.

This fragment belongs to an unknown play, but its contents are quite clear: Thetis is most displeased with Apollo for first predicting a long life for Achilles, only to then be responsible for his death at Troy. This story may well belong to a broader tradition with which even Homer was familiar,[126] but its relevance to *Ion* is certain: these are the only two instances, to my knowledge, in which Apollo is said to sing a paean, and in each case Apollo's song is directly associated with a prophecy that will reveal itself to be false: in Thetis' case it is the "long life" foreseen for Achilles, while in Creousa's song it is connected to the prophecy that had given Ion to Xouthos. Just as strikingly, each woman holds the god responsible for her child's death, and both women implicate his paean in their loss. Finally, like Creousa, Thetis emphasizes the treachery of the god's music by making a second, emphatic reference to the god in the act of singing (7: ὑμνῶν), and by juxtaposing this song to her child's death. For Thetis, just as for Creousa, Apollo's paean is a vehicle for her despair, indelibly associated with her loss.

Another striking feature of Creousa's meditation on Apollo's oracle is the enterprise that she associates with the prophecy in question. For Creousa, the bestowal of Ion to Xouthos is an act of colonization: Apollo has literally "settled" (*oikizei*) Ion in her house.[127] The phrase certainly elicits the strong associations between Apolline prophecy and colonial foundations in the Greek world.[128] But given that the term appears within a paeanic song in which Apollo is imagined singing a paean, *oikizei* also reminds us of the role paeans themselves played in establishing and propagating colonial narratives. Pindar's exploration of the

---

[126] In Homer *Iliad* 24.62–63, Hera lambasts the "ever untrustworthy" (*Iliad* 24.63: αἰὲν ἄπιστε) Apollo for disrespecting Achilles despite having been present, "lyre in hand" (*Iliad* 24.63: ἔχων φόρμιγγα) at the wedding of Thetis and Peleus. Scodel 1977 argues that Aeschylus' fragment is an allusion to these lines in the *Iliad*, which in turn implies the existence of a tradition of Apollo's *apistia*. *Contra* see J. Burgess 2004. Burgess denies both that Aeschylus' fragment is a Homeric allusion and that there was a tradition of "Apollo singing a misleading prophecy about Achilles at the wedding of Peleus and Thetis" (21). At the very least, however, it seems clear that Apolline prophecy was associated in some way with the wedding: cf. Hesiod fragment 212(b); Pindar *Nemean* 5.22–25; Euripides *Iphigenia at Aulis* 1062–1079. On Hesiod and Pindar, see esp. March 1987:12–20. But *Iphigenia at Aulis* 1062–1079 is perhaps the most compelling of these passages. Here, Chiron is said to deliver a prophecy that he received from the "Phoebic Muse" (*Iphigenia at Aulis* 1064: φοιβάδα μοῦσαν; almost certainly a priestess—perhaps Delphic?—of Apollo), according to which Achilles would become a great warrior. It is true that Apollo is not directly involved in the prophecy, and that the "prophecy does not explicitly promise a long life for Achilles and so cannot be considered deceptive" (J. Burgess 2004:26). But the combination of an Apolline prophecy at Thetis' wedding that omits any mention of Achilles' death does seem to fall in the tradition of Aeschylus' fragment.

[127] Creousa uses the same term that Thucydides does when describing the Athenian colonization of "Ionia and most of the islands" (Thucydides 1.12.4: Ἴωνας μὲν Ἀθηναῖοι καὶ νησιωτῶν τοὺς πολλοὺς ᾤκισαν).

[128] Dougherty 1993:18–21.

colonial relationship shared by Teos and Abdera in his second *Paean* is a clear example of that dynamic, but an even more intriguing (and Athenocentric) congruity exists between Creousa's words and Pindar's fifth *Paean*. In that ode, Pindar lays the roots for Athenian hegemony by noting their early colonization (39: ἔκτισαν) of the Cycladic islands and Apollo's desire that they "settle" (42: οἰκεῖν) Delos. *Oikeô* in particular is virtually synonymous with Creousa's *oikizô*,[129] so the two formulations are lexically analogous. Just as important is the conceptual similarity: Pindar claims that Apollo gave Delos to Athens and allowed it to colonize the Cyclades, while Creousa imagines Apollo giving Ion to Xouthos and colonizing the house of Erechtheus. In other words, the paeanic and prophetic are utterly entwined in Creousa's song, and insofar as Apollo's paean still casts a formidable shadow, his song is intimately associated with Ion's hostile "colonization" of Athens.

Central to this violent entanglement is the question of Ion's identity. Here it is once again a fictional one. While Creousa cannot know that her understanding of the situation is based on an entirely false premise, the audience can certainly grasp this point. As such, it must be factored into our interpretation of her ode. In this sense, Creousa's anti-paean mirrors Ion's earlier paean by expressing a false "Ionian" identity. The same can be said of Apollo's imagined paean, and of Apolline music more generally. Insofar as the god is envisioned singing a paean while colonizing the house of Erechtheus with the son of Xouthos, his paean and his music are closely related to the expression of fictional (Ionian) origins. The use of paeanic song to create and disseminate false Ionian identities is thus a salient feature of both Ion's and Creousa's monodic paeans, but also of Apollo's imagined paean. And more generally, the blend of paeanic song, Athenian autochthony, and false Ionian identities is an all-encompassing theme of the tragedy.

The paean, then, plays a substantial role in establishing and magnifying the themes that dominate the tragedy. Ion's monody is a paean that introduces his own fictional identity and, perhaps even more troubling, it mocks the power of Apolline song. The issue of identity remains squarely in the audience's mind throughout the tragedy, and though the uncomfortable critique of Apolline song passes momentarily from view, it is reintroduced with gusto by Creousa when she weaves the plot's many strands into her anti-paean. Here, she mimics Ion by using Apolline music to demonstrate the paean's potential in propagating an "Ionian" identity. At the same time, however, she emphasizes the fact that the identity propagated by a paean may well be fictional. By the end of Creousa's monody, Apolline song is expressly associated with colonial prophecies that

---

[129] Thucydides also uses the verb *oikeô* to mean "settle." Cf. Thucydides 1.8.1; 2.27.2; 6.2 *passim*.

are both false and deleterious to the purity of the house of Erechtheus and, by extension, of all Athenians. Above all, what emerges from both tragic monodies is the sense that the Apolline paean is, at least in this play, an inherently unreliable vehicle for the transmission of identity—the very act that purports to be the play's underlying concern.

4.3 Athena and the Problematic Solution to the Identity Crisis

Creousa's take on the Apolline paean leads directly to a full-blown crisis in the play. Beyond functioning as a condemnation of the god and his music, her monody helps her disclose the truth of Apollo's rape and her lost child. In this sense, it is a complete success, for she discloses the god's violent act immediately upon finishing her song (923–969). Within the context of the dramatic plot, this is problematic for a number of reasons. To begin, her revelation thwarts Apollo's intention to cover up his earlier relations with Creousa. Even more troubling is the response this revelation provokes: the *Paidagôgos* declares that Creousa must "punish the god" (972: ἀποτίνου θεόν) and proposes the radical solution of burning down Apollo's temple (974). Creousa and the *Paidagôgos* eventually adopt a more moderate course of action by deciding to poison Ion with a drop of Gorgon's blood before he can come to Athens (985–1038). But even though Apollo's temple is no longer at risk of conflagration, an act of grave sacrilege (filicide) is in the making, and even the god's modest goal of seeing Ion recognized by Creousa and receiving his due (72–74) is in serious danger of coming to naught.

The murder does not, of course, come to fruition. Ion's death is averted by the intervention of a temple bird who drinks the poison cup in his stead and dies damningly on the spot (1202–1210). The bird's intervention naturally recalls Ion's earlier aggression against this future savior,[130] but above all it marks another turning point in the tragedy. Creousa is sentenced to death (1222–1225) and seeks shelter as a suppliant at Apollo's altar (1255–1260). Ion arrives to confront her, intent on dragging Creousa from the altar and killing her (1261–1319). And lest we forget that all this is a product of mistaken identity, Creousa and Ion replay the latter's fictional identity, with Creousa accusing him of wishing to "colonize" her house (1295: ἔμελλες οἰκεῖν τἄμ'). In other words, at the very height of the dramatic crisis, Euripides employs specific language that manages to recall not only the issues of identity that resound throughout the play, but above all the paeanic song that led to this crisis.

---

[130] We may indeed be meant to understand that the dead bird is the same swan whose song Ion had earlier threatened to strangle: both birds are described via uncommon compound adjectives as having reddish feet or legs (*Ion* 162–163: φοινικοφαῆ / πόδα; *Ion* 1207–1208: φοινικοσκελεῖς / χηλας).

At this point, the confusion that has been both embodied and engendered by paeanic song requires outside intervention, and the Priestess of Delphi arrives to put an end to the quarrel. Ion greets her as his "my dear mother, though you did not give birth to me," (1324: ὦ φίλη μοι μῆτερ, οὐ τεκοῦσά περ). Ion's identity remains front and center, and the priestess' response is equally telling, for she highlights the gap that exists between those who actually are and those who are simply called Ion's parents: "I am called this, at any rate, and the name is not bitter to me" (1325: ἀλλ᾽ οὖν λεγόμεθα γ᾽· ἡ φάτις δ᾽ οὔ μοι πικρά). Finally, in a move with the potential to banish this confusion once and for all, the priestess produces the basket and belongings with which Ion was first found (1337–1339). Creousa recognizes the basket as hers and proves her maternity by identifying, sight unseen, the objects within. A joyous and lengthy recognition follows, culminating in Creousa's triumphant proclamation that "the house is established and the land has its rulers: Erechtheus has risen again!" (1464–1465: δῶμ᾽ ἑστιοῦται, γᾶ δ᾽ ἔχει τυράννους, / ἀνηβᾷ δ᾽ Ἐρεχθεύς·).

But despite Creousa's joy, the tragic crisis is not fully resolved. Ion at first still believes that Xouthos is his natural father (1468–1469), and wonders, not illogically, why Apollo "gave [me], his child, to another father, and said I was born a child of Xouthos."[131] Creousa argues that Xouthos had merely misinterpreted Apollo's prophecy; that Ion was said to be a gift to Xouthos but "born of [Apollo]" Xouthos (1535: αὐτοῦ γεγῶτα). Ion is not convinced, and he wonders whether "the god prophesies truly or in vain" (1537: ὁ θεὸς ἀληθὴς ἢ μάτην μαντεύεται;). The answer is obvious to the audience who know that Apollo has lied, but Ion's uncertainty speaks to the tension between his true and false identities that has driven the play forward to this point. Apolline prophecy, much like Apolline song (though as we have seen the distinction between the two is not so sharp), seems incapable of expressing Ion's true identity.

This inadequacy makes the possibility that Apollo will finally resolve these matters himself tantalizing. Instead, Athena arrives and precludes any chance that we may see—or at least hear from—the god who has "driven" the plot to such confusing extremes. Acting on Apollo's behalf (1556), Athena confirms Ion's Apolline paternity. As elucidated above, she takes great pains to outline the importance of this genealogical revelation both in Athens, where Ion will maintain the continuity of Erechtheus' autochthonous line, and throughout the Greek world, where his descendants will "give strength to [her] land" (cf. 1573–1594). All things considered, Athena assures us, Apollo "has done everything well" (1595: καλῶς δ᾽ Ἀπόλλων πάντ᾽ ἔπραξε). In her conception at least, Apollo

---

[131] *Ion* 1532–1533: πῶς οὖν τὸν αὐτοῦ παῖδ᾽ ἔδωκ᾽ ἄλλῳ πατρὶ / Ξούθου τέ φησι παῖδά μ᾽ ἐκπεφυκέναι;

has successfully and flawlessly carried out the promised fusion of Ionian and autochthonous ideologies.

The general levity of Athena's tone notwithstanding, her arrival and analysis by no means resolve all the play's difficulties. To begin, Athena's appearance as Apollo's "emissary,"[132] in a tragedy that is set in Delphi and which purports to present Ion as Apollo's natural son, is puzzling. While it is true that Athena's presence is in some ways "natural" for a play that concerns Athens as much as Delphi,[133] Apollo's absence, especially at this crucial juncture, only increases our doubts regarding the god's ability to control the situation.[134] The excuse Athena provides for his absence does not help his cause. According to her, Apollo does not wish "that blame for what happened earlier become public" (1558: μὴ τῶν πάροιθε μέμψις ἐς μέσον μόλη). While we cannot necessarily take this to mean that Apollo is ashamed at his prior actions,[135] his reluctance to present himself certainly reminds the audience of the criticism that Apollo has faced throughout the play, and it further undermines the imperfect solution for which he ultimately settles. Indeed, the very fact that he is avoiding blame (μέμψις) recalls Creousa's monodic blame (885: μομφάν)—blame that was cast through a paeanic medium and with criticism levied specifically at the Apolline paean. Even in his absence, the problematic nature of Apolline music bubbles to the surface.

Equally troubling is the way Athena suggests that Ion and Creousa should deal with Xouthos and the false prophecy Apollo had earlier offered:

> νῦν οὖν σιώπα παῖς ὅδ' ὡς πέφυκε σός,
> ἵν' ἡ δόκησις Ξοῦθον ἡδέως ἔχη
> σύ τ' αὖ τὰ σαυτῆς ἀγάθ' ἔχουσ' ἴῃς, γύναι.

Ion 1601–1603

> Now then, do not reveal that this child is yours,
> so Xouthos may delight in his delusion,
> and you, woman, may move on with your own blessings.

In a sense, Athena allows the audience to see the mythological fusion Hermes promised in the prologue while also granting Apollo's wish to keep his relationship with Creousa secret. But there are steep costs associated with this outcome.

---

[132] Zacharia 2003:99 and 141.

[133] Farrington 1991:125. For another recent defense of Athena's substitution of Apollo, see Swift 2008:97.

[134] Giannopoulou 2000:263.

[135] As Wilamowitz 1926:13 suggests.

This deceit is essentially a mirror-image of Xouthos' attempt to infiltrate his own son into the house of Erechtheus—a deceptive act for which Creousa had harshly condemned Apollo. In fact, it may be even more serious, for it will rely on Xouthos' false belief that Ion is his son; on the "uncertainty of paternity"[136] to which all men are subject, an issue of some concern in ancient Athens.[137]

5. Conclusions

It is certainly no coincidence that the tragedy's real dupe is also its only non-Athenian, and it is telling that the autochthonous Athenians we see on-stage are more than happy to help propagate a false notion of Ion's origins and identity simply to further their own and their city's interests. Such a notion may not have been problematic to Athenians, but there would certainly have been Ionian Greeks in the audience,[138] some of them even present as official delegates bearing the allies' annual tribute to Athens.[139] We should probably not press too far the similarities between Xouthos, whose acceptance in Athens, such as it may be, derived solely from his ability to provide military assistance (cf. *Ion* 59–61; 294–298), and the allies present at the City Dionysia. But it is reasonable to assume that the ideological fusion presented in *Ion* would be less compelling to Ionians in the audience if the only non-Athenian character, one with whom they might easily identify, is the victim of such a serious deception at the hands of his Athenian relations.

Nor do we have to imagine that "the audience feels sufficient sympathy with [Xouthos]"[140] to see that his deception casts a pall over the play's outcome. Even without this sympathy, much of the audience should have been able to recognize that this deception is the culmination of the persistent problems with Ion's many and shifting identities, for these problems are exhaustively portrayed throughout the tragedy. Ion's fictional identities threaten to cause crises of varying degrees: at first, Ion's existence as a temple slave nearly causes him to defile the sanctuary with the murder of Apollo's swan; later, the questions surrounding the prophecy which "gave" Ion to Xouthos almost results in the grotesque pollution of both Delphi and the house of Erechtheus, first by filicide and then by matricide. Here we are presented with a third fictional identity, and beyond the fact that it will lead Xouthos to raise his wife's child under

---

[136] Saxonhouse 1986:272.
[137] Cf. Lysias 1.33.
[138] Cf. Aristophanes *Acharnians* 501–503, and Σ Aristophanes *Acharnians* 503. The same point is made by Walsh 1978:310, following Meiggs 1972:290.
[139] Cf. Isocrates 8.82; Σ Aristophanes *Acharnians* 504; Raubitschek 1941; Goldhill 1990:101–104.
[140] Swift 2008:97.

the illusion that it is his own, this solution sustains and exemplifies the tension inherent in Ion's competing identities: at no point is the shadow of fiction banished.

On the contrary, insofar as Ion can only return to Athens if Xouthos believes himself to be his father, we must imagine that this deception can only function if the Athenian *polis* of the tragedy remains ignorant of Ion's true origins. In other words, Ion will continue to possess two different—and mutually exclusive—identities: his "true" autochthonous identity as the son of Apollo and Creousa, and his "false" identity as a son of Xouthos and an unknown woman, at once a bastard and a metic.[141] As Segal has argued, this "division" between appearance and reality "exposes the factitious nature of Athens' civic mythologizing ...[and] reveals the truth that the city's mythologized unity is a convenient fiction for the sake of some ulterior purpose."[142] Athens creates for itself a myth that, as Athena emphasizes, has great authority both in the city and within the sphere of external (colonial) politics. But this myth is based on the premise of a false identity. Such an accumulation of false origin-myths, all of which are propagated by Apollo, most of which are advanced within paeanic song, can hardly be a source of comfort for those who understood the role these myths played in the creation of Athenian and Ionian identities.

Ultimately, like many Euripidean tragedies, *Ion* offers its audience(s) different ways of reading the outcome. One can certainly accept the seamless fusion of Ionian and autochthonous Athenian identities that the play presents on its surface. But enough issues exist within the play, from the unreliability of Apollo's prophecies to the continual propagation of false notions of Ion's origins, to fertilize doubts about the reliability of such myths. The fact that these false identities are consistently advanced within paeanic songs is perhaps less notable for us than are Apollo's shortcomings. But for audiences accustomed to using paeans to promote mainstream notions of identity, both in local and Ionian contexts, it would certainly have been striking to see a play that so baldly advances an alternate myth of ethnic origins do so by means of fictitious paeans. We can thus see how the poetic apparatus of *Ion* has the potential to radically alter an audience's interpretation of the political questions at the heart of the play. In the following chapter, we will see how Euripides' uses another lyric genre—epinician poetry—to challenge his audience's understanding of another political problem, this time within two plays: *Alexandros* and *Heracles*.

---

[141] Drawing here on both Loraux 1993:204 and Kasimis 2018:42–48.
[142] Segal 1999:98.

2

Heracles, Alexander, and Epinician Reception in the *Polis*

O N THE SURFACE, THE EPONYMOUS protagonists of Euripides' *Heracles* and *Alexandros* could hardly be more different: the ultimate hero who set out to "tame the earth"[1] and the "bitter simulacrum of a firebrand"[2] who caused the destruction of his own city (in Euripides' words); the GOAT (Greatest of All Time) and the goat, in the parlance of our times. Recently, however, scholars have recognized that Euripides weaves similar strands of poetry and politics around these two mismatched characters. *Heracles* and *Alexandros* are both replete with epinician or encomiastic song and language,[3] and in each case the poetic subtext is closely connected to the reception of an exceptional individual (the protagonists themselves) in the dramatic *poleis* of the tragedy (Thebes and Athens in *Heracles*, Troy in *Alexandros*).[4] Still, critics have argued that the plays downplay

---

[1] Euripides *Heracles* 20: ἐξημερῶσαι γαῖαν.

[2] As he is called in *Trojan Women* (922: δαλοῦ πικρὸν μίμημ'), the third play in the trilogy in which *Alexandros* was produced.

[3] In a way, the use of the term "epinician" to designate a specific body of work perfectly encapsulates the difficulties inherent in talking about ancient Greek genres. On the one hand, of all forms of ancient lyric, epinician seems to be the most well-suited for classification, for almost all of these odes were composed with the same occasion in mind, namely the celebration of an Olympic victor. But even this rule has exceptions, as we see for example in *Pythian* 12, composed for the winner of a musical competition; *Nemean* 11, which celebrates a political appointment; and *Pythian* 4, which seems altogether an outlier among Pindar's epinicians. Moreover, epinician odes were not consistently called *epinikia* until the third century BCE (see Harvey 1955:159–164; and more recently Foster, Kurke, and Weiss 2019:3). Pindar refers to them far more often as *kômoi* ("songs for celebration"; see e.g. *Olympian* 4.9, *Olympian* 8.10, *Pythian* 5.22, etc.) or as *enkômia* ("encomiastic songs"; cf. *Pythian* 10.53, *Nemean* 1.7). All of this suggests, as other scholars have noted, that epinician was likely considered a sub-genre of encomiastic poetry in classical Greece (see e.g. Lowe 2007:167–168). In that light, and for the sake of variety, I will use "epinician" and "encomiastic" interchangeably in my discussion of *Heracles*, on the presumption that either adjective could be applied by Euripides' audience to describe the odes and language of the tragedy.

[4] On this dynamic in *Heracles*, see e.g. Swift 2010:151–156.

the typical political aspects of epinician poetry.[5] As I argue in this chapter, however, *Heracles* and *Alexandros* both seriously weigh epinician's role in dealing with the exceptional individual's reception in the *polis*, and at a time when this issue was especially pressing: *Alexandros* was performed in 415 BCE as part of the so-called "Trojan trilogy,"[6] and *Heracles* likely only a year or two earlier or later; in the midst of this, Alcibiades was racking up epinician victories at a formidable rate, and Euripides is said to have contributed an epinician ode to his ostentatious celebrations.[7] As such, these plays suggest a broad and urgent exploration of the intensely political tradition of earlier epinician poetry.

In fact, Euripides' work with epinician poetry in *Heracles* and *Alexandros* is in many ways consonant with the poetic tradition(s) he recalls. Encomiastic poetry is, by definition, deeply invested in providing poetic praise, and this is eminently visible in both plays; in *Alexandros* in particular, the epinician tones are explicitly linked to a celebration of athletic achievements. Epinician odes were typically performed by choruses[8] at the victor's home city,[9] and this also matches what we see in *Heracles* and *Alexandros*, where epinician song and celebration occur at the moment of the hero's triumphant return to the *polis*. Perhaps most importantly, Euripides follows the epinician tradition of the early fifth century by linking these songs and celebrations to the tensions that could arise between a victor and his social and civic communities. The return of athletic victors to their *poleis* seems to have been fraught in the ancient Greek world, and perhaps especially in Athens.[10] These figures were (typically) elite individuals who had left their communities to acquire even more honor and prestige, and as a result they were "potentially disruptive figure[s] who need to be reintegrated."[11] One of the main purposes of epinician poetry, then, was to assist in this process of

---

[5] For example, Swift 2010:156 suggests that *Heracles* engages in a "renegotiation of epinician values" during which the "political overtones [of the genre] are effaced." More recently, Kampakoglou 2018 develops a broader analysis of Euripides' use of epinician discourse in connection with the return of the tragic hero to their community in a number of plays (*Alcestis, Andromache, Bacchae,* and *Medea* on top of *Heracles* and *Alexandros*), arguing that "Euripides repeatedly perverts the rituals associated with epinician praise" and "throw[s] into relief the alienation of the tragic hero from his community" (p. 188).

[6] Along with *Palamedes* and *Trojan Women*. On the trilogy as a whole, see esp. Scodel 1980a.

[7] I discuss this at greater length below at pp. 58–59 and 140–142, but see Bond 1981:xxx–xxxii; and Diggle 1981:116.

[8] Malcolm Heath and Mary Lefkowitz have questioned, in a series of articles, the notion that epinician was a choral genre. Cf. Lefkowitz 1988; Heath 1988; and Heath and Lefkowitz 1991. *Contra*, see Burnett 1989; Carey 1989; Carey 1991; Morgan 1993; and Carey 2007.

[9] E.g. Kurke 1991:3–5; Swift 2010:105.

[10] Fontenrose 1968 discusses several cases in which Olympic victors encounter problematic *nostoi*. I discuss the case of Athens more specifically below at pp.*.

[11] Hornblower 2004:28.

reintegration; to facilitate an athletic victor's return to his *oikos* or *polis*.[12] By explicitly linking the epinician apparatus of *Heracles* and *Alexandros* to the politics of his protagonists' reception in these tragedies, Euripides thus hews very closely to the conventional performative and occasional contexts of epinician.

As if to mirror their protagonists, however, *Heracles* and *Alexandros* present sharply contrasting images of the manner in which epinician song can operate in relation to the heroic individual's return. Throughout *Heracles*, numerous characters use epinician song, language, and celebration as a means to advocate for Heracles' inclusion in the *polis*, and to express the need to publicly honor him and his family. In *Alexandros*, conversely, epinician song and celebration become a catalyst for hostility against Alexander, and provoke serious tensions at Troy. By looking at the two plays together, we can further understand how adeptly Euripides links politics and choral lyric in his tragedies. On the one hand, we see that these tragedies both draw upon the intimate connection between epinician poetry and the reception of elite individuals in the *polis*, and that in so doing they provide the audience with a lens through which it can examine different modes of elite/*polis* relations. At the same time, the expansive form of tragedy itself allows epinician song and celebration to, as it were, take on a role of its own: a potentially mediating force in *Heracles*, but an inflammatory one in *Alexandros*. In other words, Euripidean tragedy uses epinician not only to focalize a political question, but also to dramatize epinician poetry's power, for better or for worse, in the political arena.

1. Alcibiades, Athens, and the Urgency of Epinician

Contemporary events in Athens suggests that this exploration of epinician's political potential was fraught but urgent. Scholars have long characterized Athenian attitudes to the genre as hostile, arguing that many in Athens considered it "elitist, harmful, and inconsistent with the democratic constitution."[13]

---

[12] Crotty 1982, noting Pindar's frequent references to both athletic and heroic *nostoi*, was the first to convincingly argue that "the purpose of epinician poetry was to secure the victor's reception by his fellow citizens" (p. 108). He compares the mediation offered by epinician poetry to that of ritual initiation, insofar as both the returning victor and the young initiant have an ambiguous or liminal status (cf. Crotty 1982:112–121; and Nagy 1990:140–145). Kurke 1991 expands upon this point considerably and is by now the authority on the subject. Kurke correctly notes that the process of epinician mediation differs depending on the community to which the victor is returning, whether it be *oikos* or *polis*, or indeed a democratic *polis* or a tyrannical one, and also shows that Pindar uses a variety of poetic techniques and conceptual frameworks to facilitate these different processes.

[13] Papakonstantinou 2003:176. See also Bowra 1938:267–268; Wade-Gery 1958:247–252. Segal 1986:124 implicitly follows this view.

While recent scholars have rightly developed a more nuanced understanding of the question,[14] all evidence suggests that Athens' relation to epinician poetry was, at best, complicated. Going back to the first half of the fifth century, it appears that at least some elements of the Athenian body politic were wary of elite victors, particularly those who engaged in the equestrian competitions. This much is suggested by the discovery of *ostraka* against Megacles in which he is singled out as *hippotrophos* ("horse-breeder"), another in which his name is accompanied by a drawing of a horse and rider, and even one in which it is suggested that his horses should be ostracized with him.[15] These anxieties may have become at least slightly attenuated during the middle part of the fifth-century, with no Olympic crown-winner ostracized after Callias around 440 BCE.[16] But the question of how to deal with epinician victors certainly roared back to life in the mid-teens with Alcibiades' arrival on the scene, and his concerted efforts to transform his Olympic victory into political capital.

Neither the magnitude nor the manner of Alcibiades' exploits at Olympia in 416 BCE were likely to escape the notice of his fellow citizens: he enrolled seven chariot-teams—apparently a record at that point—and brought home the first and second prize, and either third or fourth as well.[17] He celebrated in ostentatious style, including a commission for an epinician ode (on which more below), and we have a great deal of evidence that Alcibiades' victory lap in Athens was politically charged. In Thucydides' account of the debate about the Sicilian Expedition, for example, we hear that Alcibiades claimed to have provided "a benefit to my fatherland, for the Greeks believed our city to be even more powerful than it is because of the magnificence of my delegation at Olympia."[18] Isocrates, writing in defense of Alcibiades' son around 395 BCE, makes a similar set of claims:

[14] See esp. Hornblower 2004:247–261 and Swift 2010:106–118. I expand upon this discussion below in the Epilogue at pp. 137–140.

[15] See Brenne 2002:112; Forsdyke 2005:155–156. On T 1/103 we read Μhεγ[α]κλεῖ *hιπποκράτως* |και τε *hίπōι* ("Megacles son of Hippocrates and his horses"); he is called *hippotrophos* in T 1/101-02, and T 1/104-05 refer to him as a horse-rider; the drawing of horse and rider appears in T 1/158 (for image, see Siewert 2002:524).

[16] Kyle 1993:161–163 argues that athletic achievements had become essentially decoupled from the political arena by the middle of the fifth century, and that as a consequence, Athenian anxieties about elite victories were also eased. Golden 1997:341 is less certain, and sees the possibility that athletic achievement remained a viable political tool well into the fourth century BCE. On Callias' victories (and ostentatious commemoration of them), see Papakonstantinou 2016:105–106.

[17] Thucydides 6.16.2 has Alcibiades claim first, second, and fourth prizes in the race. In Euripides' *Epinician for Alcibiades* and Isocrates 16.34, however, we hear that Alcibiades finished first, second, and third. Thucydides gives us the number of chariots entered in the race, and both Thucydides and Isocrates agree this was a record.

[18] Thucydides 6.16.1–2: τῇ δὲ πατρίδι καὶ ὠφελίαν. οἱ γὰρ Ἕλληνες καὶ ὑπὲρ δύναμιν μείζω ἡμῶν τὴν πόλιν ἐνόμισαν τῷ ἐμῷ διαπρεπεῖ τῆς Ὀλυμπίαζε θεωρίας.

ὁρῶν τὴν ἐν Ὀλυμπίᾳ πανήγυριν ὑπὸ πάντων ἀνθρώπων ἀγαπωμένην
καὶ θαυμαζομένην ... καὶ τούς τ᾽ ἀθλητὰς ζηλουμένους καὶ τὰς πόλεις
ὀνομαστὰς γιγνομένας τὰς τῶν νικώντων, καὶ πρὸς τούτοις ἡγούμενος
τὰς μὲν ἐνθάδε λῃτουργίας ὑπὲρ τῶν ἰδίων πρὸς τοὺς πολίτας εἶναι, τὰς
δ᾽ εἰς ἐκείνην τὴν πανήγυριν ὑπὲρ τῆς πόλεως εἰς ἅπασαν τὴν Ἑλλάδα
γίγνεσθαι ... ἱπποτροφεῖν δ᾽ ἐπιχειρήσας ... οὐ μόνον τοὺς ἀνταγωνιστὰς
ἀλλὰ καὶ τοὺς πώποτε νικήσαντας ὑπερεβάλετο.

Isocrates 16.32

For he saw that the Olympic festival is a source of delight and amaze-
ment for everyone ... and that the athletes are admired and the names
of the victors' cities called out. Moreover, he believed that while private
liturgies here [in Athens] are performed on behalf of private individuals for their fellow citizens, achievements at the Olympic festival are
done on behalf of the city before all of Greece. [So] he tried his hand at
horse-breeding ... and not only defeated his competitors, but indeed all
prior winners.

As in Thucydides, we see that the emphasis on Alcibiades' exceptional Olympic
performance is explicitly linked to the prestige that Athens accrued in the
eyes of other Greek cities. These claims to have aided Athens in the field of
Panhellenic relations should be taken seriously; as Gribble has argued, the
controversy around Sparta's ban from (and illegal entry into) the four-horse
chariot competition in 420 BCE suggests that the Peace of Nicias had diverted
hostilities "from the battlefield to the stadium,"[19] and shows that the stadium
was indeed a politicized space. Given the similarity of their claims, the accounts
of Thucydides and Isocrates demonstrate that at the very least, many Athenians
believed Alcibiades was exploiting his Olympic victory in order to claim he had
made a meaningful contribution to Athenian foreign policy goals. Some perhaps
even credited him with such.

Certain Athenians seem to have reacted with hostility to these attempts to
turn athletic triumph into political capital. This is again evident in Thucydides,
where Alcibiades' claim to have made Athens seem "more powerful" is clearly
arranged as a response to Nicias' earlier jibe that the Athenians should not
trust someone who yearned "to be admired for breeding horses."[20] Alcibiades'
Olympic boasts also come immediately after Thucydides' statement that his

---

[19] Gribble 2012:53.
[20] Thucydides 6.12.2: ὅπως θαυμασθῇ μὲν ἀπὸ τῆς ἱπποτροφίας. Gribble 2012:70 argues this episode
shows that "both Nicias and Alcibiades ... link the Olympic success to the Sicilian command."

main interest in sailing for Sicily was as a means to pay for his horse-breeding habit (6.15.3), and his report that the Athenian body politic would later (6.15.3: ὕστερον) become wary of Alcibiades' tyrannical ambitions (6.15.4). Thucydides thus goes to some lengths to imply that Alcibiades' Olympic expenditures had already inspired a certain amount of resentment in Athens.

We cannot simply accept Thucydides' report on Athenian receptions of Alcibiades uncritically,[21] but the discourse surrounding the ostracism of Hyperbolus in this period—the first ostracism in a generation[22]—further suggests that Alcibiades' Olympic exploits were indeed controversial. The initial vote on whether to conduct an *ostrakophoria* must have taken place around January of either 416 or 415 BCE, with the *ostrakophoria* itself coming in late February or early March of that same year.[23] The consensus is now leaning towards 415 as the year of the *ostrakophoria*,[24] but Alcibiades had been active on the chariot circuit for several years by then, including a likely victory at the Panathenaic games in 418.[25] The timing of the *ostrakophoria* thus aligns nicely with Alcibiades' open engagement with *hippotrophia*.

Regarding the vote to conduct an *ostrakophoria*, Plutarch repeatedly asserts that it was originally aimed at Alcibiades and another elite politician (Nicias or Phaeax), and that Alcibiades then teamed up with one of these two to turn the vote against Hyperbolus.[26] The story is problematic for a number of reasons,[27] but it almost certainly reflects a very real peak in political tensions in Athens and "intra-elite rivalr[ies]" at that time.[28] As one of the most prominent political

---

[21] Gribble 1999:184 argues that we should understand Thucydides' judgment of Alcibiades in 6.15 as an "anachron[istic]... narratorial intervention." See also the commentary on these sections in Hornblower 2008:339–341.

[22] For an overview of the history of ostracism in Athens before the *ostrakophoria*, see Forsdyke 2005:165–170.

[23] On the timing of the voting, see Forsdyke 2005:146–148.

[24] See Rhodes 1994:esp. 89–94; Rosenbloom 2004:77–78; Forsdyke 2005:170. Heftner 2000, conversely, argues for a date of 416 BCE.

[25] Ancient sources (reports of paintings of Alcibiades at Athenaeus 534d and Pausanias 1.22.7; a stele with a list of confiscated Panathenaic amphorae that may have belonged originally to Alcibiades) suggest that Alcibiades was victorious in the chariot race at the Pythian, Nemean and Panathenaic games between 421–418 BCE. On the date, see J. Davies 1971:21, and Golden 1997:335. On the identification of the Panathenaic amphorae as the property of Alcibiades, see Amyx 1958:183–185. For a fresh review of the evidence for these victories, see Gribble 2012:67–68.

[26] Plutarch *Nicias* 11; *Alcibiades* 11.

[27] Such as the "unnecessarily simplistic bipolar model of conflict" that is implied (Forsdyke 2005:171), and the depiction of Athenian leaders working within a paradigm similar to contemporary party politics. Opinions differ on the question of whether or not such organized voting would have been possible. See e.g. Rhodes 1994:93–97; Forsdyke 2005:171–174; Hansen 2014:381–383 and 401–402.

[28] Forsdyke 2005:175.

figures in Athens at the time, Alcibiades would inevitably have been a leading figure in those rivalries, and indeed his name appears on five of the approximately 30 *ostraka* connected to this vote (good for joint second).[29] Rosenbloom goes so far as to argue that the *ostrakophoria* itself was motivated primarily by Alcibiades' Olympic triumph.[30] The evidence directly connecting the victory to the ostracism is circumstantial, but if we can trust the hints in Thucydides and Isocrates that Alcibiades was using his victory as a means to increase his political status in Athens in 415 BCE, then it is not a stretch to imagine that these exploits became a focal point of ostracism-related discussions.

Pseudo-Andocides' speech "Against Alcibiades" ([Andocides] 4) provides strong evidence that the Olympic victory was an explosive topic in Athens at the time. The document purports to be a speech from the first half of 415 BCE[31] advocating for the ostracism of Alcibiades, and though it is likely spurious,[32] most scholars now agree that it was composed within about 20 years of the *ostrakophoria*.[33] Importantly, the author takes pains to present arguments that fit the very specific context of 415, and the text contains intimate—albeit imperfect—reports of the controversies surrounding Alcibiades in this period.[34] In other words, the document provides some of the best evidence we have concerning feelings about Alcibiades in 415.

The obsession with Alcibiades' Olympic victory in the speech is thus an important corroboration of its significance in the Athenian *zeitgeist*. Indeed, the Olympic triumph is the incident upon which the author dwells more than any other (from [Andocides] 4.25–33).[35] The introduction to this section is revealing: "I expect that [Alcibiades] will say nothing in response to [my accusations], but

---

[29] On the tally of the *ostraka*, see Brenne 2002:47, 55, 59, 64, 66. The sample size is too small to be truly meaningful—as evidenced by the fact that the actual 'winner' Hyperbolus is tied for fourth among the *ostraka* we possess—but it does provide definite confirmation that Alcibiades' name was in the mix.

[30] Rhodes 1994; Rosenbloom 2004:71–78. Gribble 2012:70 is more circumspect, noting simply that "[i]f the dating of the ostracism of Hyperbolus to 415 is correct, it is likely that it was partly precipitated by the tremendous access of prestige caused by Alcibiades' Olympic victory."

[31] The text mentions Melos (autumn of 416) but not the Sicilian expedition, nor the scandal with the Mysteries or Alcibiades' defection (summer of 415).

[32] At [Andocides] 4.22 the author refers to a son of Alcibiades by a woman enslaved during the fall of Melos (ca. November 416), impossible to reconcile with the date of the *ostrakophoria* in March of 415. Gribble 1997:379n77 argues that given our imperfect knowledge of the timing of events at Melos and of the *ostrakophoria* itself, it is possible that as many as eight months elapsed between the fall of Melos and the vote, but I share Rhodes' skepticism (1994:91).

[33] Cobetto Ghiggia 1995:69–121 has the longest discussion of the matter, and argues that the document must have been written between 415–390 BCE (*passim*). For a briefer synopsis of the problem, see Rhodes 1994:89–91.

[34] See again Cobetto Ghiggia 1995:108–109.

[35] Rosenbloom 2004:74.

will talk about his victory at Olympia instead."[36] The author may of course be drawing on the testimony provided by Thucydides and Isocrates, but the offhand manner in which the comment is made suggests that Alcibiades was famous for bringing up his victory in order to deflect accusations made against his public persona. The account of his conduct and celebration at Olympia is original (or at least not found in Thucydides and Isocrates), and deeply politicized. In particular, we hear that Alcibiades appropriated public ritual materials for his private victory celebration and then passed these off as his own, with the result that "all the foreigners ... watching our public procession believed that *we* were using *his* processional vessels."[37] Perhaps most strikingly, we hear that Ephesus, Chios, and Lesbos actually supplied Alcibiades with a massive tent, animals to sacrifice, food for his horses, and wine for himself[38]—practically transforming the annual tribute to Athens into a private one for him.[39] In sum, according to the author, Alcibiades "talks so much about the greatness of his victory, as if he had crowned the city rather than dishonoring it greatly."[40] The broader contours of the narration—that Alcibiades' behavior was extravagant and impudent—are certainly credible. But what is most important is the confirmation it offers that Alcibiades was known or remembered for boasting of his victory as a civic boon, and that some in Athens saw it as quite the opposite.[41]

One final piece of evidence remains to be discussed, one which is (curiously) ignored by Pseudo-Andocides: an epinician song commemorating Alcibiades' victory, and said to be composed by Euripides himself.[42] This is an extraordinary document, as it is the only surviving piece of classical epinician poetry that has survived from later than 450–445 BCE. Of the poem, only the opening five lines remain, plus another short fragment of two lines from some point later in the song.[43] Even from these remains, however, we can see that the song follows

---

[36] [Andocides] 4.25: ἡγοῦμαι δ᾽ αὐτὸν πρὸς ταῦτα μὲν οὐδὲν ἀντερεῖν, λέξειν δὲ περὶ τῆς νίκης τῆς Ὀλυμπίασι.

[37] [Andocides] 4.29 (emphasis mine): ὅσοι μὲν οὖν τῶν ξένων ... τὴν πομπὴν τὴν κοινὴν ὁρῶντες ὑστέραν οὖσαν τῆς Ἀλκιβιάδου τοῖς τούτου πομπείοις χρῆσθαι ἐνόμιζον ἡμᾶς.

[38] [Andocides] 4.30.

[39] Gribble 2012:61.

[40] [Andocides] 4.31: προσέτι πολλῇ τῇ νίκῃ χρῆται, ὥσπερ οὐ πολὺ μᾶλλον ἠτιμακὼς ἢ ἐστεφανωκὼς τὴν πόλιν. εἰ δὲ βούλεσθε σκοπεῖν.

[41] Gribble 2012 provides a fuller analysis of these episodes, and reaches fundamentally the same conclusions.

[42] Euripides' authorship of the epinician for Alcibiades is still a contested issue to some extent: most scholars follow the ancient attribution (see e.g. Papakonstantinou 2003:175; Hornblower 2004:28 and 56–58), but Lowe 2007:176 does argue briefly against it (see esp. n. 30). I argue in favor of Euripidean authorship at some length in the epilogue (see pp. 140–142).

[43] The first fragment is quoted at Plutarch *Alcibiades* 11; the second (and shorter) fragment at Plutarch *Demosthenes* 1.

epinician conventions: praise for Alcibiades abounds in the song's proem, as well as a reference to the victory (here, Alcibiades is said to have placed first, second, and third, as opposed to the account in Thucydides 6.16 that he finished first, second, and fourth) and the crowning ceremony. Just as important, we see in the shorter fragment that Euripides suggested "it is necessary first of all for a blessed man to have a glorious city."[44] Even removed from its immediate context, it is easy to see that this praise of Athens fits the epinician tendency to associate the victor's personal triumph with the greater glory conferred unto his *polis*; that the song is making at least some effort to mediate the relationship between victor and community. Just as our forensic and historiographical documents suggest, the fragments of the song show Alcibiades striving to insert his athletic victory into the Athenian civic and political spheres.

The emphasis on epinician celebration and the hero's return to the *polis* in both *Heracles* and *Alexandros* must be understood within the context of the political fallout of Alcibiades' athletic victories. The date of *Heracles* is a thorny question, one which will be addressed below. But we know for certain that *Alexandros* was produced in 415 BCE, some six to seven months after Alcibiades' victory at Olympia (and, presumably, Euripides' composition of his epinician for Alcibiades) and around the same time as the Athenians were debating both the Sicilian expedition and whether or not to ostracize Alcibiades. As such, this fragmentary play serves as an excellent starting point for an initial analysis of the politics of epinician in Euripidean tragedy.

2. Epinician and Alexandros

Our text of Euripides' *Alexandros* consists of 22 fragments that are quoted in other sources (primarily Stobaeus),[45] and one long (and heavily corrupted) papyrological fragment.[46] In total, we have 64 complete lines, 100 partial lines, and approximately 676 words, which likely represents 7–10% of the original text.[47] The survival of such a modest percentage (though this is actually an

---

[44] Plutarch *Demosthenes* 1: φησὶ χρῆναι τῷ εὐδαίμονι πρῶτον ὑπάρξαι τὰν πόλιν εὐδόκιμον. The last three words are certainly a quote, while the first part may have been adapted to suit Plutarch's prose-y needs. Bowra 1960:78 suggests (without total confidence) that the original lines were "χρῆν εὐδαίμονι πρῶτον ὑπάρξαι / τὰν πόλιν εὐδόκιμον."

[45] These are the fragments attributed to *Alexandros* in Collard and Cropp 2008:40–75. Of these twenty-two, seventeen are found in Stobaeus' *Anthology*.

[46] P. Strasbourg 2342–2344. For an excellent visual display of the possible arrangements of the papyrus fragments, see Huys 1986:10.

[47] The average word count in the sixteen extant Euripidean tragedies (excluding the satyr play *Cyclops* and the proto-satyric *Alcestis*, as well as the dubious *Rhesus*) is 8,544, with a maximum of 10,573 (*Orestes*) and a minimum of 6,412 (*Children of Heracles*, though it should be noted that this

abundance as far as dramatic fragments go) presents obvious challenges when it comes to reconstructing any dramatic plot, but the relatively recent discovery of a *hypothesis*[48] allows us to be fairly certain[49] about the general storylines, and even the specific dynamics and development of some episodes.

Scholars agree about the following points.[50] In the prologue, we learn of Alexander's background, in particular that he was abandoned by Hecuba and Priam at birth and that funeral games have been established in his honor. This is followed by the *parodos* and a shared lament by Hecuba and a Chorus (whose identity is uncertain), after which Alexander arrives on-stage in the guise of a slave, along with a secondary Chorus of herdsmen who accuse Alexander of excessive arrogance. These charges lead to an *agôn* between Alexander and an unknown adversary,[51] with Priam as judge. At the end of the episode Alexander is allowed to compete in the funeral games. After a choral song, a messenger relays news of Alexander's victories in the games, which in turn leads to another *agôn*, this time between Hector and his brother Deiphobus, with their mother Hecuba present. The crux of the dispute is that Deiphobus would like to kill Alexander, since it is unacceptable (in his view) that a slave should celebrate such victories, and Deiphobus ultimately persuades Hecuba to abet him in the murder. The final scenes of the play remain relatively murky even on the most general level, but we do know that Alexander seeks shelter at an altar to avoid being killed, and that he is saved when his true identity is revealed by his foster-father. At some point during all this, Cassandra also enters the scene and predicts that Alexander will be the ruin of Troy.

The first half of the play is dominated by the problem of whether or not a slave such as Alexander should be permitted to compete at all.[52] In other words, the games are, from the very beginning, inextricably linked to the question of

---

is an extreme outlier; no other tragedy has fewer than 7,314). All statistics collected from the *TLG* database.

[48] P. Oxy. 3650 col. i., on which see Coles 1974, still definitive.

[49] As noted by Hamilton 1976:67–70, we cannot simply take dramatic *hypotheseis* at their words, as comparisons between them and extant plays show that many *hypotheseis* are not entirely accurate. The errors within them, however, tend to fall into the following categories: omission of episodes; the order of episodes; and "minor inaccuracies ...[e.g.] Jason is married not engaged [in *Medea*]" (Hamilton 1976:68).

[50] I draw primarily on the most recent reconstructions, i.e. Collard and Cropp 2008:33–38; Di Giuseppe 2012:45–180; and Karamanou 2017:17–24.

[51] Karamanou 2017:182–187 provides a comprehensive account of the arguments in favor of a range of potential antagonists, namely the herdsmen, Hecuba, Deiphobus, and Alexander's foster father (another herdsman).

[52] For overviews of Alexander's problematic persona and status, see esp. Karamanou 2017:14–15. On the question of his initial status, cf. Kampakoglou 2018:204–207.

what rights Alexander should have, and how he should be viewed by the *polis*.[53] At this point in the play, epinician tones are not audible, at least not in the fragments that we possess. But the fact that athletic games are central to the plot of the tragedy would certainly have primed the audience to expect epinician song at some point in the tragedy, and indeed it does come to the foreground in the second half of the play, after Alexander's victories in the games.

It is significant that the echoes of epinician are most prominent in the episode in which the plot to murder Alexander is formed. Most of what remains from this section of the play comes from papyrological sources with numerous lacunae. But despite this fact, we can discern that epinician motifs are not only present, but indeed that Alexander's epinician celebration and reception becomes a primary catalyst of his eventual conflict with Deiphobus and Hecuba. Even before the conspiracy is formed, the Messenger suggests that the response to Alexander's victory will be a focus of the rest of the tragedy:

> ΧΟ[54] τύχῃ δ[ίδω]μι πά[ντα – x – ◡ –
> 5   ΚΗ κρείσσω‹ν› πεφυκὼς [
> ΧΟ ἦ καὶ στέφουσιν αὐτὸ[ν
> ΚΗ καί φασιν εἶναί ᾽ ἄξιον [
>
>   Euripides *Alexandros* fragment 61d Kn, 4–7

> CHORUS: we ascribe it all to fortune ...
> 5   MESSENGER: [he is] by nature superior ...
> CHORUS: And they're actually crowning him ...?
> MESSENGER: Yes, and they say that he is worthy ...

The emphasis on Alexander's exceptional *phusis* draws on an epinician trope,[55] and it is evident that Alexander is receiving a victory crown, which lends a rather celebratory tone to the affair. We also see that, for at least some people in Troy, Alexander's victories are interpreted as a sign of his worth, another notion that emerges constantly in epinician poetry. Several lines later, there may be an overt a reference to the distribution of victory prizes: εἰς τόνδε νικη. [τήρ'?] ("to him victory [prizes?]").[56] Whether or not Crönert's suggested supplement is correct, it is clear that this portion of the messenger speech focuses not so

---

53 Radding 2020.
54 Karamanou 2017:212 suggests that the Messenger's interlocutor may be either the Chorus or Hecuba. I follow here the consensus by assigning these lines to the Chorus (cf. e.g. Kannicht 2004:193), though the point is only of marginal relevance: as Scodel 1980a:31 points out, for dramatic reasons Hecuba must certainly be present for the Messenger's narration.
55 Karamanou 2017:213–214.
56 Euripides *Alexandros* fragment 61d Kn, 14, supplemented by Crönert 1922:9.

much on Alexander's victory per se, but rather on the rewards and reception he has earned with it.

Shortly thereafter, the Trojan royal family's negative reaction to Alexander's victory, and above all his celebration, becomes the focal point:

ΕΚ κε̄ῖνο̣ν μὲν—ὄνθ᾿ ὅς ἐστι—θαυμάζειν Φρύγας,
Πριάμου δὲ νικ .... γεραίρεσθαι δόμους.
ΔΕ πῶς οὖν .[3–4]λε̣ι τ̣α̣ῦ̣τ̣α̣ γ᾿ ὥστ᾿ ἔχειν καλῶς;
ΕΚ ca. 12 letters ̣ιδε χειρὶ δεῖ θανεῖν.
5   ΔΕ οὐ μὴν ἄτρωτός γ᾿ εἶσιν εἰς Ἅιδου δόμους.
ΕΚ ποῦ νυν [ἂ̣]ν̣ ε̣ἴη καλλίνικ᾿ ἔχων στέφη;
ΔΕ πᾶν ἄστυ πληροῖ Τρωϊκὸν γαυρούμενος.
ΕΚ ca. 6 δ]ε̣ῦρ᾿, εἰς βόλον γὰρ ἂν πέσοι.

Euripides Alexandros fragment 62d Kn col. ii, 1–8

HECUBA: Whoever he is, [it is clear that] the Phrygians marvel at him,
and that Priam's house is [not] honored with victory.
DEIPHOBUS: How then can we make this right again?
HECUBA: ... he must die by [this] hand
5   DEIPHOBUS: To be sure, he will not go unscathed into the house of Hades.
HECUBA: Where is he now, wearing his *kallinika* crowns?
DEIPHOBUS: He is filling the whole Trojan city with his exultations.
HECUBA: ... here, he might fall into this trap.

In the middle of this passage (lines 4–5), we see the very moment in which the conspiracy to murder Alexander crystallizes, with particular emphasis on the violence of this act ("he will not go unscathed ..."). Crucially, the murder is suggested as the only way to make up for the fact that the Alexander has usurped honors that rightfully belong to the royal family, and the admiration he has won from the Trojan people (the "Phrygians" in line 1). In other words, it is not so much the victory itself as the public celebration of it that appears to be the critical motivation for the conspiracy.

Epinician language and imagery reinforces this connection. Before Euripides, the verb *gerairô* (fragment 62d Kn col. ii, 2) appears primarily in epinician poetry, with both Bacchylides and Pindar using it to refer to the honors accorded the victor.[57] The reference to *kallinika* crowns in line five is a visual cue

---

[57]   Karamanou 2017:250. Cf. Pindar *Isthmian* 2.17 and *Isthmian* 8.63; Bacchylides 2.13, 4.3, 4.13.

which, as in fragment 61d above, asks the audience to imagine a public crowning ceremony. And the description of Alexander "filling ... Troy with his exultations" (line 8) gives a clear sense of a public victory celebration, albeit one that is viewed (at least by Deiphobus and Hecuba) as excessive. The notion of epinician celebration, accorded to Alexander and denied to the royal family, is front and center as the plot takes its shape. What we see then, is that rather than work to mediate the relationship between victor and *polis*, epinician celebration in *Alexandros* is a source of tension and envy, a primary catalyst for violence within the community.[58]

The episode, and indeed the whole play, disappears almost entirely from our view following this passage: a handful of words remain in the six lines after Hecuba expresses hope that Alexander will fall into their trap (fragment 62d Kn col. ii, 7), after which we lose 20–25 lines altogether. By the time the next column of the papyrus picks up the action, the discussion is over, and we appear to be in the midst of a dialogue between the Chorus and another character.[59] But even though the fragment is extremely fragmentary, the epinician tones of the previous episode are still audible

> δέσποινα[
> πὶ δεσποτ[
> φύλλοις ν[
> ποῦ μοι π[
> 10 Ἑκάβη, φρά[σον μοι – ◡ – x – ◡ –
> τὴν καλλ[ίνικον

Euripides Alexandros fragment 62d Kn col. iii, 6–11

> ... mistress ...
> ... to a master ...
> ... with [victor's?] leaves ...
> ... where ...
> 10 ... Hecuba, tell me ...
> ... the victory-song ...

---

[58] On the "envy" generated by Alexander's victory, as well as a possible appearance of the word φθόνος in the fragments, see Karamanou 2011:44–46. Kampakoglou 2018: 214 describes Alexander as "a locus of anxiety [who] is believed to threaten the political establishment."

[59] Collard and Cropp 2008:70–73, postulate a partially sung exchange between two semi-choruses, and Alexander. This hypothesis is suggested by the fact that two *korônides* appear in the margins of the papyrus, indicating a change of meter from iambic trimeter to a lyric meter. Similarly, Huys 1986:11 and Di Giuseppe 2012:149–152 suggest this scene may be a *kommos*.

Despite the fact that we have lost 75% of the material, it is clear from the reference to a crown that Alexander's celebration remains an issue. Moreover, the fact that a *kallinikos* song[60] is being performed confirms that the style of this celebration is fundamentally epinician. In other words, the epinician echoes in the previous passages do not just fade away, and this strengthens the notion that the plot to kill Alexander is a reaction specifically to the reception of his victory.

In the end, the fortuitous revelation of Alexander's true origins saves his life and guarantees him a place in Troy. In this way, at least, the tensions between victor and (aristocratic) community of the *polis* are ultimately resolved. But Euripides still gives us cause for pause. First of all, Alexander is saved not because of his accomplishments, and certainly not because of any epinician ideal that these accomplishments must be honored, but only thanks to his royal lineage. Despite the positive ending, then, the play seems to project an image of epinician celebration in which it exists only to provoke tension within the *polis*, and to nearly cause the Trojan royals to pollute themselves with a blood crime. In other words, rather than providing a lens through which the audience can see how hero and *polis* can benefit each other mutually, epinician in *Alexandros* becomes a poetic instrument that threatens to destroy Alexander, and to tear apart the Trojan community. It is both impossible and largely irrelevant to surmise whether or not Euripides was seeking to echo the specific dynamics of Alcibiades' controversial victory, celebration, and reception in Athens. But by dramatizing the political fallout of epinician celebration, *Alexandros* presents a confluence of poetry and politics that was strikingly topical in 415 BCE, and that would surely cause some members of the Athenian audience to reflect on the both the political and poetic aspects of epinician reception in the *polis*. As we shall see, *Heracles* provokes the audience in a similar fashion, albeit with a very different type of 'epinician backdrop.'

3. Epinician and *Heracles*

3.1 Dating *Heracles*

Although we possess the full text of *Heracles*, the date of its original production remains somewhat a mystery. Nevertheless, we can say with near certainty that the tragedy was produced either during or shortly after Alcibiades' athletic

---

[60] This hypothesis, advanced by Collard and Cropp 2008:71 and Karamanou 2017:107, seems highly probable. Cf. Euripides *Heracles* 680–681 for another example of *kallinikos* working as a feminine substantive to indicate a song.

peak. The best criteria for establishing the year in which the play was produced are, unfortunately, metrical. On this basis alone, *Heracles* seems to have fallen in the last 15 years of Euripides' career (420–406 BCE), and Bond suggests 416 and 414 as the most likely dates—within a year of the production of *Alexandros*.[61] If *Heracles* was produced after *Alexandros* and the Trojan Trilogy, the Athenian audience would naturally have been very familiar with the complexity of dealing with the return of an epinician hero. But even if it was produced a few years earlier, and thus before either Euripides' epinician for Alcibiades or the *ostrakophoria*, it is likely that these issues had already come up in the Athenian civic sphere. As mentioned above, Alcibiades seems to have won prominent victories by 418 BCE,[62] and he must have been engaging in *hippotrophia* for at least a handful of years beforehand; such is the nature of athletic competition. Moreover, it is unlikely that Alcibiades handled his early competitions and victories with much more discretion than he did the Olympic victory of 416; such, it would appear, was the nature of Alcibiades. In short, whenever *Heracles* was produced (within the very large range suggested above), the Athenian public would have been well-aware of Alcibiades' athletic ambitions—and the controversies surrounding them.

3.2 Epinician Poetics and the Question of Heracles' Integration

Unlike with *Alexandros*, Euripides does not set an athletic competition at the heart of *Heracles*. The play does, however, consistently and explicitly link epinician poetics to the political question of Heracles' reception in the various communities of the tragedy. In the first third of the play, the issue of Heracles' return and reception is reflected in the debates about whether or not his family should be killed, as Lycus insists, or whether his heroic endeavors should ensure the honor and safety of his family within the *polis*. In the middle third, Heracles' reception in the *polis* is dramatically re-enacted by the jubilant response with which the Chorus greets his return to Thebes and his defeat of Lycus. And in the final third of the tragedy, when the murder of his family threatens to obscure the

---

[61]   This is a conservative estimate. See Bond 1981:xxx–xxxii, who in fact places it between 416–406. The percentage of resolved trimeters in *Heracles* is nearly identical to that of *Trojan Women* (21.5% and 21.2%, respectively). If *Heracles* preceded *Trojan Women*, it would likely be the earliest surviving play in which Euripides uses trochaic tetrameters (*Heracles* 855–874). Beta 1999 reviews a broad range of evidence and argues that the *Heracles* we possess was actually the second Heracles play that Euripides had composed. According to Beta, the first one should be dated to 425–423 BCE, with the second and extant version produced at some point following a parody of the first *Heracles* in Aristophanes' *Wasps* (422 BCE). The notion is intriguing but likely impossible to prove. Regardless, this theory also suggests a date within the range I suggest above.

[62]   See above at p. 56.

issue of Heracles' place in the *polis*, the hero himself brings the question to the foreground:

> οὔτ' ἐμαῖς φίλαις
> Θήβαις ἐνοικεῖν ὅσιον· ἢν δὲ καὶ μένω,
> ἐς ποῖον ἱερὸν ἢ πανήγυριν φίλων
> εἶμ'; οὐ γὰρ ἄτας εὐπροσηγόρους ἔχω.
> 1285 ἀλλ' Ἄργος ἔλθω; πῶς, ἐπεὶ φεύγω πάτραν;
> φέρ' ἀλλ' ἐς ἄλλην δή τιν' ὁρμήσω πόλιν;
> κἄπειθ' ὑποβλεπώμεθ' ὡς ἐγνωσμένοι,
> γλώσσης πικροῖς κέντροισι †κληδουχούμενοι†·

Heracles 1281–1288

> It is not holy
> for me to dwell in my beloved Thebes; even if
> I did stay, to which temple or group of friends
> would I turn? For my curse is not easy to address.
> 1285 Should I go to Argos? How, as an exile from my
> own land? Then to what other city should I turn?
> When recognized I will be held in suspicion,
> and pricked by the bitter spurs of men's words.

Crucially, Heracles stresses that he will be unable to participate in religious rites—a primary aspect of inclusion within a political community.[63] Moreover, he believes that this prohibition will exist in all the *poleis* in the tragic world, and that it will be accompanied, and indeed exacerbated, by the hostile reception accorded to him by the actual inhabitants of those other cities.[64] The problem is thus universal, and the manifestation of the issue takes on the form of both institutional inhibitions and individual reactions. Heracles thus reminds us that that the question of how and in what community he may be accommodated remains central to the play.

This question of reception had already been associated with epinician throughout *Heracles*, and in numerous ways. On a general level, the entire play is imbued with references to epinician song and language that are not especially subtle. As one might expect, these references emerge most obviously in the choral odes. The first stasimon provides an instructive example of the way that the genre resounds most ostentatiously throughout the tragedy, but also of the depth of Euripides' engagement with it (*Heracles* 355–358). The song's

---

[63] See e.g. Blok 2017:esp. 57–78, and more generally Blok 2018.
[64] Yunis 1988:153.

opening lines actually suggest a dirge, beginning with the word *ailinon* (*Heracles* 348) and a dedication to "the one ... gone to the darkness."[65] This proem has led some scholars to classify it as a *thrênos*,[66] but the rest of the song is overwhelmingly encomiastic in both content and language. This combination of generic influences is by no means unique within the tragic canon,[67] but the threnodic introduction here may lend a certain power to the song that follows, almost as if the desire to praise Heracles and to celebrate his deeds simply overwhelms the impulse to mourn[68]:

> 355 ὑμνῆσαι στεφάνωμα μό-
> χθων δι᾽ εὐλογίας θέλω.
> γενναίων δ᾽ ἀρεταὶ πόνων
> τοῖς θανοῦσιν ἄγαλμα.

Heracles 355–358

> 355 I wish to sing, through fine praise,
> a crown for [Heracles'] toils.
> For the virtues of noble labors
> Are a pleasing gift to the dead.

These are the final lines of the first strophe of the *parodos*, and each is replete with epinician language and ideas. The explicit desire to praise Heracles quite obviously sets an encomiastic tone, and the references to Heracles' *ponoi* ("labors") and *mochthoi* ("toils") are conspicuous epinician *topoi*,[69] as is the focus on *aretê* ("virtue" or "excellence").[70] The metaphors also fit neatly into this epinician context. *Stephanôma* ("crown") is a term employed almost exclusively by Pindar

---

[65] *Heracles* 352–353: τὸν ... / ἐς ὄρφναν μολόντα.

[66] Both Bond 1981:146 and Carey 2012:17 classify the ode as a *thrênos*, though both also stress the abundance of encomiastic motifs that run throughout.

[67] A striking parallel can be found in the second stasimon of Euripides' *Alcestis*, where the Chorus begins to sing a *thrênos* for Alcestis only to transition into a song of praise which "evokes the conventions of encomiastic song" (*Alcestis* 393–476); cf. Swift 2012:158–161 (quote on p. 158). More generally, the juxtaposition of different generic *topoi* within a single ode was a technique commonly used by the tragic poets, as is evidenced by the fact that nearly all of the odes discussed by Swift 2010 present significant amounts of what we might call generic dissonance. On the phenomenon more generally, see Swift 2012:152–154, and Weiss 2019.

[68] Ford 2019:79–80 proposes a different reading, namely that Euripides hearkens back to a (theoretical) lyric past in which the "Linus-song" contained aspects of both mourning and celebration.

[69] Carey 1995:88–89. Carey 2012:28 argues that the lines are specifically reminiscent of Pindar.

[70] Cf. Bundy 1962, *passim*; H. Lee 1983; Hawhee 2002.

prior to *Heracles*,[71] and one which he used to refer to his songs of praise.[72] By calling their song an *agalma* ("gift," here), the Chorus confirms the proem's epinician credentials.[73] Even with the emphasis on Heracles' (presumed) death, these elements, employed together in such a condensed space, overtly signal to the audience that the song has transitioned from dirge to encomium.

The promised crown of praise lasts a full seventy-one lines (*Heracles* 359–429) before the Chorus closes the ode in the threnodic mode with which it began (*Heracles* 430–441). The encomiastic section thus takes up the vast majority of the ode. It consists of an account, practically in list form, of the twelve labors to which Amphitryon had already referred.[74] The structure and meter of the ode have Pindaric precedents,[75] and many of the terms with which Heracles' labors are described are overtly reminiscent of the epinician genre.[76] Given the Chorus' introduction to this section, there can be no doubt that it would have been understood as a praise-song in honor of Heracles. And insofar as the second and third stasima are similarly replete with epinician motifs,[77] it is clear that, as Heracles struggles to find a place in a *polis*, the choral odes work to set an encomiastic tone that could hardly escape the notice of an attentive audience.

In fact, epinician terminology abounds throughout the iambic sections of the play as well. From the outset, Euripides presents Heracles as a hero of tremendous prowess, and he is careful to mark his descriptions with epinician terminology. Amphitryon immediately stresses that Heracles is already κλεινός (*Heracles* 12: "famous"),[78] and uses the phrase "ἐξεμόχθησεν πόνους" (*Heracles* 22:

---

[71] Bond 1981:146, calls στεφάνωμα μόχθων "a Pindaric phrase for a Pindaric poem." Pindar uses *stephanôma* seven times in his epinicians. The only archaic poets to use the term are Alcaeus and Theognis (one time each). Sophocles uses the term twice, but only once prior to *Heracles* (*Antigone* 122; *Oedipus at Colonus* 684).

[72] Cf. *Isthmian* 4.44 for song as *stephanôma*. For a more complete treatment of Pindar's use of the "song as crown" metaphor, cf. Nisetich 1975.

[73] As Kurke 1991:105 notes: "epinikion ... is [both] a crown and an *agalma*." See also Segal 1967:460–469.

[74] Euripides' version of the twelve labors is: victories over the Nemean lion, the Centaurs, and the Golden Hind; taming the horses of Diomedes; defeating Cycnus; winning the Golden Apples of the Hesperides; ridding the sea of pirates; holding up the sky; victory over the Amazons and the seizure of the girdle of the Amazon queen; defeating the Hydra and Geryon; and descent into Hades for Cerberus.

[75] Barlow 1996:139.

[76] Among others, the typical references to his labors as *ponoi* (*Heracles* 388, 427); "colorful compound epithets" (Barlow 1996:139) such as ποικιλόνωτος (*Heracles* 376; Pindar *Pythian* 4.249) and ξενοδαῖκτης (*Heracles* 391; Pindar Fragment 140a); mention of "successful glories [*agalmata*] of other *dromoi*" (as translated by Padilla 1994:288).

[77] I discuss these odes separately below at pp. 79–88, but for an overview see esp. H. Parry 1965 on the second stasimon, and Swift 2010:131–133 on the third.

[78] There are fewer than fifty (non-Euripidean) uses of κλεινός before *Heracles* (all data according to the TLG), of which approximately twenty are Sophoclean. Of the remaining thirty, seventeen are

"he has toiled through labors") to denote the completion of his earlier tasks. He thus subtly imitates Pindar, who constantly recalls the toils required for athletic success in order to emphasize the victor's self-sacrifice, but also to establish a thematic connection between his *laudandi* and Heracles.[79]

The use of the adjective *kallinikos* ("gloriously triumphant") neatly encapsulates the epinician texture of the play.[80] The word was closely connected with both Heracles and athletic competition in Greek poetry. It is first attested in an Archilochean hymn that celebrated Heracles[81] and was regularly sung in honor of athletic victors at Olympia.[82] As such, the original hymn was a sort of "proto-epinician."[83] In fact, prior to *Heracles* the term *kallinikos* was used almost exclusively by Pindar to describe the Olympic victors, the reward for their toils, or the epinician song itself as a reward.[84] In total, only ten uses of this term survive prior to Euripides.[85] One of these is found in the Archilochus fragment cited above; another in an Aeschylean fragment (fragment 190); and the remaining eight are all found in Pindar, exclusively in his epinician odes. Euripides himself was quite fond of the term, using it over 30 times in his career among extant tragedies and fragments. The eight uses in *Heracles*, however, are the most of any of his tragedies.[86] Even on this granular level, then, the tragedy is sharply infused with epinician flavoring.

This is all the more apparent when one considers the variety of circumstances in which *kallinikos* is employed. We first see it in the prologue, when Amphitryon claims that he and Heracles' wife and children have taken refuge at an altar to Zeus that Heracles has set up as an offering from his "glorious spear" (*Heracles* 49: καλλινίκου δορός). It is later used to refer to the celebration of Heracles' exploits after the *gigantomachy* (*Heracles* 180), to Heracles himself (*Heracles* 582), his weapons (*Heracles* 570), and his victory over Lycus (*Heracles* 789). In the second stasimon, the Chorus actually defines their celebration of

---

Pindaric (all but one in the epinician corpus) and eight are in Bacchylides (all epinician). While Euripides himself used the adjective far too frequently to make this term truly marked in any way for his audience, it is nevertheless a term with strong epinician associations which sets the tone for the far more pronounced epinician tones that the play will develop.

[79] Carey 1995:88–89. Cf. e.g. Pindar *Olympian* 5.15; *Nemean* 7.74; *Nemean* 10.23–24; *Isthmian* 6.10–14.

[80] See also the discussions in Swift 2010:132–133 and 145–147, and in Kampakoglou 2018:188–189.

[81] Archilochus fragment 324: τήνελλα καλλίνικε χαῖρε ἄναξ Ἡράκλεις, / αὐτός τε καὶ Ἰόλαος, αἰχμητὰ δύω ("*Tênella* hail the *kallinikos* lord Heracles / and Iolaos, two warriors").

[82] Cf. Pindar *Olympian* 9.1–4, and esp. Σ *Olympian* 9.1d, in which the scholiast reports that the victor himself would sing the hymn with his *philoi* by the altar of Zeus.

[83] I borrow the term from Pavlou 2008.

[84] Describing the victor: *Pythian* 1.32; the reward: *Isthmian* 5.54; the song as reward: *Pythian* 5.106, *Nemean* 3.19.

[85] All statistics according to the data of the *TLG*.

[86] Only *Electra* (three) and *Phoenissae* (six) contain more than two instances.

Heracles as a *kallinikos* song (*Heracles* 681). Much like the epinician tones of the choral odes, the idea of Heracles as *kallinikos* echoes throughout the first half of the play, and it is closely tied both to his person and to the notion of celebrating of him.

Intriguingly, *kallinikos* continues to make its presence heard in the second half of the play, even after Heracles has killed his family. In the first instance, the Messenger reports that, in his fit of madness, Heracles "competed against nobody and proclaimed to himself his glorious victory over no one."[87] Coming as they do just as Heracles murders his family in a fit of delusion, these lines can be read as tragically ironic; certainly they "brutally reverse the chorus' celebratory imagery."[88] But in so doing, they also remind us of the fact that within the world of the play, Heracles and epinician are inextricably linked.[89] This remains true for the players in the tragedy as well: as Heracles lies unconscious in the aftermath of his descent into lunacy, the Chorus expresses their sorrow for the "*kallinikos* man" (*Heracles* 1046: τὸ καλλίνικον κάρα). Both at the moment and in the wake of his least heroic and most troubling act, the associations between Heracles, his victories, and epinician song and language remain in the foreground.

The presence of "*kallinikos*" thus provides the play with a regular injection of epinician diction, both during and around the discussions of how Heracles should be received by the *poleis* of the tragedy. Even more significant, however, is the fact that all those parties who advocate on behalf of his reception resort to language and ideals rooted in epinician poetry. At the same time, Heracles' main antagonist, Lycus, rejects both the hero and his epinician *bona fides*. As we shall see in the next section, throughout these debates, the strong association between Heracles' positive reception in the *polis* and epinician song, language, and values is at first subtle, then glaring, and finally reflected in unexpected ways after Heracles murders his family.

3.3 Epinician Advocacy: Finding a Place for Heracles in the Polis

3.3.1 Lycus, Amphitryon, and Heracles' reception in Thebes

The tragedy opens with Amphitryon standing before an unnamed altar and recalling Heracles' divine paternity, referring to himself as "a partner of Zeus'

---

[87] *Heracles* 960–961: πρὸς οὐδέν' ἡμιλλᾶτο κἀκηρύσσετο / αὐτὸς πρὸς αὑτοῦ καλλίνικος οὐδενός.

[88] Worman 1999:97.

[89] Though in fact Heracles and epinician enjoyed a close relationship outside of the world of the play as well, as Heracles is the mythical hero whom Pindar most frequently cites (cf. Nieto Hernández 1993:76 and n. 2).

bed" (*Heracles* 1: τὸν Διὸς σύλλεκτρον), a curiously elliptical formulation that will soon gain significance. The focus then shifts to Heracles and his earth-taming exploits (*Heracles* 20–25), which Amphitryon describes with generically epinician language.[90] Only after this does Amphitryon finally spell out the tragic crisis: Thebes has been convulsed by revolution, and, in Heracles' absence, the new tyrant Lycus wishes to kill Amphitryon, Megara, and Heracles' children (*Heracles* 31–41). In this context, Amphitryon finally explains the physical setting of the play: he and the rest of the family have taken refuge at "the altar of Zeus the savior, which [Heracles] set up as an offering of his *kallinikos* spear after conquering the Minyans."[91] The association between Heracles' epinician accomplishments and the possibility of salvation is, in a sense, at once oblique and direct: on the one hand, Amphitryon does not explicitly state that the family should be saved on account of Heracles' heroic deeds; but the setting and language work to forge a powerful connection between the very concept of salvation and the image of Heracles as a hero of epinician proportions. Looming in the foreground throughout the first half of the play, the altar, and Amphitryon's comments about it, prepare the audience for the argument that Heracles' earlier triumphs warrant his family's salvation.[92]

The first extensive words on the subject, however, are a rejection of the idea that Heracles' actions are worthy of recognition. Immediately after the *parodos*, Lycus comes on stage and reaffirms his intention to kill Heracles' family. The episode that follows consists primarily of a debate between Lycus, Amphitryon, and Heracles' wife Megara about the hero's legacy,[93] and it begins with Lycus' rejection of the heroic image of Heracles:

σὺ μὲν καθ᾽ Ἑλλάδ᾽ ἐκβαλὼν κόμπους κενούς
ὡς σύγγαμός σοι Ζεὺς τέκνου τε κοινεῶν,
150   σὺ δ᾽ ὡς ἀρίστου φωτὸς ἐκλήθης δάμαρ.
τί δὴ τὸ σεμνὸν σῷ κατείργασται πόσει,
ὕδραν ἕλειον εἰ διώλεσε κτανὼν
ἢ τὸν Νέμειον θῆρ᾽, ὃν ἐν βρόχοις ἑλὼν
βραχίονός φησ᾽ ἀγχόναισιν ἐξελεῖν;

---

[90] E.g. *Heracles* 22: ἐξεμόχθησεν πόνους ("he has toiled through labors").

[91] *Heracles* 48–49: βωμὸν ... τόνδε σωτῆρος Διός, / ὃν καλλινίκου δορὸς ἄγαλμ᾽ ἱδρύσατο / Μινύας κρατήσας.

[92] See Rehm 1988:302–303 on the likely placement of the altar to Zeus *Sôtêr* in the center of the orchestra throughout the first half of the play.

[93] Megara is present on-stage throughout, though there has been some debate about whether she should technically be considered an active participant in the *agôn*. On the question see esp. Hamilton 1985.

155 τοῖσδ' ἐξαγωνίζεσθε; τῶνδ' ἄρ' οὕνεκα
τοὺς Ἡρακλείους παῖδας οὐ θνήσκειν χρεών;
ὁ δ' ἔσχε δόξαν οὐδὲν ὢν εὐψυχίας
θηρῶν ἐν αἰχμῇ, τἄλλα δ' οὐδὲν ἄλκιμος

Heracles 148–158

You who toss around Greece empty boasts
that Zeus had a share of your bed and child,
150   And you who claim to be wife of the finest man:
What noble feat has your husband [Heracles] done
By wiping out a marsh-dwelling snake or killing
the Nemean beast, the one he seized with a noose
but claims to have crushed in the coils of his arms?
155   These are your arguments? And because of this
the children of Heracles ought not to die?
He's worth nothing but has a reputation of great
courage from battles with beasts, helpless in all else.

For Lycus, the point of denigrating Heracles is obviously to justify the murder of his family, and his first priority appears to be to rebut the previous depictions of the hero. He calls Amphitryon's opening claim to be "a partner of Zeus' bed" (*Heracles* 1) an "empty boast" (*Heracles* 148) and he rejects Megara's description of her "eminent marriage" to Heracles (*Heracles* 68: ἐπίσημον εὐνήν) by ridiculing the idea he accomplished anything of note. Even more obviously, he denies that Heracles' "earth-taming" endeavors merit Amphitryon's heroic characterization, at once minimizing and recasting them. These revisionist claims of Heracles' lineage and exploits must have been striking for an audience accustomed to seeing sculptural representations of his "battles with beasts" on a regular basis. A short walk from the Theater of Dionysus, for example, the hero is depicted on the Hephaisteion with the Nemean lion in the very "coils of his arm."[94] By advancing such ostentatious claims, then, Lycus draws attention to the fact that he must reject the heroic image of Heracles before he can carry out his executions.[95] We thus understand that Heracles and his family can only be

---

[94] Cf. Thompson 1962:348. It should be noted that while Heracles is using his left arm to put the lion in a stranglehold, he does stoop to using a sword with his right hand, presumably to finish the task.

[95] In a sense, perhaps, Lycus is the heir to Pindar's imagined enemies, the "envious people" who feast on words of praise (*Nemean* 8.21 ὄψον δὲ λόγοι φθονεροῖσιν) and create "hateful misrepresentation ... and malicious blame which violates the illustrious" (*Nemean* 8.32–34: ἐχθρὰ δ' ἄρα πάρφασις .../ κακοποιὸν ὄνειδος· / ἃ τὸ μὲν λαμπρὸν βιᾶται). These lines are the beginning

marginalized if the hero's credentials are successfully denied, and more broadly, that Heracles' past is intimately related to his present reception. That the two appear to be linked suggests that this is not simply a case of a tyrant behaving badly, but rather that the marginalization of Heracles and his family go hand in hand with a rejection of his heroic image.

In response to Lycus' affront, Amphitryon calls on the gods themselves to act as witnesses (*Heracles* 176: μάρτυσιν), and then turns to a description not only of Heracles' feats, but above all the manner in which they were received:

> Διὸς κεραυνὸν ἠρόμην τέθριππά τε
> ἐν οἷς βεβηκὼς τοῖσι γῆς βλαστήμασιν
> Γίγασι πλευροῖς πτήν' ἐναρμόσας βέλη
> 180   τὸν καλλίνικον μετὰ θεῶν ἐκώμασεν·

Heracles 177–180

> I call on the thunder of Zeus and the four-horsed chariot
> on which he stood against the giants,
> children of the earth, ringing their ribs with arrows,
> 180   and reveled, with the gods, the *kallinikos* celebration.[96]

Amphitryon begins by recalling one of Heracles' most famous exploits, the gigantomachy in which Heracles' contributions were crucial to the victory of the Olympian gods. The reference to Zeus' four-horsed chariot may function as a reminder both of his athletic exploits and the epinician poetry that celebrates them,[97] though the image of Heracles on a chariot during the gigantomachy would likely have been a familiar one for the Athenian audience, and perhaps even the easiest one to call to mind.[98]

---

    and end of Pindar's famous excursus on Ajax's death, on which see esp. Carey 1976:30–33; and Miller 1982.

[96]   Following Bond 1981:115 who suggests that the masculine *kallinikos* must have been implicitly understood with κῶμος, and who is certainly correct that the reference is to "the victory hymn and dance."

[97]   Padilla 1994:287. Twelve of Pindar's forty-five odes classified as epinicians were composed in honor of victories in the four-horsed chariot race, by far the most of any single competition. For Bacchylides the rate is about the same, albeit with a less meaningful sample size (three out of 13 epinicians for which it is possible to attribute an event).

[98]   The depiction of Heracles fighting with a bow, either on or near a chariot, was common in fifth-century painting and statuary. See e.g. Schwab 1996, for Heracles' depiction on the eastern metopes of the Parthenon, as well as on other roughly contemporary examples in figurative art. Moore 1995 argues that the Old Temple of Athena on the Acropolis (destroyed long before Euripides' *Heracles*, of course) featured Heracles with a bow on Zeus' chariot in the midst of the gigantomachy—the exact scene described here by Amphitryon.

The description of the aftermath of the battle, characterized as a *kallinikos kômos*, is striking in its originality[99] and obviously intended to call to mind an epinician celebration.[100] Indeed, Pindar frequently describes the victory celebration as a *kômos*,[101] refers to his song as *kallinikos*,[102] and overtly connects the two when he notes that Archilochus' "triple *kallinikos* song sufficed … for Epharmostos celebrating [*kômazonti*] with his companions."[103] In his opening gambit, then, Amphitryon pivots quickly from familiar Heraclean iconography and narratives to a description of epinician celebration. Given the context of the debate, the implication is clearly that if the Olympian gods accorded Heracles epinician honors, he has certainly earned the respect of Lycus and Thebes as well.

Before Amphitryon closes his speech, he launches a critique of the Thebans' response to Heracles' feats:

> ὦ γαῖα Κάδμου· (καὶ γὰρ ἐς σ' ἀφίξομαι
> λόγους ὀνειδιστῆρας ἐνδατούμενος),
> τοιαῦτ' ἀμύνεθ' Ἡρακλεῖ τέκνοισί τε;
> 220 Μινύαις ὃς εἷς ἅπασι διὰ μάχης μολὼν
> Θήβας ἔθηκεν ὄμμ' ἐλεύθερον βλέπειν.

Heracles 217–221

> O land of Cadmus—for I come to you as well
> to divvy up reproachful words!
> Is this how you protect Heracles and his children?
> 220 He who came as one in battle against all the Minyans
> and let Thebes look forth with free eyes?

In citing the defeat of the Minyans, and Thebes' concomitant freedom, Amphitryon accomplishes three things: he subtly recalls the setting of the scene, the altar to Zeus *Sôtêr* that Heracles had set up as an *agalma* of his *kallinikos*

---

[99] I know of no other reference to a *kallinikos kômos* occurring after the gigantomachy. Apollodorus, for example (*Bibliotheca* 1.6), mentions nothing of the sort. Even Pindar only notes that in recognition of his help, the gods granted Heracles eternal peace and the hand of *Hêbê* in marriage (*Nemean* 1.67–72).

[100] Pindar *Nemean* 1.67–72.

[101] Pindar *Olympian* 4.9, *Olympian* 6.98, *Olympian* 8.10.

[102] Pindar *Pythian* 5.106–107.

[103] Pindar *Olympian* 9.1–4: ὁ μὲν Ἀρχιλόχου μέλος / φωνᾶεν Ὀλυμπίᾳ, καλλίνικος ὁ τριπλόος / κεχλαδώς, / ἄρκεσε Κρόνιον παρ' ὄχθον ἁγεμονεῦσαι / κωμάζοντι φίλοις Ἐφαρμόστῳ σὺν ἑταίροις· ("The hymn of Archilochus resounding at Olympia, the exultation of the triple *kallinikos* [song] sufficed for Epharmostos, celebrating with his beloved companions, to lead the way along Cronos' hill.").

spear in the aftermath of that victory;[104] he emphasizes Heracles' exceptionality, particularly with the (again, innovative) reference to the fact he had defeated the Minyans on his own;[105] and he makes explicit, for the first time, the idea that the entire *polis* has benefited from Heracles' actions, and that a certain debt is owed both to him (219: Ἡρακλεῖ) and his family.

Immediately after this, Amphitryon expands the focus of his diatribe to the entirety of the Greek world, and suggesting that the inadequate reception of Heracles is not limited to Thebes or Lycus' lack of consideration:

> οὐδ' Ἑλλάδ' ᾔνεσ' (οὐδ' ἀνέξομαί ποτε
> σιγῶν) κακίστην λαμβάνων ἐς παῖδ' ἐμόν,
> ἣν χρῆν νεοσσοῖς τοῖσδε πῦρ λόγχας ὅπλα
> 225 φέρουσαν ἐλθεῖν, ποντίων καθαρμάτων
> χέρσου τ' ἀμοιβάς ὧν †ἐμόχθησας χάριν†.

Heracles 222–226

> Nor would I praise Hellas (never shall I suffer
> in silence) for she treats my son worst of all!
> She who most of all should come to these hatchlings
> 225 bearing fire, arms, and spears, compensation for his
> cleansing of land and sea, gratitude for his toils!

Rhetorically, Amphitryon repeats his maneuver from the previous passage, emphasizing the benefits conferred by Heracles' triumphs over a range of monsters—the "battles with beasts" that Lycus had just recently belittled (*Heracles* 158). By pointing out that these unrewarded exploits have been a boon not only for Thebes, but indeed for all of Hellas, he implies that the neglect of Heracles is universal and systemic.

Moreover, Amphitryon leaves no doubt that compensation for Heracles' acts is a veritable necessity, and in so doing he draws deeply on both the language and concepts of epinician poetry. The emphasis on toil (*ponos, mochthos*) is, as mentioned already, a standard epinician *topos*,[106] and Pindar posits song and

---

[104] See *Heracles* 50, the only other mention of the Minyans in the play. Intriguingly, the word "Minyans" occurs as an anapaest at the beginning of a line of iambic trimeter, a metrical formation that Euripides generally only uses for "long and intractable proper names" (Bond 1981:122). The repetition of this metrical rarity may have helped an audience more finely attuned to the rhythm of Euripides' poetry recall the earlier instance.

[105] Bond 1981:122 notes that the notion of a "μονομαχία does not occur elsewhere."

[106] On the athletes' *ponoi* in general, see H. Lee 1983; and Segal 1967:esp. 436–445.

celebration as a necessary reward for the victor's efforts.[107] Pindar also regularly suggests that the community as a whole must accord the victorious individual a positive reception. This is certainly the case in *Nemean 2*, where Pindar exhorts the Athenian citizens to provide a "glorious return for Timodemus," or in his first *Isthmian* when he claims that "he who is praised receives the greatest reward [*kerdos*]: the choicest words of citizens and strangers."[108] In *Pythian 7*, the importance of public approval is implicit when the poet "grieve[s] that *phthonos* is the reward for great deeds,"[109] a line that has generally been taken to refer to the tensions between the victor Megacles and his fellow Athenian citizens.[110]

The need to celebrate and indeed compensate the victor on a community-wide level emerges, perhaps most fully and intricately, in Pindar's second *Pythian* ode:

> ἄγει δὲ χάρις φίλων ποίνιμος ἀντὶ ἔργων ὀπιζομένα·
> σὲ δ', ὦ Δεινομένειε παῖ, Ζεφυρία πρὸ δόμων
> Λοκρὶς παρθένος ἀπύει, πολεμίων καμάτων ἐξ ἀμαχάνων
> 20   διὰ τεὰν δύναμιν δρακεῖσ' ἀσφαλές.
> θεῶν δ' ἐφετμαῖς Ἰξίονα φαντὶ ταῦτα βροτοῖς
> λέγειν ἐν πτερόεντι τροχῷ
> παντᾷ κυλινδόμενον·
> τὸν εὐεργέταν ἀγαναῖς ἀμοιβαῖς ἐποιχομένους τίνεσθαι.

Pythian 2.17–24

> Reverent gratitude leads [them], a reward for friendly deeds.
> Son of Deinomenus, the Epizephyrian Locrian maiden calls to you
> before her home, her life sheltered by your power
> 20   from the intractable toils of war.

---

[107] On the "necessity" of praise and celebration, see e.g. Bundy 1962:10–11 and 53–70; Kurke 1991:97–103. Song and praise as μισθός at *Nemean* 7.63 and *Isthmian* 1.47; as ποινή at *Pythian* 1.59; as ἄποινα at *Olympian* 7.16, *Pythian* 2.14, *Nemean* 7.16; as κέρδος at *Isthmian* 1.51; perhaps as ἀμοιβή at *Nemean* 5.48, though interpretations differ regarding the nature of the reward: Vallozza 1989:23–24 suggests it is public celebration, but Pfeijffer 1999:178 believes it is the victory itself; the two interpretations need not be mutually exclusive.

[108] *Nemean* 2.24: Τιμοδήμῳ σὺν εὐκλέϊ νόστῳ. *Isthmian* 1.50–51: εὐαγορηθεὶς κέρδος ὕψιστον δέκεται, πολιατᾶν καὶ ξένων γλώσσας ἄωτον. On these lines, see esp. Kurke 1991:209.

[109] *Pythian* 7.18–19: τὸ δ' ἄχνυμαι, / φθόνον ἀμειβόμενον τὰ καλὰ ἔργα.

[110] Bernardini, Cingano, et al. 1995:560–561 provides a synopsis of the connection between the reference to *phthonos* and Megacles' ostracism, as well as a range of scholarly interpretations of Pindar's intentions here. More recently, Athanassaki 2011 has argued that Pindar was actively working to mediate the relationship between Megacles and the Athenian citizenry in this ode.

> It is said that Ixion, by order of the gods, speaks thus
> to mortals as he is turned all round
> on his spinning wheel:
> "repay your benefactor with kind requitals."

The poem is dedicated to Hieron of Syracuse, who is addressed directly at 2.18 ("son of Deinomenus"), and in the early sections Pindar weaves together a series of myths, historical events, civic contexts, and gnomic concepts that cannot be explained here in brief.[111] Suffice it to say that given the placement of this invocation (immediately after the mention of *phila erga* and shortly before Ixion's comment about *euergetai*) and the accompanying reminder that Hieron saved Epizephyrian Locris from war only a few years prior to the poem,[112] it is clear that the tyrant prefigures as a "benefactor" who has earned *charis* and *amoibai* in his community and beyond.[113] Moreover, as Glenn Most has convincingly argued, this relationship must be understood as a three-tiered hierarchy of gods/"extraordinary men"/normal humans, within which "the inferior member displays gratitude while the superior member confers benefits."[114]

Euripides' Amphitryon draws on a similar set of language and concepts. He too points to the benefits that Heracles has conferred upon a wide array of mortals. He too emphasizes the fact that *amoibai* and *charis* are now Heracles' due. And by standing before and alluding to a monument that Heracles built to Zeus *Sôtêr* in recognition of his victory over the Minyans, he suggests that the audience is also meant to understand that like Hieron, Heracles is both benefactor and beneficiary; just as he honored Zeus in the aftermath of his victory,[115] so too should Heracles be honored by those he benefitted. In summary, in the process of arguing that Lycus, Thebes, and all of Greece must reward Heracles for his labors, Amphitryon draws deeply on epinician thought and language, and confirms that this question is central to the tragedy. The association between Heracles' reception in the *polis* and epinician song is not yet as obvious as it will be in the choral odes to come, but the foundation of these notions has already been set.

---

[111] See esp. Most 1985:60–86, which remains perhaps the most complete interpretation of the complex constellation that Pindar constructs in *Pythian 2*.

[112] On the historical context, see Bernardini, Cingano, et al. 1995:372–373.

[113] The first eight lines of the poem focus on Syracuse, and it is fairly obvious that they too are meant to publicly celebrate Hieron and to recognize the benefits his victory has conferred.

[114] Most 1985:75. See also Morgan 2015:185–186.

[115] Much like Hieron is said to have recognized Poseidon, cf. *Pythian* 2.12 and Most 1985:75.

3.3.2 Epinician reception and the return of Heracles

Heracles' inevitable return is both a source of joy for his family and a presumed resolution of the situation with Lycus, but much of the focus nevertheless remains on the question of the reception of the hero—and his deeds—within the Theban *polis*. Indeed, Heracles dedicates fewer lines to preemptively savoring his punishment of the tyrant (*Heracles* 565–567) than he does in spelling out the vengeance that he intends to visit upon the Theban citizenry:

> Καδμείων δ' ὅσους
> κακοὺς ἐφηῦρον εὖ παθόντας ἐξ ἐμοῦ
> 570   τῷ καλλινίκῳ τῷδ' ὅπλῳ χειρώσομαι,
> τοὺς δὲ πτερωτοῖς διαφορῶν τοξεύμασιν
> νεκρῶν ἅπαντ' Ἰσμηνὸν ἐμπλήσω φόνου,
> Δίρκης τε νᾶμα λευκὸν αἱμαχθήσεται.

Heracles 568–573

>   And whatever Cadmeians
> I come upon who have been wicked, despite prospering
> because of me, I'll lay them low with this *kallinikos* club;
> 570   the rest I'll tear apart with winged arrows
> and fill the whole Ismenus with gory corpses,
> while Dirce's clear waters run with blood.

The violent images here are striking, and when treated in depth have generally been related to the murderous break from reality that Heracles will soon experience;[116] certainly they prime the audience for blood. But these lines must also be read in relation to what we have seen in the play so far. Heracles draws attention to the same dynamics that Amphitryon did earlier: not just Lycus, but indeed all of Thebes has profited from his labors, and they are wrong to have turned their backs on him now. The mention of his *kallinikos* weapon is a reminder of the epinician nature of Heracles and his deeds, and the proper (celebratory) reception that Amphitryon openly demanded, the rejection of which Heracles now implies. It is a subtle reference, overshadowed perhaps by the images of corpse-strewn waters. But we nevertheless see Heracles endorse the ideas set forth in the beginning of the play, namely that the reception of his family was an obligation that touched the whole community of Thebes, and which thus demanded a communal response.

---

[116] See esp. Papadopoulou 2005:42–44, but also Luschnig 1988:102. For a synopsis of the lengthy debate about the relationship of these lines to Heracles' character and murder of his family, see Holmes 2008:249n60.

The second stasimon begins a short time later, and it draws deeply on elements of both epinician and paeanic song.[117] The song's "adherence to the conventions of encomiastic poetry"[118] recalls the various epinician elements—lexical, conceptual, and otherwise—that have thus far resounded throughout the tragedy. At the same time, the Chorus' declaration that it is engaged in the performance of a paean brings to the foreground important civic dimensions. As we shall see, the overall effect is of an encomiastic song that fits into the communal setting of the *polis*, and which becomes a crucial tool for understanding how an exceptional individual such as Heracles should be at once perceived and accepted.

These notions emerge gradually throughout the two strophic sequences. The actual praise of Heracles does not begin until the second strophic sequence, but the first antistrophe provides the framework for understanding the importance of poetic praise in the social fabric of the tragedy:

655 εἰ δὲ θεοῖς ἦν ξύνεσις
   καὶ σοφία κατ' ἄνδρας,
   δίδυμον ἂν ἥβαν ἔφερον
   φανερὸν χαρακτῆρ' ἀρετᾶς
660 ὅσοισιν μέτα, καὶ θανόντες
   εἰς αὐγὰς πάλιν ἀλίου
   δισσοὺς ἂν ἔβαν διαύλους,
   ἁ δυσγένεια δ' ἁπλοῦν ἂν
   εἶχε ζόας βίοτον,
665 καὶ τῷδ' ἂν τούς τε κακοὺς ἦν
   γνῶναι καὶ τοὺς ἀγαθούς

Heracles 655–666

655 If the gods had understanding
   and wisdom concerning men,
   they would offer a second youth
   as a visible stamp of *aretai*
660 for whoever had it, and after death

---

[117] Critical insistence on defining the song as one particular genre has led to very different conclusions. H. Parry 1965 and (implicitly, at least) Swift 2010:129–131 view it as decidedly epinician. On the other hand, Kampakoglou 2018:192 states that the second stasimon is "formally a paean but includes elements of epinician." There is no need to be so rigid in our classification of the genres (see e.g. the general comments about tragic lyric genres in Swift 2012:152). Indeed, the truth is surely that the ode could have reminded the audience of both epinician and paean-songs, given the preponderance of elements of each in the second stasimon.

[118] H. Parry 1965:374.

these men would return to the light
of the sun for a second run at life,
while base men would have
but a single course to live,
665   and in this way one might recognize
both the bad and the good.

The Chorus' main lament that human virtues (*aretai*) often go unnoticed is posed here as a general problem, but it obviously relates to Heracles' situation. We have already seen Lycus denigrate his *arete* and heard from Amphitryon that the failure to provide proper recognition for his deeds is a systemic problem. The Chorus thus doubles down on the earlier suggestions that a lack of recognition for Heracles is a central problem not only of the play, but of human existence.

Certainly we are meant to understand that against all odds, Heracles has nevertheless achieved the "stamp of *aretê*" that the Chorus longs for, and will again: he has in fact just now "return[ed] to the light," and according to tradition, he will go on to marry the goddess of Youth (*Hêbê*).[119] Nevertheless, the Chorus' use of a contra-factual condition implies a problem that extends beyond Heracles' personal situation, the "solution" to which only he possesses.[120] Heracles' unique abilities thus mark him as an individual capable of winning the recognition he deserves, but who, as a result, illuminates humanity's broader failure to grant such recognition, and the consequences of this shortcoming.

The universality of the problem is confirmed by the end of the antistrophe:

νῦν δ' οὐδεὶς ὅρος ἐκ θεῶν
670   χρηστοῖς οὐδὲ κακοῖς σαφής,
ἀλλ' εἰλισσόμενός τις αἰ-
ὼν πλοῦτον μόνον αὔξει.

Heracles 669–672

But in truth there is no clear marker
670   from the gods of either the good or bad.
Instead, time, in its turning,
    increases wealth alone.

---

[119] Cf. Scodel 1980b:308–311; Bond 1981:232; Papadopoulou 2005:33–34. On Heracles' marriage to *Hêbê*, see Hesiod *Theogony* 950–953.

[120] H. Parry 1965:367 calls this a "transition between general and particular."

The term *horos* refers to a distinct landmark or boundary—precisely the type of "visible stamp" that the Chorus calls for above. Despite Heracles' successful return from Hades, the Chorus still bemoans the lack of such a marker. This again suggests that Heracles' *aretê* is so extraordinary that he alone has earned this mark, and that it is not a solution that is adequate for all, or really any, mortals.[121] Instead, most mortals risk being cast aside by individuals—such as Lycus—whose "wealth" time has (until now) favored.[122] The first antistrophe thus eloquently articulates the difficulty of distinguishing good individuals from bad, and poses it as a universal problem. This neatly encapsulates what the audience has seen throughout the first part of the play, in which Lycus audaciously tries to cast Heracles as a *kakos*, and nearly succeeds. The hero's return restores his status, but the Chorus remains justifiably concerned that Heracles' "second youth" is not a viable measure of excellence for the rest of humanity.

It is only after highlighting the difficulty of recognizing human *aretê* that the Chorus embark on their performance of praise, a performance that is thus marked, albeit implicitly, as the solution to the problem posed above:[123]

> οὐ παύσομαι τὰς Χάριτας
> ταῖς Μούσαισιν συγκαταμει-
> 675   γνύς, ἡδίσταν συζυγίαν.
> μὴ ζῴην μετ' ἀμουσίας,
> αἰεὶ δ' ἐν στεφάνοισιν εἴην·
> ἔτι τοι γέρων ἀοιδὸς
> κελαδῶ Μναμοσύναν·
> 680   ἔτι τὰν Ἡρακλέους
> καλλίνικον ἀείδω
> παρά τε Βρόμιον οἰνοδόταν
> παρά τε χέλυος ἑπτατόνου
> μολπὰν καὶ Λίβυν αὐλόν.
> 685   οὔπω καταπαύσομεν
> Μούσας, αἵ μ' ἐχόρευσαν.

Heracles 673–686

> I will not stop blending
> the Graces with the Muses,
> 675   the sweetest union.

---

[121] Bond 1981:232: "[t]he chorus, mindful of Heracles as an *exemplum*, are in fact asking why all good people (like themselves) should not receive the distinction of a second life."

[122] H. Parry 1965:368 correctly remarks that here too the ode is drawing on epinician motifs.

[123] H. Parry 1965:369–371.

> May I not dwell among the Muse-less,
> but always be among the crowned.
> Still now, as an old singer
> I cry forth "Memory."[124]
> 680   I still sing Heracles'
> *kallinikos* [song][125]
> alongside wine-giving Bromios
> and the tune of the seven-stringed
> lyre and the Libyan flute.
> 685   Not yet shall I hold back the Muses
> who roused me to dance.

References to the Graces, to garlands (*stephanoisin*), and, naturally, to "Heracles' *kallinikos* song" all give this passage a distinctly Pindaric flavor, as does the choral use of a first-person singular *aeidô*.[126] The instruments mentioned (lyre and aulos) are the ones that generally accompanied epinician songs.[127] In short, the strophe is unmistakably epinician.

But it is the context here that is truly noteworthy: immediately after lamenting the lack of a clear "marker" for *agathoi* and *kakoi*, the Chorus dives headlong into a song of praise for Heracles. They emphasize this act by opening and closing the strophe with the statement that they will not desist from this song of praise, and by focusing on the continuity of their song: they "will not stop," they will not "hold back," they "still sing," and perhaps above all, even as "aged singer[s]" they still call forth on *Mnêmosynê*, the mother of the Muses and the divine figure who, it would appear, can ensure a proper and eternal memory of Heracles' deeds. The Chorus thus implies that its song may be the solution to the problem it has posed:[128] as long as their song of praise is audible, the proper boundary between *kakoi* and *agathoi* will be perceptible.

The coupling of this problem and solution is perfectly in line with the epinician tradition that Euripides has been evoking throughout the play. Indeed, we find in Bacchylides a wonderful parallel to the Chorus' argumentation:[129]

---

[124] I.e. *Mnêmosynê*, the mother of the Muses.

[125] Following Bond 1981:180 and 242.

[126] Pindar often speaks of the Graces accompanying or favoring his epinician poems. Among others, cf. *Isthmian* 3.8; *Pythian* 9.89; *Nemean* 4.7. For more on this point, cf. H. Parry 1965:369–372. On the *stephanos* in Pindar, see above at pp. 67–68. Pindar in fact uses the term more than all his predecessors combined. For *aeidô*, see *Olympian* 14.18; *Nemean* 10.31; *Isthmian* 2.12.

[127] Carey 2007:208.

[128] Once again, H. Parry 1965:369–371 has articulated this point at length.

[129] This parallel was first identified by H. Parry 1965:370.

ἀνδρὶ δ' οὐ θέμις, πολιὸν παρέντα
γῆρας, θάλειαν αὖτις ἀγκομίσσαι
90   ἥβαν. ἀρετᾶς γε μὲν οὐ μινύθει
βροτῶν ἅμα σώματι φέγγος, ἀλλὰ
Μοῦσά νιν τρέφει.

Bacchylides 3.88–92

For a man it is not allowed to pass over
grey old-age and to recover again blooming
90   youth. At least the splendor of mortal
excellence does not dwindle with the body,
but the Muse nurtures it.

Just like the Chorus of *Heracles*, Bacchylides notes that a second youth is impossible, but that the memory of an individual's *aretê* may nevertheless be secured by the Muse, which is to say by songs of praise. In fact, the only way that Bacchylides' formulation of the question differs from Euripides' is in his explicit expression of the solution. Pindar's understanding of the problem is also comparable. In *Nemean* 8, for example, he takes aim at the *phthoneroi* who use slander to destroy their superiors and raise themselves up—individuals essentially analogous to Lycus.[130] In the end, Pindar suggests that it is only by "praising the praiseworthy, and sowing blame for the wicked" (*Nemean* 8.39: αἰνέων αἰνητά, μομφὰν δ' ἐπισπείρων ἀλιτροῖς) that the epinician poet can ward off *phthonos* from his *laudandi*, and to thus guarantee their enduring fame.[131] In short, Pindar and Bacchylides pose the same problem as the Chorus of *Heracles*, and it is clear that Euripides is drawing on epinician conventions when he suggests that praise poetry and celebration is the only way to ensure that *aretê* may be properly recognized.

The final antistrophe of the ode continues to advance epinician motifs, but here the Chorus emphasizes the importance of the performance of celebration on a communal level:

παιᾶνα μὲν Δηλιάδες
‹ναῶν› ὑμνοῦσ' ἀμφὶ πύλας
τὸν Λατοῦς εὔπαιδα γόνον,
690   εἱλίσσουσαι καλλίχοροι·
παιᾶνας δ' ἐπὶ σοῖς μελάθροις

---

[130] As I suggest above at p. 72n95.

[131] Carey 1976:34: "the form of the expression suggests especially the role of the poet and chorus as remembrancer of great deeds."

κύκνος ὣς γέρων ἀοιδὸς
πολιᾶν ἐκ γενύων
κελαδήσω·

Heracles 687–694

The Delian maidens sing
a paean around the gates
for the noble son of Leto,
690   beautiful dancers whirling around;
so shall I, like a swan, an aged
singer, cry forth paeans
before your chambers from
greying jaws.

Here we see elements of both continuity and transition with respect to the previous strophe. On the one hand, the Chorus emphasizes that it is still the same "aged singer" who had called on *Mnêmosynê* just a few lines earlier. At the same time, the Chorus moves on from the praise of Heracles to the performance of a paean in the hero's honor. By invoking the paean, a communal song *par excellence*,[132] the Chorus subtly shifts our attention to Thebes and the city's relationship with the hero. It thus becomes implicit that the entire *polis* should, along with the Chorus, celebrate Heracles' return and his now-inevitable defeat of Lycus.

Finally, the ode finds closure by wedding this sense of communal celebration to the poetic and political questions that had been advanced thus far in both this stasimon and in the tragedy as a whole:

τᾶς δ' εὐγενίας
πλέον ὑπερβάλλων ‹ἀρετᾷ›
μοχθήσας τὸν ἄκυμον
θῆκεν βίοτον βροτοῖς
700   πέρσας δείματα θηρῶν.

Heracles 696–700

yet surpassing
even his nobility in virtue,
he labored and made a safe world
for humans, when he
700   slayed the beastly terrors

---

[132] See the lengthy discussion above at pp. 30–34.

On the one hand, the encomiastic tones of the stasimon, and of the play as a whole, remain firmly audible, with references to Heracles' toils and *aretê*. At the same time, the Chorus practically quotes Amphitryon's earlier laments about Heracles' treatment: μόχθησας is the participial equivalent of Amphitryon's ἐμόχθησας (*Heracles* 225), and refers to the same thing (Heracles' monster-slaying); more strikingly, the Chorus doubles down on Amphitryon's claim that Heracles "let Thebes gaze forth with free eyes" (*Heracles* 221: Θήβαις ἔθηκεν ὄμμ' ἐλεύθερον βλέπειν) by arguing that he "made the world habitable for humans" (τὸν ἄκυμον θῆκεν βίοτον βροτοῖς). This revisitation has several effects. On the one hand, it re-emphasizes Amphitryon's arguments concerning the benefits Heracles had bestowed, this time on an even more grandiose level. At the same time, it brings back the specter of the failure to reward acts of excellence that Amphitryon had quite explicitly lamented, and that the Chorus had just (more subtly) highlighted anew. Perhaps most importantly, and certainly most obviously, the Chorus embodies and performs the epinician celebration with which they (implicitly) suggest Heracles must be received.

The third stasimon begins a mere forty lines after the end of the second, and the short episode that lies between the two odes consists mainly of Amphitryon convincing an ever-boastful Lycus to go inside, where Heracles waits in ambush. The outcome—Lycus' death—is inevitable, and it occurs during the beginning of the third stasimon, with the tyrant's death-screams punctuating the Chorus' triumphant song. The second strophe of the third stasimon begins immediately after the Chorus announces Lycus' death (*Heracles* 760–761), and it picks up where the second stasimon left off, with a call for the whole city to join in their song:

> χοροὶ χοροὶ
> καὶ θαλίαι μέλουσι Θή-
> βας ἱερὸν κατ' ἄστυ.
> 765 μεταλλαγαὶ γὰρ δακρύων,
> μεταλλαγαὶ συντυχίας
> ‹   › ἔτεκον ἀοιδάς.

Heracles 763–767

> Dances, dances
> and celebrations enthrall
>   the holy town of Thebes.
> 765 Changes of tears,
> Changes of fortune
> ‹   › have given birth to songs.

While only implicit in the second *stasimon*, the civic dimension of the choral odes is explicit here. According to the Chorus, Heracles' victory has "given birth to songs"—presumably songs of praise and celebration. Most importantly, the entire city of Thebes is envisioned joining in this festive occasion, and it is apparent that these celebrations are warranted because the entire *polis* benefits from the "changes of fortune" wrought by Heracles.

A few lines later, the universal aspect of this celebration is even clearer— and even more clearly epinician:

> Ἰσμήν' ὦ στεφαναφόρει
> ξεσταί θ' ἑπταπύλου πόλεως
> ἀναχορεύσατ' ἀγυιαί
> Δίρκα θ' ἁ καλλιρρέεθρος,
> 785 σύν τ' Ἀσωπιάδες κόραι,
>   πατρὸς ὕδωρ βᾶτε λιποῦσαι συναοιδοί
> Νύμφαι τὸν Ἡρακλέους
> καλλίνικον ἀγῶνα.

Heracles 781–788

> Ismenus, deck yourself with garlands,
> and raise a choral dance, polished
> streets of the seven-gated city.
> Come, beautifully-flowing Dirce,
> 785 and with you the daughters of Asopus,
>   leave your father's water to sing,
> Nymphs, in harmony, of Heracles'
> kallinikon struggle.

The addressees in these lines—the Ismenus, the streets of the city, the Dirce, and the daughters of Asopus—represent the city as a whole, a metonymic strategy that Pindar regularly exploited.[133] In essence, the Chorus suggests that Thebes must welcome Heracles with song and dance, and by bearing the crown Heracles has bestowed upon the city. Since the subject of the song and dance will be Heracles' *kallinikos agôn*, it is clear that the Chorus is calling for celebration and the performance of songs of praise in his honor. The use of imperatives further

---

[133] This is obviously true of the "streets of the city"; the Ismenus and the Dirce were both bodies of water associated with the city; and the daughters of Asopus include Thebe, after whom the city is named (cf. Pindar *Isthmian* 8.15–20). Pindar and other poets frequently used Dirce to refer "metonymically" to the entire city of Thebes. Cf. Pindar *Olympian* 10.85; Bond 1981:272; Berman 2007:21–24.

implies that this act is not only desirable but indeed necessary, a notion that is ubiquitous in Pindar's work.[134]

The insistence that the Ismenus—in other words the entire city of Thebes—"deck itself with garlands" is especially suggestive. It overtly recalls the crowns with which victors were rewarded at the Olympic games, and we know that the "bearing of the crown" (i.e. *stephanêphoria*) and even the dedication of the crown in a local temple were often an integral part of epinician celebration.[135] As Kurke has argued, this act symbolized the transferal of *kudos* from victor to *polis*, a major boon for the city as a whole.[136] Pindar frequently refers to the simultaneous bestowal of crown and *kudos*, and he does so in order to both encourage and justify the accordance of poetic praise to the victor.[137] Euripides' Chorus performs a similar operation: it first draws out the image of the crown as a prize bestowed upon the entire community of Thebes, and instantly follows this by insisting upon the universal and public celebration of Heracles' victory.

The end of the strophe represents this dynamic of reciprocity in an even more overtly political manner, praising Heracles for restoring the original Theban dynasty:

> αὔξετ᾽ εὐγαθεῖ κελάδῳ
> ἐμὰν πόλιν, ἐμὰ τείχη,
> σπαρτῶν ἵνα γένος ἐφάνθη
> 795 χαλκασπίδων λόχος, ὃς γᾶν
> τέκνων τέκνοις μεταμείβει,
> Θήβαις ἱερὸν φῶς.

> *Heracles* 792–797

> Exalt my city, my walls,
> with a cheerful cry,
> where the race of Sown-men
> 795 appeared, a bronze-shielded host
> that delivers this land to its children's children,
> a sacred light for Thebes.

---

[134] Bundy 1962:54–59; Kurke 1991:97–107.

[135] On the *stephanêphoria*, see e.g. *Olympian* 8.9–10, in which the *kômos* and the *stephanêphoria* occur simultaneously: ἀλλ᾽ ὦ Πίσας εὔδενδρον ἐπ᾽ Ἀλφεῷ ἄλσος, / τόνδε κῶμον καὶ στεφαναφορίαν δέξαι. On the dedication of the crown, see Slater 1984:245 (and n. 24); Kurke 1993:140.

[136] Kurke 1991:203–209; 1993:137–141.

[137] Kurke 1991:203–209, citing Pindar's *Olympian* 4.8–12, *Olympian* 5.1–8, *Pythian* 12.4–6, and *Isthmian* 1.10–12. Kurke 1993:139 also presents later epigraphical evidence that the community's reception of the crown was equated with bestowing *kudos* upon it.

Heracles' defeat of Lycus, then, is not merely another one of his labors. Rather, it symbolizes the return of the descendants of Cadmus—Thebes' "sacred light"—to their rightful place. The concrete and beneficial civic and political effects of Heracles' return are thus fully emphasized, and communal celebration and praise of Heracles is suggested as the only logical compensation. Euripides' Chorus not only mimics Pindar's language, they also adopt his poetic and rhetorical strategy.[138] In so doing, they appear to finally resolve the problem of Heracles' acceptance in the contemporary *polis* through the performance of epinician song and celebration, and their insistence that the rest of Thebes do the same. It is, in a sense, perfect knotting of the poetic and political threads that have been dangling throughout the first half of the tragedy.

3.3.3 A new crisis, or, how Athens saves the day: epinician reciprocity and Heracles' integration in the polis

As the third *stasimon* comes to a close with one final, celebratory stanza, Iris and Lyssa ("Madness") rise above the stage. On Hera's orders, Lyssa causes Heracles to murder his wife and children.[139] Amphitryon alone survives the onslaught, and only thanks to Athena who arrives and knocks Heracles unconscious.[140] This abrupt reversal creates numerous problems for the epinician image of Heracles that Amphitryon and the Chorus had worked so hard to establish throughout the play. Obviously, Heracles is now cast as the murderer of his household rather than the savior of his city, while the tone shifts from (epinician) celebration to public mourning (see esp. *Heracles* 1045–1068). Just as troubling is the Messenger's report that, in his madness, Heracles had imagined himself to be celebrating an athletic victory moments before killing his children. Finally, as Laura Swift has noted, the Chorus' "lack of moderation" in their epinician odes may be read as the catalyst for Hera's anger at Heracles.[141] All of this creates doubt about whether Heracles will indeed find a *polis* to accept him,[142] and (more

---

[138] Bond 1981:272, notes the "encomiastic use of geography, of which there is much in Pindar," though in his analysis of the passage he does not go beyond this basic enumeration of epinician elements.

[139] The third antistrophe of the third stasimon (*Heracles* 798–814) continues to develop the encomiastic themes developed throughout the first five stanzas, referring to Heracles' divine heritage, his strength (*Heracles* 806: ἀλκάν; another direct refutation of Lycus' earlier words [cf. *Heracles* 144]), and his victory over Cerberus. We hear of Hera's role at 831–832.

[140] The event is described by a messenger at *Heracles* 910–1015.

[141] Swift 2010:149. Swift further notes (pp. 147–149) that all three choral stasima contain elements of this excess.

[142] As Heracles himself notes at *Heracles* 1281–1288, see above at p. 66.

subtly) about whether or not epinician celebration is a valid means of securing a community's acceptance.

As it turns out, both of these issues are resolved by Theseus, who arrives on-stage shortly thereafter to find Heracles covering his face in shame. Theseus immediately announces that he has come to "to give requitals" (*Heracles* 1169: τίνων δ' ἀμοιβὰς) to Heracles for saving him from Hades, a phrase that strongly recalls the Pindaric Ixion's more general injunction to "repay [*tinesthai*] one's benefactor with gentle requitals [*amoibais*]."[143] As numerous scholars have noted, Theseus emphasizes a sort of private debt that he owes to Heracles, one that is based not only on the specific act of salvation but also on the *philia* that the two heroes share.[144] But notions of a more communal cycle of benefaction and civic recognition resound even within the context of Theseus' personal offer to Heracles.

To begin with, Theseus arrives on stage with a group of "armed youths from the land of Athens" (*Heracles* 1164: ἔνοπλοι γῆς Ἀθηναίων κόροι), a visual suggestion that Theseus' private act of generosity is closely associated with the *polis*.[145] Crucially, even after learning of Heracles' slaughter of his family, Theseus stresses that Heracles has been a "benefactor to mortals and a great friend" (*Heracles* 1252: εὐεργέτης βροτοῖσι καὶ μέγας φίλος), recalling Amphitryon's earlier reminders that Heracles had wrought widespread benefits for humanity, and that he was thus owed a civic debt of gratitude. It is unclear whether *brotoisi* ("to mortals") is meant to be taken as a dative of reference with both *euergetês* and *philos*, or only with the former (from which it is inextricable). If *brotoisi* is to be taken with *euergetês* alone, then Theseus would be suggesting a distinction between his own personal bond with Heracles, and a more general relationship of benefaction between Heracles and the rest of humanity. If both substantive adjectives refer to *brotoisi*, then Theseus would be suggesting that the question of *philia*, which has suddenly become a focal point of the tragedy, is also closely related to Heracles' deeds on behalf of mortals. Regardless, we see that the obligations of *philia* that are in play go hand in hand with the notion that Heracles' benefaction to humanity warrants communal compensation. Even as the focus of the play narrows down to the private relationship between Heracles and Theseus, reminders abound that the *polis* as a whole has much at stake—and many responsibilities as well.

---

[143] *Pythian* 2.24: τὸν εὐεργέταν ἀγαναῖς ἀμοιβαῖς ἐποιχομένους τίνεσθαι. Discussed above at pp. 76–77.

[144] See e.g. Adkins 1966:214–219; Dunn 1997; J. Johnson 2002.

[145] *Contra* Dunn 1997:102–104, who argues that Theseus has no "political authority" in the play, but does not explain how to interpret his arrival with an Athenian retinue, nor indeed Theseus' later statements that show that the bestowal of civic honors upon heroic individuals was standard operating procedure for the Athens of the play (on which more below).

A short time later, Theseus brings the notion of a communal obligation to Heracles into sharper focus. He does so by proposing that Heracles come to Athens, using notions of both individual and collective reciprocity to persuade the hero to accept his offer:

> 1325 δόμους τε δώσω χρημάτων τ᾽ ἐμῶν μέρος.
> ἃ δ᾽ ἐκ πολιτῶν δῶρ᾽ ἔχω σώσας κόρους
> δὶς ἑπτά, ταῦρον Κνώσιον κατακτανών,
> σοὶ ταῦτα δώσω. πανταχοῦ δέ μοι χθονὸς
> τεμένη δέδασται· ταῦτ᾽ ἐπωνομασμένα
> 1330 σέθεν τὸ λοιπὸν ἐκ βροτῶν κεκλήσεται
> ζῶντος· θανόντα δ᾽, εὖτ᾽ ἂν εἰς Ἅιδου μόλῃς,
> θυσίαισι λαΐνοισί τ᾽ ἐξογκώμασιν
> τίμιον ἀνάξει πᾶσ᾽ Ἀθηναίων πόλις.
> καλὸς γὰρ ἀστοῖς στέφανος Ἑλλήνων ὕπο
> 1335 ἄνδρ᾽ ἐσθλὸν ὠφελοῦντας εὐκλείας τυχεῖν
>
> *Heracles* 1325–1335

> 1325 I shall give you a home and a share of my possessions.
> What I received from the citizens when I saved
> the fourteen youths and killed the Cnosian bull,
> I shall give these to you. In all the land precincts
> have been given to me; and these shall be named
> 1330 for you and will be celebrated[146] by mortals
> while you live; and when you have died and gone to Hades,
> the whole city of Athens shall lift you up,
> honored by sacrifices and marbled mounds.
> For among the Greeks it will be a beautiful crown
> 1335 for [our] citizens to earn great glory by helping a noble man.

In these eleven lines, Theseus explicitly refers to a number of concepts that are reflected throughout the epinician corpus. To begin, he asserts that the civic dimension of reciprocity is a crucial aspect of Heracles' integration into Athens. In fact, such reciprocity seems to be common in the *polis*, for the Athenian citizens had rewarded Theseus with great honors in exchange for the benefaction he provided in killing the Minotaur. In other words, Theseus had already received in Athens the communal compensation that Heracles so richly deserved

---

[146] Following Bond 1981:396.

in Thebes, and for the same beast-killing feats that Lycus had earlier mocked. Moreover, it is apparent that the honors Heracles will receive are once again to come from the community as a whole, as Theseus stresses that it is the people of Athens as a whole who will be "helping" Heracles (note the plural accusative participle *ôpheloutas*). Theseus' offer of honors in Athens is not simply a one-off, nor indeed the return of a private favor, but rather part of a pattern of recognition and recompense for heroic deeds by the Athenian *polis* as a whole.

The epinician tones emerge even more directly in the final four lines. The word *stephanos* recalls Pindar's poetry and the encomiastic backdrop of the first part of the play. Pindar variously suggests that epinician victories or the victor himself are crowns for the city, and in doing so his purpose is to emphasize the benefits bestowed by the individual on the community at large; "to make the entire polis feel that it participates in the victory won."[147] The specific notion that is presented here, namely that it is for the act of "helping" Heracles that Athens will earn a "beautiful crown," never appears in epinician, but it is clearly a descendant of these Pindaric formulations; without Heracles and his heroic deeds, there is no crown. In fact, the Euripidean Chorus seems to push it a step further, for it is only in the specific act of receiving and honoring Heracles that his glory can be refracted in Athens.

The epinician nature of Theseus' offer is also borne out in the specific honors that he guarantees. The promise of "sacrifices" and "marbled mounds" basically amounts to the establishment of a hero cult for Heracles,[148] and as Bruno Currie has argued, "epinician poetry was ... anchored to hero cult at both ends of its production: at the games where the victory was won, and at the victor's city where the ode was, most often, performed."[149] Currie suggests that the analogies between victor and hero, as frequent in Pindar as they are in *Heracles*, might be literal on a certain level; that great achievements, combined with epinician poetry, could actually "anticipate a posthumous cult of the laudandus."[150] As such, in proposing that lands be named after Heracles, and by establishing posthumous honors in order to win a crown for Athens, Theseus uses the principles found within epinician poetry to mediate the integration of Heracles into the Athenian *polis*.

[147] See Kurke 1991:203–209 for examples (quoted here from p. 208).
[148] E.g. Foley 1985:165–167, 192–195.
[149] Currie 2005:58.
[150] Currie 2005:408. This concept is, in fact, the crux of Currie's book.

It is inevitable, at this point, that Heracles will accept Theseus' invitation. The terms with which he does so once again emphasize that his assimilation into the *polis* will occur within a communal framework:

εἶμι δ' ἐς πόλιν
τὴν σήν, χάριν τε μυρίαν δώρων ἔχω.
ἀτὰρ πόνων δὴ μυρίων ἐγευσάμην

Heracles 1351–1353

I will come to your city,
and I bear great thanks [*charis*] for these countless gifts.
Truly I have tasted countless labors

The characterization of Theseus' offer as an act of *charis* can certainly be read within the context of personal *philia*, and even more specifically as compensation for Heracles' rescue of Theseus from the underworld.[151] But the passage also points to broader notions of epinician reciprocity.[152] Heracles shows that the Athenians' "countless gifts" are compensation not simply for rescuing Theseus, but also for the "countless labors" he has undertaken. And like Amphitryon before him, he relies on epinician motifs—compensation for toil—to make sense of the situation.

All this is not to say that Heracles' epinician integration into the Athenian *polis* easily resolves every issue. On the contrary, after he decides to go to Athens, the final seventy lines of the play are dominated by a different issue, namely the emotional trauma that Heracles experiences as a result of the loss of his family.[153] At this point, however, Heracles' place in the tragic *polis* is no longer under review. But as long as it remains an open question, epinician language, epinician discourse, and ideas of reciprocity and compensation that abound in Pindaric poetry are consistently used as a means to promote Heracles' civic integration. In that sense, the epinician apparatus of the play ultimately emerges as the crucial framework for resolving one of the fundamental political questions of *Heracles*.

---

[151] See e.g. Adkins 1966:215–216.

[152] While ἀτάρ might indicate that a new, unrelated thought is being introduced, Euripides' anaphoric use of *muriōn* belies that interpretation, and suggests we must consider the two lines and concepts to be connected. See the note ad loc. in Bond 1981:404.

[153] See e.g. Papadopoulou 2005:173–187; Holmes 2008:267–271.

4. Towards Some Conclusions: Heracles, Alexandros, and Euripidean Epinician

The odd and conflicting confluences of civic drama and epinician motifs in *Heracles* and *Alexandros* must be read in the light of the social and political dynamics in contemporary Athens that were outlined at the beginning of this chapter, particularly the anxieties provoked by Alcibiades' victories and celebrations in this period. Along those lines, *Alexandros* and *Heracles* show that epinician song and celebration are intimately related to the question of a hero's reception in the *polis*. But the two plays do so in deeply contrasting ways: in *Alexandros*, epinician is a source of tension that threatens to tear the community apart, whereas in *Heracles* epinician song and honors are presented as a potential, perhaps even necessary, means to achieving Heracles' civic integration. These contrasts suggest that, rather than functioning as a simple means of mediating between hero and *polis*, epinician in these two tragedies provide a poetic backdrop that allows the audience to focalize on the existence and complexity of the relationship.

Indeed, while concerns about Alexander's person and status abound in the play, it is only once he celebrates his victory in an epinician style that the focus of the tragedy moves from the individual victor to the manner in which the *polis* reacts to his victory and celebration.[154] *Alexandros* thus zooms in on a real and contemporary political drama, but the question raised is not so much whether (or to what extent) individuals such as Alexander or Alcibiades benefit the *polis*. Rather, we are asked to evaluate the community's reaction to the victory and its epinician celebration. This is, in a sense, shown to be a broader and more complex issue, for the internal fabric of the play and the broader contours of the trilogy provide conflicting answers. On the one hand, within the context of *Alexandros* alone, the emphasis on Alexander's prowess and natural attributes suggest that the Trojan people are in some sense right to celebrate his victory; conversely, the murderous reaction to his celebration by Hecuba and Deiphobus would, if successful, have resulted in a mother killing a son, and one brother another. Seen through the prism of the entire trilogy, however, we understand that the conspiracy to murder Alexander would have averted the destruction of Troy—a fact Cassandra recalls for the audience before the end of *Alexandros*.[155] Perhaps even the stain of filicide and fratricide would have been a preferable outcome. Epinician song and celebration thus emerge as powerful forces that

---

[154] Here I disagree with Kampakoglou 2018: 209, who argues that "*Alexandros* focuses on the problems caused by the victor, not his victory."

[155] Cf. the lines 26–27 of the *hypothesis*.

spark an array of reactions within, and complex outcomes for, the communities of the play. These dynamics would certainly ring true for an audience in the midst of dealing with the controversy of Alcibiades' epinician return.

As in *Alexandros*, much of the emphasis in *Heracles* is on the *polis*' reception of the epinician hero. And once again, epinician poetry catalyzes a variety of reactions. In the first half of the tragedy, epinician song, celebration, and honors are unequivocally posited as proper for a hero of Heracles' dimension, and the tragedy teases us with the specter of Heracles' successful (and epinician) integration into the Theban *polis*. After the murder of Heracles' family, however, all such notions of epinician integration—at least in Thebes—seem to be scuttled by the pollution he has brought onto himself. Despite this initial failure, the ideas set forth and embodied in the tragedy's epinician odes—ideas that are drawn from earlier epinician traditions—turn out to be crucial to Heracles' acceptance in Athens. In other words, even though they hardly represent a simple solution, epinician song and celebration ultimately do provide a figurative pathway for Heracles' integration into the tragic *polis*. Perhaps this too would have rung true for many at the City Dionysia.

To be sure, we can state with confidence that epinician in Euripidean tragedy takes on a far different role than it had in the *poleis* in which epinician lyric was originally performed. Indeed, while Pindar may claim that his epinician poetry can consistently and successfully mediate elite/*polis* relations, in Euripides it is not nearly as simple. His tragedies show both sides of the story—epinician can both smooth over tensions yet also cause them; it can be used to elevate true heroes such as Heracles, but also to celebrate individuals, such as Alexander, who will be ruinous for their communities. In short, Euripides does not undermine or depoliticize epinician discourse in any sort of consistent manner, nor does he present a consistent line of thought concerning these traditions' place in the *polis*. On the contrary, *Heracles* and *Alexandros* use epinician as a poetic lens to draw the audience's attentioan to the issue of elite integration in the *polis*, and indeed to ask the audience to ponder whether or not epinician song can be a mediating force.

In the next two chapters, I turn to *Iphigenia at Aulis*, this time to examine the use of Homer's *Iliad* and Aeschylus' *Agamemnon* as fundamental subtexts for the play. The intertextual dynamic is obviously different, for *Iphigenia at Aulis* deals not with choral lyric genres, but rather with canonical texts. Still, we shall see that this poetic interplay is just as political, and politicized, as that which we saw with the paean in *Ion* and epinician song in *Heracles* and *Alexandros*.

3

Echoes of the *Iliad* at Aulis
Agamemnon, Achilles, and
Authority among the Achaeans

WHILE THE PREVIOUS TWO CHAPTERS have considered Euripides' use of
choral lyric genres as a means to illuminate political issues in his plays, in
the following two chapters I take up a different, though closely related, phenomenon: the employment of Homer's *Iliad* (Chapter 3) and Aeschylus' *Agamemnon*
(Chapter 4) as politically charged subtexts in *Iphigenia at Aulis*. By shifting the
focus away from choral lyric, and towards specific canonical texts, we can
better see how Euripidean tragedy's engagement with the poetic tradition is
consistently related to the exploration of political issues. Moreover, as in *Ion*,
Alexandros, and *Heracles*, these political issues were of great relevance in Athens
when *Iphigenia at Aulis* was produced in 405 BCE. All of this suggests a deep and
abiding relationship between Euripides' excavation of poetic traditions and his
examination of the political present.

1. Agamemnon and Achilles at Aulis

Euripides' *Iphigenia at Aulis*[1] shares an obvious yet peculiar relationship with
Homer's *Iliad*: it is a prequel. The setting of the tragedy is the encampment at
Aulis where the Achaean army awaits a favorable wind for Troy, and the ques-
tion at hand is whether Agamemnon will sacrifice his daughter, Iphigenia, to
Artemis. This is the condition upon which the army's departure for Troy rests,

---

[1]   The manuscript tradition of *Iphigenia at Aulis* is seriously flawed. Some scholars have been particularly aggressive in their deletions, see e.g. Kovacs 2003. More recently, Collard and Morwood
2017:58 have argued in favor of "editorial tolerance." A middle ground may be found in Diggle
1994, who subdivides the text into four categories according to his estimation of their probabili-
ties of authenticity. Throughout this book, unless otherwise noted, all the passages discussed
will belong to the two categories Diggle believes most likely to be authentic. For those few
passages that do not fall into these two categories, I provide a justification of their usage.

so in a sense, the outcome of the play is predetermined by the very existence of Homer's epic. Even beyond that, the high volume of allusions to the *Iliad*, some as obvious as the choral "Catalogue of Ships" found in the *parodos*,[2] shows that Euripides is deeply engaged with the Homeric tradition. In short, the *Iliad* is embedded in the very fiber of the Euripidean tragedy.

Scholars have long noted the similarities between *Iphigenia at Aulis* and the *Iliad*, but the inevitability of Iphigenia's eventual sacrifice has suggested to some that the *Iliad*'s authority on *Iphigenia at Aulis* is "suffocating,"[3] or that "tradition has worked to close down choices and alternatives in political, social, and artistic terms."[4] This intense focus on the *Iliad*'s authority has come at the cost of understanding why the tragedy insists on reconsidering Homeric conflicts within the confines of contemporary, democratic power structures. In this chapter, I try to shift that focus. As I argue, *Iphigenia at Aulis'* relationship with the *Iliad* is not merely predicated on similarities between the two and the influence of the latter. On the contrary, the play presents a profound reassessment and even subversion of Homeric models of power and authority, all this before a democratic audience to whom these issues must have been of particular concern.

Within the tragedy, two specific issues stand out for the attention Euripides provides them, and the radical departures he makes: the conflict between Agamemnon and Achilles, which is central to the *Iliad* and ever-simmering in *Iphigenia at Aulis*; and the decision about whether to stay the course and fight the Trojans, which hovers over *Iphigenia at Aulis* and is a subject of vigorous debate in the *Iliad*. The similarities here run deep. As in Homer, the Euripidean dispute begins with a disagreement about a woman whom Agamemnon wishes to "take" from Achilles,[5] and quickly leads to questions about the standing and authority of each man. In each work, the conflict leads to urgent questions about the future of the Trojan War. Above all, in both the *Iliad* and *Iphigenia at Aulis* these two issues become prisms through which we can glimpse the dynamics of power and authority within the Achaean army.

Ultimately, the outcomes in *Iphigenia at Aulis* are superficially the same as in the *Iliad*—the quarrel between Agamemnon and Achilles is resolved, the war will

---

[2] The second half of the *parodos* is of dubious authenticity, but the first half (*Iphigenia at Aulis* 164–230) is certainly adequate evidence of the song's Homeric heritage. On the probable authenticity of the first part of the *parodos*, cf. Page 1934:142; Kovacs 2003:83.

[3] Luschnig 1988:78.

[4] Gamel 1999:320. See also Sorum 1992:542: "Agamemnon's and Iphigenia's choices cannot bear the significance necessary to tragedy because they are limited by the imposition of the myth."

[5] This time the sacrifice of Iphigenia, Agamemnon's daughter and, at least theoretically, Achilles' betrothed. I describe the situation in some detail below.

go on—but the manner in which Euripides' Achaeans reach these conclusions is decidedly un-Homeric. In the *Iliad*, the debates about whether to remain at Troy demonstrate that the *basilêes* ("kings" or leaders) of the *Iliad* retain a near-monopoly of authority at Troy. The Homeric dispute between Agamemnon and Achilles, on the other hand, results in an irresolvable "crisis of leadership,"[6] and shows that relations between different *basilêes* cannot be defined or resolved by a strict or simple hierarchy. In *Iphigenia at Aulis*, conversely, the army stages an insurrection and at once decides the question of Iphigenia's sacrifice while rendering moot the quarrel between Agamemnon and Achilles.[7]

Such a resolution would have been unimaginable in Homer's epic, but as we shall see, it is reminiscent of dynamics that existed in late fifth-century Greece, particularly among democratic bodies. In other words, *Iphigenia at Aulis* replays familiar Homeric conflicts within a contemporary setting, and updates accordingly the means by which these conflicts are resolved. Moreover, these conflicts are constructed in opposition to the *Iliad*, teasing the audience by recalling specific moments of the Homeric epic only to sharply deviate from the expectations that are set by these allusions. In so doing, *Iphigenia at Aulis* forces the audience to recognize the vast differences between the world of Homer and their own. Above all, it creates a jarring recognition of the challenges and difficulties that were unique to contemporary, democratic societies. In short, the distorted reflections of the *Iliad* become a window through which the audience can better understand the complexities of leadership, and the problems that might arise when the *dêmos* accumulates a significant amount of power.

2. Military Authority at Athens and in the *Iliad*

Around October of 406 BCE, only a few months before *Iphigenia at Aulis* was produced, the city of Athens played host to what was surely a memorable, if unsavory, event: the trial and execution of the generals who had led the Athenian navy at the battle of Arginousae. For the Athenians to punish their generals was not exceptional: at least twenty-two generals were brought to trial during the Peloponnesian War, and of those twenty-two, fourteen were sentenced to death.[8] Still, the prosecution of the Arginousae generals stands out both for the number of generals who were sentenced to death (eight), and because the Athenians had actually prevailed in the battle itself.[9] In fact, as Xenophon and

---

[6] As it is called by Donlan 1982:61.
[7] Brian Lush has recently discussed the emphasis on the army's authority in *Iphigenia at Aulis* in relation to the many changes of mind exhibited by the characters in the tragedy. Cf. Lush 2015.
[8] Hamel 1998:133.
[9] For a complete overview of the battle and the trial that followed, see Hamel 2015.

Diodorus both report, the Athenians soon regretted their actions, and punished those whom they deemed responsible for misleading the *dêmos*.[10]

It is unlikely that Euripides was alive to see the trial of the generals, much less the repentance that followed.[11] But the point here is not that he based the plot of *Iphigenia at Aulis* on the events that took place after Arginousae, but rather that the play draws on dynamics that were recognizably contemporary. As mentioned above, several Athenian generals had already been sentenced to death in the previous decades. There is also some evidence that the civic tensions that led to such prosecutions had been increasing in the years leading up to Arginousae.[12] Indeed, two of the eight generals at Arginousae simply refused to return to Athens when they were summoned to stand trial, suggesting that such an outcome was all too predictable. Similarly, Thucydides dramatizes Nicias' decision to (fatally) persist in the siege of Syracuse by emphasizing his fear that the common soldiers would accuse the generals of accepting bribes to betray the cause, and that the generals would then "be killed, unjustly, by the Athenians."[13] In short, relations between the Athenian *dêmos* and its military leaders were laden with tensions, and often culminated in violent, state-sanctioned retribution, Arginousae providing an extreme example. This fact was surely clear to the majority of the audience at the first production of *Iphigenia at Aulis*. And many of them must have recalled their own recent experiences when watching, on the tragic stage, Agamemnon and Achilles wax anxious on the possibility that their own soldiers might murder them in order to ensure the prosecution of the Trojan War.

The dynamics of military authority in the *Iliad* are rather different. The subject is complex, but while it has often been suggested that it may have been desirable for the Homeric *basilêes* to establish consensus within the army,[14]

---

[10] Xenophon *Hellenica* 1.7.35; Diodorus Siculus 13.103.1.

[11] Andrewes 1974:121 suggests that this "revulsion" must have occurred by the very beginning of 405 BCE, so at least two months before the City Dionysia at which *Iphigenia at Aulis* was produced. Euripides likely died in 407/406 BCE, that is to say at least four months before the trial of the generals. Even if this date is mistaken, it is unlikely that there would have been time to write and produce a drama that reflected the events after Arginousae in so short a time, as is suggested by van Erp Taalman Kip 1987:414–419 (examining and rejecting the possibility that Euripides' *Trojan Women* was inspired by the events on Melos the previous winter).

[12] See esp. Asmonti 2006.

[13] Thucydides 7.48.4: ἀδίκως ὑπ' Ἀθηναίων ἀπολέσθαι.

[14] Along these lines, and to varying degrees, cf. Donlan 1979; Rose 2012:93–133; Hammer 2002; Heiden 2008; Elmer 2013. Scodel 2002:182 provides a particularly nuanced example of this view: "Homeric epic is the genre of social cohesion. This cohesion requires the people to accept elite dominance but simultaneously allows them to view individual aristocrats with a critical gaze. It celebrates a shared moral perspective that gives the common people a decisive voice, even as it defines their opinions as based on ... those of the elite." *Contra* see Morris 1986; and Tandy

the power of the *basilês* over the common soldiers remains nearly absolute.[15] Numerous aspects of the political procedures make this apparent: a *basileus* such as Agamemnon may completely ignore the wishes of the rest of the army;[16] only the *basilês* are allowed to hold the floor at the assemblies;[17] at no point do the common soldiers disobey the commands of their leaders;[18] the soldiery's only means of expressing dissent is by refusing to applaud the suggestion of a *basileus*, a silence that does not have any binding or persuasive power; and the only common soldier who attempts to speak out against an Achaean *basileus*— Thersites—receives a severe thrashing for his temerity.[19] Once a *basileus* decides on a particular course of action, there is little the common soldiers can do to influence proceedings.

Debates that arise in the *Iliad* over whether or not to remain at Troy are especially indicative of the power that the Homeric leaders retain over the common soldiers, if not over each other. In book 2, for example, Agamemnon tests his army with the disingenuous suggestion that they should flee Troy (*Iliad* 2.100–141), but he instructs his fellow leaders to "restrain" (*Iliad* 2.75: ἐρητύειν) the common soldiers. As it turns out, the proposal to flee is taken up with rather too much zest by the army, and a mad rush to the ships ensues (*Iliad* 2.142–154). During the tumult, Odysseus corrals the troops and urges them to stay and fight, and in so doing he underscores the relations of power that should exist among the Achaeans.

1997:142–144 and 149–152, who insist that the *Iliad* portrays a purely "oligarchical" political landscape.

[15] Donlan 1997:40–41, considers this the distinction between "power" and "authority." He argues that while power suggests the ability to "[rule] by compulsion," authority "rules mainly through persuasion and example, and tradition."

[16] For example in *Iliad* 1, when all the other Achaeans (*Iliad* 1.22: ἄλλοι μὲν πάντες ... Ἀχαιοὶ) are in favor of returning Chryses' daughter to the priest, Agamemnon unilaterally rejects that course of action. For a Trojan example, see *Iliad* 7.345–397, in which Antenor proposes that they bring the war to an end by forcing Paris to give back Helen. Paris roundly refuses to do anything of the sort, though we learn that "the Trojans would command it" (*Iliad* 7.393: ἦ μὴν Τρῶές γε κέλονται). On this second episode, cf. Raaflaub 1988:1–5.

[17] Van Wees 1992:33; Strasburger 1997:50: "[t]he assembly of the army in the *Iliad* and the peaceful assembly of the people in the *Odyssey* are mute assemblies, in which the crowd receives announcements and instructions." This latter interpretation is perhaps an exaggeration, but a large kernel of truth lies within it.

[18] Donlan 1979, identifies forty instances in which an individual's "Leadership Authority" (i.e. command) is rejected, but none of these instances of disobedience belongs to the common soldiers.

[19] Cf. *Iliad* 2.211–75. For more on this famous episode, cf. esp. Postlethwaite 1988; Rose 1988; Thalmann 1988. For an alternative view that Thersites is not actually a common soldier, but instead a member of the elite, cf. Kirk 1985, 139; and Marks 2005.

Odysseus divides the Achaeans into two groups with which he takes two distinct approaches: the *basilêes* he persuades with "gentle words" (*Iliad* 2.189: ἀγανοῖς ἐπέεσσιν), but he beats and rebukes any common soldier (*Iliad* 2.198: δήμου τ' ἄνδρα) who crosses his path. It is obvious that the two groups are by no means equal in Odysseus' conception, but the substance of his reproaches underscores just how unequal these groups are:[20]

> δαιμόνι' ἀτρέμας ἦσο καὶ ἄλλων μῦθον ἄκουε,
> οἳ σέο φέρτεροί εἰσι, σὺ δ' ἀπτόλεμος καὶ ἄναλκις
> οὔτέ ποτ' ἐν πολέμῳ ἐναρίθμιος οὔτ' ἐνὶ βουλῇ·
> οὐ μέν πως πάντες βασιλεύσομεν ἐνθάδ' Ἀχαιοί·
> οὐκ ἀγαθὸν πολυκοιρανίη· εἷς κοίρανος ἔστω,
> 205 εἷς βασιλεύς, ᾧ δῶκε Κρόνου πάϊς ἀγκυλομήτεω
> σκῆπτρόν τ' ἠδὲ θέμιστας, ἵνά σφισι βουλεύῃσι.

Iliad 200–206

> "Good sir! Sit still and listen to the words of others,
> those who are your betters, you who are a coward and weakling
> and utterly worthless in both battle and council.
> Surely not all of us Achaeans can be kings here!
> The rule of many is no good. Let there be one ruler,
> 205 one *basileus*, to whom the son of Kronos crooked-in-counsel
> gave the scepter and authority to deliberate for his people."

Odysseus' claim that the *dêmos* is "worthless in council," is significant. While this does not precisely match what we see throughout the *Iliad* as a whole,[21] it does suggest that there is little regard for the soldiers' input on any question, let alone on whether or not to remain at war.

Of more difficult interpretation are the final lines of the passage, where Odysseus claims there should be "one ruler, one *basileus*" for all the Achaeans. Were we to take Odysseus at his word, we would understand that a strict hierarchy exists among the Greeks, with Agamemnon (presumably) at the top and all the other Achaeans subject to him. Put quite simply, this in no way conforms to what we see enacted throughout the rest of the *Iliad*.[22] A less literal, but more

---

[20] We cannot of course take Odysseus' words at face value; they are, after all, designed to persuade his audience. But as Scodel 2002:210 argues, the hierarchy he describes is not so much an invention as an exaggeration, and the efficacy of his speech attests to its verisimilitude. On this episode, see also Elmer 2013:92–93.

[21] Cf. esp. Raaflaub 1997:634–636.

[22] As for example in the other debates about whether to stay at Troy, on which see more below.

accurate, interpretation of Odysseus' comment is provided by Oliver Taplin, who argues that he "is not saying that the whole army should have one single βασιλεύς, but only that every common man should have one."[23] In other words, each *basileus* may decide when and how his own soldiers will fight, but he does not have authority over other *basilées*, nor over the personal contingents of these other *basilées*.[24]

This hypothesis fits the dynamics that are revealed in other instances where the question of whether to persist with the war arises. At the beginning of *Iliad* 9, Agamemnon again brings up the prospect of retreat (*Iliad* 9.9–28). This time, Agamemnon is completely serious, but rather than making for their ships, the entire army reacts with a stunned silence (9.29–30). Diomedes is the first *basileus* to respond to Agamemnon, and he begins by openly calling Agamemnon sense-less (*Iliad* 9.32: ἀφραδέοντι), and then by emphasizing his own right to argue against it in the assembly (*Iliad* 9.33: ἡ θέμις ἐστὶν). Diomedes then concedes that while he cannot force Agamemnon or the other *basilées* to remain at Troy, he himself will stay on and fight, along with anyone else who so wishes. In response to his speech, "all the sons of the Achaeans applauded," (9.50: οἱ δ' ἄρα πάντες ἐπίαχον υἷες Ἀχαιῶν), but even this acclaim is not sufficient to win the point;[25] Nestor must break up the assembly and suggest that the Achaean "elders" (*Iliad* 9.89: γέροντας) decide the matter in a private meeting. It is impossible to provide a complete breakdown of the power structures and hierarchies that exist in the *Iliad*, but we may make a few general points about the manner in which Homer's Achaeans decide whether or not to remain in Troy: the Achaean leaders collec-tively make the decision about whether to fight or go home; no single *basileus* can make that decision for all the Achaeans; the common soldiers have no real say in the matter.

The authority of Homer's *basilées* acquires further nuance in the dispute between Agamemnon and Achilles that begins in *Iliad* 1. Superficially at least, the possession of a captive woman is at the heart of their disagreement, as it is Agamemnon's threat to take Achilles' slave Briseis that ignites the quarrel.

---

[23] Taplin 1990:63. *Contra* see Cartledge 2009:33–39. Cartledge appears to take Odysseus' statement quite literally, though he glosses over the rather considerable contributions of the other *basilées* in the assemblies.

[24] Elsewhere, Taplin 1992:58, describes relations between Agamemnon and the other *basilées* thus: "the summoned *basilées* are committed to the supervision of [Agamemnon], who acts as a co-ordinator and spokesman. At the same time they retain substantial independence, both off the field, where they can, for instance, call together an *agorê* or *boulê*, and on, where they lead their own men."

[25] Elmer 2013:27 describes the reaction of the soldiers as "inefficient," which is to say that it does not have the persuasive force that we see when "all the *basilées* expressed *epainos*" (quoting here *Iliad* 7.344 and 9.710).

But it is clear throughout that a disagreement about authority is central to the rift. At the very moment that Agamemnon states his intention to seize Briseis (*Iliad* 1.184–187), he claims that he does so in order that Achilles may know "how much better [*pherteros*] I am than you, and others may be loath to claim they are my equals" (*Iliad* 186–187: ὅσσον φέρτερός εἰμι σέθεν, στυγέη δὲ καὶ ἄλλος / ἶσον ἐμοὶ φάσθαι). The term *pherteros* is a general one, and may simply denote that Agamemnon is "better" than Achilles, but the second part of this formulation suggests he is concerned with the "validation of his rank and of his authority as leader."[26] Indeed, the "political" basis of Agamemnon's point of view emerges more clearly in an analogous declaration of his in *Iliad* 9.160: καί μοι ὑποστήτω ὅσσον βασιλεύτερός εἰμι ("and let him submit to me, since I am more kingly"). Here, Agamemnon restates his intention of showing himself to be superior to Achilles, with a single but important change in the formulation: he is not simply *pherteros*, but indeed "*basileuteros*."[27] His aim here is fundamentally the same as it is in *Iliad* 1—to prove his superiority—but the language in this instance confirms that he is specifically concerned with the matter of his authority and Achilles' obedience.

Nestor attempts to soothe the tensions between the two feuding *basilêes*, but the reactions of the two principal actors demonstrate that the quarrel between them is a veritable power-struggle: Agamemnon accuses Achilles of wishing "to have power over everyone, to be master of everyone, to give orders to everyone," while Achilles objects that "I would be called a coward and a nobody if I yielded to you in every matter."[28] Agamemnon prevails, at least in the sense that he can claim Briseis,[29] but every other element of the episode points to the limits of Agamemnon's authority. Achilles does in fact have a choice in the matter, for he can choose to either surrender Briseis or kill Agamemnon,[30] and it is only thanks

---

[26] Donlan 1982:162; similarly, Russo 1968:284, suggests that *pherteros* here should be translated as "more powerful." *Contra* see Kirk 1985:72, who states that "[a]ttempts to give φέρτερος a more specific meaning ... are misguided." But as Pulleyn 2000:174 correctly points out, "Nestor expands on [Agamemnon's comment] at 281 saying of Agamemnon ὅ γε φέρτερος ἐστιν, ἐπεὶ πλεόνεσσιν ἀνάσσει."

[27] It is a small point, but these two lines are the only instances in which we find the combination ὅσσον + comparative adjective + εἰμι in all of the *Iliad*, a fact that implies a very close conceptual relation as well.

[28] Agamemnon at *Iliad* 1.288–289: πάντων μὲν κρατέειν ἐθέλει, πάντεσσι δ' ἀνάσσειν, / πᾶσι δὲ σημαίνειν. Achilles at *Iliad* 1.293–294: δειλός τε καὶ οὐτιδανὸς καλεοίμην / εἰ δὴ σοὶ πᾶν ἔργον ὑπείξομαι.

[29] For Donlan 1982:162, this is evidence that "Agamemnon can coerce, of course, because he is politically more powerful than Achilles."

[30] Donlan 1982:162 doubts that killing Agamemnon represents a "realistic" choice, but the possibility is realistic enough that Athena steps in to prevent Achilles from doing so (*Iliad* 1.188–222).

to Athena's intervention that he chooses the former.[31] When Achilles publicly states his intention to let Briseis go, he qualifies it by saying that he does so only because "you [plural] who gave her are taking her away" (*Iliad* 1.299: ἐπεί μ' ἀφέλεσθέ γε δόντες). He thus implicates the entire army in the decision to seize Briseis, though this is less an affirmation of the army's authority[32] than a refusal to cede openly to Agamemnon.[33] Finally, Achilles ends his short speech by threatening to kill Agamemnon should he try to seize anything else (*Iliad* 1.297–303)[34] and withdraws until Book 19. Once Achilles has declared that he will no longer obey Agamemnon,[35] Agamemnon has no ability to command either him or his Myrmidon army, proving that in fact he has no direct power over either.[36]

No other party, neither the *basilês* nor the common soldiers, can either compel one of the two heroes to yield or force a reconciliation between them. Nestor's attempt to do so is an unmitigated failure (*Iliad* 1.247–284), and no other *basileus* tries to intervene in *Iliad* 1—not even as Achilles begins to draw his sword to kill Agamemnon (*Iliad* 1.194).[37] The soldiers also make no attempt whatsoever to interfere. Donlan argues that their passivity is due to the fact

---

[31] Dodds 1951:14, has argued that Athena does not actually appear in person, but that she is rather a "projection ... of an inward monition." *Contra* see esp. Hooker 1990, who argues that, insofar as Homer frequently shows his heroes coming to decisions on their own, there is no real reason why Homer should have included the visitation unless we are to understand it as real.

[32] Few commentators have taken seriously Achilles' claim that the army is fully responsible for the distribution of war booty. Adkins 1982:300, calls this a "convenient fiction," made necessary by the fact that although "[w]e know ... that Achilles has yielded to the two goddesses ... to the others present it must appear that Achilles has backed down before Agamemnon" (p. 297). Similarly, see Taplin 1992:65. Kirk 1985:83, is less sanguine about Achilles' reasoning here, but agrees that his implication of the Achaeans is "contrive[d]." Indeed, there is every indication that the decision to take Briseis is Agamemnon's and Agamemnon's alone, and it seems as if the army's involvement in the distribution of war booty is symbolic at most: cf. van Wees 1992:299–310.

[33] Adkins 1982:300–301; Taplin 1992:58; D. Wilson 2002:64. In a sense, Achilles yields neither to the army nor to Agamemnon but to the authority of Athena and Hera (whom Athena represents), since "he must obey" the goddesses (*Iliad* 1.216: χρὴ μὲν ... εἰρύσσασθαι).

[34] Kirk 1985:83, argues that this is an "imagined case" and thus doubt the seriousness of the threat, but I see no evidence within the text itself that we should not take Achilles' words at face-value.

[35] *Iliad* 1.296: οὐ γὰρ ἔγωγ' ἔτι σοὶ πείσεσθαι ὀίω ("I think that I at least will not obey you"), directly echoing Agamemnon's earlier statement that "I think some will not obey [Achilles]" (*Iliad* 1.289: ἅ τιν' οὐ πείσεσθαι ὀίω).

[36] Generally speaking, I follow consensus in this regard. Cf. Donlan 1982:162; McGlew 1989; Hammer 2002:85–86. Raaflaub 1988:9, astutely points out that the delicacy of the situation, in which "the stronger has to subordinate himself to the more powerful ... require[s] tact and mutual respect." Lacking both these qualities, Agamemnon has no means to convince Achilles.

[37] Erbse 1986:139, argues that Athena intervenes at that moment precisely because none of the other *basileis* can.

that they do not have a direct stake in the argument,[38] but in fact, the dispute is of grave concern for them. Achilles is explicit about this when he says, early on, that "a yearning for Achilles will strike all the sons of the Achaeans ... when many fall and die before man-slaughtering Hektor."[39] As for the Myrmidons, a later episode confirms that Achilles forces them to withdraw from the war against their will.[40]

To summarize, the debates about whether or not to remain at Troy suggest that while the common soldiers may express assent or dissent, their voice is of little consequence when it comes to making decisions; ultimately, the *basilês* have complete authority when it comes to deciding the Achaeans' course of action at any particular moment. The dispute between Achilles and Agamemnon shows that the hierarchies among the leaders are less certain: while Agamemnon may hold the highest 'rank' among the Achaeans, Achilles has total autonomy over whether he (or his men) will fight. But this in turn validates the strong hierarchy that exists between *basilês* and common soldiers: despite their misgivings, once Achilles orders the Myrmidons to retire from the battlefield, they cannot return until he explicitly commands them to do so.

3. Conflict and Authority at Aulis: (Distorted) Echoes of Homer

In *Iphigenia at Aulis*, the question of Iphigenia's sacrifice leads directly to analogous controversies about military hierarchies and questions about whether or not to fight the Trojan War. Like Homer before him, Euripides uses these issues to provide a sense of the political landscape at Aulis. In reworking Homeric material as a means to approach contemporary political questions, *Iphigenia at Aulis* is hardly unique within the tragic corpus. In *Myrmidons*, Aeschylus had also taken up the theme of Achilles' contentious withdrawal from the army at Troy in order to examine the potential of contemporary "social and political practices" to resolve conflicts between aristocratic individuals and the collective.[41] In Euripides' *Helen*, performed only a few years before *Iphigenia at Aulis*, Homer's *Odyssey* functions as a subtext through which his audience might explore epistemological (and other) questions that were relevant to the contemporary Athenian world.[42] In short, we may presume that at least part of Euripides' audi-

---

[38] Donlan 1982:62.
[39] *Iliad* 1.240–243: ἦ ποτ' Ἀχιλλῆος ποθὴ ἵξεται υἷας Ἀχαιῶν / σύμπαντας ... εὖτ' ἂν πολλοὶ ὑφ' Ἕκτορος ἀνδροφόνοιο / θνήσκοντες πίπτωσι· Achilles' prediction is not inaccurate.
[40] See *Iliad* 16.200–206, which I discuss in more detail below at pp. 126–127.
[41] Michelakis 2002:22–57 (quote on 24).
[42] On this vast subject, cf. e.g. Segal 1971; Eisner 1980; Hartigan 1981; Friedman 2007.

ence was well-versed in the tragic theater's tendency to reconsider Homeric questions in a different, more contemporary light.[43]

3.1 Echoes of Homer Amidst the Suggestion of Change

Already in the prologue, *Iphigenia at Aulis'* engagement with Iliadic notions of authority makes its presence known, albeit subtly. The prologue is perhaps the most problematic passage of the tragedy's textual tradition,[44] and its authenticity has been the subject of endless discussions that have, alas, provided no perfect solution to the many questions raised by the text.[45] Nevertheless, we may at least assume that the 'original' prologue included something like the lines we possess, insofar as they are generally compatible with what we see in the rest of the tragedy.[46] Indeed, the picture they present is maintained until the middle of the first episode, at which point there is an abrupt reversal that is only explained if the tragedy had thus far presented the situation as Agamemnon does here.

As the play opens, Agamemnon cuts a lone figure in the darkness of night, brooding outside his quarters. This image is immediately reminiscent of the Homeric Agamemnon, whom we twice find in similar circumstances.[47] At this point, the audience cannot know how or to what extent this echo of the *Iliad* will relate to the dramatic plot, but it soon becomes clear that the entire expedition to Troy is at stake, and that *Iphigenia at Aulis* will show them how this question is decided. As Agamemnon recounts, the prophet Calchas has proclaimed that in order to sail to Troy, Iphigenia will have to be sacrificed to Artemis (*Iphigenia at Aulis* 89–93). According to Agamemnon, his first reaction to the news was anything but enthusiastic:

> κλύων δ' ἐγὼ ταῦτ', ὀρθίῳ κηρύγματι
> 95   Ταλθύβιον εἶπον πάντ' ἀφιέναι στρατόν,
> ὡς οὔποτ' ἂν τλὰς θυγατέρα κτανεῖν ἐμήν.

Iphigenia at Aulis 94–96

---

[43] On the possibility that late fifth-century audiences had the opportunity to see reperformances of Aeschylus' plays, see pp. 183–184.

[44] The format is odd, to say the least: it begins with a dialogue in anapaests between Agamemnon and an old slave (1–48); continues with a monologue in trimeters spoken by Agamemnon (49–114); and then returns to anapaestic dialogue in the final lines (115–163). Beyond that, the prologue presents numerous inconsistencies and occasionally awkward diction.

[45] For more on the "authenticity" of the prologue, see esp. Page 1934:131–140; Willink 1971; Knox 1972; Bain 1977; Stockert 1992 vol. 1:66–79; Kovacs 2003:80–83; Pietruczuk 2012.

[46] I exclude altogether from my discussion lines 105–110, even though they pertain to the discussions at hand, since they have been identified as the most problematic section of the prologue (see e.g. Pietruczuk 2012, but also Kovacs 2003:82).

[47] Most obviously at *Iliad* 10.1–4, but see also 9.1–12.

> When I heard this, I told Talthybius to dismiss
> 95 the whole army by direct decree,
> since I'd never dare to kill my daughter.

Agamemnon's refusal to sacrifice Iphigenia carries with it two implications: the first (and less obvious one) is that he has the authority to unilaterally dismiss the army; the second is that doing so would create a world in which the Trojan War, and by extension the *Iliad*, never existed. As many scholars have suggested, it is a foregone conclusion that Agamemnon will change his mind. The question, then, becomes how this change of mind will occur.

A similar narrative crisis, so to speak, occurs at the beginning of *Iliad* 9. There too, Agamemnon awakens at night, perturbed. There too, Agamemnon proposes that the army disband and return home. And there too, the only possible outcome is that Agamemnon must somehow change his mind. In the *Iliad*, the soldiers are silent, and Diomedes takes center-stage to rebuke Agamemnon and rally the troops, while it is Nestor who eventually convinces Agamemnon to turn his mind from flight and (at least to a degree) towards appeasing Achilles. In *Iphigenia at Aulis*, conversely, we learn that it was Menelaus who had "employed every argument" (*Iphigenia at Aulis* 97: πάντα προσφέρων λόγον) to persuade Agamemnon to summon Iphigenia. Whether this discussion occurs in the context of a broader assembly or in private quarters is, at this point, unclear. What is certain, however, is there is no mention whatsoever of the Achaean army as a whole, which implies that the soldiers at Aulis have no say in the matter. Moreover, we soon learn that Agamemnon intends to send a slave to Clytemnestra with a second letter, this time advising her and Iphigenia to stay at home (*Iphigenia at Aulis* 107–123). The question of whether or not the Trojan War will proceed thus becomes more urgent, and this time, the audience is overtly led to believe that Agamemnon's has the ability to decide the matter on his own.

The possibility that Agamemnon will call off the war is not the only Homeric issue to which Euripides alludes in the prologue; the stage is also set for another conflict between Agamemnon and Achilles. After Agamemnon claims that, but for Menelaus' persuasiveness, he had nearly sent the army home, we learn that he is luring Iphigenia to Aulis with the false promise of a marriage to Achilles (*Iphigenia at Aulis* 98–105). It is only then that he reports that he is changing his mind again, and that he will be sending another letter to his family. As he describes the contents of the second letter, the potential implications of this new decision are emphasized by the old slave who will deliver the letter:

καὶ πῶς Ἀχιλεὺς λέκτρων ἀπλακὼν
οὐ μέγα φυσῶν θυμὸν ἐπαρεῖ
σοὶ σῇ τ' ἀλόχῳ; τόδε καὶ δεινόν·

Iphigenia at Aulis 124–126

But won't Achilles, deprived of his bride,
be enraged and indignant in his heart
with you and your wife? This too is a terrible risk.

To speak of Achilles' anger at the loss of a woman is an overt allusion to the conflict over Briseis in the *Iliad*.[48] Agamemnon responds that the threat is minimal, as Achilles is "providing his name," not taking any action.[49] But the *Presbutês* disagrees, noting that Agamemnon is "taking a terrible risk by promising your child as a bride" to Achilles.[50] The specter of a showdown between Achilles and Agamemnon thus looms over the prologue, waiting only for the right moment to emerge.

If large portions of both the iambic and anapaestic sections of the prologue are Euripidean, as I suspect,[51] this would mean that the question of whether or not to go to war is highlighted twice in the prologue, and thus very much in the foreground. Even if only one of them is authentic,[52] the audience would still be made aware of the possibility of the Trojan War's "cancellation," and Agamemnon's apparently outsized influence over this decision. Regarding the Achilles/Agamemnon conflict, only the second anapaestic section contains overt allusions to that possibility. But the notion is at the very least implicit in the iambic section of the prologue: if Agamemnon is to forbid Iphigenia from coming to Aulis, Achilles will, by extension, be deprived of his (false) marriage.[53] The text is, without a doubt, deeply problematic. But it nevertheless seems certain that whatever the "original" prologue was, the audience would quickly

---

[48] Sorum 1992:532. See also Luschnig 1988:67, who notes that we are led to "understand that Briseis is not the first bride stolen from Achilles by his commander-in-chief."

[49] *Iphigenia at Aulis* 128: ὄνομ', οὐκ ἔργον, παρέχων Ἀχιλεύς.

[50] *Iphigenia at Aulis* 133–135: δεινά γ' ἐτόλμας, Ἀγάμεμνον ἄναξ, / ὃς τῷ τῆς θεᾶς σὴν παῖδ' ἄλοχον / φατίσας.

[51] Following among others, but most recently, Pietruczuk 2012.

[52] As, for example, Kovacs 2003:80–84 suggests.

[53] Even excluding all the anapaests and lines 106–114 of the iambs, as Kovacs 2003:82 suggests, we still have to imagine that Agamemnon mentions, at some point, that he is sending a second letter to Clytemnestra asking her to stay away from Aulis. Indeed, without such notice, Menelaus' entrance and assault of the *Presbutês* at the beginning of the first episode simply would not make sense.

develop a sense that Homeric conflicts and questions about power were lurking within the play.

The *parodos* that follows confirms the Iliadic backbone of the play. In a clear reference to Homer's Catalogue of Ships, the Chorus presents the audience with what can only be described as a catalogue of the heroes at Aulis. Diomedes, Odysseus, both Ajaxes, and Achilles are all present, but so too is the "obscure" Gouneus, whose mention suggests that Euripides is signaling a "purposeful intertextual connection with the *Iliad*."[54] Here again, the hierarchy seems fundamentally Homeric: of the common soldiers, only Achilles' Myrmidons are singled out for comment; the *basilês*, conversely, are explicitly said to be leading their contingents.[55] Through the first part of the play, then, Homeric structures of power remain largely intact. If anything, the distribution of power is more unequal, as the authority of Agamemnon (and perhaps Menelaus) seems essentially unfettered.

Shortly thereafter, Menelaus arrives and seizes the letter from Agamemnon's slave.[56] As one might expect, he is rather displeased to discover that Agamemnon has gone behind his back. Menelaus takes the issue up with Agamemnon, and in the debate that ensues questions of power and authority come fully to the foreground. Menelaus is the first to speak, and he begins with a general critique of Agamemnon's earlier behavior:

> οἶσθ', ὅτ' ἐσπούδαζες ἄρχειν Δαναΐδαις πρὸς Ἴλιον,
> τῷ δοκεῖν μὲν οὐχὶ χρῄζων, τῷ δὲ βούλεσθαι θέλων,
> ὡς ταπεινὸς ἦσθα, πάσης δεξιᾶς προσθιγγάνων
> 340 καὶ θύρας ἔχων ἀκλῄστους τῷ θέλοντι δημοτῶν
> καὶ διδοὺς πρόσρησιν ἑξῆς πᾶσι, κεἰ μή τις θέλοι,
> τοῖς τρόποις ζητῶν πρίασθαι τὸ φιλότιμον ἐκ μέσου,
> κᾆτ', ἐπεὶ κατέσχες ἀρχάς, μεταβαλὼν ἄλλους τρόπους
> τοῖς φίλοισιν οὐκέτ' ἦσθα τοῖς πρὶν ὡς πρόσθεν φίλος

Iphigenia at Aulis 337–344

---

[54] Torrance 2013:83.
[55] E.g. *Iphigenia at Aulis* 259–260: Λήιτος δ' ... ἄρχε ("Leitos was leading"); *Iphigenia at Aulis* 266–267: παῖς Ἀτρέως ἔπεμπε ναυβάτας / ναῶν ἑκατὸν ἠθροϊσμένους· ("Atreus' son sent a hundred ships with men he'd mustered); *Iphigenia at Aulis* 282: Εὔρυτος δ' ἄνασσε τῶνδε ("Eurytos ruled over these men").
[56] Here too Euripides does not miss a chance to emulate Homer: in a move reminiscent of Odysseus' assault on Thersites in Book Two of the *Iliad*, Menelaus threatens to "bloody" the old slave's head with his scepter. Cf. *Iphigenia at Aulis* 311: σκήπτρῳ τάχ' ἄρα σὸν καθαιμάξω κάρα (I'll bloody your head with my scepter) and *Iliad* 2.265–266: ὣς ἄρ' ἔφη, σκήπτρῳ δὲ μετάφρενον ἠδὲ καὶ ὤμω / πλῆξεν ("So [Odysseus] spoke, and he struck [Thersites'] back and shoulders with the scepter"). Luschnig 1988:88 also notes this allusion.

> You remember when you were eager to lead the Danaans to Ilium,
> wishing to at once seem willing yet not covetous—
> how humble you were! Taking each man's hand,
> 340   leaving your door unbarred to any commoner who wished,
> giving all a chance to speak, even those who didn't want to,
> striving in this way to buy the office[57] from the middle class?[58]
> But when you took control, you changed your ways
> and were no longer friendly as before to former friends.

Menelaus' point is that Agamemnon has been an unreliable leader, but he could have made this argument by simply pointing out his brother's change of mind concerning Iphigenia. Instead, Menelaus embarks on a digression about Agamemnon's actions before the tragedy. We may infer that this account is included not simply for rhetorical effect, but for the other information it conveys.

The crux of Menelaus' report is that Agamemnon has conducted a campaign to be chosen leader of the Achaean army, and that he has relied on the support of the common soldiers—the *mesos* or *dêmotai*. Such a concept is totally foreign to the *Iliad*, where Agamemnon is granted his privileged position simply because "he rules over more men."[59] But it is in many ways reminiscent of fifth-century Athens,[60] where, of course, the *dêmos* elected ten *stratêgoi* annually, and at times may even have chosen specific generals for specific expeditions.[61] Agamemnon's authority no longer resembles that of a pure autocrat, and the world of the tragedy thus shifts abruptly, and begins to subtly resemble that of Euripides' audience.

---

[57] Following e.g. Stockert 1992 vol. 2:294, who suggests that the best way to translate *philotimon* here is as "office" or "position."

[58] While this translation may seem anachronistic, the term used here (*mesos*) is the same one that Euripides gives Theseus in his famous discussion of the three "classes" of citizens (Euripides *Suppliants* 238–249; line 244: ἡ 'ν μέσῳ). Michelini 1994:226, describes this group as "a class that ideally would intervene between the quarrelling ranks of the wealthy and the poor as a stabilizing 'middle.'"

[59] As Nestor reminds Achilles at *Iliad* 1.281: ὅ γε φέρτερός ἐστιν ἐπεὶ πλεόνεσσιν ἀνάσσει.

[60] Jouan 1983:131.

[61] We know all too little about how Athenian *stratêgoi* were chosen, and hear nothing, to my knowledge, of candidates campaigning (though we do hear of candidates: cf. Demosthenes 18.285). On the question in general, cf. Piérart 1974; Rhodes 1981; and Hamel 1998:14–23. Regarding the possibility that Athenians held special elections in which they would choose one or more generals for specific expeditions, cf. *IG* I³ 93b 2–3 (= Meiggs/Lewis 78b; cited by Rhodes 1981:130); and Hamel 1998:15–19.

This shift is both confirmed and characterized by the term with which Menelaus describes Agamemnon's objective: *to philotimon* (*Iphigenia at Aulis* 342). Most literally, *philotimia*[62] meant a "love of honor," but it was often used to denote individual ambition or even political office more generally. By the end of the fifth century, the term was laden with both positive and negative connotations. Thucydides' Pericles, for example, comforts the parents of fallen Athenian soldiers by reminding them that *philotimia* alone is "ageless" (ἀγήρων), and that "to be honored" (τὸ τιμᾶσθαι) is that which renders old age most enjoyable (2.44.4). A short time later, however, Thucydides laments that Pericles' successors adopted policies that were ruinous for the city because they pursued "personal *philotimia*" (2.65.7: τὰς ἰδίας φιλοτιμίας). In general, it appears that *philotimia* could be considered useful when applied to the public good, harmful when it was limited to the realm of personal ambition, and was a topic of great relevance to fifth-century Athenians.[63] The portrait of Agamemnon seeking to "buy" *philotimia* thus raises grave doubts about the quality of his leadership. In short, at the very moment that notions of contemporary politics enter the drama, so too does the notion that these power structures are less than ideal.

Nevertheless, as Menelaus fills in more details about the plot's background, the power of the Achaean leaders still seems firmly entrenched. As it turns out, when the winds had first turned at Aulis, "the Danaans began to argue that the fleet should be disbanded" (*Iphigenia at Aulis* 352–353: Δαναΐδαι δ' ἀφιέναι / ναῦς διήγγελλον). According to Menelaus, Agamemnon was greatly distressed at the thought of "being deprived of his command" and losing his shot at glory, so the army's permanence at Aulis suggests that Agamemnon's will had in fact prevailed. Moreover, the question of Iphigenia's sacrifice seems as if it will be decided by the two men on-stage, with the army and the rest of the *basilêes* (again) excluded from the decision-making process. Neither man is willing to budge, and we find ourselves at an impasse. Indeed, if one looks past the brief reference to Agamemnon's political campaign, the tragic *agôn* is in many ways

---

[62] *Philotimia* and *to philotimon* are fundamentally equivalent. Cf. Hornblower 1991:313.

[63] Whitehead 1983:59, notes that *philotimia* was "a basic feature of the society and economy of democratic Athens." Similarly, Green 2001:42, argues that "[p]hilotimia in fifth century Athens was nothing less than intense contest for leadership of the *polis*." This competition had both positive and negative connotations. By the mid-fourth century, it seems to have become a less controversial topic, as it most often referred to the private outlay of expenditures that were crucial to the functioning of the *polis* (cf. Dover 1974:230–233). In the fifth century, however, feelings about *philotimia* were more fraught. Pindar, in perhaps the earliest known use of the term, says that "in *poleis* men are all too interested in *philotimia*, [and] they cause obvious suffering" (fragment 210: ἄγαν φιλοτιμίαν μνώμενοι ἐν πόλεσιν ἄνδρες· ἱστᾶσιν ἄλγος ἐμφανές). Euripides calls it "the worst of *daimones*" (*Phoenissae* 532: τῆς κακίστης δαιμόνων). And the subject of *philotimia* was controversial enough that Protagoras dedicated an entire treatise to it (Περὶ φιλοτιμίας, mentioned in Diogenes Laertius 9.55, cited by Whitehead 1983:57).

analogous to the quarrel between Achilles and Agamemnon in Book One of the Iliad: each dispute revolves around a woman's fate; both Agamemnon (*Iphigenia at Aulis* 396–399) and Achilles (*Iliad* 1.152–160) protest that the whole reason for the war—the recovery of Helen—is one that doesn't truly concern them; and above all, just as in the *Iliad*, the quarrel between Menelaus and Agamemnon appears to be an irresolvable clash between two *basilês*. Despite the earlier suggestion that Agamemnon was chosen by the army, the situation, the hierarchy of decision-making, and the relations between individuals at Euripides' Aulis seem generally analogous to those at Homer's Troy.

3.2 Power to the People at Aulis?

The parallels between *Iphigenia at Aulis* and the *Iliad* begin to quickly break down when a messenger enters to announce the arrival of Clytemnestra and Iphigenia at Aulis (*Iphigenia at Aulis* 414–439). Agamemnon weeps with despair at the knowledge that Iphigenia's death is imminent, and wonders how he will break the news to his wife. In truth, he finds no shortage of reasons to feel sorry for himself, and he suggests that such suffering is the fate of all leaders:

> ἡ δυσγένεια δ' ὡς ἔχει τι χρήσιμον·
> καὶ γὰρ δακρῦσαι ῥᾳδίως αὐτοῖς ἔχει
> ἅπαντά τ' εἰπεῖν· τῷ δὲ γενναίῳ φύσιν
> ἄνολβα πάντα· προστάτην δὲ τοῦ βίου
> 450 τὸν ὄγκον ἔχομεν τῷ τ' ὄχλῳ δουλεύομεν.
>
> *Iphigenia at Aulis* 446–450

> Low birth does possess some advantages:
> for it is easier for them to cry and speak
> of anything, while to the high-born man
> all sorrows come, but we're obliged to weigh
> 450 the dignity of life, slaves to the mob.

While Agamemnon's plaint is by no means unique within the Euripidean corpus,[64] it certainly signals a radical departure from the image of authority that had thus far been projected in the play. Up until now, every indication has been that the choice to sacrifice Iphigenia would lie with Agamemnon and his fellow *basilês*, if not with Agamemnon and Menelaus alone. Here, however, the Achaean leader suggests that he may have to reckon with the mass of the army as well.

---

[64] For the complaint that it is better to be "low-born," cf. Euripides fragment 285; on "enslavement to the mob" cf. Euripides *Hecuba* 868 (also noted by Stockert 1992 vol. 2:331).

Furthermore, Euripides' choice of the term *ochlos* is a loaded one. The term *ochlos* was unknown to Homer,[65] but by the fifth century it was quite common. Thucydides, for example, uses it 27 times in his *History*, either in a neutral manner (i.e. "mass") or with negative connotations (i.e. "mob").[66] Given the sentiment expressed here—that Agamemnon is a "slave" to the *ochlos*—it is implicit that we are dealing with a "mob," and reasonable to suppose that Euripides' audience would have understood it as such. This is another subtle erosion of our initial impression that the soldiery at Aulis is as passive as Homer's Achaean army—another small, almost imperceptible contemporization of affairs, one that would be unremarkable were it to occur in isolation. But it comes in the midst of a larger paradigm shift.

This shift becomes even more obvious as the debate between the two Atreids reaches its climax. Agamemnon's tears inspire pity in Menelaus, and in a surprising reversal he urges Agamemnon not to kill Iphigenia (*Iphigenia at Aulis* 473–503). Even more astonishing, however, is Agamemnon's own change of mind:

> ΑΓ ἀλλ' ἥκομεν γὰρ εἰς ἀναγκαίας τύχας,
> θυγατρὸς αἱματηρὸν ἐκπρᾶξαι φόνον.
> ΜΕ πῶς; τίς δ' ἀναγκάσει σε τήν γε σὴν κτανεῖν;
> ΑΓ ἅπας Ἀχαιῶν σύλλογος στρατεύματος.
> 515 ΜΕ οὔκ, ἤν νιν εἰς Ἄργος ‹γ'› ἀποστείλῃς πάλιν.
> ΑΓ λάθοιμι τοῦτ' ἄν, ἀλλ' ἐκεῖν' οὐ λήσομεν.
> ΜΕ τὸ ποῖον; οὔτοι χρὴ λίαν ταρβεῖν ὄχλον.
> ΑΓ Κάλχας ἐρεῖ μαντεύματ' Ἀργείων στρατῷ.
> ΜΕ οὔκ, ἤν θάνῃ γε πρόσθε· τοῦτο δ' εὐμαρές.

Iphigenia at Aulis 511–519

> AGAMEMNON: We've reached the point where fortune forces me to carry out my daughter's bloody murder.
> MENELAUS: What? Who compels you to kill her?
> AGAMEMNON: The whole assembly of the Achaean host.
> 515 MENELAUS: Not if you send her back again to Argos.
> AGAMEMNON: I might get away with that, but not this ...

---

[65] Homer used a great variety of terms to describe the soldiery, ranging from *laos* and *dêmos* to *homilos* or *stratos*, but never *ochlos*. For more on the Homeric terminology, see Welskopf 1981.

[66] Hunter 1988. I discuss Thucydides' "negative" uses of the term in greater detail below. Lush 2015:214 calls it "pejorative," as does Saïd 2013:202. But my sense is that Thucydides uses it frequently enough in a neutral manner (e.g. at 1.80.3 and 3.87.3) to suggest that it is not strictly derogatory.

MENELAUS: What? One must not fear the mob too much.
AGAMEMNON: Calchas will tell the Argive army his
prophecies.
MENELAUS: Not if he dies first. A simple task, that.

Unlike his earlier, vague ruminations about the *ochlos*, Agamemnon here describes exactly how he might become a "slave to the mob": the army might force him to sacrifice Iphigenia (line 514). Superficially at least, Menelaus is less concerned about this threat. But the reasons for his insouciance in fact confirm Agamemnon's concerns about the army: he first suggests that Agamemnon might get away with simply sending Iphigenia home, and when Agamemnon worries that Calchas might inform the army of the prophecy,[67] Menelaus proposes to kill the seer before he can do so. Implicit in this reasoning is that the army's ignorance must be maintained, for it is the only thing that stands between Iphigenia and the sacrificial altar.

Such dynamics are, of course, very different from the hierarchies depicted in the *Iliad*. And as the conversation continues, even starker images of the new order emerge:

ΑΓ τὸ Σισύφειον σπέρμα πάντ' οἶδεν τάδε.
525 ΜΕ οὐκ ἔστ' Ὀδυσσεὺς ὅτι σὲ κἀμὲ πημανεῖ.
ΑΓ ποικίλος ἀεὶ πέφυκε τοῦ τ' ὄχλου μέτα.
ΜΕ φιλοτιμίᾳ μὲν ἐνέχεται, δεινῷ κακῷ.
ΑΓ οὔκουν δοκεῖς νιν στάντ' ἐν Ἀργείοις μέσοις
λέξειν ἃ Κάλχας θέσφατ' ἐξηγήσατο,
530 κἄμ' ὡς ὑπέστην θῦμα, κᾆτ' ἐψευδόμην
Ἀρτέμιδι θύσειν; οὐ ξυναρπάσας στρατόν,
σὲ κἄμ' ἀποκτείναντας Ἀργείους κόρην
σφάξαι κελεύσει; κἂν πρὸς Ἄργος ἐκφύγω,
ἐλθόντες αὐτοῖς τείχεσιν Κυκλωπίοις
535 ἀναρπάσουσι καὶ κατασκάψουσι γῆν.

Iphigenia at Aulis 524–535

---

[67] The "secret prophecy" motif has been hotly contested for some time, most recently and extensively by Kovacs 2003 and Pietruczuk 2012. The strongest argument in favor of assessing all mentions of a secret prophecy to an interpolator remains the internal inconsistencies regarding the matter in *Iphigenia at Aulis*, but problems with consistency remain, in my view, even if we do eliminate all mentions of a secret prophecy; for a review of the problems that exist on both sides of the debate, see Collard and Morwood 2017 vol. 2:241–243. In any case, regarding this passage in particular it is clear that no dilemma exists unless the army remains ignorant of something, whether that be of the prophecy or of Iphigenia's arrival at Aulis.

AGAMEMNON: The child of Sisyphus knows all this.
525 MENELAUS: There's no way for Odysseus to hurt us.
AGAMEMNON: He has always been most cunning with the
mob.
MENELAUS: He is obsessed with honor, a terrible evil.
AGAMEMNON: Then don't you think he'll stand amidst the
Argives
to tell them the prophecies Calchas prescribed,
530 that I lied and promised to sacrifice a victim
to Artemis? That he'll seize the army, and order
the Argives to kill you and me and to slaughter
the girl? And then, even if I flee to Argos,
they'll come as far as the Cyclopean walls
535 to carry off [Iphigenia] and destroy the land.

Odysseus' ability to "seize" the army and "order" the soldiers to kill Agamemnon and his family suggests that at least one Homeric *basileus* would retain some form of authority. But once again, Menelaus and, at least implicitly, Agamemnon dismiss the possibility that another Greek elite—this time Odysseus—might sway the outcome of the Iphigenia-question on his own. Instead, the real peril lies in the possibility that Odysseus will inform the army of the various machinations at hand. Once that fact is known, the army is liable to act swiftly, violently, and above all decisively in bringing about Iphigenia's sacrifice. The fact that the army could pursue Agamemnon to Argos shows that Agamemnon runs the risk of losing authority "even [in] the region in which he holds institutional standing."[68] All of this indicates a total breakdown in the Homeric power structures that guaranteed that each *basileus* would at least have total authority over his own contingent.

Indeed, a neat frame through which to view this evolution of authority is the manner in which Calchas and Odysseus operate. The presence of the prophet Calchas, and in particular the adversarial nature of his relationship with Agamemnon that emerges in this scene, is strongly reminiscent of Book 1 of the *Iliad*.[69] But in order to even speak in the *Iliad*, Calchas had to beg for protection from Achilles for fear of (presumably violent) retribution from Agamemnon.[70]

---

[68] Lush 2015:212.

[69] Cf. *Iliad* 1.106, where Agamemnon famously calls Calchas a "prophet of ills" (μάντι κακῶν) for pointing out that he must return Chryses' daughter.

[70] Cf. *Iliad* 1.80–82: κρείσσων γὰρ βασιλεὺς ὅτε χώσεται ἀνδρὶ χέρηϊ· / εἴ περ γάρ τε χόλον γε καὶ αὐτῆμαρ καταπέψῃ, / ἀλλά τε καὶ μετόπισθεν ἔχει κότον, ὄφρα τελέσσῃ ("for a *basileus* is more powerful when he is angry with a lesser man, and even if he chokes down his anger for a day, he will hold onto his wrath until he satisfies it later"). Hammer 2002:83 argues that Calchas'

There, his prophecy is pivotal not because he wins over the common soldiers[71] but because Agamemnon sees that it is better to return Chryses' daughter than to allow his whole army to die (cf. *Iliad* 1.68–116). Here at Aulis, however, Calchas' prognostication has not convinced Agamemnon to sacrifice Iphigenia.[72] But his ability to speak to and move the Achaean *ochlos* looks to be a decisive factor. The dynamics of Calchas' intervention are thus entirely upended, and the fact that he will speak not to Agamemnon but to the *ochlos* suggests a substantial modification of the mechanisms of authority among the Achaeans.

Odysseus' role also speaks to this transition. As in Book Fourteen of the *Iliad* (cf. 14.82–102), Odysseus looks set to stand up to Agamemnon and force the war to continue. But whereas at Troy he had intervened by directly rebuking Agamemnon, here, just like Calchas, he represents a threat because he is able to appeal directly to the army. Moreover, it does not seem that Odysseus will be able to mobilize the army through threats and violence, as he does in *Iliad* 2, but rather because he is *poikilos* with the *ochlos*—"cunning with the mob" (*Iphigenia at Aulis* 526). This implies that his power at Aulis comes from rhetorical and persuasive excellence[73] rather than status or physical prowess. While the ability to persuade may have been desirable for Homeric *basilêes*, it was absolutely necessary for leaders in democratic Athens,[74] so Odysseus appears to be a leader more in the mold of Euripides' contemporaries than his Homeric antecedents. This modernity is further confirmed by the description of him "standing amidst the Argives" to incite them, as well as the fact that, just like Agamemnon, he too is obsessed with *philotimia*.

With regards to both Odysseus and Calchas, then, allusions to the *Iliad* come hand-in-hand with radical breaks from the Homeric tradition, thus emphasizing, in the starkest of manners, the new dynamics at Aulis. At the same time,

---

reticence illustrates the fact that "Agamemnon's ability to command obedience rests on a fear of retribution." Euripides' Menelaus might allude to this episode by suggesting that it would be easy to kill the prophet (*Iphigenia at Aulis* 519), as if to provide the retribution Calchas feared in the *Iliad*. Homer's epic is ever-present, even, or perhaps especially, when Euripides deviates from that model.

71   The soldiers in *Iliad* 1 are present as silent and passive spectators, and had in fact urged Agamemnon to ransom the girl a full ten days earlier (cf. *Iliad* 1.22–23)—a recommendation that Agamemnon had roundly and rashly ignored.

72   At least not on second thought: as Menelaus (*Iphigenia at Aulis* 358–363) tells us, Agamemnon had first agreed whole-heartedly to sacrifice Iphigenia, only to later change his mind. On this, cf. Gibert 1995:210–217.

73   Isocrates, for example, implies that *poikilia* is an integral part of rhetorical persuasiveness: cf. Isocrates 5.27; 12.4; 15.47. For the overtly negative connotations of Odysseus' *poikilia*, cf. my discussion at pp. 164–166.

74   Among many others, see for example Ober 1989:113: "[s]kill in public address was sine qua non for the [Athenian] politician"; Yunis 1996: *passim* but esp. 11–12; and Yunis 1998.

these new conditions are placed in the least flattering of lights. The outcomes envisioned by Agamemnon—the murder of Iphigenia, his own assassination, the sack of Argos—amount to a violent military coup and a total disintegration of military hierarchies. It is a striking image of the evolution of the Achaean army. Agamemnon's sense of obligation to sacrifice Iphigenia, his fears about the Achaean army and Odysseus' ability to stoke the flames of revolt, even Menelaus' hopes to suppress the army's knowledge, rather than their actions: all these suggest that it is no longer simply desirable to obtain the consensus of the common soldiers, but rather that their will is actually decisive in the debate about whether or not to bring war to Troy.

3.3 Military Authority at Athens and at Aulis

The dynamics of authority that emerge in the conversation between Agamemnon and Menelaus certainly appear strange within the context of Homer's Achaean army, but our evidence suggests that it was not uncommon for the Athenian *dêmos* to force generals to lead campaigns. One intriguing (if inadequately attested) parallel to the situation at Aulis seems to have occurred in 433 BCE. As Plutarch tells us (*Pericles* 29.2), after the Athenians had decided to enter into an alliance with Corcyra, Pericles "persuaded the *dêmos*" (ἔπεισε τὸν δῆμον) to send ten ships as aid and appoint Cimon's son Lacedaemonius to lead them "against his will" (μὴ βουλόμενον). Plutarch reports that the appointment was intended as an insult (29.2: οἷον ἐφυβρίζων), and while political or diplomatic considerations may have been the true motive for sending Lacedaemonius,[75] the story reflects a belief that Athenians generals were subject to the whims of the demos.

A pair of Thucydidean episodes confirm that this belief was rooted in reality. In 425 BCE, when Cleon demanded that the current generals (of which he was not one) lead an expedition against Spartan soldiers stranded on Sphacteria. Nicias, one of the elected generals that year, responded to Cleon's call by resigning and telling Cleon "to lead the campaign himself with whatever force he wished."[76] This caught Cleon off guard. According to Thucydides, Cleon had never actually wanted the command,[77] and he now attempted to get out of it by reminding everyone that Nicias was the real general (Thucydides 4.28.2). When Nicias reiterated his resignation and indifference, Cleon was backed into a corner. At this point, the Athenian *dêmos*, acting "just as an *ochlos* is wont to do ... demanded

---

[75] As suggested by Kagan 1969:243–44; Stadter 1989:266; Hamel 1998:18.
[76] Thucydides 4.28.1: ἥντινα βούλεται δύναμιν λαβόντα τὸ ἐπὶ σφᾶς εἶναι ἐπιχειρεῖν.
[77] While we must be cautious when it comes to Thucydides' portrayal of Cleon, there is less reason to believe he is distorting the basic dynamics of the debate, especially since Thucydides may well have been present, as is suggested by Westlake 1974:225.

that Nicias resign his command and shouted at Cleon to lead the expedition."[78] Cleon was thus forced to accept the appointment (Thucydides 4.28.4).

Nicias' aforementioned decision to continue the siege at Syracuse in 413 BCE is equally suggestive. Thucydides reports that the Athenian generals at Syracuse disagreed about the course of action they should take: Demosthenes advocated that they return to Athens immediately; Nicias, conversely, insisted that they persist with the siege until they wore the city down. According to Thucydides, Nicias argued that they should remain for the following reasons: "the Athenians would never approve of their departing without having voted on it themselves";[79] the common soldiers would accuse the generals of accepting bribes to betray the cause (Thucydides 7.48.4); because "knowing the nature of the Athenians, he did not wish ... to be killed, unjustly, by the Athenians;"[80] and because he was convinced that the Syracusans were "even worse off" (ἔτι ἥσσω) than the Athenian forces (7.48.5).

Curiously, according to Thucydides, Nicias neglects to mention the real reason that he wished to stay, namely that he had inside information about a faction within Syracuse that wished to betray the city (Thucydides 7.48.2). But perhaps this was because, in Thucydides' mind, Nicias realized that such argumentation would not win the day, that Demosthenes would have remained adamantly opposed to the idea of staying at Syracuse. Demosthenes was, however, persuaded by the notion that they "must not withdraw the troops without a vote of the Athenians," and suggested instead that they go to another part of Sicily.[81] Thucydides could not, of course, have certain knowledge of any of these things. But as a former general, one who had in fact been punished by the Athenian people, his reconstruction of the debate is a meaningful indicator of the manner in which Athenian generals might approach the decision-making process. Clearly, the reactions of the army and the *dêmos*, and the very real risk of being punished by them, were crucial factors.

To be sure, there are notable differences between all of these episodes, and between Agamemnon's situation at Aulis; in none of the historical examples is a general summarily executed by his army, as Agamemnon fears. But there are a number of remarkable similarities. With all of the generals (Agamemnon, Cleon, Nicias, Demosthenes, even Cimon's son Lacedaemonius) it is suggested that

---

[78] Thucydides 4.28.3: οἱ δέ, οἷον ὄχλος φιλεῖ ποιεῖν ἐπεκελεύοντο τῷ Νικίᾳ παραδιδόναι τὴν ἀρχὴν καὶ ἐκείνῳ [scil. τῷ Κλέωνι] ἐπεβόων πλεῖν.

[79] Thucydides 7.48.3: Ἀθηναῖοι σφῶν ταῦτα οὐκ ἀποδέξονται, ὥστε μὴ αὐτῶν ψηφισαμένων ἀπελθεῖν.

[80] Thucydides 7.48.4: οὔκουν βούλεσθαι αὐτός γε ἐπιστάμενος τὰς Ἀθηναίων φύσεις ... ἀδίκως ὑπ' Ἀθηναίων ἀπολέσθαι.

[81] Thucydides 7.49.2: δεῖ μὴ ἀπάγειν τὴν στρατιὰν ἄνευ Ἀθηναίων ψηφίσματος.

they are compelled to conduct a military operation against their better judgment or will.[82] In each case, we see a divergence of interests among leaders—Agamemnon and Odysseus at Aulis, Nicias and Cleon at Athens, Nicias and Demosthenes at Syracuse, presumably between Pericles and Lacedaemonius as well—and a certain amount of gamesmanship that takes place between them. And while we do not know the specific pressures that Cleon faced in Athens, nor indeed whether Nicias truly feared the possibility of execution, it is implicit that this concern pushes (Thucydides') Demosthenes to modulate his stance in the debate at Syracuse. In short, the fear of capital punishment was not only plausible, as evidenced by the numerous instances in which it was meted out, but was also acknowledged by generals at the time. Euripides thus did not need to find inspiration in specific events. He could simply draw on a pervasive set of notions about how decisions about war were made, and the consequences leaders might face.

Returning strictly to the situation at Aulis, Agamemnon's explicit fear of the army's wrath and his capitulation to their presumed will is important for two reasons. First of all, it represents a radical shift in the politics of authority in the play. Whereas the earlier image of Agamemnon campaigning did not suggest that his power, once elected, was fundamentally diminished with respect to that of a Homeric *basileus*, at this point that illusion is totally broken: generals no longer make decisions about war; the common soldiers do. Second, it is at the very moment that this illusion is broken that the politics of military decision-making also begins to seem highly problematic. This is conveyed quite starkly by Agamemnon's vision of the army rising up to kill not only Iphigenia but also himself and Menelaus. And it is further implied by the language that is used throughout this passage: the army is twice referred to as an *ochlos* (517 and 526)—and here it is unquestionable that the "pejorative" sense of the word is in play; at the same time, both Calchas and Odysseus are said to be pursuing *philotimia*,[83] which is further characterized as "evil." The overall effect is striking: the mirage of Homeric hierarchies that had been maintained in the first part of the play is shattered, and a powerful portrayal of contemporary power structures achieves a sharp and negative definition.

Nor is this the only occasion in which *Iphigenia at Aulis* emphasizes the contemporary and troubling aspects of the political dynamics at Aulis. At first

---

[82] Even if Nicias' real reason for staying at Syracuse was not the potential backlash he would face from the army and *dêmos*, we might recall that his very presence in Sicily was one that was forced upon him by the Athenian people. See Thucydides 6.8–14 and 6.19–25; Hamel 1998:20–21.

[83] Odysseus at *Iphigenia at Aulis* 527 (see above at p. 113), but also Calchas at *Iphigenia at Aulis* 520: [Agamemnon] ὸ μαντικὸν πᾶν σπέρμα φιλότιμον κακόν ("the whole *philotimos* race of seers is evil").

glance, the arrival of Clytemnestra and Iphigenia marks a change of course in the play's trajectory, and Agamemnon's decision to simply appease the army and sacrifice his daughter suggests that the matter might be resolved. But this is far from the climax of the tragedy's meditation on the nature of authority at Aulis, for the appearance of Agamemnon's erstwhile rival Achilles complicates matters severely.

3.4 Achilles' Entrance and the Complete Recalibration of Homeric Power Structures

When Achilles finally enters the scene in the third episode of the play, he is met by Clytemnestra, who greets him as a son-in-law (*Iphigenia at Aulis* 835–836). The subsequent confusion that this meeting and greeting engenders is resolved only by the reappearance of the *Presbutês* with whom we first saw Agamemnon conversing in the prologue, and who immediately discloses Agamemnon's plot to Clytemnestra. Clytemnestra's only recourse, at this point, is to call on Achilles to protect Iphigenia. And when Achilles accedes to this appeal, (*Iphigenia at Aulis* 900–974), the prospect of another Agamemnon-Achilles dispute now looms large.

Just as importantly, the terms of the dispute fall along the same lines as in the *Iliad*, as Achilles' grounds for accepting Clytemnestra's appeal explicitly recall the reasons behind the Homeric conflict and his own stance in the *Iliad*:[84]

> καὶ τοῖς Ἀτρείδαις, ἢν μὲν ἡγῶνται καλῶς,
> πεισόμεθ', ὅταν δὲ μὴ καλῶς, οὐ πείσομαι.

---

[84] I will be working with these lines even though virtually the entirety of Achilles' monologue (*Iphigenia at Aulis* 919–974) is of disputed authenticity. Diggle 1994:ad loc. gives it his second-lowest authenticity-ranking ("vix Euripidei"); Page 1934:175–179, deletes almost the entirety of Achilles' speech (919–1035) on grounds of language and style; while Kovacs 2003:91–93 excises large swaths because they lack any "relevant point" (919–31), on account of "oddities" (932–943), or because of repetitions and irrelevance (955–969). *Contra* see esp. Ritchie 1978 (who also provides a fine synthesis of the history of editorial deletions of those lines); as well as Jouan 1983:141, and Stockert 1992 vol. 2:463, who follow Ritchie. In general, the deletions of Achilles' speech are based on questions of style and aesthetics. Given the relative weakness of such evidence, and insofar as the plot of the tragedy requires that Achilles explain his decision to intervene on behalf of Iphigenia, by far the best option seems to me to work with the text we possess. Regarding more specifically the lines I have cited above, Ritchie (186) points out that 928–931 were "the only part of the speech which no one has yet held to be spurious," though Kovacs 2003 has since argued that Achilles' "exordium [i.e. 919–31] ... makes no recognizably relevant point" and labeled his statements "abstractions" that are "[not] tied to any concrete action or decision" (p. 91). Of course, were we to eliminate all the "abstractions" from Euripidean speeches, we would find ourselves committed to the excision of a number of passages that are surely authentic.

930 ἀλλ' ἐνθάδ' ἐν Τροίᾳ τ' ἐλευθέραν φύσιν
   παρέχων

Iphigenia at Aulis 928–931

> When they lead well, I'll obey the Atreids,
> but when they lead poorly I will not.
> 930 Instead, I will maintain my free nature
> both here and in Troy

Achilles here provides a perspective on Agamemnon's authority that is similar to his attitude in the *Iliad*, when he boldly proclaims he will not simply "yield [to Agamemnon] in every matter" (*Iliad* 1.294: πᾶν ἔργον ὑπείξομαι).[85] His submission to Agamemnon, both here and in the *Iliad*, is conditional, and will depend on the manner in which Agamemnon uses his authority. Moreover, Achilles mentions he will maintain this attitude in Troy as well—an obvious allusion to the "Homeric Achilles"[86]—and he even directly recalls his words in the *Iliad* with a double-use of the future-middle of *peitho*.[87]

As Achilles elaborates on his reasons for standing against Agamemnon, he continues to describe the brewing conflict in a manner reminiscent of the *Iliad*:[88]

   οὐ τῶν γάμων ἕκατι—μυρίαι κόραι
960 θηρῶσι λέκτρον τοὐμόν—εἴρηται τόδε·
   ἀλλ' ὕβριν ἐς ἡμᾶς ὕβρισ' Ἀγαμέμνων ἄναξ.

···

968 νῦν δ' οὐδέν εἰμι, παρὰ δὲ τοῖς στρατηλάταις
   ἐν εὐμαρεῖ με δρᾶν τε καὶ μὴ δρᾶν κακῶς.

Iphigenia at Aulis 959–961, 968–969

> I say this not because of the wedding
> 960 —so many women do long for my hand—
> but since lord Agamemnon's insulted me!

---

[85] On which, see above at p. 102.

[86] Ritchie 1978:186.

[87] See *Iliad* 1.296: οὐ γὰρ ἔγωγ' ἔτι σοὶ πείσεσθαι ὀΐω (see also above at p. 103n35).

[88] Kovacs 2003:92, deletes the entirety of 953–969 on the grounds that they are "irrelevant" (959–961) or because they repeat Achilles' comments in lines 944–947. The relevance of the first three lines is adequately attested by the fact they are an overt reference to the Homeric quarrel. Kovacs' deletion of 968–969 makes little difference to my argument, since what I say of them is equally true of lines 944–945, which Kovacs upholds. Regarding 962–967 (not quoted here), Kovacs and the vast majority of commentators are probably correct that these lines have been subject to some form of interpolation. Ritchie 1978:193–195, gamely tries to salvage them, but his attempt is less than convincing.

....

968   ... And now I'm nothing, and the generals
       don't care whether they treat me well or ill.

The first two lines of this passage are a direct allusion Homer's embassy, where Achilles rejects Agamemnon's offer of a daughter in marriage on the grounds that he could have his pick of "many Achaean women" (*Iliad* 9.395–396: *pollai Achaiides kourai*).[89] The lines thus serve to both recall the dispute in Homer while at the same time emphasizing the fact that, just as in Homer, the quarrel between Agamemnon and Achilles relates only superficially to the woman in question. The accusation of hubris is also the same term with which Achilles describes Agamemnon's actions in the *Iliad*, so we are further reminded of the epic.[90] Finally, we come to the real reason Achilles has decided to come to Iphigenia's defense: to protect his reputation. Just as in the *Iliad*, Achilles fears that he will be seen as a "nobody" (here: *ouden*; at *Iliad* 1.293: *outidanos*).[91] And once again, it is Agamemnon's (and here also Menelaus') disregard for him that diminishes his reputation and thus arouses his anger. In short, the dispute between the two heroes at Aulis comes amidst a volley of allusions to the *Iliad*. The audience is primed to expect a retelling of the intractable conflict between Achilles and Agamemnon in the *Iliad*, and once again, the twin problems of authority and status appear central to a conflict between two *basilées*.

Achilles then suggests that Clytemnestra should first attempt to persuade Agamemnon to spare Iphigenia, noting that he will intervene if Agamemnon should resist (*Iphigenia at Aulis* 1015–1016)—an intervention we are surely meant to anticipate at this point. The following episode shows Clytemnestra gamely following Achilles' advice as she tries to change her husband's mind. Agamemnon is not without pity, but as he informs his wife and daughter, his hands are tied:

       ὁρᾶθ' ὅσον στράτευμα ναύφρακτον τόδε
1260   χαλκέων θ' ὅπλων ἄνακτες Ἑλλήνων ὅσοι,
       οἷς νόστος οὐκ ἔστ' Ἰλίου πύργους ἔπι
       οὐδ' ἔστι Τροίας ἐξελεῖν κλεινὸν βάθρον,
       εἰ μή σε θύσω, μάντις ὡς Κάλχας λέγει.

---

[89] Noted by, among others, Ritchie 1978:192; and Jouan 1983:142.
[90] *Iliad* 1.203: ὕβριν; repeated by Athena in *Iliad* 1.214: ὕβριος. Luschnig 1988:67, and Ritchie 1978:193, also note this allusion. These are in fact the only two instances in which the noun *hubris* appears in the *Iliad*, so the reference is perhaps more obvious than one might initially expect.
[91] Ritchie 1978:195.

μέμηνε δ' Ἀφροδίτη τις Ἑλλήνων στρατῷ
1265 πλεῖν ὡς τάχιστα βαρβάρων ἐπὶ χθόνα
παῦσαί τε λέκτρων ἁρπαγὰς Ἑλληνικῶν·
οἳ τὰς ἐν Ἄργει παρθένους κτενοῦσί μου
ὑμᾶς τε κἀμέ, θέσφατ' εἰ λύσω θεᾶς.

Iphigenia at Aulis 1259–1268

You see how great this ship-fenced army is,
1260 how many masters of the bronze-clad Greeks
who, unless I sacrifice you as the prophet
Calchas says, will never make the journey
to the towers of Ilium, nor sack the famous seat of Troy.
Some Aphrodite is inciting the Greek army
1265 to sail as soon as possible to that barbarian land,
and to stop the abductions of Greek brides.
And if I defy the decree of Artemis, they will kill
our daughters in Argos, as well as you and me.

The scene that Agamemnon imagines here very closely resembles his closing statement in his debate with Menelaus (see above at p. 114). In both cases, Agamemnon predicts that a violent rebellion by his troops will lead directly to the deaths of his daughter(s), himself, and his interlocutor (here Clytemnestra; before Menelaus). Here too it seems that if need be, the Achaean army will travel to Argos to carry out Iphigenia's sacrifice. And as in the first episode, Agamemnon believes that resistance is futile.

These similarities between the two episodes are obvious, but the differences between the accounts are also glaring. Perhaps most notably, Calchas and Odysseus, the two individuals whom Agamemnon initially feared most, have been stripped of any agency. In Agamemnon's new assessment of the situation, the mutinous army will not even require the guidance of a *basileus*. Instead, the leaders are so peripheral to the affair that even though both *basilêes* and the common soldiers—the *anaktes* and the *strateuma*—would be deprived of the glory of the Trojan expedition, Agamemnon is concerned only about the possibility that the army (*stratos*) will rise up against him. In this new conception, the army's voice is not simply a decisive one in the debate; it is the only one that counts.

The Achaean army not only expropriates all decision-making power, it also acquires, for the first time, a good deal of characterization. To begin, Euripides uses the rare term *nauphraktos* to emphasize the fact that this army is specifically a naval one. More poignantly, we find out their motivation for rebelling:

"some Aphrodite" has fallen upon the Argives and impels them to sail for Troy. The peculiarity of this formulation recalls Thucydides' similar evaluation of the Athenian *dêmos* as they voted to set sail for Sicily in 415 BCE:[92]

καὶ ἔρως ἐνέπεσε τοῖς πᾶσιν ὁμοίως ἐκπλεῦσαι, τοῖς μὲν γὰρ πρεσβυτέροις ὡς ἢ καταστρεψομένοις ἐφ' ἃ ἔπλεον ἢ οὐδὲν ἂν σφαλεῖσαν μεγάλην δύναμιν, τοῖς δ' ἐν τῇ ἡλικίᾳ τῆς τε ἀπούσης πόθῳ ὄψεως καὶ θεωρίας, καὶ εὐέλπιδες ὄντες σωθήσεσθαι· ὁ δὲ πολὺς ὅμιλος καὶ στρατιώτης ἔν τε τῷ παρόντι ἀργύριον οἴσειν καὶ προσκτήσεσθαι δύναμιν ὅθεν ἀΐδιον μισθοφορὰν ὑπάρξειν. ὥστε διὰ τὴν ἄγαν τῶν πλεόνων ἐπιθυμίαν, εἴ τῳ ἄρα καὶ μὴ ἤρεσκε, δεδιὼς μὴ ἀντιχειροτονῶν κακόνους δόξειεν εἶναι τῇ πόλει ἡσυχίαν ἦγεν.

Thucydides 6.24.3–4

And an *erôs* fell equally upon everyone to set sail. For the older men [were convinced] they would either overrun the lands to which they were sailing, or that at the very least a force of this size could not be defeated. The men of fighting age[93] [were seized] by a desire for distant sights and spectacles, and had great faith that they would survive. And the main body of the troops [yearned] to bring home money in the present and besides that to gain the potential for unlimited income in the future.[94] So that due to the excessive desire for the expedition, if there was anyone to whom it did not appeal, fearing that by voting against it they might seem ill-disposed to the city, they remained silent.

The proceedings described by Thucydides here are strikingly similar to the situation in *Iphigenia at Aulis*: in each case, a crucial decision must be about made whether or not to embark on a long and costly military expedition; at both Aulis and Athens, the overriding motivation for the expedition turns out to be an irrational lust for war;[95] in both cases, this passion acts upon the common soldiers, whose will turns out to be the decisive—perhaps even only—factor in the decision-making process; and finally, Agamemnon's reaction may be compared

---

[92]   Stockert 1992 vol. 2:554, also notes this similarity.
[93]   Hornblower 2008:362, believes Thucydides is referring here to the "officer class."
[94]   Following Hornblower 2008:362.
[95]   *Erôs* for Thucydides, "some Aphrodite" for Euripides, though in fact earlier in the play, at a less suspect moment (*Iphigenia at Aulis* 808–809: οὕτω δεινὸς ἐμπέπτωκ' ἔρως / τῇσδε στρατείας) Achilles had used Thucydides' formulation. The secondary goals here are different—Thucydides' troops want money while Euripides' seek to "stop the abductions of Greek brides"—though of course it would hardly be appropriate for Agamemnon to convince Clytemnestra that Iphigenia must be sacrificed in order to satisfy the army's greed.

to those few who opposed the Sicilian expedition, for just as the dissenting Athenians are cowed into maintaining their silence, Agamemnon is too intimidated by the army's excessive passion to speak out against the sacrifice of his daughter. In summary, Euripides' image of a passionate soldiery that is in full command of the situation confirms that a metaphorical gulf lies between his Aulis and Homer's Troy, and that *Iphigenia at Aulis* hews much closer instead to the world of fifth-century Athens.

As a result of this new vision of Achaean power-structures, it is now only Achilles that can save Iphigenia. Given the hero's prowess, one might find some comfort in knowing that he is Iphigenia's last line of defense. But as the final episode of the tragedy opens, Iphigenia catches hold of an inauspicious sight: a mass of Achaean soldiers is making their way toward Iphigenia and Clytemnestra, and they are once again called an *ochlos* (*Iphigenia at Aulis* 1338).[96] Neither their appearance nor Iphigenia's definition of them as a mob bodes well. On the contrary, it suggests that Agamemnon's prediction is coming true, and that the army will simply assert itself and demand Iphigenia's sacrifice.

This sensation is immediately confirmed by Achilles' account of all that has happened behind the scenes:

> 1345 ΑΧ ὦ γύναι τάλαινα, Λήδας θύγατερ ...
> ΚΛ οὐ ψευδῆ θροεῖς.
> ΑΧ δείν' ἐν Ἀργείοις βοᾶται ...
> ΚΛ τίς βοή; σήμαινέ μοι.
> ΑΧ ἀμφὶ σῆς παιδός ...
> ΚΛ πονηρῶν εἶπας οἰωνὸν λόγον.
> ΑΧ ὡς χρεὼν σφάξαι νιν.
> ΚΛ †κοὐδεὶς ἐναντία λέγει;†
> ΑΧ ἐς θόρυβον ἐγώ τιν' αὐτὸς ἤλυθον ...
> ΚΛ τίν', ὦ ξένε;
> 1350 ΑΧ σῶμα λευσθῆναι πέτροισι.
> ΚΛ μῶν κόρην σῴζων ἐμήν;
> ΑΧ αὐτὸ τοῦτο.
> ΚΛ τίς δ' ἂν ἔτλη σώματος τοῦ σοῦ θιγεῖν;
> ΑΧ πάντες Ἕλληνες.

---

[96] I regard as highly unlikely the suggestion made by Stockert 1992 vol. 2:574, that this *ochlos* refers to the handful of "faithful soldiers" who remain by Achilles' side (cf. *Iphigenia at Aulis* 1358, in which we learn that at least two comrades are on hand to arm Achilles). The term *ochlos*, which appears a full eight times in *Iphigenia at Aulis* (191, 450, 517, 526, 735, 1030, 1338, 1546), is in every other instance used in reference to the Achaean army as a whole.

ΚΛ στρατὸς δὲ Μυρμιδὼν οὔ σοι παρῆν;
ΑΧ πρῶτος ἦν ἐκεῖνος ἐχθρός.

Iphigenia at Aulis 1345–1353

1345   ACHILLES: O wretched woman, daughter of Leda.
CLYTEMNESTRA: You do not speak falsely.
ACHILLES: The Argives are shouting terrible things.
CLYTEMNESTRA: Shouting what? Explain this to me.
ACHILLES: About your child ...
CLYTEMNESTRA: The words you say are an evil omen.
ACHILLES: That they must slaughter her.
CLYTEMNESTRA: And no one speaks up against this?
ACHILLES: I myself risked it against their uproar.
CLYTEMNESTRA: Risked what?
1350   ACHILLES: Death by stoning.
CLYTEMNESTRA: For defending my child?
ACHILLES: Yes, exactly.
CLYTEMNESTRA: But who would dare take hold of you?
ACHILLES: All the Greeks.
CLYTEMNESTRA: And your Myrmidon army wasn't there?
ACHILLES: They were my first enemy.

Earlier in the play, when Achilles was pondering the issue with Clytemnestra, he had framed the question of Iphigenia's sacrifice as a dispute between himself and Agamemnon, or at most between himself and other Greek *basilêes*;[97] at no point had he even spoken of the common soldiers, let alone considered their opinion to be of any consequence.

The scene he describes, however, utterly defies these expectations. Instead of taking the matter up directly with Agamemnon or the other *basilêes*, Achilles finds himself face to face with the entire army. The impact of the army's intervention can hardly be understated: Achilles' objections to Agamemnon's exercise of power, and his displeasure with his loss of status, are effectively rendered moot. Instead, Achilles must choose between allowing the sacrifice to go ahead as planned, or losing his life at the hands of the Achaean *ochlos*. Having already decided the question of Iphigenia's sacrifice, it appears as if the army will simply render any dispute between Agamemnon and Achilles irrelevant. Once again, *Iphigenia at Aulis* shows us a Homeric problem resolved through a

[97]   Conflict specifically between Achilles and Agamemnon: *Iphigenia at Aulis* 961; between Achilles and the Atreids: *Iphigenia at Aulis* 928–929; or between Achilles and the "generals": *Iphigenia at Aulis* 968.

radical inversion of the traditional hierarchies and power-structures among the Achaean army.

One detail perfectly illustrates this evolution of authority at Aulis: Achilles tells us that his Myrmidons were not only involved in this uprising, but that they actually led the rebellion. As discussed above, despite the complexities of the relations between the different *basilêes* in the *Iliad*, it is a general rule that the Achaean soldiers follow their collective lead. With regard to any individual army (i.e. the Myrmidons, the Boeotians, etc.), the situation is even simpler: each army follows the orders of its *basileus* (or *basilêes*). In fact, the strict hierarchical relationship between a Homeric *basileus* and his own soldiers is best illustrated by none other than Achilles and the Myrmidons, as we see in Book Sixteen when Achilles finally addresses his army:

> 200 Μυρμιδόνες μή τίς μοι ἀπειλάων λελαθέσθω,
> ἃς ἐπὶ νηυσὶ θοῇσιν ἀπειλεῖτε Τρώεσσι
> πάνθ' ὑπὸ μηνιθμόν, καί μ' ἠτιάασθε ἕκαστος·
> "σχέτλιε Πηλέος υἱὲ χόλῳ ἄρα σ' ἔτρεφε μήτηρ,
> νηλεές, ὃς παρὰ νηυσὶν ἔχεις ἀέκοντας ἑταίρους·
> 205 οἴκαδέ περ σὺν νηυσὶ νεώμεθα ποντοπόροισιν
> αὖτις, ἐπεί ῥά τοι ὧδε κακὸς χόλος ἔμπεσε θυμῷ."

> *Iliad* 16.200–206

> 200 "Myrmidons: let no one forget those constant threats
> that you uttered against the Trojans beside the swift ships
> when I was in my wrath, and how each of you condemned me,
> 'Cruel son of Peleus! Your mother must have nursed you on anger.
> You are ruthless, you keep your comrades besides the ships against their will.
> 205 We should go home again in our seafaring ships
> since this awful anger has descended on your spirit.'"

It is evident here that the withdrawal Achilles had imposed on his troops in the *Iliad* was by no means pleasing to them. Nevertheless, at no point had they taken the issue up with him directly, choosing instead to direct criticism at him from behind his back. And neither their unhappiness nor their latent criticism appears to have had any effect whatsoever. While the Myrmidons may wish to either enter the fray or return home, they have instead been doing just as Achilles ordered: standing idly by their ships. The situation at Aulis, on the contrary, is the reverse—as soon as the Myrmidons disagree with their leader, they rise up against him—and serves as another example of *Iphigenia at Aulis'* deliberate inversion of Homeric power structures.

The type of behavior that Achilles attributes to the Achaeans also provides decisive information. Achilles begins by telling Clytemnestra that the army is "shouting" that Iphigenia needs to die, and a few lines later, he tells us that this shouting turned into a veritable *thorubos* (line 1349: "tumult" or "uproar") when he attempted to speak in Iphigenia's defense. Euripides' use of the term is significant. Much like *ochlos*, the word *thorubos* was a decidedly contemporary word.[98] It could refer to the tumult in battle when opposing armies clashed,[99] but just as frequently we hear of *thorubos* occurring in the context of debate, where it was common for members of the public to "shout down" (*thorubein*) a speaker with whom they disagreed. The latter dynamic is certainly what Achilles has described.

The fact that a popular *thorubos* resolves the debate at Aulis lends to the proceedings an air that is at once contemporary and decidedly democratic. Indeed, resolution-by-*thorubos* was especially prevalent in democratic *poleis*.[100] In fact, it seems to have been, in a certain sense, an essential mechanism of ancient democracies.[101] In Athens, for example, it was a common occurrence both in the law-courts and at assemblies where policy was debated.[102] In all likelihood, *thorubos* was the easiest, if not only, way for the vast majority of Athenian citizens to actively engage in or "regulate" public debate and to express a "negative" opinion regarding a specific proposal.[103] Indeed, in a situation that is again analogous to proceedings at Aulis, it was a *thorubic* intervention that had forced

---

[98] It never once appears in Homer, or for that matter in any pre-classical author with the exception of Aesop *Proverbia* 107 and 152. Among authors of the classical era, Thucydides, Euripides, Aristophanes, Xenophon, Plato, and Demosthenes all use the term regularly.

[99] E.g. Thucydides 2.4.2, 4.127.1; Herodotus. 8.91.

[100] This is implied by the fact that almost all classical-era descriptions of *thoruboi* in the context of debate are in reference to Athenian democratic practices, as indeed are modern analyses of the phenomenon. Confirmation of the fundamentally "democratic" nature of *thorubos* may also be seen in its suppression during the oligarchic coups in Athens in 411 and 404 BCE, as is pointed out by Wallace 2004:226.

[101] On the widespread practice of *thorubos* in democratic Athens in general, see Wallace 2004; Schwartzberg 2010:461–465; and Balot 2004:243–246. Contra, see Hansen 1990:350: "[t]*horybos*, heckling, was ideologically to be avoided ... it was only a tolerated and not an intentional part of Athenian political discourse" [emphasis in original]. But Hansen's argument suffers, in my view, from his emphasis that there was a single ideology of "discourse" in Athens, an orthodoxy that I believe is belied by, among other things, the widespread existence of *thorubos* itself, particularly in the law-courts and the assembly.

[102] On *thorubos* during legal proceedings, see esp. Bers 1985; and E. Hall 1995:43–44. Regarding episodes of *thorubos* in the assembly itself, cf. Tacon 2001; but also Hansen 1991:146–147.

[103] Wallace 2004:225–226.

a reluctant Cleon to take command during the Pylos affair in 425 BCE.[104] And the very recent precedent of the execution of the generals after Arginousae—an event both Xenophon and Diodorus agree was replete with *thorubic* activity[105]— was surely a poignant example. In other words, the primary method through which the Achaean *ochlos* resolves the central conflict of *Iphigenia at Aulis* is a technique that an Athenian audience would have easily recognized as imported from their own *polis*.

Even beyond the simple fact that the army is threatening to kill Achilles, its *thorubic* activity is cast in a particularly negative light. This is evident from the manner in which the Achaean *ochlos* intends to enact the execution: death by stoning. The threat itself is not exceptional, as stoning was a commonly proposed sanction in the Greek literary tradition, especially in tragedy.[106] But the situation in *Iphigenia at Aulis* stands out for the manner in which the punishment is threatened. In nearly all other tragic instances in which a character risks being stoned, the sentence is decided and delivered by a figure (or figures) in a legitimate position of power.[107] The example that provides the most relevant contrast concerns another tragic version of Achilles himself, that of Aeschylus' *Myrmidons*. In *Myrmidons*, it is suggested that Achilles might be stoned by the Achaean army (fragment 132c)[108] for refusing to fight at Troy. On the surface,

---

[104] Wallace 2004:224. Thucydides is indeed emphatic that *thorubos* plays a crucial role here: it is only "when the Athenians had begun to clamor at [4.28.1: ὑποθορυβησάντων]" Cleon's unwillingness to actually lead the expedition that Nicias 'offered' to set aside the generalship in his favor; and it is only in the midst of the *ochlos*' shouting (4.28.3: οἱ δέ, οἷον ὄχλος φιλεῖ ποιεῖν ... ἐπεβόων) that Cleon felt obliged to accept.

[105] Diodorus relates that those who wished to defend the generals were unable to speak because of a *thorubos* (*Bibliotheca* 13.101.6: συνθορυβοῦντες), while Xenophon (*Hellenica* 1.7.14–15) states that the *prytaneis* were cowed into allowing a (possibly illegal) mass vote on the generals' culpability amidst a great deal of shouting and clamor.

[106] On the literary tradition more generally, see esp. Steiner 1995. The most notable example, at least within the context of this study, is *Iliad* 3.56–57, where Hector claims that if they were not cowards, the Trojans would have already stoned Paris for stealing Helen. But the fact that the Trojans have not stoned Paris suggests this is not a realistic possibility.

[107] Either by a tribunal, as in Euripides *Orestes* 49–50, or by a group's leader or leaders, as in Euripides *Ion* 1111–1112; *Bacchae* 355–357; Sophocles *Antigone* 36; *Ajax* 251–255. The only exceptions are in Euripides' *Iphigenia in Tauris* 240–339, in which a group of shepherds uses stones to attack Orestes and Pylades for killing their livestock, though this seems less an instance of "justice" being sought through stoning than a group of people using the only weapons at their disposal to attack armed men; and Aeschylus *Agamemnon* 1616, in which the Chorus suggests that Aegisthus will eventually be stoned by the people of Argos.

[108] This fragment is from a papyrus, and it is itself fragmentary and of difficult interpretation. Even its Aeschylean provenance has been doubted, e.g. by Page 1942:137–139. More recent commentators have generally seen the fragment as genuine, though they have differed in their interpretations of it. In general, I follow the reconstruction and analysis provided by Michelakis 2002:22– 57, as this is the most extensive recent treatment of the *Achilleis*. For other viewpoints, cf. Snell 1964:1–22; Moreau 1996; and Sommerstein 2010:242–245.

this is very similar to the uprising at Aulis, but unlike in *Iphigenia at Aulis*, Aeschylus suggests that a "judicial process" is used to arrive at the decision,[109] and the news is brought to Achilles by an emissary from Agamemnon, possibly Phoenix,[110] conferring a certain amount of legitimacy on the proceedings. Furthermore, in *Myrmidons*, Achilles practically scoffs at the threat,[111] and the sanction serves only to make Achilles "more obdurate," for it is now "psychologically impossible for Achilles to rejoin battle."[112] In *Iphigenia at Aulis*, conversely, the impetus to stone Achilles arises from the masses and is taken most seriously by Achilles, who flees. While Euripides is likely alluding to the Aeschylean precedent, he also differs in numerous and meaningful ways from his predecessor's treatment of the stoning.

But while the situation in *Iphigenia at Aulis* is exceptional when compared to tragic precedents, it is strikingly similar to at least one contemporary example of stoning.[113] When large Spartan and Argive contingents (and their respective allies) set up for battle near Argos in 418 BCE, the Spartan king Agis and the Argive general Thrasylus brokered a truce, but without consulting their armies or allies. The soldiers on both sides were unhappy with the accord, not least because it was struck without their input. At least superficially, then, the situation resembles the one at Aulis, where a single leader (Achilles) attempts to scuttle the soldiery's desire for war.

Thucydides' account of the soldiers' reactions to the truce is fascinating for the contrasts, both subtle and obvious, that distinguish the Spartans and Argives:[114]

οἱ δὲ Λακεδαιμόνιοι καὶ οἱ ξύμμαχοι εἵποντο μὲν ὡς ἡγεῖτο διὰ τὸν νόμον, ἐν αἰτίᾳ δ' εἶχον κατ' ἀλλήλους πολλῇ τὸν Ἆγιν ... τὸ μὲν οὖν στρατόπεδον οὕτως ἐν αἰτίᾳ ἔχοντες τὸν Ἆγιν ἀνεχώρουν τε καὶ διελύθησαν ἐπ' οἴκου ἕκαστοι, Ἀργεῖοι δὲ καὶ αὐτοὶ ἔτι ἐν πολλῷ πλέονι αἰτίᾳ εἶχον τοὺς σπεισαμένους ἄνευ τοῦ πλήθους ... τόν τε Θράσυλον ἀναχωρήσαντες ἐν τῷ Χαράδρῳ, οὗπερ τὰς ἀπὸ στρατείας δίκας πρὶν

---

[109] Michelakis 2002:24.

[110] Moreau 1996, 14; Sommerstein 2010:242–243.

[111] Achilles notes that he is "everything for the Achaean army" (fragment 132c 11: ἐγὼ τὰ πάντ' Ἀχαιϊκῷ στρατῷ).

[112] Snell 1964, 3.

[113] To be clear, stoning was not a common practice in archaic and classical Greece. It seems to have been deployed only rarely, and usually against deposed tyrants or army leaders who ran afoul of their soldiers (see Gras 1984:83–85). The episode in *Iphigenia at Aulis* could clearly be classified as the latter.

[114] The segments I have deleted from the Thucydidean passage merely relate the reasons the armies were upset (namely that each side fancied its chances). A second account of this incident is found in Diodorus Siculus 12.78.5–6, and it falls along the general lines of Thucydides' narration.

ἐσιέναι κρίνουσιν, ἤρξαντο λεύειν. ὁ δὲ καταφυγὼν ἐπὶ τὸν βωμὸν περιγίγνεται· τὰ μέντοι χρήματα ἐδήμευσαν αὐτοῦ.

Thucydides 5.60.2, 5.60.4–6

The Spartans and their allies followed [Agis'] lead out of respect for the law, but amongst themselves they blamed him loudly [for denying them certain victory] ... the army therefore withdrew blaming Agis, and returned to their respective homes. The Argives, on the other hand, were even louder in blaming those who had made the truce without consulting the people ... and when they had withdrawn, they began to stone [Thrasylus] in the Charadrus, the very place they hold military trials before entering the city. He survived by fleeing to the altar. Nevertheless, they confiscated his property.[115]

The differences in the behaviors of the two armies is highlighted by the fact that both sides consider their leaders to be "responsible" (*en aitiai*) for costing them the battle. The Spartans and their allies return to their cities unhappy, but they do not rebel against or otherwise punish Agis.[116] The Argives, on the other hand, look at Thrasylus' action as a betrayal of the collective will, and they react with incomparably greater severity by attempting to stone their leader to death.

The fact that this stoning took place in the normal venue for military trials lends a veneer of legitimacy to the Argives' actions, but reading between the lines we see that Thucydides suggests otherwise. To begin, he specifically emphasizes that the Spartans had maintained their collective cool "out of respect for the law"; no such explanation is supplied for the Argives' reaction, and we may thus infer that Thucydides sees the stoning as a deviation from legal standards. Moreover, had this stoning actually been mandated by the military tribunal (such as it may have been), it is unlikely that fleeing to an altar would have been sufficient to guarantee Thrasylus' long-term survival. In fact, Diodorus tells us that it was not the altar that saved him, but a great deal of supplication (Diodorus Siculus 12.78.5: πολλῆς δεήσεως), and Forsdyke correctly points out that this amounts to an "emotional appeal ... rather than a formal defence."[117] This in turn suggests that neither the stoning nor the pardon occurred within the context of a legal procedure. Finally, the fact that his property was subsequently confiscated shows that an actual legal ruling was made,

---

[115] I am indebted to Richard Crawley's translation for a number of these turns of phrase.

[116] Diodorus says that the Spartans took legal action against Agis, but that he escaped punishment by promising to make up for his error (*Bibliotheca* 12.78.6).

[117] Forsdyke 2008:30.

and it did not result in an execution. As such, the stoning of Thrasylus appears to be an example of spontaneous and extra-legal activity, one that is enacted against a general by his army. Most importantly, this anecdote suggests that the stoning would push at least some members of the audience to recognize that the Achaean army at Aulis is acting beyond the limits of legal behavior.

This dubious characterization of the Achaean army at Aulis is further enhanced by other information that we learn during the course of Achilles' conversation with Clytemnestra. Achilles remains firm in his intention to defend Iphigenia's life, and he has brought with him the weapons to prove it. As he prepares to make his stand, he provides one final piece of testimony that returns us to the question of authority at Aulis, and completes the *Iphigenia at Aulis*'s critical re-evaluation of the Achaean army's power structures:

> ΚΛ ἥξει δ' ὅστις ἅψεται κόρης;
> ΑΧ μυρίοι γ', ἄξει δ' Ὀδυσσεύς.
> ΚΛ ἆρ' ὁ Σισύφου γόνος;
> ΑΧ αὐτὸς οὗτος.
> ΚΛ ἴδια πράσσων ἢ στρατοῦ ταχθεὶς ὕπο;
> ΑΧ αἱρεθεὶς ἑκών.
> ΚΛ πονηράν γ' αἵρεσιν, μιαιφονεῖν.
> ΑΧ ἀλλ' ἐγὼ σχήσω νιν.
> ΚΛ ἄξει δ' οὐχ ἑκοῦσαν ἁρπάσας;
> ΑΧ δηλαδὴ ξανθῆς ἐθείρας.

Iphigenia at Aulis 1361–1366

CLYTEMNESTRA: Who will come to seize the girl?
ACHILLES: Thousands, and Odysseus will lead her away.[118]
CLYTEMNESTRA: The son of Sisyphus?
ACHILLES: The very one.
CLYTEMNESTRA: Pursuing his own interests, or appointed by the army?
ACHILLES: He was chosen willingly.
CLYTEMNESTRA: Murder is a poor choice indeed.
ACHILLES: But I will keep him at bay.

---

[118] Following the note by Stockert 1992 vol. 2:581. Stockert argues that ἄξει is in reference only to Clytemnestra's question of "[τὶς] ἅψεται κόρης," but not in reference to the μύριοι, who are themselves the answer to Clytemnestra's first question ([τὶς] ἥξει). This is feasible on a grammatical level—the particle δὲ suggests we have two short, separate clauses—but it is especially convincing in light of line 1364, which shows that a rather peculiar relationship exists between Odysseus and the *ochlos*.

> CLYTEMNESTRA: What, will he drag her off against her will?
> ACHILLES: By her golden hair if need be.

Two things immediately stand out in this passage: the first is the extreme violence of the affair, exemplified by Odysseus' willingness to drag Iphigenia off by her hair;[119] the second is the return of Odysseus to the center of the fray. As it turns out, the Myrmidons, and indeed the rest of the Achaeans, are not acting entirely on their own, but in concert with another *basileus*.

At first glance, this revelation might seem to bring us a touch closer to the idea of elite authority that we have seen disintegrate at Aulis; after all, one can now say that the Achaeans are at least following a *basileus*. But Odysseus is not acting as a Homeric leader would.[120] The wording of 1363-1364 is crucial. Clytemnestra first asks whether Odysseus is "pursuing his own interests, or [has been] sent by the army." Neither of these choices suggests that Odysseus is providing inspiring leadership for the Achaeans. This is obvious in the case that he has been "sent" by the army, in which case he would actually be following their orders.[121] But even if he is coming of his own volition, Clytemnestra's suggestion that he is *prassôn idia* is equally alarming. *Ta idia* were regularly juxtaposed to *ta koina*[122] ("public matters"), and in fifth-century Greece a very clear strain of thought emerges that sees the two as fundamentally incompatible: that the pursuit of private interests was deleterious to the interests of the community.[123] Regardless of whether Odysseus is following the *ochlos* or leading them in pursuit of his own interests, it is certain that he exemplifies a negative model of leadership.

And according to Achilles, Odysseus is actually both leading and following: having been "chosen willingly," he is now pursuing his own interests and being led by the mob.[124] In this way, Odysseus is remarkably similar to Athens' post-Periclean leaders who, at least according to Thucydides, began by looking

---

[119] Stockert 1992 vol. 2:582 points out that such an act is similar to the "humiliation" to which prisoners of war are subject, as for example in Euripides *Trojan Women* 881-882, and Euripides *Andromache* 401-402. Such comparisons hardly put the actions of the Achaean army in a positive light, in particular since they are theoretically seeking to "prevent the abductions of Greek brides" (*Iphigenia at Aulis* 1266: παῦσαί τε λέκτρων ἁρπαγὰς Ἑλληνικῶν,) that they are about to commit.

[120] As is also suggested by Griffin 2007:200.

[121] Lush 2015, 217 also highlights "the passivity of the participles" here.

[122] Stockert 1992 vol. 2:581.

[123] Cf. Thucydides 2.61.4; 4.59.4–60.1; 6.12.2; 8.83.3; Sophocles *Oedipus Tyrannus* 634–636; Euripides *Hecuba* 641–643. Though naturally Pindar claims to further both private and public interests at once: *Olympian* 13.49.

[124] Lush 2015:217, describes this as "the dialectical and mutually dependent relationship of popular demagogue to constituent mass."

towards their "private ambition and personal profit" (2.65.7: κατὰ τὰς ἰδίας φιλοτιμίας καὶ ἴδια κέρδη) and ended by "surrendering the affairs of the state to the whims of the *dêmos*" (2.65.10: ἡδονὰς τῷ δήμῳ καὶ τὰ πράγματα ἐνδιδόναι). Everything we hear about Odysseus in *Iphigenia at Aulis*—his obsession with *philotimia*, his eagerness to pursue his personal interests, his willingness to follow the Achaean mob—all of this serves to depict him as a contemporary paradigm of a poor leader.

4. Conclusions

Throughout his report to Clytemnestra, Achilles confirms virtually all of Agamemnon's earlier fears, and he definitively characterizes the Achaean army at Aulis as one which is thoroughly contemporary, and also thoroughly in control of the situation. Achilles' attempt to speak in Iphigenia's defense results in *thorubos*, an outcome that was unimaginable in the world of the *Iliad* yet common in fifth-century Athens. This *thorubos* then quickly devolves into an attempt to stone Achilles, one that recalls a rare yet significant episode of stoning from only a few years prior. Finally, Achilles' description of Odysseus' particular role in this furious mob closely resembles Thucydides' condemnation of Athenian leaders during the Peloponnesian War.

The contemporary and democratic nature of the structures of power and authority at Aulis would thus have been clear to many in the audience at the Theater of Dionysus. How precisely the audience might have reacted to it is, of course, impossible to know with certainty, but we may make some educated guesses. First of all, there must have been a great variety in responses: those who saw the situation as Thucydides did would surely have seen the Euripides' Achaeans as a negative example of a democratic mob gone astray, while those who eagerly participated in ecclesiastic *thoruboi*, or advocated violent reprisals of Athenian generals, may have been unperturbed, or indeed delighted to see such representations on stage. But we may imagine that these scenes would have struck a particular chord within members of the audience whose remorse regarding the Arginousae generals was still fresh. And here, Euripides' use of the Homeric subtext would have been a powerful factor. Seeing the Achaean *ochlos* very nearly kill Achilles himself, an act that surely would have doomed their chances to succeed in the Trojan war, not only throws into relief the subversion of Homer's power structures: it also demonstrates, at a safe distance, the potentially devastating consequences of democratic approaches to military leadership.

4

Duplicity at Aulis

Euripides, Aeschylus, and the Gendering of Deceptive Speech

WHILE IN THE PREVIOUS CHAPTER, I focused exclusively on the manner in which Euripides recasts the conflicts of the *Iliad* in *Iphigenia at Aulis*, in this chapter I shift the focus onto the manner in which the tragedy engages with Aeschylus' *Agamemnon*.[1] The connection between the two plays is natural and, one could say, almost inevitable. The central question of *Iphigenia at Aulis*—the sacrifice of Iphigenia—is the event that precipitates the dramatic action of Aeschylus' *Agamemnon*. This event is described by the Chorus in the parodos of Aeschylus' play (Aeschylus *Agamemnon* 160–247), and it is invoked as the primary reason for Clytemnestra's murder of her husband (Aeschylus *Agamemnon* 1412–1418, 1432, but cf. also 154–155).[2] In *Iphigenia at Aulis*, conversely, Euripides essentially unpacks the parodos of *Agamemnon*, turning 100 lines into 1600 and breathing life into Agamemnon's indecision and Iphigenia's death, all while providing us with a surprising glimpse of Agamemnon's relationship with Clytemnestra before the sacrifice. Much like it does to the *Iliad*, Iphigenia at Aulis functions as a narrative prequel to Aeschylus' play.

---

[1] This is by no means the only play in which Euripides reworks *Agamemnon*. Garner 1990:165 notes that *Agamemnon* is "the most frequent source of imitation" in several of Euripides' plays. On top of *Iphigenia at Aulis*, Garner also points to *Trojan Women*, *Iphigenia in Tauris*, and *Helen*.

[2] Though Iphigenia's sacrifice is not given as the motive for the murder of Agamemnon in Homer (cf. *Odyssey* 1.35–40; 3.262–272; 11.405–434), by the end of the fifth century BCE nearly every account of the affair stresses the relationship between Agamemnon's death and Iphigenia's sacrifice. Besides Aeschylus, cf. Pindar *Pythian* 11.17–27, (Pindar wonders whether it was the sacrifice of Iphigenia or Clytemnestra's adulterous ways that led the queen to commit murder); Sophocles *Electra* 534–551; and Euripides *Electra* 1011–1031. In all likelihood, the tragedians are in fact drawing on an earlier tradition present in Stesichorus: see Davies and Finglass 2014:489–490.

As I argue in this chapter, however, *Iphigenia at Aulis* does not simply offer an earlier episode in the lives of Aeschylus' characters: he radically alters the roles that the characters themselves play, casting Agamemnon as the deceiver, and Clytemnestra as the deceived. The play thus rejects Aeschylus' portrayal of verbal treachery as the province of female speakers, and projects it onto the leading male figure of the play. In the process, *Iphigenia at Aulis* mirrors contemporary Athenian concerns about the use of false speech in the political arena. The play's intertextual relationship with *Agamemnon* is thus another case in which Euripides uses a canonical text as a backdrop against which to illuminate a crucial political issue for his audience.

1. Aeschylus' *Agamemnon* as Sub-text:
Evidence and Interpretations

Aeschylus' *Agamemnon* is an inevitable and ever-present subtext for *Iphigenia at Aulis*, and Euripides goes out of his way to call his audience's attention to this fact, filling his drama with dramatic elements that recall Aeschylus' tragedy. The fact that Clytemnestra shares the stage with Agamemnon throughout the play is significant in and of itself, for one can hardly help but be reminded of their famous encounter in Aeschylus' play. Following Aeschylus, Euripides makes Argos, rather than the traditional Mycenae, the home of Agamemnon and Clytemnestra,[3] a detail Euripides dwells on to the extent that he mentions Argos more times in *Iphigenia at Aulis* alone than Aeschylus does in the entire *Oresteia*. And with Clytemnestra's entrance on a wagon, he "evoke[s] the ominous arrivals for a sacrificial death of Agamemnon and Cassandra at Argos in Aeschylus' *Agamemnon*."[4] Before Clytemnestra speaks her first lines, we are already reminded of the royal couple's Aeschylean showdown.

Specific verbal allusions add to the sense that Euripides' play is, at its most basic level, playing off of Aeschylus' *Agamemnon*. When Euripides' Agamemnon comes to the conclusion that Iphigenia must be sacrificed, he refers to it as "the yoke of necessity" (*Iphigenia at Aulis* 443), paraphrasing the words that Aeschylus' Agamemnon (*Agamemnon* 218) when he comes to that very conclusion.[5] In both plays, Agamemnon's first form of address to Clytemnestra is "offspring of Leda" (Euripides *Iphigenia at Aulis* 686 and 1106; Aeschylus *Agamemnon* 914: Λήδας

---

[3] Eisner 1979:161. Sophocles, of course, moves his *Electra* back to Mycenae.

[4] Foley 1985:70–71; Aélion 1983:106, makes the same connection. Diggle 1994 doubts the authenticity of the entrance, though it is by no means certain that her entrance by chariot is a later invention simply because the text itself is interpolated.

[5] Garner 1990:174; Sorum 1992:537 (I borrow Sorum's translation here).

γένεθλον).[6] The use of the matronymic is on the whole very rare in Euripides,[7] and this particular moniker appears nowhere else in extant Greek literature, so this seems to be an intentional reclamation of the Aeschylean appellation. And perhaps no allusion is more obvious than Clytemnestra threatening to kill Agamemnon upon his return (*Iphigenia at Aulis* 1180–1182), the very act she accomplishes in Aeschylus' play. These allusions make it very likely that an audience familiar with *Agamemnon*, as was Euripides', would certainly have recognized the references to Aeschylus' play.[8]

Scholars have also long observed Euripides' reclamation of Aeschylean themes and language, but they have often seen *Agamemnon*'s influence on *Iphigenia at Aulis* as unilateral and overwhelming. An emblematic assessment is provided by Sorum, who argues that the inflexibility of tradition is most visible in Clytemnestra's attempt to alter it.[9] This analysis is consistent with the critical consensus,[10] but it overlooks the fact that Clytemnestra's failure to persuade Agamemnon is in and of itself a major departure from Aeschylus' play. Indeed, it is her very ability to persuade her husband through the use of deceptive speech that is perhaps her most marked quality in Aeschylus' play. Euripides may be constrained by tradition on the level of plot, but he faces no such constraints when it comes to the characterization, speech, and the relationships of the main players. And indeed, much of the dramatic action in *Iphigenia at Aulis* involves a recasting of the Agamemnon/Clytemnestra relationship, whereby Clytemnestra becomes the deceived victim, and Agamemnon the deceiver. By looking closely at *Iphigenia at Aulis*' portrayal of Clytemnestra and—even more importantly—Agamemnon, we may also understand just how radically Euripides engages with the Aeschylean tradition.

---

[6]   Garner 1990:174.

[7]   Stockert 1992 vol. 2:211.

[8]   The question of whether or not Aeschylus' plays were re-performed at the City Dionysia in the last quarter of the fifth century is still debated. Among recent scholars, Revermann 2006a:72–73 and Csapo 2010:97 argue in favor of reperformance at the City Dionysia, while Lamari (2015 and 2017:76) is cautiously in favor. Biles 2006 argues against such reproductions at the City Dionysia, but even he agrees that the "potential role [of the Rural Dionysia] in keeping Aeschylus alive during the fifth century is a point that should be kept in mind" (p. 211). (For more on the Rural Dionysia, see e.g. Csapo and Wilson 2015:319–328.) Regardless of the venue and frequency of reproductions, we see that Aristophanes can presume a high level of "audience competence" throughout the Aeschylus-Euripides *agôn* of *Frogs* (see Revermann 2006b:esp. 119–120). Since *Frogs* and *Iphigenia at Aulis* were both performed in 405, we can confirm that at least some of the audience of *Iphigenia at Aulis* must have been able to pick up on even subtle allusions to Aeschylean tragedy, let alone the very open engagement that Euripides creates throughout his play.

[9]   Sorum 1992:538.

[10]   Along these same lines, see also: Foley 1985:97; Luschnig 1988:77–78; and Gamel 1999:320.

2. Aeschylus' Clytemnestra:
The Epitome of the Deceptive Woman

Numerous scholars have by now demonstrated that in *Agamemnon*, Clytemnestra is a consummately persuasive woman, one who gains her ends primarily through deceit and guile. Among many others, Simon Goldhill has written extensively about Clytemnestra's striking and successful use of "multivalent language."[11] Aeschylus makes Clytemnestra a paradigm of deception within a context of explicit antagonism between male and female,[12] to the extent that she comes to epitomize the extreme danger that women represent to men, a danger that must be suppressed.[13] Furthermore, Clytemnestra is a threat precisely because of her ability to manipulate and deceive the men around her, and Aeschylus emphasizes that her capacity for *dolos* ("cunning" or "treachery") is a specifically feminine trait. When the exiled Aegisthus is finally allowed to come on stage, he responds to the deluge of comments on his cowardice by noting that it was only natural that Clytemnestra be in charge of the *dolos*: τὸ γὰρ δολῶσαι πρὸς γυναικὸς ἦν σαφῶς (*Agamemnon* 1636: "setting the trap was clearly the woman's job"). The comment mirrors other references in the play to Clytemnestra (and her actions) as *dolios*[14] ("treacherous") and confirms that not only is Clytemnestra dangerous, but that she is dangerous in a paradigmatically feminine way.

The threat represented by Clytemnestra's ability to deceive is emphasized throughout the play by both her speech and actions. Clytemnestra herself acknowledges as much:

> πολλῶν πάροιθεν καιρίως εἰρημένων
> τἀναντί' εἰπεῖν οὐκ ἐπαισχυνθήσομαι.
> πῶς γάρ τις ἐχθροῖς ἐχθρὰ πορσύνων, φίλοις

---

[11] See esp. Goldhill 1984:68–79; Goldhill 1986:1–32. Numerous other scholars have also treated the issue of Clytemnestra's speech: Neustadt 1929; Betensky 1978; Sevieri 1991; McClure 1997 and 1999:73–79; Foley 2001:207–234.

[12] On this, see Goldhill 1992:37–40. Goldhill provides a useful catalogue of instances in *Agamemnon* in which the male/female polarity is explicitly stressed.

[13] As Zeitlin 1978 argues, Clytemnestra's attempt to seize power in Agamemnon symbolizes the mythical "Rule of Women," wherein male is to be subjugated to the female.

[14] Clytemnestra is called treacherous (δολία) in the parados (*Agamemnon* 155); Agamemnon is said to die by a "treacherous fate" (*Agamemnon* 1495, 1519: δολίωι μόρωι); Cassandra foresees that Agamemnon will die in "a basin of murderous treachery" (*Agamemnon* 1129: δολοφόνου λέβητος); Clytemnestra herself obliquely refers to her treachery when she falsely claims that her excuse for Orestes' absence is credible because it "holds no *dolos*" (*Agamemnon* 886: οὐ δόλον φέρει).

1375   δοκοῦσιν εἶναι, πημονῆς ἀρκύστατ' ἂν
φράξειεν, ὕψος κρεῖσσον ἐκπηδήματος

Agamemnon 1372–1376

Having said, earlier, many things opportune,
I will not now be ashamed to say the opposite.
How else could one, tending evil for enemies
1375   seeming as friends, secure dense nets
of ruin at a height too great to be overleapt.

Shortly after murdering Agamemnon, Clytemnestra makes two crucial admissions: that she has engaged in deceptive speech throughout the first three quarters of the play; and that she has done so with the specific aim of betraying and destroying her (male) adversary.

Clytemnestra's actions are no less tricky than her words, and they support the notion that Aeschylus is portraying a specifically feminine type of deceit. Once Agamemnon arrives, evidently persuaded by the duplicitous message Clytemnestra had sent him, a verbal contest takes place on-stage. Clytemnestra must convince her husband to walk upon colorful garments against his objections, and it is implicit that his defeat in this *agôn* represents his death. Once inside, Clytemnestra will entangle him in another garment as he exits his bath,[15] thus ensuring that Agamemnon can "neither flee nor ward off his fate"[16] as she kills him. The use of woven garments in her plot is significant. As Jenkins notes, "the female art of weaving provided a natural metaphor for the art of deception,"[17] and it had been exploited by other mythical women in order to overcome male adversaries.[18] Aeschylus provides Clytemnestra with a murderous plot that is peculiarly feminine, and this femininity is emphasized repeatedly: Clytemnestra does not mention the weapon she uses to actually *kill*

---

[15] Or perhaps it is the same garment upon which Agamemnon had just trodden. Cf. Taplin 1977:314–315.

[16] *Agamemnon* 1381: ὡς μήτε φεύγειν μήτ' ἀμύνεσθαι μόρον.

[17] Jenkins 1985:115.

[18] Most notably Penelope in the *Odyssey*, but the story of Procne and Philomela is another early example of women weaving deceit. Procne's husband Tereus had raped Philomela and cut out her tongue to ensure her silence. Not to be outdone by her brother-in-law's treachery, Philomela wove a garment depicting the events and sent it to her sister Procne. The two then teamed up to kill Procne's son (who is, of course, also Tereus' child) and "boiled him down and served him to an unwitting Tereus." Cf. Apollodorus *Bibliotheca* 3.14.8.

her husband,[19] yet she dwells on her description of this treacherous *peplos*.[20] In total, it is mentioned five times by four different characters,[21] and it is the garment that, in all likelihood, covers Agamemnon's dead body when he is brought out on stage.[22]

Aeschylus thus captures his audience's imagination with descriptions and, in the end, a display of this *peplos*, leaving no doubt as to the feminine nature of Clytemnestra's treachery. This powerful poetic creation has reverberations that extend well beyond the world of the drama. First of all, Clytemnestra presents a formidable paradigm for deceptive and dangerous women. The power and influence of this paradigm is illustrated by the imitations Aeschylus' Clytemnestra would spawn, especially in Greek tragedy. Among others, Euripides' Medea and Hecuba, and Sophocles' Deianeira all use deception in order to bring about the death of a man; all of them are described as committing *doloi*,[23] and all three use garments as part of their plots. All of these can be seen as dramatic descendants of Aeschylus' Clytemnestra. This proliferation of deadly and deceptive women is a testament to the power of the Aeschylean paradigm in the fifth century BCE.

Moreover, the motif of the deceptive woman is not simply a cause for concern for male characters in drama; its implications extend out to the world of the audience. As Goldhill notes, "[l]anguage, when Clytemnestra uses it, becomes frightening. The uncertainty she introduces is not merely verbal, but works also towards the death of her husband, the king—the overthrow of social order."[24] This dynamic is obvious within the context of the Argive monarchy: Agamemnon loses both his life and throne, and Argos comes to be, in essence, ruled by a female usurper. But it is equally troubling within the context of Athenian democracy, a form of government that relied upon public speech in order to inform political decisions and legal judgments. As Laura McClure has shown, in fact, the rest of the *Oresteia* enacts the resolution of this problem, culminating in Athena "supplant[ing] the ambiguous and deceptive speech of Clytemnestra" with "a powerful form of persuasion stripped of feminine

---

[19] *Agamemnon* 1384–1386: Clytemnestra describes "striking" Agamemnon twice, and then a third time, but does not say with what.

[20] According to her, it is a "boundless net" (*Agamemnon* 1382: ἄπειρον ἀμφίβληστρον) and an "evil wealth of cloth" (*Agamemnon* 1383: πλοῦτον εἵματος κακόν).

[21] Respectively Cassandra (twice), Clytemnestra, the Chorus, and Aegisthus (*Agamemnon* 1115–1116 and 1126; 1383; 1492; 1580). The obsession with this device continues in *Choephoroi*, as both Electra and Orestes cannot resist but mention it (*Choephoroi* 494, 999–1000). For a fuller discussion of all these references to the *peplos*, see Seaford 1984:247–254.

[22] Taplin 1977:325; Seaford 1984:250.

[23] Cf. Sophocles *Trachiniae* 850; Euripides *Medea* 783 and *Hecuba* 1269.

[24] Goldhill 1986:14.

guile."[25] In short, Aeschylus' Clytemnestra shows us that the type of speech in which she engages, whether it be categorized as deceptive female speech or more broadly as an outsider's "manipulation of public and persuasive speech genres out of self-interest,"[26] represents an existential threat to the basic functioning of democracy.

It is difficult to say whether this gendered depiction of deceptive speech matched Athenian expectations when the *Oresteia* was produced, as we have very little evidence about mainstream attitudes towards these questions in 458 BCE. We have much more evidence for the final quarter of the fifth century, but nearly all of it suggests that these concerns were not necessarily linked to women, but were instead focalized on the problem of deceptive speech within the (male) political sphere. This anxiety seems to have been increasing throughout the latter half of the fifth century, spurred by the influence of rhetoric within democratic Athens and, perhaps, by sophistic theories that equated persuasive speech with deception.[27] The existence of the trope that "words" (*logoi*) were often inconsistent with the basic facts (*erga*) of reality[28]—a trope upon which *Iphigenia at Aulis* draws heavily—suggests that these anxieties would have been broadly familiar to an Athenian audience.

The events after the battle of Arginousae are again instructive in this regard. As discussed in the previous chapter, six of the generals who had led the Athenians to victory at Arginousae were brought to trial on charges that they had neglected to pick up the men who had been shipwrecked during the battle (Xenophon *Hellenica* 1.7.4). After a series of reversals—the generals had almost talked themselves out of trouble before nightfall, and a festival, intervened—they were all condemned to death and executed (Xenophon *Hellenica* 1.7.4–34).

---

[25] McClure 1999:110–111.

[26] McClure 1999:111.

[27] Cf. Gorgias *Encomium of Helen* 11: "Many speakers on many subjects persuade and have persuaded many people by molding false arguments" (ὅσοι δὲ ὅσους περὶ ὅσων καὶ ἔπεισαν καὶ πείθουσι δὲ ψευδῆ λόγον πλάσαντες). There is no agreement as to whether or not Gorgias believed that all persuasion is a form of deception, or if he simply emphasized the natural gulf that lay between the reality of things and the way that they are described in language (for varying views see e.g. Kerferd 1981:78–81; Verdenius 1981; Porter 1993; and Valiavitcharska 2006). But the fact that he addresses such issues in the few writings of his that survive suggests that such discussions were *en vogue*, at least in some circles in the late fifth century.

[28] A. Parry 1981:48, states that this concept "becomes common coin in the Vth century." The dichotomy between *ergon* and *logos* is seen as especially problematic in Thucydides, on which cf. A. Parry 1970:3–20; A. Parry 1981:*passim*; Ober 1998:53–63. Outside of Thucydides, the juxtaposition between *logos* and *ergon* comes up frequently in oratory (cf. Antiphon *On the Choreutes* 47.5 and *On the Murder of Herodes* 84.12; Isocrates 3.1.8 and 8.134.2) philosophy (cf. Plato *Apology* 32a and 32d and *Gorgias* 450d), and also drama (cf. Euripides *Alcestis* 339, *Phoenician Women* 389; Sophocles *Electra* 357, 893). Euripides had even made this contrast the central conceit of *Helen* (cf. Segal 1971), a tragedy produced only a few years before *Iphigenia at Aulis*.

In the aftermath, however, the Athenian citizens "repented," and lashed out at those who had urged the execution. The charge against these men was that they had "deceived the *dêmos*."[29] Both Xenophon and Diodorus provide accounts of this incident, and although they diverge on many important details,[30] they agree that the Athenian *dêmos* felt it had been deceived, and that specific charges of deception were subsequently levied against those who had urged the prosecution of the generals. This is crucial, since it represents the "only certain instance of *probolai* against deceivers of the demos" in fifth-century Athens.[31] That fact alone would seem to indicate that the anxiety about elite deception had come to a head in 405 BCE, when *Iphigenia at Aulis* was produced.

Xenophon adds several details which, even if not entirely accurate,[32] nevertheless indicate that an atmosphere of distrust had permeated Athens. For example, the historian claims that Theramenes, one of the leaders of the motion to prosecute the generals, went so far as to hire people to appear at the assembly and impersonate the relatives of those who had died at Arginousae (Xenophon *Hellenica* 1.7.8) in order to inflame the *dêmos*. Xenophon also reports that Theramenes bribed a certain Callixenus to speak before the assembly and propose the extraordinary (and "probably illegal"[33]) measure of trying all the generals together (Xenophon *Hellenica* 1.7.9–10). After this, another man addressed the assembly and claimed to have survived the shipwreck by chance, and to have been urged by his drowning companions "to report to the *dêmos* that the generals had not picked up the men who had done the most in service of the fatherland."[34] As if to confirm the pervasive anxiety about the use of deceptive speech in this public sphere, the one defense speaker whom Xenophon records (Euryptolemus) prefaces his remarks with the comment that that he will "advise [the assembly] in such a way that you cannot be deceived

---

[29] Xenophon *Hellenica* 1.7.35: τὸν δῆμον ἐξηπάτησαν; Diodorus Siculus 13.103.2: τὸν δῆμον ἐξηπατηκώς.

[30] Most notably in their explanation of Theramenes' role in the conviction of the eight generals. For a concise analysis of the divergences in the two accounts, the questions that these divergences raise, and some possible solutions (especially concerning our interpretations of Theramenes), see Andrewes 1974.

[31] Christ 1992, 340 fn 20. Kremmydas 2013, 51, adds to this tally the prosecution of Miltiades as described in Herodotus 6.136.

[32] Andrewes 1974 tends to cast doubt on these claims; Sordi 1981 is more sanguine about Xenophon's accuracy.

[33] Roberts 1977, 111.

[34] Xenophon *Hellenica* 1.7.11: ἀπαγγεῖλαι τῷ δήμῳ ὅτι οἱ στρατηγοὶ οὐκ ἀνείλοντο τοὺς ἀρίστους ὑπὲρ τῆς πατρίδος γενομένους. Xenophon does not actually say that this man was planted, but the structure of the narrative and the nature of the remarks suggest that he was.

either by me or by anyone else."[35] Whether or not Xenophon is correct about all the details of the pre-trial debate, his narration implies a belief that numerous underhanded measures had been taken and, even more importantly, that the Athenian citizenry expected this to be the case.

These events took place in the months directly preceding *Iphigenia at Aulis*, and while Euripides died shortly before this incident occurred, and so cannot possibly be referring to it directly, the episode must have weighed heavily in the minds of the audience. Perhaps more importantly, it speaks to the feelings of mistrust that imbued Athenian democratic discourse at the time. Moreover, other episodes confirm that the concerns about deceptive speech in the public sphere had been peaking for some time. A classic example is provided by Thucydides in his description of the Mytilenian debate. Nominally, at least, the Athenian assembly had met to revisit the decision to execute the entire population of Mytilene. In Thucydides' retelling, however, the discussion quickly devolves into a broader controversy about the extent to which deceptive speech pervades the Athenian democracy. Cleon argues that whoever speaks "will try to mislead" the people (Thucydides 3.38.2: παράγειν πειράσεται), while the people themselves are "the best at being deceived by a fancy turn of phrase."[36] Speaking against Cleon on the subject of the executions, Diodotus manages to confirm his rival's indictment of democratic discourse, claiming that all speakers must lie to the assembly in order to be believed (Thucydides 3.43.2), and that in Athens itself "it is impossible to do good without resorting to deceit."[37]

In *Knights*, Aristophanes also casts serious doubt upon the integrity of public discourse in democratic Athens. The main characters of the play are a thinly disguised Cleon and a fictional rival (the Sausage Seller) who compete to become the leading politician in Athens. Instances of both Cleon and the Sausage Seller telling blatant and self-serving lies are so abundant in *Knights* that it would be impossible to mention them all. The two characters square off in specious *agônes* before both the *boulê* (not shown on-stage) and the *Dêmos*. At the *boulê* level, we hear that Cleon invents outlandish—yet "most persuasive" (*Knights* 629: πιθανώταθ')—tales of conspiracies until the Sausage Seller, seeing the *boulê* "deceived by this crookery" (*Knights* 633: τοῖς φενακισμοῖσιν ἐξαπατωμένην), steps in. He distracts them with the news of a steep drop in the price of sardines, an initiative clever enough to bring him victory. The Chorus celebrates the Sausage Seller's victory by claiming that with his *poikiloi doloi* (*Knights* 686), he is more than a match for Cleon. The evidence available

---

[35] Xenophon *Hellenica* 1.7.19: συμβουλεύω δ' ὑμῖν, ἐν οἷς οὔθ' ὑπ' ἐμοῦ οὔθ' ὑπ' ἄλλου οὐδενὸς ἔστιν ἐξαπατηθῆναι ὑμᾶς.

[36] Thucydides 3.38.5: μετὰ καινότητος μὲν λόγου ἀπατᾶσθαι ἄριστοι.

[37] Thucydides 3.43.2–3: εὖ ποιῆσαι ἐκ τοῦ προφανοῦς μὴ ἐξαπατήσαντα ἀδύνατον·

in Aristophanes, alongside that presented by Thucydides and the accounts of events after Arginousai, all suggest that *Iphigenia at Aulis* was produced within an atmosphere in which there was deep skepticism about the credibility of political speech.

3. Clytemnestra and Agamemnon at Aulis: Inverting the Aeschylean Model

3.1 Prologue: Agamemnon's First Deceptions

Long before Clytemnestra arrives to reprise the famous *agôn* from *Agamemnon*, Euripides suggests that his characters at Aulis may reflect real-life concerns about deceitful politicians. Agamemnon is actually the first to admit that he has not been entirely truthful during the events leading up to Iphigenia's sacrifice, and it does not take long for him to do so. Indeed, we first find out about his dishonesty in the iambic section of the prologue:

> κἀν δέλτου πτυχαῖς
> γράψας ἔπεμψα πρὸς δάμαρτα τὴν ἐμὴν
> 100 πέμπειν Ἀχιλλεῖ θυγατέρ' ὡς γαμουμένην,
> τό τ' ἀξίωμα τἀνδρὸς ἐκγαυρούμενος,
> συμπλεῖν τ' Ἀχαιοῖς οὕνεκ' οὐ θέλοι λέγων,
> εἰ μὴ παρ' ἡμῶν εἶσιν ἐς Φθίαν λέχος·
> πειθὼ γὰρ εἶχον τήνδε πρὸς δάμαρτ' ἐμήν,
> 105 ψευδῆ συνάψας †ἀντὶ παρθένου†[38] γάμον.

Iphigenia at Aulis 98–105

> I wrote a letter
> and sent it to my wife, asking her to send
> 100 our daughter here to wed Achilles,
> while also boasting of the man's reputation
> and saying he would not sail with the Achaeans
> unless a bride came from us to his bed in Phthia.
> This is how I managed to persuade my wife:
> 105 by contriving a false marriage for the girl.

Here, Agamemnon comes clean to a trusted slave (referred to henceforth as the *Presbutês*), but only because he needs him to deliver a new letter to Clytemnestra

---

[38] Diggle marks these two words (ἀντὶ παρθένου) with cruces, but this must certainly be the point.

telling her to remain at home (*Iphigenia at Aulis* 115–123). As such, a mere 100 lines into the play we learn that Agamemnon has already perpetrated a series of deceptions: he has lured Clytemnestra and Iphigenia to Aulis with the promise of a "false marriage" to Achilles, and he has compounded this lie by inventing a story about Achilles' insistence on the arrangement. The purpose of this false marriage—this *dolos* as it will later be called[39]—is to arrange the sacrifice of his daughter (cf. *Iphigenia at Aulis* 89–98), and the efficacy of these lies quickly becomes evident. When Clytemnestra finally arrives with Iphigenia, Clytemnestra is particularly curious to know more about Achilles' provenance and the plans for the wedding (*Iphigenia at Aulis* 698–722). Agamemnon's lies have clearly been persuasive thus far.

Furthermore, his pre-play machinations are not limited to the deceit of his wife and daughter. As we soon learn, he has not been entirely honest with Achilles either. When the *Presbutês* warns him that Achilles may be enraged to be left "bereft of his marriage,"[40] Agamemnon brushes off this concern on the grounds that Achilles doesn't even know about the arrangement:[41]

> ὄνομ', οὐκ ἔργον, παρέχων Ἀχιλεὺς
> οὐκ οἶδε γάμους, οὐδ' ὅτι πράσσομεν,
> 130   οὐδ' ὅτι κείνῳ παῖδ' ἐπεφήμισα
>
> *Iphigenia at Aulis* 128–130

> Achilles is providing his name, not the act,
> and knows not of the wedding, nor of what
> 130   we are doing, nor that I have pledged my child to him

Agamemnon refers quite overtly to the contemporary trope that words and speech (*logos*, but also commonly *onoma*,[42] as we see here) have only a tenuous relationship to fact or reality (*ergon*). Euripides' audience surely would have recognized this reference to such a "popular distinction."[43] But while the gulf between *logos* and *ergon* was a source of anxiety for many Athenians,[44] Agamemnon

---

[39] *Iphigenia at Aulis* 898, 1457.

[40] *Iphigenia at Aulis* 124–126: καὶ πῶς Ἀχιλεὺς λέκτρων ἀπλακὼν / οὐ μέγα φυσῶν θυμὸν ἐπαρεῖ / σοὶ σῇ τ' ἀλόχῳ;

[41] Foley 1985:68 notes that this may have been a Euripidean invention.

[42] *Onoma* was regularly substituted for *logos* and equally antithetical to the notion of *ergon*. Cf. A. Parry 1981:11–13. In general, the authors who juxtapose *onoma* and *ergon* are the same ones who do so with *logos* and *ergon* as well (e.g. Thucydides, Herodotus, Euripides, Isocrates, Xenophon etc.).

[43] A. Parry 1981:18–19 opposes this "popular distinction" of the *logos*/*ergon* antithesis to the "literary distinction" and the "philosophical distinction."

[44] As argued above, but on this specific subject see e.g. A. Parry 1981:76–89; and Ober 1998:53–63, but esp. 58.

seems untroubled by it; for him it is a trifling matter to manipulate *logoi* when it suits his purposes. In this, he resembles Aeschylus' Clytemnestra—both are only too happy to say "opportune things" when it suits their purposes[45]—but also politicians such as Cleon who, as we have seen, is depicted in a similar way by Thucyidides and Aristophanes.

The *Presbutês*, for his part, is unimpressed: "you've dared a terrible thing" (*Iphigenia at Aulis* 133: δεινά γ' ἐτόλμας), he tells Agamemnon, implying that he should be less cavalier about his manipulation of *logos*. Achilles' later response to the situation lends credence to the *Presbutês*' concerns, for when he eventually learns of the elaborate wedding ruse, Achilles finds little consolation in the fact that "only" his name was used to effect it:

> οὐ γὰρ ἐμπλέκειν πλοκὰς
> ἐγὼ παρέξω σῷ πόσει τοὐμὸν δέμας.
> τοὔνομα γάρ, εἰ καὶ μὴ σίδηρον ἤρατο,
> τοὐμὸν φονεύσει παῖδα σήν. τὸ δ' αἴτιον
> 940   πόσις σός. ἁγνὸν δ' οὐκέτ' ἐστὶ σῶμ' ἐμόν,
> εἰ δι' ἔμ' ὀλεῖται διά τε τοὺς ἐμοὺς γάμους

Iphigenia at Aulis 936–941

> I shall not give my person over
> to your husband so he can weave his webs.
> For even if it does not raise the sword,
> my name will murder your child. Your husband
> 940   is responsible. But my body will no longer be
> pure if she dies through me and my marriage

Achilles is clearly displeased that, unbeknownst to him, his hand in marriage has been used as bait for Agamemnon's trap. He blames Agamemnon, but notes very specifically that his name will be the murderer, and that he himself can no longer be considered chaste—in fact, he will no longer consider himself an unmarried man.[46] He too is aware of the relationship between *logos* and *ergon*, but in a manner that is more reminiscent of Thucydides or Gorgias, both of whom understood that "λόγος is opposed to ἔργα, but it can act itself as an ἔργον."[47] It is clear that the deceptive use of Achilles' name for this plot is not merely a white lie for which there will be no consequences; on the contrary, Achilles'

---

[45] As in Aeschylus *Agamemnon* 1372; see above at p. 138–139.
[46] Foley 1982:162–163.
[47] A. Parry 1981:45. Parry here refers to Gorgias, but given his analysis of Thucydides' understanding of the *logos/ergon* dynamic (cf. pp. 76–89), the words seem applicable to both.

reaction shows that Agamemnon's tendency to lie is a serious and objectionable matter. Moreover, the fact that Achilles describes Agamemnon as "weaving a web" casts Agamemnon's *dolos* in feminine terms, another reminder of his once and future killer.

Beginning in the prologue, then, the audience learns that Agamemnon has been willing to bring about his daughter's sacrifice by any (dishonest) means necessary. These include actively deceiving his wife and daughter in order to lure them to Aulis, and concealing from Achilles the fact that he has used his name as bait. Both of these lies are cast in a nefarious light, and in defending himself, Agamemnon refers to fifth-century concerns about deceptive speakers. Audience and reader alike are alerted to the possibility that this kind of deceitful behavior is central to the play. As the tragedy unfolds, two additional points will become increasingly clear: that deception is Agamemnon's primary mode of communication; and that Euripides intentionally presents him as an individual analogous to Aeschylus' Clytemnestra, the embodiment of feminine guile. While the latter of these only becomes obvious once Clytemnestra arrives near the middle of the play, the former is emphasized in the first episode.

3.2 Episode One: Agamemnon and Deceptive Speech in the Political Sphere

The parodos momentarily distracts us from the implications of Agamemnon's deceit, but Menelaus' arrival on stage brings his gamesmanship swiftly back into focus. It is only natural, though again hardly forthright of him, that Agamemnon has not told his brother that he plans to call off the wedding/sacrifice. After all, as we learned in the prologue, it was Menelaus who had insisted that they sacrifice Iphigenia.[48] When Menelaus catches the *Presbutês*, secret letter in hand, he is furious to learn that his brother has gone behind his back and back on his word. "Your mind is warped" (*Iphigenia at Aulis* 332: πλάγια γὰρ φρονεῖς), he roars, before berating Agamemnon for being οὐ βέβαιος (*Iphigenia at Aulis* 334: "inconsistent")—another key term in the *logos/ergon* dichotomy.[49] For his part, Agamemnon insists that he should be able to "manage his own household" (*Iphigenia at Aulis* 331: τὸν ἐμὸν οἰκεῖν οἶκον) as he sees fit. Given Agamemnon's earlier account of his own reticence and Menelaus' endorsement of the sacrifice, the interaction plays out in a fairly predictable manner.

---

[48] *Iphigenia at Aulis* 97–98: οὗ δή μ' ἀδελφὸς πάντα προσφέρων λόγον / ἔπεισε τλῆναι δεινά ("At which point my brother, bringing forth every argument / convinced me to dare this terrible deed").

[49] Cf. A. Parry 1981:67–68.

Menelaus' narration of prior events at Aulis, however, suggests that there is more to the case than Agamemnon's testimony. Most obviously, while Agamemnon had previously stated that he had ordered the army to disband at once (*Iphigenia at Aulis* 94–96), Menelaus' recollection is rather different:

> ἐπεὶ Κάλχας ἐν ἱεροῖς εἶπε σὴν θῦσαι κόρην
> Ἀρτέμιδι, καὶ πλοῦν ἔσεσθαι Δαναΐδαις, ἡσθεὶς φρένας
> 360 ἄσμενος θύσειν ὑπέστης παῖδα· καὶ πέμπεις ἑκών,
> οὐ βίᾳ—μὴ τοῦτο λέξῃς—σῇ δάμαρτι παῖδα σὴν
> δεῦρ' ἀποστέλλειν, Ἀχιλλεῖ πρόφασιν ὡς γαμουμένην.

Iphigenia at Aulis 358–362

> When Calchas said the Danaans could sail
> if you sacrificed your daughter to Artemis, you rejoiced
> 360 and were happy to promise to sacrifice a child.
> You willingly—not by force; make no such claim—told your wife
> to send your child here, her marriage to Achilles a pretense.

Menelaus' version of the pre-tragic events is in many ways similar to Agamemnon's. Both brothers agree that Calchas had said that Iphigenia must be sacrificed to Artemis, and both brothers note that the ruse by which they lured Iphigenia to Aulis is a fake marriage to Achilles.[50] But they differ on one crucial point, and that is Agamemnon's willingness to kill his daughter: where Agamemnon claims that he had at first refused to sacrifice her, only to be persuaded otherwise by Menelaus, the latter insists, in no uncertain terms, that Agamemnon had been only too happy to do so.

Menelaus does not necessarily come off as the most reliable of narrators,[51] but of the two contradictory accounts of Agamemnon's reaction in the (imaginary) time before the play, there is substantial evidence we should have more faith in that of Menelaus.[52] When given the chance, for instance, Agamemnon does not disavow this accusation. It is also more likely that he would gloss over his enthusiasm to the *Presbutês*, who was not present when Calchas made his prophecy (and thus could not know how Agamemnon reacted), than that

---

[50] In fact, even the precise language that the two brothers use is very similar: ὡς γαμουμένην appears in both lines 100 and 362; πέμπεις ... σῇ δάμαρτι (360-361) and ἔπεμψα πρὸς δάμαρτα τὴν ἐμήν (99);

[51] See e.g. Saïd 2002:74.

[52] Much of the argumentation that follows belong to van Erp Taalman Kip 1996:532; Siegel 1981:260 also believes that Menelaus' version is closer to the truth.

Menelaus would lie so baldly to Agamemnon (who of course knows full well how he reacted). Furthermore, since (as we discover) the *Presbutês'* first allegiance is to Clytemnestra, it would be ruinous (for Agamemnon) if he discovered how callously Agamemnon had at first acted.[53] So even if Menelaus is exaggerating in depicting Agamemnon as gleefully unpaternal in his response to the prophecy, it seems safe to conclude that Agamemnon's characterization of his reaction was far from honest. Within the first 400 lines, then, we have already discovered that Agamemnon has lied to his wife and daughter in order to bring them to Aulis; lied (by omission) to Achilles regarding the use of his name; and lied to the *Presbutês*—and by extension the audience—about his reaction to the news about the sacrifice.

Other aspects of Menelaus' account confirm that Agamemnon's use of language has been most untrustworthy. In the prologue, Agamemnon had suggested that he and the other Achaean leaders had (passively) received Calchas' divinations in their state of *aporia* (*Iphigenia at Aulis* 89). Now, however, we learn that Agamemnon had been desperate "not to be deprived of [his] command or to lose his beautiful glory" (*Iphigenia at Aulis* 357: ὥστε μὴ στερέντα σ' ἀρχῆς ἀπολέσαι καλὸν κλέος). This line immediately precedes the description of Calchas' prophecy and Agamemnon's initial (and positive) reaction to it, so it is clear that his desire to lead the army drives his enthusiasm for Iphigenia's sacrifice—and his willingness to lie to achieve it. Importantly, this also confirms that the question of Iphigenia's sacrifice is not one that simply concerns Agamemnon's household, but that he himself had originally seen it as a means to realizing his own ambition to lead. In other words, for Agamemnon, Iphigenia's sacrifice is a personal and a political issue.

Moreover, Menelaus had already implied that Agamemnon's propensity for deception was characteristic of his approach to leadership and—as the following passage suggests—politics more generally:

> οἶσθ', ὅτ' ἐσπούδαζες ἄρχειν Δαναΐδαις πρὸς Ἴλιον,
> τῷ δοκεῖν μὲν οὐχὶ χρῄζων, τῷ δὲ βούλεσθαι θέλων,
> ὡς ταπεινὸς ἦσθα, πάσης δεξιᾶς προσθιγγάνων
> 340 καὶ θύρας ἔχων ἀκλήστους τῷ θέλοντι δημοτῶν
> καὶ διδοὺς πρόσρησιν ἑξῆς πᾶσι, κεἰ μή τις θέλοι,
> τοῖς τρόποις ζητῶν πρίασθαι τὸ φιλότιμον ἐκ μέσου,

---

[53] Soon after Clytemnestra arrives, the *Presbutês* informs her of Agamemnon's plan to kill Iphigenia, noting "I am well-disposed to you [Clytemnestra], and less so to your husband" (*Iphigenia at Aulis* 871: καὶ σοὶ μὲν εὔνους εἰμί, σῷ δ' ἧσσον πόσει.). This is because he had come to Agamemnon's house as part of Clytemnestra's dowry (cf. *Iphigenia at Aulis* 869–70), which of course Agamemnon knows perfectly well (this is obvious, but cf. *Iphigenia at Aulis* 46–48).

κᾆτ', ἐπεὶ κατέσχες ἀρχάς, μεταβαλὼν ἄλλους τρόπους
τοῖς φίλοισιν οὐκέτ' ἦσθα τοῖς πρὶν ὡς πρόσθεν φίλος,

Iphigenia at Aulis 337–344

You remember when you were eager to lead the Danaans to Ilium,
wishing to at once seem willing yet not covetous—
how humble you were! Taking each man's hand,
340   leaving your door unbarred to any commoner who wished,
giving all a chance to speak, even those who didn't want to,
striving in this way to buy the office from the middle class?[54]
But when you took control, you changed your ways
and were no longer friendly as before to former friends.

As I discuss above in Chapter Three (see pp. 109–110), Menelaus describes a process of selecting generals that overtly mirrors contemporary Athenian practices. Within this apparently democratic context, we see two striking examples of political dissemblance. The first is Agamemnon's wish to disguise his ambition to lead the Achaean army, cloaking himself in false humility in order to be elected general. The second is his overall approach to the soldiers: where at first he was warm and welcoming, Menelaus implies that Agamemnon's true (and aloof) nature was only revealed after he had gained power. As in the description of Agamemnon's despondence in the face of adverse winds, Menelaus' emphasis here is on Agamemnon's desire to lead (337: ἄρχειν; 343: ἀρχάς). Considered in conjunction with the false letter to Clytemnestra and his lies of omission regarding Achilles, the overriding image that emerges is of a leader who is prepared to use varying levels of deceit in order to satisfy his ambitions.

3.3 Flipping Aeschylus' Script: Agamemnon, Clytemnestra, and Iphigenia at Aulis

3.3.1 Clytemnestra at Aulis

When Clytemnestra arrives in the second episode, the audience is primed to see her take up the role that Agamemnon had played in Aeschylus' play: the victim of a duplicitous plot. For just as Aeschlyus had done for Clytemnestra in *Agamemnon*, Euripides spends the first half of *Iphigenia at Aulis* establishing

---

[54] I discuss this passage in Chapter Three as well; see above (at p. 109n58) on the translation of these lines.

Agamemnon's capacity for deception in preparation for the arrival of his spouse. As in Aeschylus' play, the life of an Atreid is at stake (this time Iphigenia's, rather than Agamemnon's). And here too, the outcome of this domestic drama will have serious political consequences, this time the prosecution of the Trojan War, and Agamemnon's position as the leader of the Achaeans. The stage is thus set for the Aeschylean roles to be reversed in a manner that mirrors contemporary concerns about the use of deceptive speech for political ends.

Euripides manages to immediately evoke Clytemnestra's duplicitous past while also forming a strong contrast with it. Her arrival by wagon is reminiscent of her husband's ill-fated entrance in *Agamemnon*.[55] In both plays it is the first yet long-anticipated meeting between husband and wife, and each encounter begins with Clytemnestra asking Agamemnon a series of questions. But whereas in Aeschylus' play these are trick questions which serve to change the terms of their discussion and persuade him to walk voluntarily to his own death, in *Iphigenia at Aulis*, Clytemnestra's queries are undeniably plain and transparent: "where is Achilles from?"; "who are his parents?"; "when will the wedding be?"[56] These serve not to trick her husband but to learn the details of Iphigenia's wedding and the background of her future son-in-law, emphasizing her belief in the fiction that Agamemnon had created. Moreover, as we shall see, it is Agamemnon who consistently dissembles in response. In essence, in her first encounter with Agamemnon in *Iphigenia at Aulis*, Clytemnestra is the antithesis of her Aeschylean analogue, a contrast that will be reinforced throughout the rest of the tragedy.

Soon thereafter, an incidental encounter with Achilles leads Clytemnestra to discover that her husband is secretly planning to sacrifice Iphigenia. This conspiracy is quite similar to Clytemnestra's undisclosed intention to "sacrifice" Agamemnon in *Agamemnon*, but Achilles presents a solution to the problem: Clytemnestra should "persuade" Agamemnon to "think better."[57] This suggestion reminds us, of course, of Clytemnestra's peithotic prowess in *Agamemnon*, and Achilles' reliance on her to convince her husband seems analogous to Aegisthus' willingness to allow her to take care of "setting the trap."[58] The audience is thus reminded both of *Agamemnon* on a general level, but also of

---

[55] On this allusion, see above at p. 136.

[56] I am paraphrasing here, but this is the gist of the series of questions that Clytemnestra asks Agamemnon in *Iphigenia at Aulis* 695–720.

[57] *Iphigenia at Aulis* 1011: πειθώμεν αὖθις πατέρα βέλτιον φρονεῖν. While Achilles uses the first-person plural as if to suggest that he and Clytemnestra will work together to convince Agamemnon of his folly, it soon becomes clear that he really means Clytemnestra should do it herself (*Iphigenia at Aulis* 1015–18).

[58] *Agamemnon* 1636, on which see above at p. 138.

Clytemnestra's rather unique way with words in that tragedy, and from this point on, the entanglements between the Euripidean and Aeschylean Clytemnestras become ever more marked and complex, at once parallel and divergent.

Indeed, one might imagine that if we were dealing with the same woman who so successfully ensnared Agamemnon, Clytemnestra would have made short work of her husband's resistance in *Iphigenia at Aulis*. But this is not the case in Euripides' tragedy. Clytemnestra's failure to carry out Achilles' plan is the most obvious indication that she is not the force of persuasion that she was in Aeschylus' drama, but there are signs throughout that Euripides' queen no longer traffics in deceit and deception. Above all, her speech is consistently marked by frankness. This becomes rapidly apparent during her attempt to dissuade Agamemnon from sacrificing their daughter. Here, her first line of attack is to simply ask after her husband's plans: "Do you intend to kill your child and mine?" (*Iphigenia at Aulis* 1131: τὴν παῖδα τὴν σὴν τήν τ' ἐμὴν μέλλεις κτανεῖν;). Subtle this is not, but such directness is entirely typical of the way she communicates in *Iphigenia at Aulis*.

Agamemnon responds to this frank question with a weak lie, which only angers Clytemnestra. This anger, however, does not lead to deceit. Instead, as Agamemnon continues to dance around the subject, Clytemnestra's language becomes even more transparent. She bemoans her fate and Iphigenia's (*Iphigenia at Aulis* 1137), and declares bluntly that she already knows everything, that it is no longer worth it for Agamemnon to lie (*Iphigenia at Aulis* 1141–1143). All this suggests that Clytemnestra's communication techniques have evolved significantly with respect to her portrayal in *Agamemnon*.

This evolution is at once signaled and epitomized by the beginning of the speech with which Clytemnestra attempts to dissuade Agamemnon: "Hear me now, for I shall unveil my words / and no longer employ obscure riddles" (*Iphigenia at Aulis* 1146–1147: ἄκουε δή νυν· ἀνακαλύψω γὰρ λόγους / κοὐκέτι παρῳδοῖς χρησόμεσθ' αἰνίγμασιν.) This statement is crucial for several reasons: first, Euripides openly emphasizes the fact that his Clytemnestra will employ frankness rather than dishonesty; second, Clytemnestra has heretofore neither veiled her words nor employed obscure riddles, an irony which only heightens the emphasis on her directness; and finally, her words are highly reminiscent of the first lines of iambic trimeter that Cassandra speaks in Aeschylus' *Agamemnon*:[59]

---

[59] I am indebted to Sarah Nooter for first bringing this to my attention. Garner 1990:174, also points out this allusion.

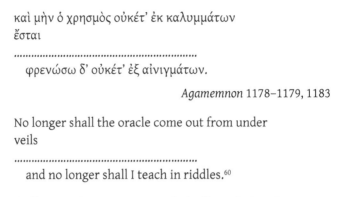

καὶ μὴν ὁ χρησμὸς οὐκέτ' ἐκ καλυμμάτων
ἔσται

....

φρενώσω δ' οὐκέτ' ἐξ αἰνιγμάτων.

Agamemnon 1178–1179, 1183

No longer shall the oracle come out from under
veils

....

and no longer shall I teach in riddles.[60]

Two striking similarities between Cassandra's formulation in *Agamemnon* and Clytemnestra's in *Iphigenia at Aulis* suggest that Euripides is purposefully drawing an analogy between the two characters: the twin usage of the term αἴνιγμα; and the identical metaphorical use of "unveiling" one's speech in order to be understood (χρησμὸς ἐκ καλυμμάτων vs. ἀνακαλύψω γὰρ λόγους). Both of these locutions are relatively rare,[61] and in fact, *Agamemnon* and *Iphigenia at Aulis* contain the only two extant passages in which they are used together. Moreover, the combination of αἴνιγμα and unveiled speech is not the only way in which these two passages are similar. Clytemnestra's use of the verb χράω (χρησόμεθα) mirrors Cassandra's χρησμός,[62] and both women insist that they will no longer (οὐκέτι) use such enigmatic, oracular speech. It is clear that with Clytemnestra's

---

[60] I have excluded four lines from this passage because, while they are indeed part and parcel of Cassandra's declaration that she will engage in clear speech, they manage, in their own inimitably Aeschylean oracularity, to at the same time be nearly impenetrable in their opacity. Cf. Goldhill 1984:85: "the expression of clarity comes through an extremely complex interplay of meanings of the central term for 'clear', which, through the cumulative refraction of the structure of the similes, undercuts the very desire for clarity."

[61] Prior to *Iphigenia at Aulis*, in fact, only nineteen uses of the noun αἴνιγμα are found in the *TLG*, and seven of these are in reference to Oedipus and the Sphynx (Euripides *Phoenician Women* 48, 1049, 1688, 1731, 1759; Sophocles *Oedipus Tyrannus* 393, 1525), which is quite clearly not what Clytemnestra is talking about. The metaphorical concept of "unveiling" one's language is even rarer: I have found only five instances in extant classical Greek literature, including the two cited above. (This tally factors not only the uses of ἀνακαλύπτω and the expression ἐκ καλυμμάτων, as in the above passages, but also those of the verb ἐκκαλύπτω.) The other three are: Aeschylus *Prometheus Bound* 196; Critias fragment 1 Snell; and, curiously enough, *Iphigenia at Aulis* 872. Indeed, Clytemnestra uses a similar expression (ἐκκάλυπτε ... οὕστινας στέγεις λόγους) when she insists that the *Presbutês* inform her of the plot to kill Iphigenia, to which he has been alluding. This second use of such a rare expression again points to a general preoccupation, in *Iphigenia at Aulis*, with the potential ubiquity of deceptive speech.

[62] The two words are etymologically related, and the verb, translated here as "employ," is also commonly used in reference to oracles and prophetic speech.

first words in her attempt to persuade Agamemnon, she alludes to Cassandra's famous speech in *Agamemnon.*

Despite Euripides' mimetic precision, this verbal parallel may not have been easy for his audience to perceive on the spot. But this is not the only way in which Clytemnestra's speech echoes Cassandra's. As a prophetess, Cassandra is concerned with revealing the future, but she begins by revealing "crimes committed long ago"[63]—specifically the murder of Thyestes' children and the banquet at which they were served to him—before going on to predict Agamemnon's death at the hands of his wife.[64] In *Iphigenia at Aulis*, Clytemnestra also reaches into the past before discussing the future. After describing Agamemnon's past transgressions—namely his shocking murder of Clytemnestra's child from an earlier marriage[65]—Clytemnestra goes on to issue a not-so-subtle warning to her husband. With a prediction that no one in the audience could have overlooked, she recalls the future acts already dramatized by Aeschylus:

ἐπεὶ βραχείας προφάσεως ἐνδεῖ μόνον,
ἐφ' ᾗ σ' ἐγὼ καὶ παῖδες αἱ λελειμμέναι
δεξόμεθα δέξιν ἥν σε δέξασθαι χρεών.

Iphigenia at Aulis 1180–1182

Only a small pretense is wanting
for me and your abandoned daughters
to receive you with the reception you deserve.

As Smith quite elegantly put it, Euripides' Clytemnestra is "threatening Agamemnon with *Agamemnon*."[66] With her talk of a fitting reception, she foresees, some ten years in advance, exactly what Aeschylus' Cassandra does: the murder of Agamemnon. Furthermore, the "small pretense" (*Iphigenia at Aulis*

---

[63] *Agamemnon* 1184–1185: κακῶν / ... τῶν πάλαι πεπραγμένων.

[64] *Agamemnon* 1219, 1222: παῖδες θανόντες ὡσπερεὶ πρὸς τῶν φιλῶν / ... ὧν πατὴρ ἐγεύσατο ("Just like children, killed by loved ones / ... whom their father tasted").

[65] *Iphigenia at Aulis* 1148–1156. Euripides has either invented or used an uncommon variant of the story of Agamemnon and Clytemnestra's marriage. In this version, we find out that Clytemnestra was already married when she and Agamemnon first met. Undeterred by this trifling detail, Agamemnon apparently killed her husband (a curiously named Tantalus) and her infant child, risking death at the hands of Castor and Pollux but ultimately procuring for himself the hand of Clytemnestra. Cf. Gibert 2005 for the most complete discussion of this novel version of the myth.

[66] W. Smith 1979:178.

1180) yet lacking is almost certainly Cassandra herself,[67] who will eventually arrive in Argos as a replacement bride.[68]

Euripides' Clytemnestra thus draws on Cassandra's prophetic speech in three important ways: she echoes the words and meaning of Cassandra's introductory iambic lines; she adopts Cassandra's technique of highlighting past transgressions as a context for future consequences; and she does so for the same revelatory purpose, to prophesize both the act of and the motivation for Agamemnon's death. In doing so, she reminds the audience of Cassandra's future arrival at her house, the very circumstance in which, according to the tragic tradition, Cassandra will make the speech that Clytemnestra is now imitating in *Iphigenia at Aulis*. Such strong parallels in both style and substance can hardly be a coincidence. Euripides is clearly drawing a connection between his Clytemnestra and Aeschylus' Cassandra.

This connection is profoundly relevant to any comparison between Euripides' Clytemnestra and Aeschylus' version of the queen. In *Agamemnon*, Cassandra embodies "the inverse of Clytemnestra."[69] She first stands by silently as Clytemnestra weaves her web of lies around her husband, leading him to his (and eventually Cassandra's) certain death. She then wordlessly resists Clytemnestra's attempts to coax her inside, fending off her powerful *peithô* with an equally powerful silence (*Agamemnon* 1035–1071).[70] When Cassandra finally does speak, her speech is very much the opposite of Clytemnestra's: she says nothing but the truth. Unfortunately, the outcome of her speech is also radically different, for where Clytemnestra is utterly convincing, Cassandra can persuade no one.[71] In each of these ways, Cassandra differs dramatically from Aeschylus' Clytemnestra, and is at the same time most similar to Euripides' version of the queen.

The Euripidean Clytemnestra's strong resemblance to Cassandra is emblematic of the manner in which Euripides marks the differences between his queen and Aeschylus', namely through the contrast in their modes of communication. This contrast remains intact throughout Clytemnestra's long monologue (*Iphigenia at Aulis* 1146–1208). The specific purpose of this speech is to persuade Agamemnon, but rather than being laden with trickery and deceit, Clytemnestra's

---

[67] As the prophetess well understood, Aeschylus' Clytemnestra will "redeem her abduction with death" (*Agamemnon* 1263: ἐμῆς ἀγωγῆς ἀντιτείσασθαι φόνον).

[68] On Cassandra being presented as a bride in Aeschylus' *Agamemnon*, cf. Taplin 1977:302–306; on the "bridal imagery" that abounds throughout Cassandra's time on-stage, see Seaford 1987:125–128, and Mitchell-Boyask 2006.

[69] Thalmann 1985:229. For a more thorough list of the ways in which Cassandra and Clytemnestra function as opposites in *Agamemnon*, cf. McClure 1997:121–124; and McClure 1999:92–93.

[70] Thalmann 1985:228–229; Goldhill 1986:23–26.

[71] Thalmann 1985:229: "it is one of the terrible ironies of this play that [Cassandra] is cursed with the inability to *persuade* ... whereas Clytemnestra's talent for persuasion is formidable" [italics in original].

words are consistent with the frankness she has thus far manifested. This is especially apparent in the way that she predicts that Agamemnon will receive the reception he deserves if he kills Iphigenia, a threat that Clytemnestra never dares to utter in Aeschylus' play. What is striking about this moment—and what should have stood out for the audience—is that the two Clytemnestras' modes of speech differ on the very same subject: Aeschylus' Clytemnestra cannot help but lie about her plans for Agamemnon's return; Euripides', on the other hand, tells the truth about the event even though she is by no means forced to.

In summary, in both episodes in which Clytemnestra and Agamemnon appear on-stage together in *Iphigenia at Aulis*, Euripides goes to great length to emphasize the fact that his character is significantly different from Aeschylus' version of the queen. These contrasts are evident above all in their different modes of speech: the trick questions of *Agamemnon* become the forthright ones of *Iphigenia at Aulis*; the Aeschylean Clytemnestra's ambiguous ritual language becomes, in Euripides' tragedy, an unveiled threat; and while Aeschylus' queen is depicted as fundamentally antithetical to his Cassandra, Euripides emphasizes the similarities between his Clytemnestra and the prophetess. In short, where the queen of *Agamemnon* is the embodiment of feminine guile, one whose ability to manipulate speech represents a grave danger to her husband and to male society, the Clytemnestra of *Iphigenia at Aulis* seems to have forgotten how to either lie or persuade. All this serves to emphatically underline that Agamemnon is the true agent of deceitful speech in *Iphigenia at Aulis*.

3.3.2 Agamemnon and Iphigenia

As boldly as Euripides flouts the Aeschylean tradition by portraying Clytemnestra as a frank wife and loving mother, his treatment of Agamemnon is even more arresting. In Aeschylus' play, Agamemnon appears on-stage for a scant 200 lines, barely enough time to be bested by his wife in a contest of words and led blindly to a grisly fate. While many conflicting reasons have been given to explain Agamemnon's submission, it is at least clear that when it comes to manipulative speech, Agamemnon is the prey to Clytemnestra's predator. Euripides dispels the possibility of seeing this dynamic again in *Iphigenia at Aulis* by making his Clytemnestra avoid any of the "multivalent" language which she so fluently delivered in *Agamemnon*.

We have already seen how Agamemnon's speech patterns are marked by duplicity in the first part of the play, albeit subtly. Once he engages with Clytemnestra and Iphigenia, his tendency to resort to deceptive—and even multivalent—language becomes obvious to all observers. Moreover, like Aeschylus' Clytemnestra, he uses this speech to effectively bring about the death of a family member, and to maintain power in the world of the play. The result is that in *Iphigenia at Aulis*, it becomes obvious that it is no longer feminine guile that threatens to corrupt the *oikos* and the *polis*, but rather the treachery of the male protagonists.

Upon learning that Clytemnestra and Iphigenia have arrived at Aulis, Agamemnon's stated goal is to keep them from uncovering his plot so that Iphigenia's sacrifice may be accompanied by "the fewest tears possible" (*Iphigenia at Aulis* 541: ἐπ' ἐλαχίστοις δακρύοις). To this end, he orders both Menelaus and the Chorus to keep quiet (*Iphigenia at Aulis* 542). Silence will not suffice, however, for Agamemnon. Instead, he must resort to manipulative language to delude first Iphigenia and then Clytemnestra. He begins with simple evasive tactics when Iphigenia wonders why he is not happy to see her, but as she begins to press him for the details of her future, he becomes more and more mendacious:

ΙΦ εἴθ' ἦν καλόν †μοι σοί τ' ἄγειν σύμπλουν ἐμέ†.
ΑΓ ἔτ' ἔστι καὶ σοὶ πλοῦς, ἵν' †μνήσῃ† πατρός.
ΙΦ σὺν μητρὶ πλεύσασ' ἢ μόνη πορεύσομαι;
ΑΓ μόνη, μονωθεῖσ' ἀπὸ πατρὸς καὶ μητέρος.
670 ΙΦ οὖ πού μ' ἐς ἄλλα δώματ' οἰκίζεις, πάτερ;
ΑΓ ἐατέ·· οὐ χρὴ τοιάδ' εἰδέναι κόρας.
ΙΦ σπεῦδ' ἐκ Φρυγῶν μοι, θέμενος εὖ τἀκεῖ, πάτερ.
ΑΓ θῦσαί με θυσίαν πρῶτα δεῖ τιν' ἐνθάδε.
ΙΦ ἀλλὰ ξὺν ἱεροῖς χρὴ τό γ' εὐσεβὲς σκοπεῖν.
675 ΑΓ εἴσῃ σύ· χερνίβων γὰρ ἐστήξεις πέλας.

Iphigenia at Aulis 666–675

IPHIGENIA: If only it was right for you to bring me by ship.
AGAMEMNON: A voyage still awaits you, a memory of your father.[72]
IPHIGENIA: Will I sail with mother or be taken alone?
AGAMEMNON: Alone, isolated from your father and mother.
670 IPHIGENIA: Are you then settling me in a new home, father?
AGAMEMNON: Enough; a girl need not know these things.
IPHIGENIA: Hurry back from Phrygia, father, once you've prevailed.
AGAMEMNON: First I must sacrifice a certain sacrifice here.
IPHIGENIA: Yes, one must look to the sacred with holy rites.
675 AGAMEMNON: You will see, for you'll be near the libations.

---

[72] The true meaning of this line appears unsalvageable.

Throughout the exchange, Agamemnon's ability to convey lies via half-truths is especially reminiscent of Aeschylus' Clytemnestra.[73] Agamemnon tells the truth, in the broadest sense of the word, when he says that Iphigenia will soon take a trip by boat (*Iphigenia at Aulis* 667), though presumably she imagines she will be sailing the high seas and not the river Styx. While it is accurate to say that she will, on this voyage, be separated from her mother and father (*Iphigenia at Aulis* 669), Agamemnon is hardly explicit about the permanence of this state. His most honest statement is his third (671), when he simply refuses to answer Iphigenia's question. But when she begs of him to make a speedy return from Troy (highly unlikely), Agamemnon mentions, in the vaguest terms possible, that he must "sacrifice a sacrifice." This is not a lie, but the full meaning is again impossible for Iphigenia to know. Euripides is obviously drawing attention to Agamemnon's dissimulation by using this emphatic—and ridiculously ambiguous—formulation.[74] To pound the point home, the tragedian then has Agamemnon note that Iphigenia will be able to "see" the sacred rites herself, since she will be standing "near the libations" (an understatement if ever there was one). Had anyone in the audience heretofore failed to notice Agamemnon's exploitation of multivalent and deceptive language, surely this last comment would have startled them into recognition. At the same time, Iphigenia's pathetically naïve excitement at the prospect of leading the dances around the altar emphasizes, yet again, how effectively Agamemnon can manipulate language.

3.3.3 Agamemnon and Clytemnestra

Having convinced Iphigenia that everything is as it should be does not mean that Agamemnon can cease dissembling. He must now face his wife and attempt to convince her that nothing is amiss. Even before this encounter begins, it is already reminiscent of the famous husband-wife *agôn* in Aeschylus' *Agamemnon*; the roles have simply been reversed. This time, it is Clytemnestra, rather than Agamemnon, who arrives by wagon,[75] summoned to her spouse by a duplicitous message.[76] And before Clytemnestra can even get a word in edgewise, Agamemnon has already lied to her: he apologizes for his sour mood and once again shrouds the truth in ambiguity by noting that although Iphigenia's

---

[73] I am indebted to Shadi Bartsch-Zimmer for both this phrase and the broader point.

[74] In fact, it is one that he will use again in a short time, cf. *Iphigenia at Aulis* 721 and my discussion below at pp. 159–160.

[75] Aélion 1983:106; Foley 1985:70–71.

[76] In *Agamemnon*, this function is fulfilled by a messenger who takes Clytemnestra's hypocritical greeting to her husband. In *Iphigenia at Aulis*, this is done not by a verbal message but by a letter, though on a dramatic level, it fulfills essentially the same function.

"dispatch is a happy one,"[77] it is always sad for parents to see their children leave (*Iphigenia at Aulis* 688-690). His sadness is reminiscent of Clytemnestra's "joy" at the news of her husband's imminent return in *Agamemnon*;[78] in each case the feeling may be true, but the underlying motive is falsely implied. Agamemnon thus sets the terms of their exchange from the beginning: Agamemnon will play the deceiver, and Clytemnestra the deceived. At stake is Iphigenia's life.

Despite this inauspicious start, and despite the reminders (both textual and dramatic) of the royal couple's traditionally rocky relationship, the conversation begins on good terms. Clytemnestra asks after the provenance of Iphigenia's (presumed) future husband, and Agamemnon answers with candid ease. The natural simplicity of their dialogue is almost enough to make one forget that it is based on a lie. But when Clytemnestra brings up Iphigenia's wedding, Agamemnon must dissemble once more:

> ΚΛ ἀλλ' εὐτυχοίτην. τίνι δ' ἐν ἡμέρᾳ γαμεῖ;
> ΑΓ ὅταν σελήνης ἐντελὴς ἔλθῃ κύκλος.
> ΚΛ προτέλεια δ' ἤδη παιδὸς ἔσφαξας θεᾷ;
> ΑΓ μέλλω· 'πὶ ταύτῃ καὶ καθέσταμεν τύχῃ.
> 720 ΚΛ κἄπειτα δαίσεις τοὺς γάμους ἐς ὕστερον;
> ΑΓ θύσας γε θύμαθ' ἁμὲ χρὴ θῦσαι θεοῖς.

Iphigenia at Aulis 716–721

> CLYTEMNESTRA: May they prosper! Which day will they marry?
> AGAMEMNON: When the circle of the moon is full.
> CLYTEMNESTRA: Have you slain the child's offerings to the goddess[79]?
> AGAMEMNON: I will soon. It is for this act I am now prepared.
> 720 CLYTEMNESTRA: And then you'll serve the wedding feast?
> AGAMEMNON: After I've sacrificed the sacrifices I must sacrifice to the gods.

Clytemnestra's first line—wishing the future newlyweds well—is yet another testament to the efficacy of Agamemnon's lies; much like Agamemnon when

---

[77] *Iphigenia at Aulis* 688: ἀποστολαὶ γὰρ μακάριαι.

[78] Aeschylus *Agamemnon* 264–267.

[79] Gamel 1999:466: "Klytemnestra probably means Hera, who is the principal female deity of Argos, but Agamemnon and the audience would think of Artemis, also associated with marriage." Clytemnestra's misconceptions, constantly fostered by Agamemnon, take place even on this minute level.

he arrives home in Aeschylus' play, she still believes in her spouse's good faith. Agamemnon's words, however, betray her trust. Even more so than in his discussion with Iphigenia, each of his responses is full of treachery. Knowing what we know, it is obvious to the audience that the full moon will not be blessing the wedding of Iphigenia and Achilles. It also seems unlikely that Agamemnon will get around to setting up Iphigenia's marriage feast. Moreover, Euripides again accentuates the ambiguity of Agamemnon's language by giving him an absurd line (721) in which he uses three words stemming from θύω (to sacrifice). This is obviously very similar to the line he uses to deflect Iphigenia's attention, and it is once again an ostentatious allusion to the deception he is perpetrating; a way of calling the audience's attention to the fact that Agamemnon is systematically using veiled ritual language to disguise his intentions.

Nevertheless, perhaps the most loaded exchange in this scene concerns the *proteleia* to the goddess on behalf of Iphigenia. Clytemnestra is obviously referring to the prenuptial sacrifices that would take place before any wedding,[80] and naturally, Agamemnon takes advantage of this misconception: it is true he will soon perform *proteleia*, but not the ones that Clytemnestra is asking about, nor to the goddess (Hera) whom Clytemnestra has in mind.[81] Agamemnon thus fosters misunderstanding on every level. But aside from the fact that he clearly takes advantage of the multivalent nature of the word in order to deceive his wife, this is also a sly allusion, on Euripides' part, to *Agamemnon*. Indeed, the only prior extant uses of *"proteleios"* had occurred in Aeschylus' play.[82] And although only one of these concerns a sacrifice,[83] this sacrifice—the *proteleia*—is none other than Iphigenia herself: "an offering on behalf of ships."[84]

---

[80] Oakley and Sinos 1993:11: "[s]acrifices to the gods preceded every major undertaking in ancient Greece, and the wedding was no exception." By the fourth century, Oakley and Sinos continue, "it was especially important to pay respect to the gods by performing prenuptial sacrifices, called *proteleia*." Although *Iphigenia at Aulis* was first produced before any other known reference to these prenuptial sacrifices as *proteleia* (according to the TLG, after *Iphigenia at Aulis* the earliest certain use of *proteleia* in this manner is Plato *Laws* 774e9: ὅσα δὲ προτέλεια γάμων), it is reasonable to assume that the audience would interpret these *proteleia* as such; Clytemnestra is, after all, primarily interested in the wedding at this point. Furthermore, her follow-up question (*Iphigenia at Aulis* 720: "and then you'll serve the wedding feast?") is perfectly in line with actual ceremonial procedures. See again Oakley and Sinos 1993:22: "[e]very wedding included a feast, with abundant meat provided by the prenuptial sacrifices performed by both families."

[81] Gamel 1999:466.

[82] According to the TLG. Cf. Aeschylus *Agamemnon* 65, 227, 720. On Aeschylus' uses of *proteleia* (and the audience's understanding of it), cf. Fraenkel 1950:40–41; Zeitlin 1965:464–467.

[83] *Agamemnon* 227: προτέλεια ναῶν. Here too *proteleia* takes a genitive complement to convey the meaning of a sacrificial offering on behalf of a person or thing.

[84] Garner 1990:174, also notes this allusion. Euripides had already alluded to the first line of the choral strophe from which these lines come by referring to the "yoke of necessity" which Agamemnon donned in his eponymous play. (Cf. above p. 136; Garner 1990:174; and Sorum

To summarize, Euripides invents a situation that is bound to remind much of the audience of Aeschylus' play. He creates a sort of reverse *Agamemnon*, one in which it is now Agamemnon who attempts to ensnare Clytemnestra with his words. He first draws attention to Aeschylus' tragedy by having Clytemnestra arrive on-stage by wagon and under the false impressions created by her spouse. He then alerts the audience that Agamemnon will continue with his earlier treacherous use of language by showing him brazenly manipulate Iphigenia, and by having him lie to Clytemnestra before the *agôn* even begins. Then, even in the midst of the *agôn*, even as we see Agamemnon hoodwink Clytemnestra much like she had him in Aeschylus' play, Agamemnon takes advantage of the ambiguity of a rare term from *Agamemnon*, one that Aeschylus used to describe the very sacrifice which he is at such pains to conceal. There can be no doubt that Euripides is intentionally and openly using *Agamemnon* as the backdrop against which to cast his depiction of his utterly untruthful king. He brings this point home by closing the husband-wife *agôn* just as Aeschylus does: "obey!" demands Agamemnon (*Iphigenia at Aulis* 739: πιθοῦ). This is the very same word with which Clytemnestra springs the trap she had set for her husband in *Agamemnon* (Aeschylus *Agamemnon* 943). Euripides has systematically overturned one of the primary dynamics of Aeschylus' play: the male is now the deceiver, the female the deceived; Agamemnon has become Clytemnestra.

3.4 The Dissolution of Agamemnon's Duplicity

In the fourth and final scene in which Agamemnon appears (episode three), his consistent distortion of facts and language continues—at least until he realizes the game is up. Clytemnestra has, by now, learned that her husband's true intention is to sacrifice Iphigenia. Nevertheless, unaware that the *Presbutês* has sold him out to Clytemnestra,[85] Agamemnon still attempts to conceal the truth from Clytemnestra. He speaks as if the wedding preparations are proceeding without a hitch; he refers to Iphigenia as a "bride-to-be" (*Iphigenia at Aulis* 1108: τὰς γαμουμένας); and he talks, in great detail, of the sacrifices which must be completed "before the wedding" (*Iphigenia at Aulis* 1113: πρὸ γάμων). Clytemnestra is hardly pleased with this, and her response to Agamemnon's duplicity provides more context: "with names [*onomasin*] you speak well, but

---

1992:537.) In fact, *Iphigenia at Aulis* itself is arguably a massive elaboration of these ten Aeschylean lines, a process that is neatly illustrated by the fact Euripides directly alludes to both the first and last lines of this strophe.

[85] Contrary to his earlier claim to be completely trustworthy; *Iphigenia at Aulis* 44–45: φέρε κοίνωσον μῦθον ἐς ἡμᾶς. / πρὸς ‹δ᾽› ἄνδρ᾽ ἀγαθὸν πιστόν τε φράσεις· ("Come now, share with me your tale; you'll be speaking to a good and loyal man.").

in naming your deeds / I know not how to speak well of them."[86] This some-what awkward play on words calls our attention to the fact that Clytemnestra is using the exact same juxtaposition between logos (here again, *onoma*) and *ergon* that Agamemnon and Achilles did before. And just as for Achilles, the gulf between Agamemnon's words and his deeds is a matter of grave concern for Clytemnestra. As such, we can see that it is a central theme of this tragedy; a way to emphasize the dishonesty that characterizes Agamemnon's speech, and to frame it within the context of a contemporary debate on the reliability of speech in the political arena.

Once Agamemnon can no longer invent words to disguise his deeds, there is little left for him to say. Soon after Clytemnestra hints at the distance between his words and deeds, she reveals that she knows what his plot is. After a brief exclamation of despair (*Iphigenia at* Aulis 1140: ἀπωλόμεσθα), he declares that he will "be silent" (*Iphigenia at Aulis* 1144: σιωπῶ). It is almost as if, with lies no longer available to him, his power of speech abandons him; honest words, perhaps, do not become him. His final statement of the play comes some one-hundred lines later, after both his wife and daughter have, to no avail, sought to dissuade him from the sacrifice. Forced to make a final decision, Agamemnon claims that Iphigenia must be sacrificed for Hellas, to ensure that "the Greeks" (*Iphigenia at Aulis* 1275: Ἕλληνας) not be deprived of their wives at the hands of barbarians (*Iphigenia at Aulis* 1269–1275). Critics have endlessly tried to assess the sincerity of this sudden emphasis on Panhellenic unity. There is no way of knowing whether these sentiments are honest, though critical consensus leans towards disbelieving Agamemnon;[87] certainly we are primed to be skeptical of anything he says at this point.[88] The question is only of limited importance here. More relevant is the fact that at the crucial moment of the play, Agamemnon confirms that the decision about whether or not to sacrifice his daughter is primarily a political issue.[89] Within that context, the undeniable consistency with which he uses deceit and deceptive speech throughout *Iphigenia at Aulis* is striking. His dishonesty is pervasive, and while his performance may not be as smooth as that of Aeschylus' Clytemnestra, Agamemnon ultimately

---

[86] *Iphigenia at Aulis* 1115–1116: τοῖς ὀνόμασιν μὲν εὖ λέγεις, τὰ δ' ἔργα σου / οὐκ οἶδ' ὅπως χρή μ' ὀνομάσασαν εὖ λέγειν.

[87] Most recently, Foley 1985:98 and D. Burgess 2004:48 have argued in favor of his sincerity (at least to a certain degree). Less sanguine about his honesty are Siegel 1981:264–265; Saïd 2002:74–78; and Synodinou 2013. Markantonatos 2011, even though he argues against an ironic or critical reading of Iphigenia's enthusiastic adoption of the Panhellenic argument, still calls Agamemnon's advancement of the same an act of "pathetic self-justification" in which he "us[es] the mask of patriotism to defend illogical and immoral actions" (p. 210).

[88] Nancy 1981:23.

[89] As Blume 2011:184 puts it, "policy quickly gains the upper hand over family ties."

accomplishes his goals: the death of Iphigenia, and his own command of the Trojan War.

4. Conclusion: The Agamemnon/Clytemnestra Inversion and Its Reverberations at Aulis

As we have seen, *Iphigenia at Aulis* brings to the foreground Agamemnon's proclivity for deception through a comparison to Aeschylus' Clytemnestra. Moreover, this inversion of the Agamemnon-Clytemnestra relationship is accomplished in the midst of a decision that proves, above all, to be a political one. Here, it is important to recall again the broader context of the play. The Achaean army camp is, essentially, "the polis' military analogue."[90] Given the great extent to which the political apparatus of the play reflects the world of his Athenian audience, it is apparent that the army operates as an analogue for the *dêmos*, while Agamemnon and other Achaean *basilées* stand in for democratic leaders.[91]

Within this political context, it is evident that the Achaean leaders rely heavily on deceit. Agamemnon's lies about Iphigenia's sacrifice and his deceptive exchanges with Clytemnestra are the most blatant examples of manipulative language in the play, and indeed the only ones that take place on stage. But from what we learn of the communications that occur off-stage, deception is typical of the way that Agamemnon and the rest of the Greek leaders deal with the Achaean army. Menelaus' description of Agamemnon's campaign to be elected as general (*Iphigenia at Aulis* 337–344, discussed above) is especially meaningful, for it suggests that he does not simply use deception in settling the Iphigenia question, but that this is in fact Agamemnon's standard operating procedure in the realm of (democratic) politics. This tendency is confirmed by Agamemnon's negligence in reporting Calchas' prophecy to the army,[92] another obvious attempt to mislead the mass of soldiers.

This dynamic of self-interested and deceptive leadership is a motif that Euripides explores with the other leaders of the Greek army. Agamemnon, for one, points his accusing finger at his partners in politics at a pivotal moment in the first episode, shortly after convincing Menelaus that they should not sacrifice Iphigenia. When the news of Clytemnestra's arrival prompts Agamemnon to believe he has no choice but to kill his daughter, Menelaus, justifiably enough,

---

[90]   Carter 2010:49.

[91]   I argue this throughout Chapter Three, and several recent analyses of the play also focus on this general dynamic, e.g. Markantonatos 2011 and Lush 2015.

[92]   The authenticity of the "secret prophecy" motif is contested, but see my comments above in Chapter Three (p. 113n67).

wonders why; after all, the army is as yet unaware of all these machinations. The answer is that Agamemnon fears that his authority over the army will be usurped by his former ally Odysseus:

525 ΜΕ οὐκ ἔστ' Ὀδυσσεὺς ὅτι σὲ κάμὲ πημανεῖ.
ΑΓ ποικίλος ἀεὶ πέφυκε τοῦ τ' ὄχλου μέτα.
ΜΕ φιλοτιμίᾳ μὲν ἐνέχεται, δεινῷ κακῷ.
ΑΓ οὔκουν δοκεῖς νιν στάντ' ἐν Ἀργείοις μέσοις
λέξειν ἃ Κάλχας θέσφατ' ἐξηγήσατο,
530 κἄμ' ὡς ὑπέστην θῦμα, κᾆτ' ἐψευδόμην,
Ἀρτέμιδι θύσειν; οὐ ξυναρπάσας στρατόν,
σὲ κἄμ' ἀποκτείναντας Ἀργείους κόρην
σφάξαι κελεύσει;

Iphigenia at Aulis 525–533

AGAMEMNON: The child of Sisyphus knows all this.
525 MENELAUS: There's no way for Odysseus to hurt us.
AGAMEMNON: He has always been most cunning with the mob.
MENELAUS: He is obsessed with honor, a terrible evil.
AGAMEMNON: Then don't you think he'll stand amidst the Argives
to tell them the prophecies Calchas prescribed,
530 that I lied and promised to sacrifice a victim
to Artemis? That he'll seize the army, and order
the Argives to kill you and me and to slaughter the girl?

Even though Agamemnon does not claim that Odysseus will lie in order to persuade the army, his description nevertheless alludes to a deep anxiety about the ease with which he could manipulate the "mob."

To begin, the word *poikilos* ("many-colored," "intricate," but also "wily") has many negative connotations. It was often used to describe woven fabrics, and in fact it is the very term used to describe one of the "tricky" garments discussed earlier in this chapter: the "carpet" which leads Agamemnon to his death (cf. Aeschylus *Agamemnon* 923, 926, 936). When used to describe humans, *poikilos* "indicate[s] ... a man of cunning, full of inventive ploys ... and tricks of every kind."[93] Homer's Odysseus, Hesiod's Prometheus, and the divine trick-

---

[93] Detienne and Vernant 1991:19.

ster Hermes are all characterized as endowed with *poikilia*.[94] Within the context of archaic epic, this was sometimes portrayed as a positive, or at least useful, attribute. But within the arena of public discourse—the context within which Odysseus' *poikilia* is described in *Iphigenia at Aulis*—this was not the case.

Alcaeus, for example, maligns his rival Pittacus because "like a *poikilo*-minded fox foretold an easy outcome and hoped to escape notice."[95] Since the figure of the fox in Greek poetry had heretofore enjoyed "a broadly positive profile" and "instantiat[ed] a laudable cunning,"[96] it appears to be the term *poikilos* alone that conveys the negative connotations of Alcaeus' remarks. In a set of lines directed at an unnamed target, Theognis lambasts a former friend for keeping a "cold and *poikilos* serpent within your breast."[97] In Euripides' *Hecuba*, the Chorus uses a compound form of the same adjective to describe another tragic version of Odysseus as a "*poikilos*-minded [*poikilophrôn*], glib, sweet-talking *dêmos*-pandering"[98] individual who persuades the army that it is necessary to sacrifice Polyxena (another young woman). The dramatic parallels to *Iphigenia at Aulis* are striking, but so too is the fact that both plays use the adjective *poikilos* (or a compound) to describe Odysseus' ability to manipulate the crowd. Aristophanes draws on the same lexical tradition in his *Knights*, a comedy which, as we have seen, is similar to *Iphigenia at Aulis* in its preoccupation with deceptive speech. In *Knights*, the characters Cleon and the Sausage Seller represent the ubiquity and danger of deceptive speech and flattery in Athenian political discourse,[99] and Aristophanes calls each of these men *poikiloi*.[100] Even more compellingly, he refers to their methods of persuasion as *doloi poikiloi* (*Knights* 685).

A speaker who is *poikilos*, then, is one who is able to twist words in order to be persuasive, and this is exactly what is implied of Odysseus when he is described as such. Furthermore, his reasons for using rhetorical *poikilia* are clearly self-interested: he is *philotimos*—ambitious—a term which, even when not qualified as "a terrible evil" (as it is here) was already rife with negative connotations.[101]

---

94 The Homeric Odysseus is regularly described with the compound ποικιλομήτης (cf. Homer *Odyssey* 3.163, 7.168, 22.115, etc.); Prometheus receives a variety of *poikilo*-compounds (Hesiod *Theogony* 511: ποικίλος αἰολόμητις; *Theogony* 521: ποικιλόβουλος); and Hermes is also called ποικιλομήτης (*Homeric Hymn to Hermes* 155, 514).

95 Alcaeus fragment 69: ὁ δ' ὡς ἀλώπα [... / ποικ[ι]λόφρων εὐμάρεα προλέξα[ις / ἤλπ[ε]το λάσην.

96 Cf. Steiner 2010:100.

97 Theognis 599–602: ψυχρὸν ὃς ἐν κόλπῳ ποικίλον εἶχες ὄφιν.

98 Euripides *Hecuba* 131–132: ὁ ποικιλόφρων / κόπις ἡδυλόγος δημοχαριστής.

99 Cf. Sommerstein 1981:2; Hesk 2000:255–258; Scholtz 2004.

100 Also noted by Bowie 1993:54. Cf. Aristophanes *Knights* 685 (the Sausage Seller), and 758 (Cleon). In the play, Cleon is in fact considered dangerous specifically because he is a *poikilos anêr*.

101 Cf. LSJ; Pindar, fragment 210; Thucydides 2.65.7: Thucydides speaks of "private *philotimia*" (ἰδίας φιλοτιμίας) as being one of the downfalls of the Athenians in the Peloponnesian War. While

Finally, it is evident that Odysseus' *poikilia* allows him to exert considerable influence over the army—in Agamemnon's words to "seize" (*Iphigenia at Aulis* 531: ξυναρπάσας) the army. The use of this verb suggests an act of violence, one that is essentially analogous to Paris' theft of Helen, which is also described in *Iphigenia at Aulis* with *harpazô*-compounds.[102] In other words, the terms with which Agamemnon describes Odysseus reflect, ironically enough, a deep anxiety on his part about his rival's use of questionable rhetoric for his gain. Much like, for example, Cleon in Thucydides' Mytilenian Debate, Agamemnon complains bitterly about his rival's use of the same deceptive tactics he employs.

Even though Agamemnon is not the most trustworthy source, and despite the fact that we never see Odysseus in action, Achilles' testimony at the end of the play confirms that Odysseus has succeeded in doing just what Agamemnon feared. After the exposure of Agamemnon's lies, the passionate pleas for Iphigenia's life, and Agamemnon's eventual rejection of the same, Achilles bursts onto the scene and announces that the Argive army is hot on his heels, and that Odysseus is prepared to take Iphigenia to the altar. Clytemnestra then asks whether Odysseus is "pursuing his own interests, or ordered by the army?" Achilles' responds by saying that "he was chosen willingly,"[103] a pithy formulation, suggesting that both options presented by Clytemnestra are true: Odysseus is acting only at the army's forbearance, but also with his own self-interests in mind.

While we cannot know exactly how Odysseus managed to be chosen, there is some evidence that the information he gave the army is not altogether accurate. Achilles, who had been at the camp and who describes a scene similar to an Athenian assembly,[104] reports that the army is furious with him for protecting

---

Euripides does not specifically qualify Odysseus' *philotimia* as "private," it seems safe to say, from this passage, that he is perceived to be pursuing his own interests. See also Thucydides 3.82 and 8.89 (not terribly dissimilar in sentiment from 2.65); Euripides *Phoenician Women* 531–32; and of course *Iphigenia at Aulis* 342 (cited above on p. 110) and *Iphigenia at Aulis* 520. Euripides and Thucydides are, essentially, the first authors to use these terms (*philotimos, philotimia* etc.) with any frequency.

[102] *Iphigenia at Aulis* 75–76: ἐρῶν ἐρῶσαν ᾤχετ' ἐξαναρπάσας / Ἑλένην. Iphigenia, when she explains her reasons for accepting her own sacrifice, also uses a *harpazô*-compound to describe Helen's kidnapping (*Iphigenia at Aulis* 1382: ἣν ἀνήρπασεν Πάρις). She even argues that it is right that she be sacrificed specifically because it is necessary to stop the barbarians from seizing other Greek women (*Iphigenia at Aulis* 1381: ἁρπάζειν). See also Herodotus 1.2–4, in which he constantly uses the terms *harpazô* and *harpagê* to describe the exchange of kidnappings that preceded the Trojan War. In all of these cases, including the one that relates to Odysseus, forms of *harpazô* clearly denote acts of violence.

[103] *Iphigenia at Aulis* 1363–1364: *Clytemnestra*: ἴδια πράσσων, ἢ στρατοῦ ταχθεὶς ὕπο; / *Achilles*: αἱρεθεὶς ἑκών.

[104] Achilles notes that he had attempted to speak out against the plan to sacrifice Iphigenia, but had been shouted down by a general *thorubos* (uproar, clamor). This kind of popular uproar is

Iphigenia because, according to them, "it is necessary to slaughter her" (*Iphigenia at Aulis* 1348: χρεὼν σφάξαι νιν). Even Achilles' own men have turned against him and are calling him "a slave to marriage" (*Iphigenia at Aulis* 1354: οἵ με τὸν γάμων ἀπεκάλουν ἥσσον') believing that he is choosing his marriage over their war. Neither of these claims is exactly true, since we know it is really a choice between sacrificing Iphigenia and returning home (cf. *Iphigenia at Aulis* 89–93), and that Achilles wishes to save Iphigenia not in order to marry her, but rather to clear his name (*Iphigenia at Aulis* 935–947). It is possible that the army has come to these conclusions on their own, without Odysseus' encouragement. But since we already know that he is a crafty speaker, that he has been charged by the army to lead this endeavor, and that the army has used misinformation to malign and shout down Achilles in an assembly-like atmosphere, the implication is that Odysseus has planted these ideas in the army's (collective) head. At once *poikilos* and *philotimos*, Odysseus embodies a demagogue.[105]

A third leader of the Greeks, the seer Calchas, is described in even less flattering and ambiguous terms. Like Odysseus, Agamemnon accuses him (and his ilk) of being an "ambitious evil" (*Iphigenia at Aulis* 520: φιλότιμον κακόν). Later on, Achilles asks "what kind of man is a seer? One who says a few true things, and many false."[106] While he is not a central character in *Iphigenia at Aulis*, this brief characterization helps evince the idea that the Greek leaders, as evidenced by Agamemnon's behavior on stage, are ever willing to lie and deceive in order to win the glory that only Iphigenia's sacrifice can enable.

Athenian preoccupations about political speakers using these very types of deceitful tactics and manipulative speech had deep roots by the time *Iphigenia at Aulis* was produced. This anxiety is easily visible in both Thucydides' description of the Mytilenian debate and Aristophanes' *Knights*. In these texts, it appears to be a concern that is central to the Athenian polis. But these are not the only texts in which one can detect this apprehension concerning the use of deceit by elite males. Aristophanes' *Acharnians*, for example, is another comedy in which this is quite openly depicted.[107] And Thucydides' Melian dialogues goes so far as to suggest that not only were the Athenians suspicious of their orators, so

---

described by Plato (*Republic* 492B) as being frequent occurrences at "assemblies, law courts, theaters, or military camps," (εἰς ἐκκλησίας ἢ εἰς δικαστήρια ἢ θέατρα ἢ στρατόπεδα) and it is undoubtedly the type of commotion to which Xenophon refers in *Hellenica* 1.7.12–13 when he describes the people's uproar at the thought that they should not be permitted to "do as they please" (πράττειν ὃ ἂν βούληται). On the frequency of such *thoruboi* in democratic Athens, cf. above, pp. 127–128; Bers 1985; Tacon 2001.

[105] This is also true of Odysseus' appearances in other tragedies of the period. See esp. Montiglio 2011:8–11.

[106] *Iphigenia at Aulis* 956–957: τίς δὲ μάντις ἔστ' ἀνήρ, / ὃς ὀλίγ' ἀληθῆ, πολλὰ δὲ ψευδῆ λέγει.

[107] On *Acharnians*, see J. Hall 2010:25–26.

too were the other Greeks. Indeed, the entire reason that the dialogue occurs, as the Athenian ambassadors state in their opening sentence, is because the Melians will not allow them to speak before the people, lest they "be deceived at once upon hearing [the Athenians'] alluring and irrefutable words" (Thucydides 5.85.1: μὴ ... ἐπαγωγὰ καὶ ἀνέλεγκτα ἐσάπαξ ἀκούσαντες ἡμῶν ἀπατηθῶσιν).

Nor were these the only authors or genres that address contemporary anxieties about deceptive political speech. Antiphon's *Tetralogies* highlight another problem that Sophistic theory faced in the late fifth century. In these speeches, Antiphon all but gives up trying to establish what actually happened in the hypothetical incidents, focusing heavily on what is "likely" (τὸ εἰκός) or what is "credible" (τὸ πιστός). A recurring theme in Antiphon's work is the relationship between *logos* and *ergon*, and what emerges is "an alignment of probability, discourse, and law on the one hand against direct evidence, facts, and nature on the other."[108] Sophocles' *Philoctetes* is another tragedy that foregrounds the problem of deceit and sophistic rhetoric.[109] And Critias fragment 19 portrays another instance of an individual using deceptive means in a coercive manner. The speaker of this fragment postulates that the gods were invented by "some man, cunning and clever in judgment" (line 12: πυκνός τις καὶ σοφὸς γνώμην ἀνήρ) as a means of scaring other humans into behaving well. It is explicit that this was achieved by "concealing the truth with false speech" (v. 26: ψευδεῖ καλύψας τὴν ἀλήθειαν λόγῳ). And although the outcome (good behavior) is theoretically a positive one, it is nevertheless another example of the disconnect between *logos* and *ergon*, particularly in persuasive speech. The nonchalance with which the speaker describes this act, and the fragment's conformity with mainstream sophistic thought on deceitful rhetoric, demonstrate that such means were considered common.[110] We can thus see that in *Iphigenia at Aulis*, Euripides addresses concerns that we see constantly in other late fifth-century Athenian documents.

Euripides differs from these other writers, however, by framing this contemporary concern against the background of Aeschylus' *Agamemnon*. By embedding an earlier and canonical tragedy within his own, he places *Iphigenia at Aulis* within a longer tradition of tragic reflection on the subject of problematic speech, and he signals that his own tragedy will delve deeply into the subject. Just as importantly, by drawing on the tragic figure who, perhaps more than any other, inspired fear with her speech,[111] Euripides heightens the

---

[108] Gagarin 2002:134.

[109] Cf. e.g. Rose:1976.

[110] On this fragment cf. Hesk 2000:180–188; O'Sullivan 2012; and Whitmarsh 2014.

[111] See Thalmann 1993:130: "conventions have a way of being realized in particularly memorable form in certain texts, and their use later will inevitably evoke those texts ...[F]or Euripides and

tension that results from Agamemnon's persistent use of deceptive language. Much as it does with the *Iliad*, *Iphigenia at Aulis* effectively uses the poetic canon as a means to shine a light on a very real political issue at the heart of both the play and contemporary Athenian culture, and to destabilize the perceptions created by his predecessor. Agamemnon's deceit of Clytemnestra, in all its contrasts to the Aeschylean tradition, reverberates through every scene and relates to every aspect of *Iphigenia at Aulis*, reinforcing an image of democratic leaders who are willing to use all manners of manipulation to further their interests. In so doing, Euripides also rejects Aeschylus' idea that deceptive female speech is an evil that represents "the overthrow of social order"[112] and fundamental threat to democracy. Indeed, it is through the contrast with *Agamemnon* that *Iphigenia at Aulis* emphasizes the manner in which *male* deceit is the main catalyst for instability.

---

his audience, as well as for us, the *Oresteia* was such a text because of its historical significance as a major summing-up of Athenian culture."

[112] Goldhill 1986:14 on Clytemnestra in *Agamemnon*. Quoted in full above on p. 140.

Epilogue

Reversing the Lens and
Reimagining Poetry in the *Polis*

WE HAVE SEEN HOW EURIPIDEAN tragedy consistently employs external poetic traditions and genres in order to draw attention to specific political issues that are central to the tragedies themselves. In this chapter, I reverse the lens, so to speak, and focus not on the political issues that Euripides throws into relief by engaging with external poetic traditions, but rather on how these plays simultaneously challenge the reception of these poetic traditions in the Athenian *polis*. Posing the question this way, what is striking is how deftly Euripides eludes simple characterization. At times, as in dealing with paeans, he appears to challenge mainstream considerations of the genre. With epinician, he comes off as a traditionalist, abandoning the softened form that had occurred over previous decades in favor of using the genre, once again, to explore the relationship between a returning hero and his political community. With the poetry of Homer and Aeschylus, on the other hand, Euripides seems to place himself as a competitor, suggesting that his own poetry is better adapted to the social and political milieu of late fifth-century Athens. By taking this holistic look at the different ways in which Euripidean tragedy engages with and exploits a variety of poetic forms, we can better understand the range of approaches Euripides takes in relation to the poetic traditions he inherited. Ultimately, as I argue at the end of this chapter, what emerges is an image of a post-modern poet in Umberto Eco's sense of the term: one who is aware of prior traditions, and also of his audience's awareness of these traditions; an awareness that is not necessary to enjoy Euripidean tragedy, but one that can offer new avenues for interpretation.[1]

---

[1] See especially Eco 1984:37–41.

1. *Ion*'s Paeans and the Athenian *polis*

Euripides' employment of paeans in *Ion* presents perhaps the most straight-forward case of his reconsideration of the mainstream uses of poetry in the Athenian *polis*. As I detail at length in Chapter 1, our evidence shows that the paean was the poetic vehicle *par excellence* for constructing Ionian identity in the fifth century.[2] Athens in particular seems to have exploited paeans, above all at sanctuaries to Apollo, in order to propagate notions of Ionian identity that subtly justified its hegemonic role in the Delian League.[3] While the evidence for purely Athenian paeans has essentially all been lost, by analogy with paeans composed for other Greek *poleis*, we can surmise that these songs fulfilled the important function of expressing "local" identity (or identities) in Athens as well.[4] All of this suggests that large portions of Euripides' audience would intuitively feel a close relationship between the performance of paean-songs in Apolline contexts, and the expression of identity and of notions of shared (mythological) origins.

For many, then, it would have been striking to see *Ion*'s paeans insistently present fictionalized Ionian identities and persistently undermine the divinity that is their patron. Since Athenians and Ionians regularly made use of paeans in order to propagate the same compelling genealogical relationships advanced by *Ion*, and since these relationships served to provide a strong mythological foundation to the Delian League, the perverse nature of these tragic paeans takes on a profound meaning. In short, it becomes clear that, at least in the world of the play, paeans are unreliable vehicles for the very articulation of identities and origins in which the tragedy is supposedly engaged. Indeed, even though the play claims to offer a successful merger of Athenian and Ionian identity, the means by which this relationship could be cemented and promoted remain controversial and questionable: the paean seems in no way capable of performing a shared Athenian/Ionian identity, only of pointing to the cracks in its foundation. At a time when the (geo)political stakes of Athenian/Ionian solidarity were inordinately high outside of *Ion*'s tragic world, the play challenges the credibility, indeed the viability, of the primary poetic vehicle for achieving such unity both inside and outside of the dramatic setting.

---

[2]   Above, pp. 23–29; see also Kowalzig 2007:81–110.
[3]   Above on pp. 23–28; Kowalzig 2007:114–118.
[4]   For the scant evidence we have coming directly from Athens, see above, pp. 30–31. For examples of the paean functioning to express local identities outside of Athens, see e.g. Dougherty 1994; Herda 2011.

2. Epinician in the Light of *Heracles* and *Alexandros*

The case of epinician is more complex, not only because we have seen Euripidean tragedy deal with the genre in very different ways, but also because the reception of epinician poetry in Athens is not entirely clear. As we shall see, however, Euripides' employment of epinician in conjunction with the hero-*polis* relationship appears to be a deviation from Athenian norms. First of all, with the notable exception of Euripides' epinician for Alcibiades (to which we will return again below), the genre appears to have become "functionally extinct" in the Greek world some thirty years prior to *Heracles* and *Alexandros*.[5] Athletic victors seemed to have simply stopped commissioning new epinician odes to celebrate their victories, and it is thus self-evident that epinician odes were no longer regularly used—or consumed—as a form of mediation between elite individuals and their communities. That is not to say that Athenians were unfamiliar with the genre. Quotations of Pindar and Simonides in Aristophanes would not make sense if at least part of the audience were not intimately familiar with specific poems, and the frequency of allusions suggests that the epinician repertoires of these poets were still widely known in Athens.[6] The genre was also featured regularly on the tragic stage, as has been discussed by numerous scholars in recent years.[7] But in tragedy, at least, epinician poetry was often disassociated from questions of civic integration, becoming, as Carey puts it, "a simple—even simplistic—exercise in celebration."[8] Generally speaking, then, in the decades preceding the productions of *Heracles* and *Alexandros*, the notion that epinician poetry was also a form of mediation between victor and *polis* may not have seemed especially relevant to an Athenian audience.[9]

Just as importantly, long before its decline in popularity in the Greek world, Athenian attitudes towards epinician poetry, and perhaps athletics more generally, seem to have been fraught. The traditional view has long been that

---

[5] Quoting Alley 2019:30, but see also Swift 2010:108.

[6] Pindar fragment 105a S-M at *Birds* 924–930, and Simonides fragment 507 PMG at *Clouds* 1354–1358, both discussed by Swift 2010:112–114. For more on Aristophanic quotations of and allusions to Simonides, see esp. Rawles 2013.

[7] Swift 2010 and 2012; Carey 2012; Kampakoglou 2018.

[8] Carey 2012:27. The essay also provides a survey of epinician in all three surviving tragedians, including in *Heracles* and (briefly) *Alexandros*. With these two plays, Carey is most interested in the generic hybridity of the odes in *Heracles* (see pp. 15–19) and a possible "*phthonos* motif" in *Alexandros* (p. 23). Kampakoglou 2018 takes a different approach in his survey of Euripidean plays in which epinician song and motifs are employed, arguing that Euripides typically "employs epinician imagery to throw into relief the alienation of the tragic hero from his community and accentuate the violent reversal of his fate" (p. 188).

[9] Perhaps this is also indicated by Pheidippides' dismissal of Simonides' poetry in Aristophanes' *Clouds* (cf. *Clouds* 1353–1362).

democratic Athens was naturally "hostile" to epinician poetry.[10] This stance has recently and justifiably been questioned by various scholars, who note (among other things) that the three or four epinicians composed for Athenian victors are more than can be found for other major cities at the time;[11] that non-poetic honors were accorded to athletic victors that put them on a par with generals and politicians in Athens;[12] and that athletes appear to have been widely admired.[13] These points have provided an important corrective to what was surely an over-simplified view of the reception of epinician in democratic Athens, but other evidence shows us that Athens' relationship with the genre was nevertheless unusual.[14] Unlike other Greek *poleis*, Athens did not permit statues of athletic victors to be erected in the *agora*.[15] There is considerable evidence of hostility in Athens towards the breeding of horses for athletic competition (*hippotrophia*),[16] the very activity Pindar sees as the most worthy of his epinician praise.[17] And in a famous Euripidean fragment from the satyr play *Autolycus*, we see a fully articulated critique of athletes that is replete with tropes that are found in both later and earlier authors.[18] The Euripidean critique certainly does not reflect the

[10] As espoused by Bowra 1938:267–268; and Wade-Gery 1958:247–252. Segal 1986:124 implicitly follows this view when he argues that "Pindar writes for aristocratic patrons at a time when in many parts of the Greek world they are embattled against a rising wave of democratic feeling." This dichotomy has been examined more recently, and in a more nuanced manner, by Papakonstantinou 2003. Aloni 2012 presents a different (yet still constitutionally driven) reason for Athens' relative lack of interest in epinician, namely that (like Sparta) Athens had a "total-ising regime" (p. 30) that privileged collective or civic identities in lieu of celebrations of families and individuals.

[11] Swift 2010:107.

[12] IG I² 77 confirms that *sitêsis*, the practice of providing state-funded meals, was a reward for athletic victors at least as far back as the 430s BCE, and it is likely that the right of *proedria* (seats of honor at the theater) was also granted at this time. On the inscription see esp. Morrissey 1978:124 who points out that "*sitêsis* seems not to have been given without *proedria* until Roman times." Pritchard 2010:66 makes the point that these honors were also granted to "victorious generals ... and politicians who had performed an extraordinary service for the city."

[13] See Kyle 1993:124–41; and Pritchard 2010.

[14] This is arguably true of every ancient Greek city, though of course our evidence for basically every *polis* besides Aegina is extremely limited.

[15] Currie 2005:145; Swift 2010:110; Aloni 2012:27. The ancient evidence regarding the lack of statues is admittedly scarce, and consists essentially of a contrast made by Lycurgus between Athens and other cities in which one "will find [statues] of athletes erected in the *agora*," while the Athenians reserve this right for "generals and the tyrant-killers" (Lycurgus 1.51: εὑρήσετε δὲ παρὰ μὲν τοῖς ἄλλοις ἐν ταῖς ἀγοραῖς ἀθλητὰς ἀνακειμένους, παρ' ὑμῖν δὲ στρατηγοὺς ἀγαθοὺς καὶ τοὺς τὸν τύραννον ἀποκτείναντας).

[16] Hornblower 2004:250–251, but see also my discussion of *ostraka* cast for Megacles above in Chapter 2 (p. 54).

[17] Kurke 1991:185–187.

[18] Euripides fr. 282 Kn. For other examples see Xenophanes fragment B 2 DK, and Plato *Apology* 36d. On the connections between these three texts, see Harris 2009:163–166. For evidence that other texts (both earlier and later) draw on the same tropes as the Euripidean fragments, cf. García

sentiments of all Athenians—and perhaps not even those of its author—but its very existence indicates that this type of hostility towards athletes had entered the mainstream. All of this evidence dates from the fifth century, and it contributes to the image of athletics as a topic that was, at the very least, a sensitive one in Athens.

Moreover, certain peculiar elements of Athenian epinician odes suggest that the songs themselves inspired complex reactions in fifth-century Athens. The case of Pindar's Seventh *Pythian*, composed for Megacles, is instructive. The ode was almost certainly composed soon after Megacles had been ostracized, and as such was not performed in Athens, at least not originally.[19] Unlike most Pindaric odes, it makes no reference to public celebration, and the tone of the poem is relatively subdued when it comes to praise for the victor himself, with only the barest mention of Megacles' penchant for horse-breeding and chariot-racing.[20] The implication, as Athanassaki has argued, is that the ode actually warns against ostentatious celebration of particular athletic achievements.[21] The injunction was likely a prudent one, considering the fact that Megacles was later ostracized a second time, and numerous *ostraka* have been found that specifically refer to him as a *hippotrophos*.[22]

Bacchylides 10, an undatable[23] epinician written for an unknown Athenian victor, features other anomalies. In particular, we find no mention of the victor's family or ancestors, but Bacchylides does explicitly name the *phylê* (civic tribe) to which the victor belonged, noting that he has "brought *kudos* to broad Athens and fame [*doxan*] to the Oeneidae."[24] On this basis, Aloni argues that the ode privileges civic institutions over family connections.[25] Aloni may be going too far here, not least because the fragmentary state of the poem prevents us from knowing with any certainty whether the victor's family is also singled out for praise.[26] But given the singularity of Bacchylides' tribal reference, it is fair to

---

Soler 2010. Pritchard 2012:11 calls it "the fullest critique of athletics in any genre of Athenian literature."

[19] See Bernardini, Cingano et al. 1995:560–561. Athanassaki 2011:257–262 argues that it was intended for reperformance at symposia.

[20] Athanassaki 2011:243–245. Although the song is in celebration of Megacles' victory in the four-horse chariot race at the Pythian games, Pindar only refers to horses once, and only after declaring that "the great city of Athens is the finest prelude" for his song.

[21] Athanassaki 2011:245.

[22] See T 1/101-02, and T 1/104-05 in Brenne 2002:112.

[23] Following Hornblower 2004:257 whose skepticism in this case seems prudent. Contra cf. Aloni 2012:33.

[24] Bacchylides 10.17–18: κῦδος εὐρείαις Ἀθάναις / θῆκας Οἰνείδαις τε δόξαν.

[25] Aloni 2012:33.

[26] Though Aloni 2012:33n69 argues that it is "unlikely on the basis of the legible remnants that the verses contain anything more than the victor's name."

believe that he is modifying essential elements of the epinician tradition in order to conform to the peculiar civic reality of Athenian democracy.[27]

Pindar's second *Nemean*, conversely, follows epinician conventions in repeatedly naming the victor and his family,[28] and the final lines include one of the most straightforward calls for community-wide celebration that can be found in his poetry.[29] But here too it is very much in question whether the song was actually performed before Athenian citizens: due to its brevity, Gelzer has suggested it was intended for performance at Nemea; Instone has argued that it was never performed at all.[30] Most recently, Aloni has ingeniously proposed that the ode was performed not in the urban center of Athens, but in Timodemus' "rural deme" of Acharnae,[31] which Pindar singles out for praise (*Nemean* 2.16–17) in what is the only other mention, besides that in Bacchylides *Ode* 10, of a specific civic subdivision in lieu of the *oikos* or *polis*. In short, there is no consensus on the question of where—or even if—Pindar's ode was performed. But *Nemean* 2 is certainly another case in which traditional epinician motifs appear to be elided and modified in a concession to Athenian civic institutions.

In summary, each of these Athenian epinicians suggests that the genre's status in the city was peculiar, particularly with respect to its role as mediator between victor and *polis*. It is into this quagmire that Euripides appears to have entered, not only with *Heracles* and *Alexandros*, but also with an epinician poem composed for Alcibiades. As noted above,[32] Euripidean authorship of the fragment has been contested by some scholars.[33] It should in my view be considered probable.[34] Our fragments come from two later authors, Plutarch, who quotes it twice (*Demosthenes* 1 and *Alcibiades* 11), and Athenaeus, who cites it once (3a). Plutarch expresses some doubt about the authorship in one instance, referring to "the author ... of the encomium for Alcibiades, whether it was Euripides, as

---

[27] My thanks to Jonathan Hall for his insight on this question.
[28] Timodemus is named in *Nemean* 2.14 and 2.24; his father (Timonous) is named in 2.10; and even his children (2.18: the "Timodemidai") are singled out for praise.
[29] *Nemean* 2.24 (on which, see also above p. 76): τόν [scil. Δία], ὦ πολῖται, κωμάξατε Τιμοδήμῳ σὺν εὐκλέϊ νόστῳ.
[30] Gelzer 1985:109; Instone 1996:144–145.
[31] Aloni 2012:34–35.
[32] At p. 58n42.
[33] Most recently by Lowe 2007:176, though his arguments against authenticity are brief and confined to a section of a footnote (n. 30). Other recent scholars do not contest the attribution but remain essentially non-committal, e.g. Swift 2010:115–116; Aloni 2012:36.
[34] For the longest argument in favor of authenticity, cf. Bowra 1960. Scholars who accept the Euripidean attribution include Page 1962:391; Nagy 1990:187; Papakonstantinou 2003:175; Hornblower 2004:28 and 56–58; Budelman 2012:180.

most believe, or someone else."[35] But on the other occasion, in which he quotes the ode more fully, he expresses no such reservations, and the same is true of Athenaeus, who merely notes that "Euripides wrote an epinician" for Alcibiades' victory in the chariot race.[36] On balance then, out of three citations we have two unequivocal statements of Euripidean authorship and one tepid endorsement of it, and we know that Euripidean authorship was widely believed around 100 CE (Plutarch tells us this much).

While such late attributions are not irrefutable evidence that Euripides wrote the ode for Alcibiades, other considerations also point in that direction. Bowra has identified several stylistic points in the extant lines of the ode that suggest Euripidean authorship,[37] and though such interpretations are to some extent subjective, we can at least say that the fragments do not give us any reason to believe Euripides was *not* the author. Moreover, there is a third argument for authenticity that has not yet, to my knowledge, been made. To wit, insofar as the very purpose of commissioning an epinician ode was to bolster one's reputation, it seems exceedingly likely that Alcibiades would have hired a poet of great repute. While Euripides was not the only such poet active in Athens at this time, he was certainly one of a select few. And if another famous poet, for example Agathon, had written these lines, it seems *unlikely* that later generations would have so broadly attributed the ode to Euripides when the actual author was in fact quite well-known.

Regarding the contents of the ode, despite the fact that the surviving fragments are scant,[38] there is no doubt that it traffics in standard epinician tropes: in the first line, Euripides bestows upon Alcibiades a phrase of unadulterated praise ("I marvel at you, son of Cleinias"[39]), after which he announces the unprecedented nature of Alcibiades' victory. The song was obviously intended to enhance its subject's reputation in Athens, and in this sense it is a fairly straightforward revival of what appears to have been, by then, a long-extinct genre. Moreover, one of the fragments specifically refers to the victor's desire to belong to a "glorious city,"[40] implying that Alcibiades' relationship with Athens was an issue with which the poem dealt. This fits neatly into the model of epinician mediation that is broadly

---

[35] Plutarch *Demosthenes* 1: Ὁ μὲν γράψας τὸ ... εἰς Ἀλκιβιάδην ἐγκώμιον, εἴτ᾽ Εὐριπίδης ὡς ὁ πολὺς κρατεῖ λόγος, εἴθ᾽ ἕτερός τις ἦν.

[36] Plutarch *Alcibiades* 11.3: λέγει δ᾽ ὁ Εὐριπίδης; Athenaeus 3a: Εὐριπίδης ἔγραψεν ἐπινίκιον.

[37] Bowra 1960:76–79.

[38] The opening six lines, plus another line or two from a later point in the song. Bowra 1960 remains the most complete treatment of the remaining fragments.

[39] Euripides *Epinician for Alcibiades* fragment 1.1-2: σὲ δ᾽ ἄγαμαι, / ὦ Κλεινίου παῖ.

[40] As quoted in Plutarch *Demosthenes* 1: τὰν πόλιν εὐδόκιμον. On the reconstruction of the passage, see esp. Bowra 1960:78.

visible in Pindar's poetry, and as such it also appears to be a deviation from the norms of Athenian epinician, for as discussed above, in their Athenian odes, both Pindar and Bacchylides are hesitant to focus on their victors' relationship with the *polis* as a whole.

Seen in this light, Euripides' epinician dabblings in *Heracles* and *Alexandros* suggest a persistent interest in exploring the political potential of epinician, at a time when this question was undeniably charged on account of Alcibiades' equestrian triumphs.[41] As we saw in Chapter 2, the two plays' treatments of epinician are neither consistent with each other, nor indeed does either employ a straightforward model of epinician mediation. *Alexandros* shows a community's hostile reception to epinician celebration, while *Heracles* suggests both the civic potential and pitfalls of epinician song. What the plays do have in common, however, is a definite interest in the reception of such songs in the *polis*. Together, and alongside the ode for Alcibiades, these plays achieve a sort of re-politicization of epinician poetry in the Athenian civic space. In Euripides' hands, the genre is no longer purely celebratory, nor does it simply set in relief some sort of tragic reversal. Instead, Euripidean epinician deviates from both prior and contemporary Athenian norms and organizes the focus of these songs around a traditional theme: the hero's reception in the *polis*.

3. Iphigenia at Aulis and Homeric Epic in Athens

As I argue in Chapter 3, the Iliadic subtext running throughout *Iphigenia at Aulis* prompts troubling questions about the dynamics of power within a democratic body. Here, I contend that, by dramatizing the dissimilarity between Homeric and democratic armies, *Iphigenia at Aulis* wades into a contemporary debate about the usefulness of Homeric poetry as "educational" texts in classical Athens. In particular, *Iphigenia at Aulis*' manipulation of the *Iliad* can be seen as a reaction to the contemporary usage of Homer's poetry for didactic purposes, something that appears to have been broad-ranging throughout the late-archaic and classical eras.[42] Xenophanes, for example, claims that "from the beginning, all men have learned from Homer."[43] Herodotus notes that it is from Homer and Hesiod that the Greeks first learned of the gods' origins, names, and functions.[44] And Plato speaks of those who praise Homer because "the poet

---

[41] I discuss this at length above in Chapter 2 at pp. 54–59.

[42] For general approaches to Homer's role in ancient Greek education, see Marrou 1965:31–41 and 246–47; Verdenius, 1970; Robb 1994, 159–82, who argues that "to convey an oral paideia was the fundamental cultural purpose of Homeric speech" (p. 166); and Murray 1996:19–24.

[43] Xenophanes fragment B 10 DK: ἐξ ἀρχῆς καθ' Ὅμηρον ἐπεὶ μεμαθήκασι πάντες.

[44] Herodotus 2.53.2. As is correctly pointed out by Ford 2002:99, Herodotus does not mean to "praise the poets' omniscience ... but [to form] a historical argument that Greek images and conceptions of divinity derive from them."

has educated Greece," and is a worthy example for the "ordering and culture of human affairs."[45] In all likelihood, the use of Homer for didactic purposes had been disputed for much of this time: the same Xenophanes also criticizes Homer (and Hesiod) for providing negative examples of the gods' engaging in unsavory acts,[46] while Plato cites those who praise Homer only to categorically reject the presence of any poetry besides hymns and encomia to good men in his ideal city (*Republic* 607a). In short, Homer's poetry was seen as an educational tool by the Greeks, but not without controversy.

This seems to have been particularly true concerning beliefs about Homer's ability to teach lessons on military and civic leadership.[47] Certainly some in Athens believed his poetry was replete with such knowledge: as Aeschylus asks in Aristophanes' *Frogs*, "how else did divine Homer win honor and glory, if not from teaching the most useful things: battle lines, brave deeds, and the arming of men."[48] Aristophanes may be making fun of the idea that Homer could "teach" such things, but unless the notion held some currency, there would be nothing to make fun of.[49] Other takes on the subject abounded. In Xenophon's *Symposium*, for example, Niceratus suggests that "whoever might wish to become ... a leader of people or a general ... should consult [him, i.e. Niceratus]," thanks to his thorough command of Homer's poetry.[50] It eventually becomes clear that Niceratus is speaking in jest,[51] but once again, the joke is only funny if we assume that some of his contemporaries truly believed the Homeric texts to be repositories of knowledge of warfare and leadership.

Naturally, Plato's Socrates also has something to say on the subject. In the midst of a broader refutation of Homer's didactic qualities in the *Republic* (cf. 598d–600e), Socrates singles out "wars, generalships, governing cities and educating

---

[45] Plato *Republic* 606e: τὴν Ἑλλάδα πεπαίδευκεν οὗτος ὁ ποιητὴς καὶ πρὸς διοίκησίν τε καὶ παιδείαν τῶν ἀνθρωπίνων πραγμάτων.

[46] See especially fragments B 11 DK and B 12 DK, as well as the commentary provided by Lesher 1992:81–85. Lesher notes that even the seemingly complimentary words of fragment 10 are "probably best understood as [Xenophanes] complaining (in a Platonic vein) about the extent of Homer's influence on customary thought and conduct." For an overview of the Xenophanes' hostility towards Homer, see esp. Ford 2002:46–66.

[47] For a good overview of the question, see Klooster and van den Berg 2018:8–13.

[48] Aristophanes *Frogs* 1034–1036: ὁ δὲ θεῖος Ὅμηρος / ἀπὸ τοῦ τιμὴν καὶ κλέος ἔσχεν πλὴν τοῦδ' ὅτι χρήστ' ἐδίδαξεν, / τάξεις ἀρετὰς ὁπλίσεις ἀνδρῶν;

[49] Cf. e.g. Graziosi 2002:177 who argues that that these lines show that Homer was taken to be adept at "teaching how to organise mass fighting," even in the context of classical Athens.

[50] Xenophon *Symposium* 4.6: ὅστις ἂν οὖν ὑμῶν βούληται ... ἢ δημηγορικὸς ἢ στρατηγικὸς γενέσθαι ... ἐμὲ θεραπευέτω. We know from Xenophon *Symposium* 3.5 that Niceratus' education had consisted of memorizing the Homeric epics in their entirety.

[51] See Ford 2002:205–207.

people" as the "finest" (*kallistôn*) subjects about which Homer speaks.[52] Almost immediately, Socrates dismisses the notion of Homeric expertise by asking, rhetorically, whether any city claims to have been better governed thanks to Homer, or any war better fought (*Republic* 599e–600a). Nevertheless, the fact that Plato would go to such lengths in constructing this argument constitutes decisive evidence that many people truly did believe that the Homeric texts contained valuable lessons on leadership.

Still, it is in *Ion* that Plato most strongly implies the existence of a wide-spread belief in Homer's ability to teach leadership. The dialogue as a whole serves, among other things, to refute the existence of poetic and rhapsodic *technê*.[53] And to a certain extent, Socrates' rejection of the notion that Ion has learned the art of generalship (*ta stratiôtika* or *ta stratêgika*) from Homer is part and parcel with this project. But it is striking that while Ion immediately relinquishes any claim to knowledge, via Homer, of charioteering, medicine, or the types of things a wool-spinner or shepherd might say,[54] he is adamant that Homer has taught him a great deal about being a general (*Ion* 540d). In fact, not only does Ion insist that he would know how a general would exhort his soldiers,[55] he even goes so far as to claim that, thanks to his study of Homer, he is likely to be the finest general in all of Greece:

> ΣΩ ἀλλ' ἐκεῖνο μὴν δοκεῖ σοι, ὅστις γε ἀγαθὸς ῥαψῳδός, καὶ
> στρατηγὸς ἀγαθὸς εἶναι;
> ΙΟΝ πάνυ γε.
> ΣΩ οὐκοῦν σὺ τῶν Ἑλλήνων ἄριστος ῥαψῳδὸς εἶ;
> ΙΟΝ πολύ γε, ὦ Σώκρατες.
> ΣΩ ἦ καὶ στρατηγός, ὦ Ἴων, τῶν Ἑλλήνων ἄριστος εἶ;
> ΙΟΝ εὖ ἴσθι, ὦ Σώκρατες· καὶ ταῦτά γε ἐκ τῶν Ὁμήρου μαθών.

> Plato *Ion* 540e–541b

---

[52] Plato *Republic* 599c–d: πολέμων τε πέρι καὶ στρατηγιῶν καὶ διοικήσεων πόλεων, καὶ παιδείας πέρι ἀνθρώπου.

[53] For a brief overview, see esp. Murray 1996:8–10.

[54] When asked whether "you [Ion] or a chariot-driver would better understand" (Plato *Ion* 538b: σὺ κάλλιον γνώσῃ ἢ ἡνίοχος) whether Nestor's charioteering advice in Book 23 was sound, Ion concedes, without argument, that a chariot-driver would. He is equally agreeable concerning the subjects of medicine, fishing, etc., and how shepherds or wool-spinners would talk about their crafts. (cf. *Ion* 538d–540d)

[55] Plato *Ion* 540d: *Socrates:* ἀλλ' οἷα ἀνδρὶ πρέπει εἰπεῖν γνώσεται στρατηγῷ στρατιώταις παραινοῦντι; *Ion:* ναί, τὰ τοιαῦτα γνώσεται ὁ ῥαψῳδός. (*Socrates:* But a rhapsode will know the types of things a general should say while exhorting his soldiers? *Ion:* Yes, such things he will know.)

> SOCRATES: But this at least seems true to you, that whoever is a good
>   rhapsode is also a good general?
> ION: Absolutely.
> SOCRATES: And are you not the finest rhapsode of the Greeks?
> ION: By far, Socrates.
> SOCRATES: Then are you also the best general of the Greeks, Ion?
> ION: Count on it, Socrates; this at least I have learned from Homer.

Socrates does, ultimately, force Ion to concede that he is merely "inspired" (θεῖος) by Homer, without possessing any true knowledge.[56] But Ion never actually relinquishes his claim to have developed expertise in warfare through Homer.[57] And above all, the fact that this is a sticking point for him, alongside the other gestures we have seen to Homer's specific abilities to teach the art of generalship, suggests that similar claims were made with at least some seriousness, and with some frequency to boot.

Indeed, the evidence suggests that the individuals who invoked this Homeric expertise were most variegated. This emerges in unexpected ways and places, for instance in the treatise that is known to us as the *Certamen* between Homer and Hesiod.[58] The surviving work can be dated to the Roman era, but it is almost certainly based on a tradition going at least as far back as the fourth century BCE, and as such it is indicative of attitudes to Homer in classical Greece (and by extension, Athens). The basic and obviously fictional conceit of the treatise is that Homer and Hesiod met at Aulis and engage in a poetic competition. All this would be of little concern to the matter at hand, except that the passage that Homer chooses as his "finest" passage[59] is most unusual: *Iliad* 13.126–33 and 339–44, lines which have been seen "as an interpolated or at best problematic depiction of hoplite-tactics."[60] The choice of this unique passage seems to confirm that Homer was regarded as a teacher of hoplite battle tactics, and thus especially germane to the world of fifth-century Athens. Going even further, Barbara Graziosi argues that "in democratic Athens Homer becomes the poet of communal fighting."[61] Despite the starkly different realities of war and leadership that existed in the Homeric epics and fifth-century Athens, the Athenians were nevertheless able to accommodate Homer as a teacher of these arts in a democratic society.

---

[56] Cf. *Ion* 542b.

[57] As is also pointed out by Weineck 1998:26.

[58] On this curious work, see e.g. West 1967; Richardson 1981; and Graziosi 2002:168–180.

[59] *Certamen Homeri et Hesiodi* 12: τὸ κάλλιστον ἐκ τῶν ἰδίων ποιημάτων. Note that "Homer" here seems to agree with Plato, insofar as both claim that his poems' "finest" (*kallistos*) moments involve lessons on warfare.

[60] Janko 1992:59; cited by Graziosi 2002:175.

[61] Graziosi 2002:180.

At the same time, we can also see the exploitation of Homeric texts by those who were ideologically opposed to Athenian democracy. Two passages, in fact, attest to the utilization of Homeric poetry within what we may call "oligarchic" contexts. The first is from Xenophon's *Memorabilia*, where the author discusses the accusations made against Socrates in the trial that led to his execution. One of these charges is that Socrates used to "choose the basest passages of the finest poets and use them as lessons to teach his companions to be criminals and tyrants."[62] Xenophon then goes on to cite one of these so-called base passages, and it turns out to be none other than the lines that Odysseus speaks to the *basilées* and to the *dêmos* in Book Two of the *Iliad*, including the ones cited above in which the *dêmos* are said to be "of no account whatever in battle or council."[63] The obvious implication is that these lines were seen as fundamentally undemocratic, and that they were wont to be used by individuals who argued in favor of oligarchy or tyranny.

Confirmation of this dynamic comes from Theophrastus' *Characters*, where we find an even more strikingly politicized example of Homeric citation. In his caricature of the "Oligarchic Man," Theophrastus states that this is the type of person who "of Homer's words remembers only this, that '[l]ordship for many is no good thing. Let there be one ruler.'"[64] These are, again, taken from the very same episode to which Socrates' "accusers" refer, that is the passage in which Odysseus rebukes the Achaean army as it flees. Theophrastus' diagnosis of oligarchic exploitations of Homer is not subtle, and in order to be a caricature, it has to present characteristics that are quite recognizable. In the light of this evidence, it is virtually certain that Homer, and in particular this passage of Homer, was used or cited by opponents of democracy as a "lesson" in how power and authority should be exercised in an ideal society.

Iphigenia at Aulis' consistent manipulation of the Homeric text should be read in the context of this highly charged debate concerning the educational merits and uses of Homer's poetry. By presenting the dynamics of the Achaean army in an overtly contemporary manner, the tragedy certainly throws into relief certain problematic aspects of leadership in democratic Athens. At the same time, by depicting a world in which leadership functions in an utterly

---

[62] Xenophon *Memorabilia* 1.2.56: ἔφη δ' αὐτὸν ὁ κατήγορος καὶ τῶν ἐνδοξοτάτων ποιητῶν ἐκλεγόμενον τὰ πονηρότατα καὶ τούτοις μαρτυρίοις χρώμενον διδάσκειν τοὺς συνόντας κακούργους τε εἶναι καὶ τυραννικούς. Once again, it is Graziosi who brings this passage to my attention (2002:178–179)

[63] Xenophon *Memorabilia* 1.2.58, citing *Iliad* 2.188–191, 198–203.

[64] Theophrastus *Characters* 26.2: καὶ τῶν Ὁμήρου ἐπῶν τοῦτο ἓν μόνον κατέχειν, ὅτι 'Οὐκ ἀγαθὸν πολυκοιρανίη, εἷς κοίρανος ἔστω." This passage was brought to my attention by Ober 1998:365–366.

different manner, the play also wades into a contemporary debate concerning the practicality of using the *Iliad* to impart lessons on leadership and military authority. In fact, Achilles' plight exemplifies the irrelevance of the Homeric text. The young hero, who sees the conflicts along very much the same lines as his Homeric counterpart, discovers almost too late that he is living in a new world, one in which his elite status does not even grant him authority over his own Myrmidons, much less the rest of the Achaeans. As we watch Achilles complete this journey of discovery, and as the distance that lies between Athenian society and the world of Homer becomes ever more apparent, it becomes difficult to see how the Homeric texts might provide any insight at all into "wars, generalships, [and] the administration of cities." Deeply embedded within the text, the *Iliad* functions not so much as an ineluctable force that drives the plot to its inevitable conclusion, but rather as a distorted mirror that reflects the dramatic evolution the Achaean army has undergone from Homer to Aulis, and, by extension, the utter impracticality of using Homeric epic to impart lessons on authority and leadership. For the purposes of late fifth-century Athenians, Euripidean tragedy would appear to provide a better sounding board.

4. Reconsidering a Cultural Touchstone: The Case of Agamemnon and Clytemnestra

Perhaps no less than the *Iliad*, Aeschylus' *Agamemnon* was, for both Euripides and his Athenian audience, a cultural touchstone.[65] Aeschylus' plays were surely reperformed in Athens with some regularity, if not at the City Dionysia itself, then at least through reperformances at rural festivals to Dionysus or recitations in private settings.[66] Indeed, the constant riffing on Aeschylean style in the famous *agôn* of Aristophanes' *Frogs* essentially requires the presence of an audience able to grasp these refined allusions.[67] In *Clouds*, conversely, we see Aristophanes precede Euripides by replaying the Agamemnon-Clytemnestra showdown, this time with Socrates inhabiting Clytemnestra's role as a

---

[65] Thalmann 1993:130 suggests that for Euripides and his audience the *Oresteia* was considered "a major summing-up of fifth-century Athenian culture," and the *parodos* of *Agamemnon* in particular was "a deeply but creatively problematical text for Euripides" (p. 127).

[66] For a recent and thorough evaluation of the question, see Lamari 2015. The father-son skirmish at the end of Aristophanes' *Clouds*, a dispute about whether or not the songs of Aeschylus or Euripides should be performed at a private banquet (*Clouds* 1364–1372), suggests that symposia were another venue at which at least portions of Aeschylean tragedy could be reperformed. On this, see e.g. Lai 1997. Biles 2006:229 argues that symposia may not have been the only informal public venue at which Aeschylus' poetry was present, and that "reciting Aeschylus was a natural and even socially acceptable thing to do."

[67] See Revermann 2006b:120.

dangerously persuasive speaker.[68] Even more strikingly, *Wasps* includes a set of allusions to the *Oresteia*, including to *Agamemnon*'s famous "carpet scene," and it does so within the context of a metatheatrical competition with Aeschylus.[69] Once again, in order to make these sophisticated intertextual moments worth Aristophanes' efforts, a reasonable portion of the audience must have been capable of perceiving them, and at least some of them must have grasped the stakes of this poetic engagement.

The Athenian public must have brought similar sets of expertise to the theater when *Iphigenia at Aulis* was first produced. Even beyond the fact that there must have been substantial crossover between the spectators of *Iphigenia at Aulis* and *Frogs* (both performed in 405 BCE, though at different festivals), Euripidean audiences would have been accustomed to the tragedian's penchant for engaging with the *Oresteia* in general,[70] and *Agamemnon* in particular. *Hecuba* engages deeply with *Agamemnon*, and in so doing contests Aeschylus' ideas about war and male violence against female victims.[71] In *Trojan Women*, Cassandra's song and monologue work to "undermin[e] the religious and cosmic pattern of the *Agamemnon*."[72] And *Iphigenia at Tauris*, which presents itself as a sequel to the *Oresteia*,[73] had recently treated audiences to a similar examination of some of the complex dynamics, including those of gender, that were central to Aeschylus' *Agamemnon*.[74] In short, Athenian audiences were accustomed to seeing Euripidean tragedy "re-enact" elements of *Agamemnon* in order to inspire deep and subtle reflections on the cultural and political questions embedded and explored within Aeschylus' play. Not everyone in the audience would have been willing or able to engage with *Iphigenia at Aulis* on this level, but those who were would likely have been drawn in by the lengths to which the tragedy calls attention to its reversal of Agamemnon and Clytemnestra's modes of communication.

How then, might we imagine that an experienced and engaged audience would understand *Iphigenia at Aulis*' use of *Agamemnon* as a textual backdrop

---

[68] Telò 2016:142.

[69] Wyles 2020.

[70] Thalmann 1993:127.

[71] Thalmann 1993.

[72] Brillet-Dubois 2015:168 (for the quote, but argumentation passim).

[73] As suggested by Burnett 1971:71.

[74] Sansone 1975:292 argues that *Iphigenia in Tauris* was "an answer to, and rejection of, the theology of the *Oresteia*" (specifically regarding the 'evolution' of the gods as seen in the trilogy). Zeitlin 2005 sees the play as providing a refutation of Aeschylus' "radical solution" (p. 218) to the problem of matricide. Torrance 2011 argues that in *Iphigenia in Tauris*, the recognition scene, rich in allusions to *Agamemnon*, serves not only to provide a plot reversal (Orestes is saved), but also to emphasize that Euripides is "revers[ing] the anomaly of female killing male which had been so significant in *Agamemnon*" (p. 196).

against which to frame its political questions? To begin, we might think again about the confrontation between Aeschylus and Euripides in Aristophanes' *Frogs*, performed in Athens just a couple of months prior. Given the comedic nature of the scene, the evidence it provides is of limited help in understanding the true relationship between Euripidean and Aeschylean tragedy. But it can tell us how an Athenian audience might plausibly think about Euripides' relation to Aeschylus. In particular, as Ralph Rosen points out, the very existence and terms of the *agôn* suggest that the question of "which [poet] is better" was one that was being asked in Athens at the time.[75] This does not necessarily mean that Euripides himself was interested in this question, but given the frequency with which he openly engaged with Aeschylean tragedy,[76] and the long tradition of competition in almost all ancient Greek poetic arenas,[77] the notion is not far-fetched. Regardless, from the moment that Clytemnestra arrives at Aulis and begins to square off against Agamemnon, the audience must have been heavily primed, perhaps even eager, to see Euripides openly challenging Aeschylus for poetic supremacy.[78]

This poetic competition can be seen separately from the political issue for which it serves as a backdrop, but it need not be. On the one hand, it is easy to imagine the role-reversal in *Iphigenia at Aulis* as a form of pure entertainment; anyone can savor the delight of seeing Agamemnon try—and especially fail—to adopt Clytemnestra's tricky speech for murderous ends. At the same time, the Euripidean role-reversal is overtly political in nature: the contest arises within a political setting (the Achaean camp at Aulis); the question—whether or not to go to war—is one that affects all the soldiers present (and one that Athenians had ample experience weighing); there is much hand-wringing throughout the play about the manner in which this and other political issues are decided; and perhaps above all, Agamemnon's newfound tendency toward deception, both in his debate with Clytemnestra and in other moments of the play, clearly reflects contemporary Athenian concerns about deceptive speech in the democratic *polis*.

As such, the contest that Euripides stages between himself and Aeschylus can be understood not simply as a question of "who staged it better," but also

---

[75] Rosen 2004:319.

[76] Beyond the examples listed above, see also Zeitlin 1980:53, who notes that Euripides' *Orestes* "is formulated as a reaction [against the *Oresteia*] ... Nor is this the first time that Euripides has done battle with the Aeschylean elephant both as an artist and as a thinker."

[77] Griffith 1990.

[78] As Winnington-Ingram 1969, 136 notes, "[t]he number of people in the audience who enjoyed a hit at Aeschylus may not have been large, but need not have been small." Indeed, these meta-theatrical contests with Aeschylus, and in particular with the *Oresteia*, may well have been considered part of Euripides' "brand" at this point in his career, to draw on the language and observations of Wright 2013 (see esp. p. 220) with respect to Aristophanes.

as a debate about which of the two poets can speak with more relevance to the present audience. Indeed, here again Aristophanes' plays can provide important insight into this competitive phenomenon. In *Wasps*, we see Aristophanes imply that not only is his comedy better than tragedy, it can also speak more constructively to the city's cultural moment than, for example, Aeschylus.[79] In the famous *agôn* of *Frogs*, conversely, the one thing on which Euripides and Aeschylus actually seem to agree is that it was the poet's job "to make the cities' people better."[80] None of this proves that Euripides (or Aristophanes, for that matter) either believed or was intent on proving that he was a better citizen-coach than Aeschylus.[81] But it does provide crucial evidence regarding the existence of a contemporary discourse surrounding tragedy's "didactic" potential.[82] Above all, it strongly suggests that Athenian audiences could easily believe that when it came to speaking to and about the politics of the contemporary moment, Euripides was suggesting that his own poetry was far more relevant than that of Aeschylus.

5. Final Reflections on a "Post-modern" Euripides

As the evidence from Aristophanes suggests, Euripides' "competition" with Aeschylus in *Iphigenia at Aulis* must have been seen by some in the audience as a classic Euripidean gambit. Moreover, both Euripides and at least part of his audience must have been aware of the political contexts and stakes involved with challenging Aeschylean tragedy's canonical place in Athenian consciousness; otherwise, Aristophanes' comments—sarcastic or not—about a poet's role in the city would make no real sense. Given Euripides' penchant for playing around with the *Iliad*, epinician, and even paeanic song, many members of the audience would also have been able recognize Euripidean tragedy's engagement with these poetic traditions, and indeed the political stakes of this engagement. Much of the public was, of course, intimately familiar with these poetic forms, and with the political milieus in which they were either expressed or invoked.

It is in this sense that we can begin to see Euripides as a post-modern poet, in the way that Umberto Eco defines the term: a poet who recognizes that "the past, since it cannot be destroyed ... must be revisited: with irony, and not in an innocent way."[83] As with the post-modernism of which Eco speaks, two

---

[79]   Wright 2013:208; Wyles 2020.

[80]   Aristophanes *Frogs* 1009–1010: βελτίους τε ποιοῦμεν / τοὺς ἀνθρώπους ἐν ταῖς πόλεσιν.

[81]   In fact, Wright 2010:167–171 effectively shows that, within the actual Euripidean corpus, there is little evidence of interest in the social ramifications of his tragedies or of poetry more broadly.

[82]   Rosen 2005:264.

[83]   Eco 1984:39.

interpretive paths would have been available to his audience: an audience that understood the depths of Euripides' engagement could "play, consciously and with pleasure, the game of irony." But it was "also possible to not understand the game and to take it seriously, which is a characteristic (a risk) of irony. For there is always someone who takes ironic discourse seriously."[84] Euripides, however, plays this game of irony on two levels: on the first level, once we recognize, either consciously or unconsciously, the poetic intertexts of Euripidean tragedy, we can engage more critically with the political apparatus of the plays. But it is only when we have understood that game that we can access the secondary level, and see the irony that lies beneath Euripides' engagement with the poetic tradition, a politicized engagement which serves also as a means to comment on and challenge the ways in which the poetic past, and indeed present, was received and perceived in the Athenian *polis*.

---

[84] Eco 1984:39.

Bibliography

Adkins, A. W. H. 1966. "Basic Greek Values in Euripides' *Hecuba* and *Hercules Furens*." *Classical Quarterly* 16:193–219.

———. 1982. "Values, Goals, and Emotions in the *Iliad*." *Classical Philology* 77:292–326.

Aélion, Rachel. 1983. *Euripide Héritier d'Eschyle*. Vol. 1. Paris.

Allen, Danielle. 2000. *The World of Prometheus: The Politics of Punishing in Democratic Athens*. Princeton.

Alley, Dennis. 2019. *Talking to Tyrants: Poetic Autonomy in Pindaric Lyric*. PhD diss., Cornell University.

Aloni, Antonio. 2012. "Epinician and the *Polis*." *Bulletin of the Institute of Classical Studies* 55:21–37.

Alty, John. 1982. "Dorians and Ionians." *Journal of Hellenic Studies* 102:1–14.

Amyx, D. A. 1958. "The Attic Stelai: Part III. Vases and Other Containers." *Hesperia* 27:163–254.

Andrewes, A. 1961. "Philochoros on Phratries." *Journal of Hellenic Studies* 81:1–15.

———. 1974. "The Arginousai Trial." *Phoenix* 28:112–122.

———. 1982. "The Tyranny of Pisistratus." *The Cambridge Ancient History*. Vol. 3, part 3. Ed. John Boardman and N. G. L. Hammond, 392–416. Cambridge.

Asmonti, Luca A. 2006. "The Arginusae Trial, the Changing Role of *Strategoi* and the Relationship between *Demos* and Military Leadership in Late–Fifth Century Athens." *Bulletin of the Institute of Classical Studies* 49:1–21.

Athanassaki, Lucia. 2011. "Song, Politics, and Cultural Memory: Pindar's *Pythian* 7 and the Alcmaeonid Temple of Apollo." In Athanassaki and Bowie 2011:235–268.

Athanassaki, Lucia, and Ewen Bowie, eds. 2011. *Archaic and Classical Choral Song: Performance, Politics, and Dissemination*. Leiden.

Athanassaki, Lucia, Richard P. Martin, and John F. Miller, eds. 2009. *Apolline Politics and Poetics*. Athens.

Bacon, Helen H. 1994–1995. "The Chorus in Greek Life and Drama." *Arion* 3:6–24.

Bain, David. 1977. "The Prologues of Euripides' *Iphigeneia in Aulis*." *Classical Quarterly* 27:10–26.

Bakola, E., L. Prauscello, and M. Telò, eds. 2013. *Greek Comedy and the Discourse of Genres*. Cambridge.

Balot, Ryan K. 2004. "Free Speech, Courage, and Democratic Deliberation." In *Free Speech in Classical Antiquity*, ed. Ineke Sluiter and Ralph M. Rosen, 233–259. Leiden.

Barlow, Shirley A. 1971. *The Imagery of Euripides: A Study in the Dramatic Use of Pictorial Language*. London.

––––, ed. 1996. *Euripides: Heracles*. Warminster.

Barron, John P. 1962. "Milesian Politics and Athenian Propaganda c. 460–440 B.C." *Journal of Hellenic Studies* 82:1–6.

–––––. 1964. "Religious Propaganda of the Delian League." *Journal of Hellenic Studies* 84:35–48.

Berman, Daniel W. 2007. "Dirce at Thebes." *Greece and Rome* 54:18–39.

Bernardini, P., E. Cingano, B. Gentili, and P. Giannini, eds. *Pindaro: Le Pitiche*. Verona.

Bers, Victor. 1985. "Dikastic *Thorubos*." In *Crux: Essays in Greek History Presented to G. E. M. de Ste. Croix on His 75th Birthday*, ed. P. A. Cartledge and F. D. Harvey, 1–15. London.

Beta, Simone. 1999. "Madness on the Comic Stage: Aristophanes' *Wasps* and Euripides' *Heracles*." *Greek, Roman, and Byzantine Studies* 40:135–157.

Betensky, Aya. 1978. "Aeschylus' *Oresteia*: The Power of Clytemnestra." *Ramus* 7:11–25.

Biles, Zachary P. 2006–2007. "Aeschylus' Afterlife: Reperformance by Decree in 5th c. Athens?" *Illinois Classical Studies* 31–32:206–242.

Blok, Josine. 2017. *Citizenship in Classical Athens*. Cambridge.

———. 2018. "Retracing Steps: Finding Ways into Archaic Greek Citizenship." In *Defining Citizenship in Archaic Greece*, ed. Alain Duplouy and Roger W. Brock, 79–101. Oxford.

Blume, Horst-Dieter. 2011. "Euripides' *Iphigenia at Aulis*: War and Human Sacrifice." In Markantonatos and Zimmermann 2011:181–187.

Boegehold, Alan L. 1994. "Perikles' Citizenship Law of 451/0 B.C." In Boegehold and Scafuro 1994:57–66.

Boegehold, Alan L., and Adele C. Scafuro, eds. *Athenian Identity and Civic Ideology*. Baltimore.

Bond, Godfrey W., ed. 1981. *Euripides: Heracles*. Oxford.

Bowie, A. M. 1993. *Aristophanes: Myth, Ritual, and Comedy*. Cambridge.

Bowra, C. M. 1938. "Xenophanes and the Olympic Games." *American Journal of Philology* 59:257–279.

———. 1960. "Euripides' Epinician for Alcibiades." *Historia: Zeitschrift für Alte Geschichte* 9:68–79.

———. 1964. *Pindar*. Oxford.

Bremmer, Jan N. 1997. "Myth as Propaganda: Athens and Sparta." *Zeitschrift für Papyrologie und Epigraphik* 117:9–17.

Brenne, S. 2002. "Die Ostraka (487–ca. 416 v. Chr.) als Testimonien (T1)." In Siewert 2002:36–166.

Brillet-Dubois, Pascale. 2015. "A Competition of *Choregoi* in Euripides' *Trojan Women*: Dramatic Structure and Intertextuality." *Lexis* 33:168–180.

Budelman, Felix. 2012. "Epinician and the *Symposion*: A Comparison with the *Enkomia*." In *Reading the Victory Ode*, ed. Peter Agócs, Chris Carey, and Richard Rawles, 173–190. Cambridge.

Bundy, Elroy. 1962. *Studia Pindarica*. Berkeley.

Burgess, Dana L. 2004. "Lies and Convictions at Aulis." *Hermes* 132:37–55.

Burgess, Jonathan S. 2004. "Untrustworthy Apollo and the Destiny of Achilles: *Iliad* 24.55–63." *Harvard Studies in Classical Philology* 102:21–40.

Burkert, Walter. 1983. *Homo Necans: The Anthropology of Ancient Greek Ritual and Myth*. Trans. Peter Bing. Berkeley.

Burnett, Λ. P. 1971. *Catastrophe Survived: Euripides' Plays of Mixed Reversal*. Oxford.

———. 1985. *The Art of Bacchylides*. Cambridge, MA.

———. 1989. "Performing Pindar's Odes." *Classical Philology* 84:283–293.

Caedel, E. B. 1941. "Resolved Feet in the Trimeters of Euripides and the Chronology of the Plays." *Classical Quarterly* 35:66–89.

Calame, Claude. 2009. "Apollo in Delphi and in Delos: Poetic Performances between Paean and Dithyramb." In Athanassaki, Martin, and Miller 2009:169–197.

Carey, Christopher. 1976. "Pindar's Eighth *Nemean* Ode." *Proceedings of the Cambridge Philological Society* 22:26–41.

———. 1989. "The Performance of the Victory Ode." *American Journal of Philology* 110:545–565.

———. 1991. "The Victory Ode in Performance: The Case for the Chorus." *Classical Philology* 86:192–200.

———. 1995. "Pindar and the Victory Ode." In *The Passionate Intellect: Essays on the Transformation of the Classical Tradition*, ed. Lewis Ayres, 85–103. New Brunswick.

———. 2007. "Pindar, Place, and Performance." In Hornblower and Morgan 2007: 167–176.

———. 2012. "The Victory Ode in the Theatre." In *Receiving the Komos: Ancient and Modern Receptions of the Victory Ode*, ed. Peter Agócs, Chris Carey, and Richard Rawles, 1–29. London.

Carter, David M. 2007. *The Politics of Greek Tragedy*. Bristol.

———. 2010. "The Demos in Greek Tragedy." *Cambridge Classical Journal* 56:47–94.

———, ed. 2011. *Why Athens? A Reappraisal of Tragic Politics*. Oxford.

Cartledge, Paul. 2009. *Ancient Greek Political Thought in Practice*. Cambridge.

Ceccarelli, Paola. 2013. "Circular Choruses and the Dithyramb in the Classical and Hellenistic Period: A Problem of Definition." In Kowalzig and Wilson 2013:153–170.

Christ, Matthew R. 1992. "Ostracism, Sycophancy, and Deception of the Demos: [Arist.] *Ath. Pol.* 43.5." *Classical Quarterly* 42:336–346.

Clay, Andreana. 2004. "Keepin' It Real: Black Youth, Hip-Hop Culture, and Black Identity." *American Behavioral Scientist* 46:1346–1358.

Cobetto Ghiggia, Pietro, ed. 1995. *[Andocide] Contro Alcibiade*. Pisa.

Coles, R. A. 1974. *A New Oxyrhynchus Papyrus: The Hypothesis of Euripides' Alexandros*. Bulletin Supplement 32. London.

Collard, Christopher and Martin Cropp, eds. 2008. *Euripides: Fragments*. Vol. 7. Cambridge, MA.

Collard, Christopher, and James Morwood, eds. 2017. *Euripides: Iphigenia at Aulis*. 2 vols. Liverpool.

Comparetti, D. 1898. "Les Dithyrambes de Bacchylide." In *Mélanges Henri Weil: Receuil de Mémoires*, ed. A Fontemoing, 25–38. Paris.

Connor, W. Robert. 1993. "The Ionian Era of Athenian Civic Identity." *Proceedings of the American Philosophical Society* 137:194–206.

———. 1994. "The Problem of Athenian Civic Identity." In Boegehold and Scafuro 1994:34–44.

Constantakopoulou, Christy. 2007. *The Dance of the Islands: Insularity, Networks, the Athenian Empire, and the Aegean World*. Oxford.

Crawley, Richard, trans. 1910. *Thucydides: History of the Peloponnesian War*. London.

Cromey, R.D. 2006. "Apollo Patroos and the Phratries." *L'Antiquité Classique* 75:41–69.

Crönert, Wilhelm. 1922. *Griechische literarische Papyri aus Strassburg, Freiburg und Berlin*. Göttingen.

Crotty, Kevin. 1982. *Song and Action: The Victory Odes of Pindar*. Baltimore

Crouch, Stanley. 1989. "Do the Race Thing: Spike Lee's Afro-Fascist Chic." *The Village Voice*, June 20, 1989. https://www.villagevoice.com/2019/07/01/do-the-race-thing-spike-lees-afro-fascist-chic/.

Csapo, Eric. 2010. *Actors and Icons of the Ancient Theater*. Malden, MA.

Csapo, Eric, and Peter Wilson. 2015. "Drama Outside Athens in the Fifth and Fourth Centuries BC." *Trends in Classics* 7:316–395.

Currie, Bruno. 2005. *Pindar and the Cult of Heroes*. Oxford.

D'Alessio, G. B. 1991. "Osservazioni e paralipomeni ad una nuova edizione dei frammenti di Pindaro." *Rivista di Filologia e di Istruzione Classica* 119:91–117.

———. 1992. "Immigrati a Teo e ad Abdera (SEG XXXI 985: Pind. fr. 52b Sn.-M.)." *Zeitschrift für Papyrologie und Epigraphik* 92:73–80.

———. 1994. Review of *Paian: Studien zur Geschicte einer Gattung* by Lutz Käppel. *The Classical Review* 44:62–65.

———. 2009. "Defining Local Identities in Greek Lyric Poetry." In *Wandering Poets in Ancient Greek Culture: Travel, Locality and Pan-Hellenism*, ed. Richard Hunter and Ian Rutherford, 137–177. Cambridge.

———. 2013. "'The Name of the Dithyramb': Diachronic and Diatopic Variations." In Kowalzig and Wilson 2013:113–132.

D'Angour, Armand. 1997. "How the Dithyramb Got Its Shape." *Classical Quarterly* 47:331–351.

Davies, J. K. 1971. *Athenian Propertied Families 600–300 B.C.* Oxford.

Davies, M., and P. J. Finglass, eds. 2014. *Stesichorus: The Poems*. Cambridge.

de Schutter, Xavier. 1987. "Le culte d'Apollon Patrôos à Athènes." *L'Antiquité Classique* 56:103–129.

Detienne, Marcel, and Jean-Pierre Vernant. 1991. *Cunning Intelligence in Greek Culture and Society*. Trans. Janet Lloyd. Chicago.

Diggle, J., ed. 1981–1994. *Euripidis Fabulae*. 3 vols. Oxford.

Di Giuseppe, Lidia. 2012. *Euripide: Alessandro*. Lecce.

Dodds, E.R. 1951. *The Greeks and the Irrational*. Boston.

Donlan, Walter. 1979. "The Structure of Authority in the *Iliad*." *Arethusa* 12:51–70.

———. 1982. "Reciprocities in Homer." *The Classical World* 75:137–175.

———. 1997. "The Relations of Power in the Pre-State and Early State Polities." In *The Development of the Polis in Archaic Greece*, ed. Lynette G. Mitchell and P. J. Rhodes, 39–48. London.

Dougherty, Carol. 1993. *The Poetics of Colonization from City to Text in Archaic Greece*. Oxford.

———. 1994. "Pindar's Second Paean: Civic Identity on Parade." *Classical Philology* 89:205–218.

———. 1996. "Democratic Contradictions and the Synoptic Illusion of Euripides' *Ion*." In *Dêmokratia: A Conversation on Democracies, Ancient and Modern*, ed. Josiah Ober and Charles Hedrick, 249–270. Princeton.

Dover, Kenneth. 1974. *Greek Popular Morality in the Time of Plato and Aristotle*. Oxford.

Driscoll, C. M., M. R. Miller, and A. B. Pinn, eds. 2019. *Kendrick Lamar and the Making of Black Meaning*. Abingdon, England.

Dunn, Francis M. 1997. "Ends and Means in Euripides' *Heracles*." In *Classical Closure: Reading the End in Greek and Latin Literature*, ed. Deborah H. Roberts, Francis M. Dunn, and Don Fowler, 83–111. Princeton.

Eco, Umberto. 1984. *Postille a Il nome della rosa*. Milan.

Eisner, Robert. 1979. "Euripides' Use of Myth." *Arethusa* 12:153–174.

———. 1980. "Echoes of the *Odyssey* in Euripides' *Helen.*" *Maia* 32:31–37.

Elmer, David F. 2013. *The Poetics of Consent: Collective Decision Making in the Iliad.* Baltimore.

Erbse, Hartmut. 1986. *Untersuchungen zur Funktion der Götter im homerischen Epos.* Berlin.

Farrington, Andrew. 1991. "ΓΝΩΘΙ ΣΑΥΤΟΝ: Social Self-Knowledge in Euripides' *Ion.*" *Rheinisches Museum für Philologie* 134:120–136.

Fearn, David. 2007. *Bacchylides: Politics, Performance, Poetic Tradition.* Oxford.

———. 2011. "The Ceians and Their Choral Lyric: Athenian, Epichoric, and Pan-Hellenic Perspectives." In Athanassaki and Bowie 2011: 207–236.

———. 2013. "Athens and the Empire: The Contextual Flexibility of Dithyramb, and Its Imperialist Ramifications." In Kowalzig and Wilson 2013: 133–152.

Fernández Delgado, José Antonio. 2012. "Luces y Sombras en la Comunicación con Apolo, de la Monodia de Ión a la de Creúsa." *Journal of Classical Philology* 16:17–34.

Foley, Helene P. 1982. "Marriage and Sacrifice in Euripides' *Iphigeneia in Aulis.*" *Arethusa* 15:159–180.

———. 1985. *Ritual Irony: Poetry and Sacrifice in Euripides.* Ithaca.

———. 2001. *Female Acts in Greek Tragedy.* Princeton.

Fontenrose, Joseph P. 1968. "The Hero as Athlete." *California Studies in Classical Antiquity* 1:73–104.

Ford, Andrew. 2002. *The Origins of Criticism: Literary Culture and Poetic Theory in Classical Greece.* Princeton.

———. 2006. "The Genre of Genres: Paeans and Paian in Early Greek Poetry." *Poetica* 38:277–296.

———. 2019. "Linus: The Rise and Fall of Lyric Genres." In Foster, Kurke, and Weiss 2019:57–81.

Forsdyke, Sara. 2005. *Exile, Ostracism, and Democracy: The Politics of Expulsion in Ancient Greece.* Princeton.

———. 2008. "Street Theatre and Popular Justice in Ancient Greece: Shaming, Stoning, and Starving Offenders inside and outside the Courts." *Past and Present* 201:3–50.

Foster, Margaret, Leslie Kurke, and Naomi Weiss. "Introduction." In Foster, Kurke, and Weiss 2019:1–28.

Foster, Margaret, Leslie Kurke, and Naomi Weiss, eds. 2019. *Genre in Archaic and Classical Greek Poetry: Theories and Model.* Leiden.

Fraenkel, Eduard, ed. 1950. *Aeschylus: Agamemnon.* 3 vols. Oxford.

Friedman, Rachel D. 2007. "Old Stories in Euripides' 'New' *Helen:* ΠΑΛΑΙΟΤΗΣ ΓΑΡ ΤΩΙ ΛΟΓΩΙ Γ'ΕΝΕΣΤΙ ΤΙΣ (*Hel.* 1056)." *Phoenix* 61:195–211.

Furley, William D. 1999–2000. "Hymns in Euripidean Tragedy." *Illinois Classical Studies* 24–25:183–198.

Furley, William D., and Jan Maarten Bremer. 2001. *Greek Hymns: Selected Cult Songs from the Archaic to the Hellenistic Period.* 2 vols. Tübingen.

Gagarin, Michael. 2002. *Antiphon the Athenian: Oratory, Law, and Justice in the Age of the Sophists.* Austin.

Gamel, Mary-Kay. 1999. "Introduction: *Iphigenia at Aulis.*" In *Women on the Edge: Four plays by Euripides,* ed. Ruby Blondell, Mary-Kay Gamel, Nancy Sorkin Rabinowitz, and Bella Zweig, 305–328. New York.

García Soler, María José. 2010. "Euripides' Critique of Alcibiades in *Autolykus,* fr. 282 N²." *Nikephoros* 23:139–153.

Garner, Richard. 1990. *From Homer to Tragedy: The Art of Allusion in Greek Poetry.* London.

Gause, Charles Phillip. 2003. Review of *Performing Identity/Performing Culture: Hip Hop as Text, Pedagogy, and Lived Practice* by Greg Dimitriadis. *Urban Education* 38:134–140.

Gelzer, Thomas. 1985. "Μοῦσα αὐθιγενής: Bemerkungen zu einem Typ Pindarischer und Bacchylideischer Epinikien." *Museum Helveticum* 42:95–120.

Giannopoulou, Vasiliki. 1999–2000. "Divine Agency and *Tyche* in Euripides' *Ion*: Ambiguity and Shifting Perspectives." *Illinois Classical Studies* 24–25:257–271.

Gibert, John. 1995. *Change of Mind in Greek Tragedy*. Göttingen.

———. 2005. "Clytemnestra's First Marriage: Euripides' *Iphigenia in Aulis*." In Pedrick and Oberhelman 2005:227–248.

Gibson, Casarae L. 2017. "'Fight the Power': Hip Hop and Civil Unrest in Spike Lee's *Do the Right Thing*." *Black Camera* 8:183–207.

Gill, Jon. 2019. "From 'Blackness' to Afrofuture to 'Impasse': The Figura of the Jimi Hendrix/Richie Havens Identity Revolution as Faintly Evidenced by the Work of Kendrick Lamar and More Than a Nod to Lupe Fiasco." In Driscoll, Miller, and Pinn 2019:191–211.

Golden, Mark. 1997. "Equestrian Competition in Ancient Greece: Difference, Dissent, Democracy." *Phoenix* 51:327–344.

Goldhill, Simon. 1984. *Language, Sexuality, Narrative: the Oresteia*. Cambridge.

———. 1986. *Reading Greek Tragedy*. Cambridge.

———. 1990. "The Great Dionysia and Civic Ideology." In *Nothing to Do with Dionysus? Athenian Drama in Its Social Context*, ed. John J. Winkler and Froma I. Zeitlin, 97–129. Princeton.

———. 1992. *Aeschylus: The Oresteia*. Cambridge.

Gorman, Vanessa B. 2001. *Miletos, the Ornament of Ionia: A History of the City to 400 B.C.E.* Ann Arbor.

Graf, Fritz. 1979. "Apollon Delphinios." *Museum Helveticum* 36:2–22.

———. 2009. *Apollo*. London.

Gras, Michel. 1984. "Cité grecque et lapidation." *Publications de l'École française de Rome* 79:75–89.

Graziosi, Barbara. 2002. *Inventing Homer: The Early Reception of Epic*. Cambridge.

Green, Ricky K. 2001. *Democratic Virtue in the Trial and Death of Socrates: Resistance to Imperialism in Classical Athens*. New York.

Grenfell, Bernard P., and Arthur S. Hunt. 1908. *The Oxyrhynchus Papyri.* Vol. 5. London.

Gribble, David. 1997. "Rhetoric and History in [Andocides] 4, *Against Alcibiades.*" *Classical Quarterly* 47:367–391.

———. 1999. *Alcibiades and Athens: A Study in Literary Presentation.* Oxford.

———. 2012. "Alcibiades at the Olympics: Performance, Politics, and Civic Ideology." *Classical Quarterly* 62:45–71.

Griffin, Jasper. 2007. "Desperate Straits and the Tragic Stage." In *Hesperos: Studies in Ancient Greek Poetry Presented to M. L. West on His Seventieth Birthday,* ed. P. J. Finglass, C. Collard, and N. J. Richardson, 189–203. Oxford.

Griffith, Mark. 1990. "Contest and Contradiction in Early Greek Poetry." In *Cabinet of the Muses: Essays on Classical and Comparative Literature in Honor of Thomas G. Rosenmeyer,* eds. M. Griffith and D. J. Mastronarde, 185–207. Atlanta.

Guillory, Margarita Simon. 2019. "Can I Be *Both?* Blackness and the Negotiation of Binary Categories in Kendrick Lamar's *Section.80.*" In Driscoll, Miller, and Pinn 2019: 25–36.

Hall, Edith. 1995. "Lawcourt Dramas: The Power of Performance in Greek Forensic Oratory." *Bulletin of the Institute of Classical Studies* 40:39–58.

———. 1999. "Actor's Song in Tragedy." In *Performance Culture and Athenian Democracy,* ed. Simon Goldhill and Robin Osborne, 96–122. Cambridge.

Hall, Jonathan M. 1997. *Ethnic Identity in Greek Antiquity.* Cambridge.

———. 2010. "Autochthonous Autocrats: The Tyranny of the Athenian Democracy." In *Private and Public Lies: The Discourse of Despotism and Deceit in the Graeco-Roman World,* ed. Andrew J. Turner, James H. Kim On Chong-Gossard, and Frederik Juliaan Vervaet, 11–28. Leiden.

Hamel, Debra. 1998. *Athenian Generals: Military Authority in the Classical Period.* Leiden.

———. 2015. *The Battle of Arginusae: Victory at Sea and Its Tragic Aftermath in the Final Years of the Peloponnesian War.* Baltimore.

Hamilton, Richard. 1976. Review of *A New Oxyrhynchus Papyrus: The Hypothesis of Euripides' Alexandros* by R. A. Coles. *American Journal of Philology* 97:65–70.

———. 1985. "Slings and Arrows: The Debate with Lycus in the Heracles." *Transactions of the American Philological Association* 115:19–25.

———. 1990. "The Pindaric Dithyramb." *Harvard Studies in Classical Philology* 93:211–222.

Hammer, Dean C. 2002. *The Iliad as Politics: The Performance of Political Thought.* Norman, Ok.

Hansen, M. H. 1990. Review of *Mass and Elite in Democratic Athens: Rhetoric, Ideology, and the Power of the People* by Josiah Ober. *Classical Review* 40:348–356.

———. 1991. *The Athenian Democracy in the Age of Demosthenes: Structure, Principles, and Ideology.* Oxford.

———. 2014. "Political Parties in Democratic Athens?" *Greek, Roman, and Byzantine Studies* 54:379–403.

Harris, John P. 2009. "Revenge of the Nerds: Xenophanes, Euripides, and Socrates vs. Olympic Victors." *American Journal of Philology* 130:157–194.

———. 2012. "The Swan's Red-Dipped Foot: Euripides, *Ion* 161–9." *Classical Quarterly* 62:510–522.

Harrison, Anthony Kwame. 2012. "Post-Colonial Consciousness, Knowledge Production, and Identity Inscription within Filipino American Hip Hop Music." *Perfect Beat* 13:29–48.

Hartigan, Karelisa V. 1981. "Myth and the *Helen*." *Eranos* 79:23–31.

Harvey, A. E. 1955. "The Classification of Greek Lyric Poetry." *Classical Quarterly* 5: 157–175.

Hawhee, Debra. 2002. "Agonism and *Aretê*." *Philosophy and Rhetoric* 35:185–207.

Heath, Malcolm. 1988. "Receiving the κῶμος: The Context and Performance of Epinician." *American Journal of Philology* 109:180–195.

Heath, Malcolm, and Mary Lefkowitz. 1991. "Epinician Performance." *Classical Philology* 86:173–191.

Hedrick, Charles W., Jr. 1988. "The Temple and Cult of Apollo Patroos in Athens." *American Journal of Archaeology* 92:185–210.

Heftner, Herbert. 2000. "Zur Datierung der Ostrakisierung des Hyperbolos." *Rivista storica dell'antichità* 30:27–46.

Heiden, Bruce. 2008. "Common People and Leaders in *Iliad* Book 2: The Invocation of the Muses and the Catalogue of Ships." *Transactions of the American Philological Association* 138:127–154.

Herda, Alexander. 2006. *Der Apollon-Delphinios-Kult in Milet und die Neujahrsprozession nach Didyma.* Mainz am Rhein.

———. 2011. "How to Run a State Cult: The Organization of the Cult of Apollo Delphinios in Miletos." In *Current Approaches to Religion in Ancient Greece,* ed. Matthew Haysom and Jenny Wallensten, 57–81. Stockholm.

Herrera, Patricia. 2016. "*Hamilton,* Democracy, and Theatre in America." *HowlRound* (Blog). May 13, 2016. https://howlround.com/hamilton-democracy-and-theatre-america. Accessed April 1, 2020.

Hesk, John. 2000. *Deception and Democracy in Classical Athens.* Cambridge.

Hill, Marc Lamont. 2009. *Beats, Rhymes, and Classroom Life: Hip-Hop Pedagogy and the Politics of Identity.* New York.

Hoffer, Stanley E. 1996. "Violence, Culture, and the Workings of Ideology in Euripides' *Ion.*" *Classical Antiquity* 15:289–318.

Hooker, J. T. 1990. "The Visit of Athena to Achilles in *Iliad* I." *Emerita* 58:21–32.

Holmes, Brooke. 2008. "Euripides' Heracles in the Flesh." *Classical Antiquity* 27:231–281.

Hornblower, Simon. 1991–2008. *A Commentary on Thucydides.* 3 vols. Oxford.

———. 1992. "The Religious Dimension of the Peloponnesian War, or, What Thucydides Does Not Tell Us." *Harvard Studies in Classical Philology* 94:169–197.

———. 2004. *Thucydides and Pindar: Historical Narrative and the World of Epinikian Poetry.* Oxford.

Hornblower, Simon, and Catherine Morgan, eds. 2007. *Pindar's Poetry, Patrons, and Festivals: From Archaic Greece to the Roman Empire*. Oxford.

Humphreys, S. C. 1974. "The Nothoi of Kynosarges." *Journal of Hellenic Studies* 94:88–95.

Hunter, Virginia. 1988. "Thucydides and the Sociology of the Crowd." *The Classical Journal* 84:17–30.

Huys, Marc. 1986. "The Plotting Scene in Euripides' *Alexandros*: An Interpretation of Fr. 23, 23A, 23B, 43 Sn. (cf. Hypothesis, ll. 23–25)." *Zeitschrift für Papyrologie und Epigraphik* 62:9–36.

Ibrahim, Awad El Karim M. 1999. "Becoming Black: Rap and Hip-Hop, Race, Gender, Identity, and the Politics of ESL Learning." *TESOL Quarterly* 33:349–369.

Ieranò, G. 1989. "Il ditirambo XVII di Bacchilide e le feste apollinee di Delo." *Quaderni di storia* 30:157–183.

———. 1997. *Il ditirambo di Dioniso: le testimonianze antiche*. Pisa.

Instone, Stephen, ed. 1996. *Pindar: Selected Odes*. Warminster.

Janko, Richard. 1992. *The Iliad: A Commentary*. Vol. 4. Cambridge.

Jauss, Hans Robert. 1982. *Toward an Aesthetic of Reception*. Trans. Timothy Bahti. Minneapolis.

Jenkins, I. D. 1985. "The Ambiguity of Greek Textiles." *Arethusa* 18:109–132.

Johnson, Mat. 2011. *Pym*. New York.

Johnson, James F. 2002. "Compassion and Friendship in Euripides' *Herakles*." *The Classical Bulletin* 78:115–129.

Jouan, François, ed. 1983. *Euripide: Iphigénie à Aulis*. Paris.

Kagan, Donald. 1969. *The Outbreak of the Peloponnesian War*. Ithaca.

Kajikawa, Loren. 2018. "'Young, Scrappy, and Hungry': *Hamilton*, Hip Hop, and Race." *American Music* 36:467–486.

Kampakoglou, Alexandros. 2018. "Epinician Discourse in Euripides' Tragedies: The Case of *Alexandros*." In *Paths of Song: The Lyric Dimension of Greek Tragedy*, eds. Rosa Andújar, Thomas R. P. Coward, and Theodora A. Hadjimichael, 187–218. Berlin.

Kannicht, Richard, ed. 2004. *Tragicorum Graecorum Fragmenta*. Vol. 5. Göttingen.

Käppel, Lutz. 1992. *Paian: Studien zur Geschichte einer Gattung*. Berlin.

Karamanou, Ioanna. 2011. "The Hektor-Deiphobos Agon in Euripides' *Alexandros* (frr. 62a-b K.: P. Stras. 2342, 2 and 2343)." *Zeitschrift für Papyrologie und Epigraphik* 178:35–47.

———. 2017. *Euripides, Alexandros: Introduction, Text, and Commentary*. Berlin.

Kasimis, Demetra. 2018. *The Perpetual Immigrant and the Limits of Athenian Democracy*. Cambridge.

Kerferd, G. B. 1981. *The Sophistic Movement*. Cambridge.

Kirk, G. S., ed. 1985. *The Iliad: A Commentary*. Vol. 1. Cambridge.

Klimek-Winter, Rainer. 1996. "Euripides in den dramatischen Agonen Athens: Zur Datierung des *Ion*." *Gymnasium* 103:289–297.

Klooster, Jacqueline and Baukje van den Berg. 2018. "Homer and the Good Ruler in Antiquity and Beyond: Introduction." In *Homer and the Good Ruler in Antiquity and Beyond*, 1–19. Leiden.

Knox, Bernard M. W. 1972. "Euripides' *Iphigenia in Aulide* 1–163 (in that order)." In *Yale Classical Studies* 22:239–261.

———. 1979. *Word and Action: Essays on the Ancient Theater*. Baltimore.

Kovacs, David. 2003. "Toward a Reconstruction of *Iphigenia Aulidensis*." *Journal of Hellenic Studies* 123:77–103.

Kowalzig, Barbara. 2007. *Singing for the Gods: Performances of Myth and Ritual in Archaic and Classical Greece*. Oxford.

Kowalzig, Barbara, and Peter Wilson, eds. 2013. *Dithyramb in Context*. Oxford.

Kraus, Walther. 1989. "Textkritische Erwägungen zu Euripides' *Ion*." *Wiener Studien* 102:35–110.

Kremmydas, Christos. 2013. "The Discourse of Deception and Characterization in Attic Oratory." *Greek, Roman, and Byzantine Studies* 53:51–89.

Kurke, Leslie. 1991. *The Traffic in Praise: Pindar and the Poetics of Social Economy.* Ithaca.

———. 1993. "The Economy of *Kudos.*" In *Cultural Poetics in Archaic Greece,* ed. Carol Dougherty and Leslie Kurke, 131–163. Cambridge.

———. 2005. "Choral Lyric as 'Ritualization': Poetic Sacrifice and Poetic Ego in Pindar's Sixth Paian." *Classical Antiquity* 24:81–130.

Kyle, Donald G. 1993. *Athletics in Ancient Athens.* Leiden.

Lai, Alberta. 1997. "La circolazione delle tragedie Eschilee in ambito simposiale." *Lexis* 15:143–148.

Lamari, Anna A. 2015. "Aeschylus and the Beginning of Tragic Reperformances." *Trends in Classics* 7:189–206.

———. 2017. *Reperforming Greek Tragedy: Theater, Politics, and Cultural Mobility in the Fifth and Fourth Centuries BC.* Berlin.

Lape, Susan. 2010. *Race and Citizen Identity in the Classical Athenian Democracy.* Cambridge.

Larson, Sarah. 2014. "'Do the Right Thing' at Twenty-Five." *The New Yorker,* July 4, 2014. https://www.newyorker.com/culture/sarah-larson/do-the-right-thing-at-twenty-five.

Larue, Jene. 1963. "Creousa's Monody: *Ion* 859–922." *Transactions of the American Philological Association* 94:126–136.

Lawall, Mark L. 2009. "The Temple of Apollo Patroos Dated by an Amphora Stamp." *Hesperia* 78:387–403.

Lee, Hugh M. 1983. "Athletic Arete in Pindar." *The Ancient World* 7:31–37.

Lee, K. H., ed. 1997. *Euripides: Ion.* Warminster.

Lee, Spike, dir. 1989. *Do the Right Thing.* Universal City, CA.

Lefkowitz, Mary R. 1988. "Who Sang Pindar's Victory Odes?" *American Journal of Philology* 109:1–11.

Lesher, J. H., ed. 1992. *Xenophanes of Colophon, Fragments: A Text and Translation with Commentary*. Toronto.

Loraux, Nicole.1993. *The Children of Athena: Athenian Ideas about Citizenship and the Division between the Sexes*. Trans. Caroline Levine. Princeton.

———. 2000. *Born of the Earth: Myth and Politics in Athens*. Trans. Selina Stewart. Ithaca.

Lowe, N. J. 2007. "Epinikian Eidography." In Hornblower and Morgan 2007:167–176.

Luschnig, C. A. E. 1988. *Tragic Aporia: A Study of Euripides' Iphigenia at Aulis*. Victoria, Australia.

Lush, Brian V. 2015. "Popular Authority in Euripides' *Iphigenia in Aulis*." *American Journal of Philology* 136:207–242.

Maehler, Herwig. 1997. *Die Lieder des Bakchylides*. Vol. 2. Leiden.

March, Jennifer R. 1987. *The Creative Poet: Studies on the Treatment of Myths in Greek Poetry*. London.

Markantonatos, Andreas. 2011. "Leadership in Action: Wise Policy and Firm Resolve in Euripides' *Iphigenia at Aulis*." In Markantonatos and Zimmermann 2011:189–218. Berlin.

Markantonatos, Andreas, and Bernhard Zimmermann, eds. 2011. *Crisis on Stage: Tragedy and Comedy in Late Fifth-Century Athens*. Berlin.

Marks, J. 2005. "The Ongoing *Neikos*: Thersites, Odysseus, and Achilleus." *American Journal of Philology* 126:1–31.

Marrou, Henri. 1965. *Histoire de l'éducation dans l'antiquité*. Paris.

Martin, Gunther. 2010. "On the Date of Euripides' *Ion*." *Classical Quarterly* 60:647–651.

Mastronarde, Donald J. 1999–2000. "Euripidean Tragedy and Genre: The Terminology and its Problems." *Illinois Classical Studies* 24–25: 23–39.

McClure, Laura. 1997. "*Logos Gunaikos*: Speech, Gender, and Spectatorship in the *Oresteia*." *Helios* 24:112–135.

———. 1999. *Spoken Like a Woman: Speech and Gender in Athenian Drama.* Princeton.

McGlew, James F. 1989. "Royal Power and the Achaean Assembly at *Iliad* 2.84–393." *Classical Antiquity* 8:283–295.

Mead, Rebecca. 2015. "All about the Hamiltons." *The New Yorker*, February 2, 2015. https://www.newyorker.com/magazine/2015/02/09/hamiltons.

Meiggs, Russell. 1972. *The Athenian Empire.* Oxford.

Meiggs, Russell, and David Lewis, eds. 1969. *A Selection of Greek Historical Inscriptions to the End of the Fifth Century B.C.* Oxford.

Merkelbach, R. 1973. "Päonische Strophen bei Pindar und Bakchylides." *Zeitschrift für Papyrologie und Epigraphik* 12:45–55.

Michelakis, Pantelis. 2002. *Achilles in Greek Tragedy.* Cambridge.

Michelini, Ann N. 1994. "Political Themes in Euripides' *Suppliants*." *American Journal of Philology* 115:219–252.

Miller, Andrew M. 1982. "*Phthonos* and *Parphasis*: The Argument of *Nemean* 8.19–34." *Greek, Roman, and Byzantine Studies* 23:111–120.

Mirto, Maria Serena, ed. 2009. *Euripide: Ione.* Milan.

Mitchell, W. J. T. 1990. "The Violence of Public Art: *Do the Right Thing*." *Critical Inquiry* 16:880–899.

Mitchell-Boyask, Robin. 2006. "The Marriage of Cassandra and the *Oresteia*: Text, Image, Performance." *Transactions of the American Philological Association* 136:269–297.

Montanari, Enrico. 1981. *Il mito dell'autoctonia: linee di una dinamica mitico-politica ateniese.* Rome.

Montiglio, Silvia. 2011. *From Villain to Hero: Odysseus in Ancient Thought.* Ann Arbor.

Moore, Mary B. 1995. "The Central Group of the Gigantomachy of the Old Athena Temple on the Acropolis." *American Journal of Archaeology* 99:633–639.

Moreau, Alain. 1996. "Eschyle et les tranches des repas d'Homère: La trilogie d'Achille." In *Panorama du théâtre antique: d'Eschyle aux dramaturges d'Amérique Latine*, 3–27. Montpelier.

Morgan, Kathryn A. 1993. "Pindar the Professional and the Rhetoric of the ΚΩΜΟΣ." *Classical Philology* 88:1–15.

———. 2015. *Pindar and the Construction of Syracusan Monarchy in the Fifth Century B.C.* Oxford.

Morris, Ian. 1986. "The Use and Abuse of Homer." *Classical Antiquity* 5:81–138.

Morrissey, Edmond J. 1978. "Victors in the Prytaneion Decree (*IG* I² 77)." *Greek, Roman, and Byzantine Studies* 19:121–125.

Most, Glenn. 1985. *The Measures of Praise: Structure and Function in Pindar's Second Pythian and Seventh Nemean Odes*. Göttingen.

Mueller, Melissa. 2010. "Athens in a Basket: Naming, Objects, and Identity in Euripides' *Ion*." *Arethusa* 43:365–402.

Murray, Penelope, ed. 1996. *Plato on Poetry*. Cambridge.

Nagy, Gregory. 1990. *Pindar's Homer: The Lyric Possession of an Epic Past*. Baltimore.

Nancy, Claire. 1983. "Φάρμακον Σωτηρίας: Le mécanisme du sacrifice humain chez Euripide." In *Théâtre et spectacles dans l'antiquité: actes du colloque de Strasbourg 5-7 novembre 1981*, ed. Hubert Zehnacker, 17–30. Leiden.

Neustadt, Ernst. 1929. "Wort und Geschehen in Aischylos *Agamemnon*." *Hermes* 64:243–265.

Nieto Hernández, M. P. 1993. "Heracles and Pindar." *Mètis* 8:75–102.

Nisetich, Frank J. 1975. "*Olympian* 1.8-11: An Epinician Metaphor." *Harvard Studies in Classical Philology* 79:55–68.

Noel, Anne-Sophie. Forthcoming. "Playing Make Believe with Objects: Counterfactual Imagination and Psychodrama in Greek Tragedy."

Oakley, John H., and Rebecca H. Sinos. 1993. *The Wedding in Ancient Athens*. Madison.

Ober, Josiah. 1989. *Mass and Elite in Democratic Athens: Rhetoric, Ideology, and the Power of the People*. Princeton.

————. 1998. *Political Dissent in Democratic Athens: Intellectual Critics of Popular Rule*. Princeton.

Ogden, Daniel. 1996. *Greek Bastardy in the Classical and Hellenistic Periods*. Oxford.

Oliver, James H. 1936. "The Sarapion Monument and the Paean of Sophocles." *Hesperia* 5:91–122.

Osborne, Robin. 2004. "Competitive Festivals and the *Polis*: A Context for Dramatic Festivals at Athens." In *Athenian Democracy*, ed. P. J. Rhodes, 207–224. Edinburgh.

O'Sullivan, Patrick. 2012. "Sophistic Ethics, Old Atheism, and 'Critias' on Religion." *The Classical World* 105:167–185.

Owen, A. S., ed. 1939. *Euripides: Ion*. Oxford.

Padilla, Mark W. 1994. "Heroic Paternity in Euripides' *Heracles*." *Arethusa* 27:279–302.

Page, Denys L. 1934. *Actors' Interpolations in Greek Tragedy: Studied with Special Reference to Euripides' Iphigenia in Aulis*. Oxford.

————, ed. 1942. *Select Papyri*. Vol. 3. Cambridge, MA.

————, ed. 1962. *Poetae Melici Graeci*. Oxford.

Papadopoulou, Thalia. 2005. *Heracles and Euripidean Tragedy*. Cambridge.

Papakonstantinou, Zinon. 2003. "Alcibiades in Olympia: Olympic Ideology, Sport and Social Conflict in Classical Athens." *Journal of Sport History* 30:173–182.

————. 2016. "Sport, Victory Commemoration and Elite Identities in Archaic and Early Classical Athens." *Classica et Mediaevalia* 65:87–126.

Parke, H. W. 1977. *Festivals of the Athenians*. Ithaca.

Parry, Adam. 1970. "Thucydides' Use of Abstract Langauge." *Yale French Studies* 45:3–20.

————. 1981. *Logos and Ergon in Thucydides*. New York.

Parry, Hugh. 1965. "The Second Stasimon of Euripides' *Heracles* (637–700)." *American Journal of Philology* 86:363–374.

Patterson, Cynthia B. 1990. "Those Athenian Bastards." *Classical Antiquity* 9:40–73.

———. 2006. "Athenian Citizenship Law." In *The Cambridge Companion to Ancient Greek Law*, ed. Michael Gagarin and David Cohen, 267–289. Cambridge.

Pavlou, Maria. 2008. "Metapoetics, Poetic Tradition, and Praise in Pindar *Olympian* 9." *Mnemosyne* 61:533–567.

———. 2012. "Bacchylides 17: Singing and Usurping the Paean." *Greek, Roman, and Byzantine Studies* 52:510–539.

Pedrick, Victoria, and Steven M. Oberhelman, eds. 2005. *The Soul of Tragedy: Essays on Athenian Drama*. Chicago.

Pfeijffer, Ilja Leonard. 1999. *Three Aeginetan Odes of Pindar: A Commentary on Nemean V, Nemean III & Pythian VIII*. Leiden.

Piérart, Marcel. 1974. "À propos de l'élection des stratèges athéniens." *Bulletin de Correspondance Hellénique* 98:125–146.

Pietruczuk, Katarzyna. 2012. "The Prologue of *Iphigenia Aulidensis* Reconsidered." *Mnemosyne* 65:568–583.

Porter, James I. 1993. "The Seductions of Gorgias." *Classical Antiquity* 12:267–299.

Postlethwaite, N. 1988. "Thersites in the *Iliad*." *Greece & Rome* 35:123–136.

Pritchard, David M. 2010. "Sport, War and Democracy in Classical Athens." In *Sport in the Cultures of the Ancient World*, ed. Zinon Papakonstantinou, 64–97. London.

———. 2012. "Athletics in Satyric Drama." *Greece & Rome* 59: 1–16.

Pulleyn, Simon, ed. 2000. *Homer: Iliad I*. Oxford.

Raaflaub, Kurt A. 1988. "Homer and the Beginning of Political Thought in Ancient Greece." *Proceedings of the Boston Area Colloquium in Ancient Philosophy* 4:1–25.

———. 1997. "Homeric Society." In *A New Companion to Homer*, ed. Ian Morris and Barry B. Powell, 624–648. Leiden.

Radding, Jonah. 2020. "Status sociale e identità civile: l'*Alexandros* di Euripide e i limiti dell'ideologia." In *The Forgotten Theatre II: Mitologia, drammaturgia e tradizione del dramma frammentario greco-romano*, ed. Luca Austa, 115–138. Freiburg.

———. 2021. "Communal Voices and Communal Bonds in Pindar's Paeans." *Transactions of the American Philological Association* 151:265–293.

Radt, Stefan Lorenz. 1958. *Pindars zweiter und sechster Paian: Text, Scholien und Kommentar*. Amsterdam.

Raubitschek, A. E. 1941. "Two Notes on Isocrates." *Transactions of the American Philological Association* 72:356–364.

Rawles, Richard. 2013. "Aristophanes' Simonides: Lyric Models for Praise and Blame." In Bakola, Prauscello, and Telò 2013:175–202.

Reger, Gary. 2004. "The Aegean." In *An Inventory of Archaic and Classical Poleis*, ed. M. H. Hansen and T. H. Nielsen, 732–793. Oxford.

Rehm, Rush. 1988. "The Staging of Suppliant Plays." *Greek, Roman, and Byzantine Studies* 29:263–307.

Revermann, Martin. 2006a. *Comic Business: Theatricality, Dramatic Technique, and Performance Contexts of Aristophanic Comedy*. Oxford.

———. 2006b. "The Competence of Theatre Audiences in Fifth- and Fourth-Century Athens." *Journal of Hellenic Studies* 126:99–124.

Rhodes, P. J. 1981. "Notes on Voting in Athens." *Greek, Roman, and Byzantine Studies* 22:125–132.

———. 1994. "The Ostracism of Hyperbolus." In *Ritual, Finance, Politics: Athenian Democratic Accounts Presented to David Lewis*, ed. R. Osborne and S. Hornblower, 85–98. Oxford.

Richardson, N.J. 1981. "The Contest of Homer and Hesiod and Alcidamas' Mouseion." *Classical Quarterly* 31:1–10.

Ritchie, W. 1978. "Euripides, *Iphigenia at Aulis* 919–974." In *Dionysiaca: Nine Studies in Greek Poetry*, ed. R. D. Dawe, J. Diggle, and P. E. Easterling, 179–203. Cambridge.

Robb, Kevin. 1994. *Literacy and Paideia in Ancient Greece*. Oxford.

Roberts, Jennifer Tolbert. 1977. "Arginusae Once Again." *The Classical World* 71:107–111.

Robertson, Noel. 1988. "Melanthus, Codrus, Neleus, Caucon: Ritual Myth as Athenian History." *Greek, Roman, and Byzantine Studies* 29:201–261.

Rose, Peter W. 1988. "Thersites and the Plural Voices of Homer." *Arethusa* 21:5–25.

———. 2012. *Class in Archaic Greece*. Cambridge.

Rosen, Ralph M. 2004. "Aristophanes' *Frogs* and the *Contest of Homer and Hesiod*." *Transactions of the American Philological Association* 134:295–322.

———. 2005. "Aristophanes, Old Comedy, and Greek Tragedy." In *A Companion to Tragedy*, ed. R. Bushnell, 251–268. Malden, MA.

Rosenbloom, David. 2004. "*Ponêroi* vs. *Chrêstoi*: The Ostracism of Hyperbolos and the Struggle for Hegemony in Athens after the Death of Perikles, Part I." *Transactions of the American Philological Association* 134:55–105.

Rosivach, Vincent J. 1987. "Autochthony and the Athenians." *Classical Quarterly* 37:294–306.

Rubin, Joel. 2016. "Hip Hop Videos and Black Identity in Virtual Space." *Journal of Hip Hop Studies* 3:74–85.

Russo, Joseph A. 1968. "Homer against His Tradition." *Arion* 7:275–295.

Rutherford, Ian C. 1990. "Paeans by Simonides." *Harvard Studies in Classical Philology* 93:169–209.

———. 1993. "Paeanic Ambiguity: A Study of the Representation of the παιάν in Greek Literature." *Quaderni urbinati di cultura classica* 44:77–92.

———. 1995. "Apollo in Ivy: The Tragic Paean." *Arion* 3:112–135.

———. 2000. "State Pilgrimage and the Performance of *Paean 4.*" In *Poesia e religione in Grecia: Studi in onore di G. Aurelio Privitera*, ed. Maria Cannatà Fera and Simonetta Grandolini, 605–612. Naples.

———. 2001. *Pindar's Paeans: A Reading of the Fragments with a Survey of the Genre.* Oxford.

———. 2004. "Χορὸς εἷς ἐκ τῆςδε τῆς πόλεως (Xen. *Mem.* 3.3.12): Song-Dance and State-Pilgrimage at Athens." In *Music and the Muses: The Culture of Mousikê in the Classical Athenian City*, ed. Penelope Murray and Peter Wilson, 67–90. Oxford.

———. 2013. *State Pilgrims and Sacred Observers in Ancient Greece: A Study of Theôriâ and Theôroi.* Cambridge: Cambridge University Press.

Saïd, Suzanne. 2002. "Greeks and Barbarians in Euripides: The End of Differences?" In *Greeks and Barbarians*, ed. Thomas Harrison, 62–100. Edinburgh.

———. 2013. "Thucydides and the Masses." In *Thucydides between History and Literature*, ed. M. Tamiolaki and A. Tsakmakis, 199–224. Berlin.

Sansone, David. 1975. "The Sacrifice-Motif in Euripides' *IT.*" *Transactions of the American Philological Association* 105:283–95.

Saxonhouse, Arlene W. 1986. "Myths and Origins of Cities: Reflections on the Autochthony Theme in Euripides' *Ion.*" In *Greek Tragedy and Political Theory*, ed. J. Peter Euben, 252–273. Berkeley.

Schmidt, D. A. 1990. "Bacchylides 17: Paean or Dithyramb?" *Hermes* 118:18–31.

Scholtz, Andrew. 2004. "Friends, Lovers, Flatterers: Demophilic Courtship in Aristophanes' *Knights.*" *Transactions of the American Philological Association* 134:263–293.

Schröder, Stephan. 1999. *Geschichte und Theorie der Gattung Paian: Eine kritische Untersuchung mit einem Ausblick auf Behandlung und Auffassung der lyrischen Gattungen bei dem alexandrischen Philologen.* Stuttgart.

———. 2000. "Das Lied dem Bakchylides von der Fahrt des Theseus nach Kreta (C. 17 M) und das Problem seiner Gattung." *Rheinisches Museum für Philologie* 143:128–160.

Schwab, Katherine A. 1996. "Parthenon East Metope XI: Herakles and the Gigantomachy." *American Journal of Archaeology* 100:81–90.

Schwartzberg, Melissa. 2010. "Shouts, Murmurs, and Votes: Acclamation and Aggregation in Ancient Greece." *The Journal of Political Philosophy* 18:448–468.

Scodel, Ruth. 1977. "Apollo's Perfidy: *Iliad* ω59–63." *Harvard Studies in Classical Philology* 81:55–57.

———. 1980a. *The Trojan Trilogy of Euripides*. Göttingen.

———. 1980b. "Hesiod Redivivus." *Greek, Roman, and Byzantine Studies* 21:301–320.

———. 2002. *Listening to Homer: Tradition, Narrative, and Audience*. Ann Arbor.

Seaford, Richard. 1984. "The Last Bath of Agamemnon." *Classical Quarterly* 34:247–254.

———. 1987. "The Tragic Wedding." *Journal of Hellenic Studies* 107:106–130.

Segal, Charles. 1967. "Pindar's Seventh *Nemean*." *Transactions of the American Philological Association* 98:431–480.

———. 1971. "The Two Worlds of Euripides' *Helen*." *Transactions of the American Philological Association* 102:553–614.

———. 1986. *Pindar's Mythmaking: The Fourth Pythian Ode*. Princeton.

———. 1999. "Euripides' *Ion*: Generational Passage and Civic Myth." In *Rites of Passage in Ancient Greece: Literature, Religion, Society*, ed. Mark W. Padilla, 67–108. Lewisburg, PA.

Sevieri, Roberta. 1991. "Linguaggio consapevole e coscienza individuale di Clitennestra nell'*Agamennone* di Eschilo." *Dioniso* 61:13–31.

Shapiro, H. Alan. 2009. "Apollo and Ion on Classical Athenian Vases." In Athanassaki, Martin, and Miller 2009:265–284.

Siegel, Herbert. 1981. "Agamemnon in Euripides' *Iphigenia at Aulis*." *Hermes* 109:257–265.

Siewert, P., ed. 2002. *Ostrakismos-Testimonien*. Vol. 1, *Die Zeugnisse antiker Autoren der Inschriften und Ostraka über das athenische Scherbengericht aus vorhellenistischer Zeit (487–322 v. Chr.)*. Stuttgart.

Slater, William J. 1984. "*Nemean One*: The Victor's Return." In *Greek Poetry and Philosophy: Studies in Honor of Leonard Woodbury*, ed. Douglas E. Gerber, 241–264. Chico, CA.

Smith, Christopher Holmes. 1997. "Method in the Madness: Exploring the Boundaries of Identity in Hip-Hop Performativity." *Social Identities* 3:345–374.

Smith, W. D. 1979. "Iphigenia in Love." In *Arktouros: Hellenic Studies presented to Bernard M. W. Knox on the occasion of his 65th birthday*, ed. Glen W. Bowersock, Walter Burkert, and Michael C. J. Putnam, 173–180. Berlin.

Snell, Bruno. 1964. *Scenes from Greek Drama*. Berkeley.

Sommerstein, Alan H., ed. 1981. *Aristophanes: Knights*. Warminster.

———. 2010. *Aeschylean Tragedy*. London.

Sordi, Marta. 1981. "Teramene e il processo delle Arginuse." *Aevum* 55:3–12.

Sorum, Christina Elliot. 1992. "Myth, Choice, and Meaning in Euripides' *Iphigenia at Aulis*." *American Journal of Philology* 113:527–542.

Stadter, Philip A. 1989. *A Commentary on Plutarch's Pericles*. Chapel Hill.

Steiner, Deborah T. 1995. "Stoning and Sight: A Structural Equivalence in Greek Mythology." *Classical Antiquity* 14:193–211.

———. 2010. "Framing the Fox: Callimachus' Second *Iamb* and Its Predecessors." *Journal of Hellenic Studies* 130:97–107.

Stockert, Walter. 1992. *Euripides: Iphigenie in Aulis*. 2 vols. Vienna.

Strasburger, Hermann. 1997. "The Sociology of the Homeric Epics." In *Homer: German Scholarship in Translation*, ed. and trans. G. M. Wright and P. V. Jones, 47–70. Oxford.

Swift, L. A. 2008. *Euripides: Ion*. London.

———. 2010. *The Hidden Chorus: Echoes of Genre in Tragic Lyric*. Oxford.

———. 2012. "Paeanic and Epinician Healing in Euripides' *Alcestis*." In *Greek Drama IV: Texts, Contexts, Performance*, ed. David Rosenbloom and John Davidson, 149–168. Oxford.

Synodinou, Katerina. 2013. "Agamemnon's Change of Mind in Euripides' *Iphigeneia at Aulis*." *Logeion* 3:51–65.

Tacon, Judith. 2001. "Ecclesiastic *Thorubos*: Interventions, Interruptions, and Popular Involvement in the Athenian Assembly." *Greece & Rome* 48:173–192.

Tandy, David W. 1997. *Warriors into Traders: The Power of the Market in Early Greece*. Berkeley.

Taplin, Oliver. 1977. *The Stagecraft of Aeschylus: The Dramatic Use of Exits and Entrances in Greek Tragedy*. Oxford.

———. 1990. "Agamemnon's Role in the *Iliad*." In *Characterization and Individuality in Greek Literature*, ed. Christopher Pelling, 60–82. Oxford.

———. 1992. *Homeric Soundings: The Shaping of the Iliad*. Oxford.

Telò, Mario. 2016. *Aristophanes and the Cloak of Comedy: Affect, Aesthetics, and the Canon*. Chicago.

Thalmann, William G. 1985. "Speech and Silence in the *Oresteia* 2." *Phoenix* 39:221–237.

———. 1988. "Thersites: Comedy, Scapegoats, and Heroic Ideology in the *Iliad*." *Transactions of the American Philological Association* 118:1–28.

———. 1993. "Euripides and Aeschylus: The Case of the *Hekabe*." *Classical Antiquity* 12:126–159.

Thompson, Homer A. 1937. "Buildings on the West Side of the Agora." *Hesperia* 6:1–226.

———. 1962. "The Sculptural Adornment of the Hephaisteion." *American Journal of Archaeology* 66:339–347.

Torrance, Isabelle. 2011. "In the Footprints of Aeschylus: Recognition, Allusion, and Metapoetics in Euripides." *American Journal of Philology* 132:177–204.

———. 2013. *Metapoetry in Euripides*. Oxford: Oxford University Press.

Tsagalis, Christos C. 2009. "Blurring the Boundaries: Dionysus, Apollo, and Bacchylides 17." In Athanassaki, Martin, and Miller 2009:199–215.

Valiavitcharska, Vessela. 2006. "Correct *Logos* and Truth in Gorgias' *Encomium of Helen*." *Rhetorica* 24:147–161.

Vallozza, Maddalena. 1989. "Il motivo dell'invidia in Pindaro." *Quaderni urbinati di cultura classica* 31:13–30.

van Erp Taalman Kip, A. Maria. 1987. "Euripides and Melos." *Mnemosyne* 40:414–419.

———. 1996. "Truth in Tragedy: When Are We Entitled to Doubt a Character's Words?" *American Journal of Philology* 117:517–536.

van Oeveren, C. D. P. 1999. "Bacchylides Ode 17: Theseus and the Delian League." In *One Hundred Years of Bacchylides*, ed. I.L. Pfeijffer and S. R. Slings, 31–42. Amsterdam.

van Wees, Hans. 1992. *Status Warriors: War, Violence, and Society in Homer.* Amsterdam.

Verdenius, W.J. 1970. *Homer, the Educator of the Greeks.* Amsterdam.

———. 1981. "Gorgias' Doctrine of Deception." In *The Sophists and Their Legacy*, ed. G. B. Kerferd, 116–128. Wiesbaden.

Wade-Gery, H. T. 1958. *Essays in Greek History.* Oxford.

Wallace, Robert W. 2004. "The Power to Speak—and not to Listen—in Ancient Athens." In *Free Speech in Classical Antiquity*, ed. Ineke Sluiter and Ralph M. Rosen, 221–232. Leiden.

Walsh, George B. 1978. "The Rhetoric of Birthright and Race in Euripides' *Ion*." *Hermes* 106:301–315.

Wasserman, Felix M. 1940. "Divine Violence and Providence in Euripides' *Ion*." *Transactions of the American Philological Association* 71:587–604.

Weaver, Jace. 2012. Review of *Pym: A Novel* by Mat Johnson. *Studies in American Indian Literatures* 24:133–136.

Weineck, Silke-Maria. 1998. "Talking About Homer: Poetic Madness, Philosophy, and the Birth of Criticism in Plato's *Ion*." *Arethusa* 31:19–42.

Weiss, Naomi. 2019. "Generic Hybridity in Athenian Tragedy." In Foster, Kurke, and Weiss 2019:167–190. Leiden.

Welskopf, E. C. 1981. "Die Bezeichnungen λαός, δῆμος, ὅμιλος, πληθύς, ἔθνος in den homerischen Epen." In *Untersuchungen ausgewählter altgriechischer sozialer Typenbegriffe*. Vol. 3:163–192. Berlin.

West, M. L. 1967. "The Contest of Homer and Hesiod." *Classical Quarterly* 17:433–450.

Westlake, H. D. 1974. "The Naval Battle at Pylos and Its Consequences." *Classical Quarterly* 24:211–226.

Whitehead, David. 1983. "Competitive Outlay and Community Profit: *Philotimia* in Democratic Athens." *Classica et Mediaevalia* 34:55–74.

Whitmarsh, Tim. 2014. "Atheistic Aesthetics: The Sisyphus Fragment, Poetics and the Creativity of Drama." *The Cambridge Classical Journal* 60:109–126.

Wilamowitz-Moellendorff, Ulrich von. 1922. *Pindaros*. Berlin.

———. 1926. *Euripides: Ion*. Berlin.

Willink, C. W. 1971. "The Prologue of *Iphigenia at Aulis*." *Classical Quarterly* 21:343–364.

Wilson, Donna F. 2002. *Ransom, Revenge, and Heroic Identity in the Iliad*. Cambridge.

Wilson, Peter. 2000. *The Athenian Institution of the Khoregia: The Chorus, the City and the Stage*. Cambridge.

———. 2007. "Performance in the *Pythion*: The Athenian Thargelia." In *The Greek Theatre and Festivals: Documentary Studies*. Oxford.

Winnington-Ingram, R. P. 1969. "Euripides: *Poiêtês Sophos*." *Arethusa* 2:127–142.

Wohl, Victoria. 2015. *Euripides and the Politics of Form*. Princeton.

Wolff, Christian. 1965. "The Design and Myth in Euripides' *Ion*." *Harvard Studies in Classical Philology* 69:169–194.

Worman, Nancy. 1999. "The Ties That Bind: Transformations of Costume and Connection in Euripides' *Heracles*." *Ramus* 28:89–107.

Wright, Matthew. 2010. "The Tragedian as Critic: Euripides and Early Greek Poetics." *Journal of Hellenic Studies* 130:165–184.

———. 2013. "Comedy versus Tragedy in *Wasps*." In Bakola, Prauscello, and Telò 2013:205–225.

Wyles, Rosie. 2020. "The Aeschylean Sting in *Wasps*' Tale: Aristophanes' Engagement with the *Oresteia*." *Classical Quarterly* 70:529–540.

Yunis, Harvey. 1988. *A New Creed: Fundamental Religious Beliefs in the Athenian Polis and Euripidean Drama*. Göttingen.

———. 1996. *Taming Democracy: Models of Political Rhetoric in Classical Athens*. Ithaca.

———. 1998. "The Constraints of Democracy and the Rise of the Art of Rhetoric." In *Democracy, Empire, and the Arts in Fifth-Century Athens*, ed. Deborah Boedeker and Kurt A. Raaflaub, 223–240. Cambridge, MA.

Zacharia, Katerina. 1995. "The Marriage of Tragedy and Comedy in Euripides' *Ion*." In *Laughter down the Centuries*, ed. S. Jäkel and A. Timonen, 45–63. Turku.

———. 2003. *Converging Truths: Euripides' Ion and the Athenian Quest for Self-Definition*. Leiden.

Zeitlin, Froma I. 1965. "The Motif of Corrupted Sacrifice in Aeschylus' *Oresteia*." *Transactions of the American Philological Association* 96:463–508.

———. 1978. "The Dynamics of Misogyny: Myth and Mythmaking in the *Oresteia*." *Arethusa* 11:149–184.

———. 1980. "The Closet of Masks: Role-Playing and Myth-Making in the *Orestes* of Euripides." *Ramus* 9:51–77.

———. 1996. *Playing the Other: Gender and Society in Classical Greek Literature*. Chicago.

———. 2005. "Redeeming Matricide? Euripides Rereads the *Oresteia*." In Pedrick and Oberhelman 2005:199–226.

Index Locorum

Index of Subjects